DEBORAH SMITH

Blue
Willow

BANTAM BOOKS
New York Toronto London Sydney Auckland

BLUE WILLOW

A Bantam Book/February 1993

Grateful acknowledgment is made for permission to reprint from "Georgia on My Mind" by Hoagy Carmichael and Stuart Gorrell. Copyright © 1930 by Peer International Corporation. Copyright Renewed and Assigned to Peermusic Ltd. International Copyright Secured. All Rights Reserved. Used by permission.

All rights reserved.
Copyright © 1993 by Deborah Smith.

DESIGN AND ORNAMENTATION BY PATRICE FODERO

No part of this book may be reproduced or transmitted in any form or by any means, electronic or mechanical, including photocopying, recording, or by any information storage and retrieval system, without permission in writing from the publisher. For information address: Bantam Books.

If you purchased this book without a cover you should be aware that this book is stolen property. It was reported as "unsold and destroyed" to the publisher and neither the author nor the publisher has received any payment for this "stripped book."

ISBN 0-553-29690-6

Published simultaneously in the United States and Canada

Bantam Books are published by Bantam Books, a division of Random House, Inc. Its trademark, consisting of the words "Bantam Books" and the portrayal of a rooster, is Registered in U.S. Patent and Trademark Office and in other countries. Marca Registrada. Bantam Books, 1540 Broadway, New York, New York 10036.

PRINTED IN THE UNITED STATES OF AMERICA

OPM   0   9   8

Many thanks to my sister-in-law, Myra, for her expert advice on matters botanical, to Mother, Jack, and Ann for their love and unwavering family support, and, most of all, much love to my husband, Hank, for being my consultant on architecture and engineering, and for always reminding me that llamas spit.

Blue
Willow

Part One

Other arms reach out to me,
Other eyes smile tenderly,
Still in peaceful dreams I see,
The road leads back to you.

Hoagy Carmichael

One

Money, power, respect. Artemas Colebrook looked down on the proof of all he'd achieved in thirty-eight years but saw only the desire he could never fulfill.

Six generations of Colebrook history had reached a pinnacle. The bloodlines of a poor immigrant English potter had survived more than 150 years of ambition, triumph, and scandal. A fortune lost and regained. It had begun with a handful of pure white clay in the Georgia mountains. Now, it ended and began again in the glittering, neo-Gothic splendor of Colebrook International's new headquarters in the moneyed crescent of Atlanta's suburbs.

He stood alone and unmoving, painfully lost in the scene below him, a tall, big-shouldered man in formal attire who had inherited a legacy of fine china to which he'd added a prosperous industrial ceramics empire. Thick black hair framed a rugged face. There was an inward elegance to him, a grace of manner that gentled the haphazardly cut cheekbones and rakish black brows. Large gray eyes were locked in brooding concentration, revealing all the strength but little of the innate kindness behind them.

The atrium of Colebrook International's new offices

plunged down from his spot on an upper balcony. A few stories below him was a masterpiece of architecture. The serpentine bridge seemed to float across a lobby packed with people. Looking down, men in tuxedos and women in beautiful evening gowns crowded the bridge. Artemas gazed past them, at more guests, at liveried servers carrying silver trays filled with hors d'oeuvres and glasses of champagne, at an orchestra playing Mozart, at the lobby's centerpiece garden and the magnificent blue-green willow tree that dominated it.

Artemas stared at the tree and clenched his hands on the balcony's railing. *Salix cyaneus "MacKenzieii."* As a boy, he'd climbed ones so similar to it, along the MacKenzies' creek. A blue willow. A mutant. A botanical mystery. A marvel.

One of Lily's trees.

He waited, his chest aching with anticipation and restraint. Finally she appeared from under the willow's delicate, draping limbs. She was laughing, her head tilted back as if by the weight of the mane of red hair drawn up in a soft, chic bundle. She was so tall, she stood out even among the luscious jungle of plants surrounding the willow, her simple black gown catching heedlessly on the fronds and branches as she strode through the greenery. Her body was rangy and full-figured, her face vibrant, fascinating, with strong features. Men scrutinized her as if she were some queenly Amazon.

She carried her giggling red-haired son over one shoulder, one strong bare arm braced across his back, her diamond bracelet catching the light. She held him with the careful confidence of a woman who'd grown up shouldering sacks of feed and fertilizer. People around the garden's marble border laughed awkwardly and stared.

Lily had never given a damn for appearances.

Artemas watched her with the desperate knowledge that after tonight's opening ceremonies there would be no reason for her to set foot in his presence again, no reason for her to endure even the most innocent contact with him.

She was not part of his family, not one of the five Colebrook siblings whom he spotted on the bridge or in the lobby below. She did not work for him—not anymore, now that the garden she'd designed was finished. She would never curry his favor like the politicians and business leaders, like the executives from companies owned by Colebrook International, not even like her own husband and her husband's partner, the architects who'd designed this building.

Lily MacKenzie Porter. Her son was not his. Her life was not his. She was another man's wife.

But she had belonged to Artemas since the day she was born.

"Help! I'm caught in the zipper."

"Hold on, mister, you'll rip off something important. We'd have to call you Stephanie instead of Stephen." Kneeling in the loamy mulch among the plants, trying to ward off her six-year-old's helpful hands, Lily tucked and zipped, then straightened his child-sized tuxedo. "Next time you have to pee, you tell me before you get desperate. This place has more toilets than the Atlanta stadium. I'll find one for you. Okay?"

"Okay. But I want to see Daddy give his talk."

"Daddy's just going to go up on the bridge and say, 'Yep, we built the whole doggoned thing. Thank you very much.'"

"Him and Frank and Mr. Grant and *you*."

"I just did the garden."

"I like the garden best of all."

"That's because you've got farmer blood in you." Lily ruffled his red hair. "Can't let you look *too* neat," she whispered, grinning at him. "Daddy wouldn't recognize you."

She led Stephen from the garden, and they sat on the marble edge while she slipped her feet back into the high-heeled black shoes she'd dumped there. Her back, though covered by the gown's sheer black yoke, felt exposed and cold. A bead of perspiration crept down her spine.

She wondered if Artemas was still high above them,

watching. After tonight, thank God, she could retreat from the memories and the unceasing sense of accusation.

The number of times they'd seen and spoken to each other over the past few years could be counted on the fingers of one hand. And each time he'd been unfailingly polite, even distant. No hint of their history had escaped, no ungallant invitation to forget her marriage vows, no attempt to remind her that he'd given this project to Richard's firm because he thought it fulfilled an old debt of honor to her.

He'd done nothing to make her think about him when she made love to her husband. Yet he probably hoped she did. That was a torment she'd never admit to anyone and had fought with every ounce of loyalty to Richard.

"Where have you two been?" asked Richard, walking out of the crowd around them and clamping a hand on their son's shoulder. "I like to know where you are."

Lily looked up into her husband's flushed face. Big and stocky—he could have played football in college if he'd had the kind of brutal streak the sport demanded— Richard was, instead, as gentle and dependable as a tame bear. She loved him, even if she wanted to shake him sometimes just to hear a growl.

Brown hair shagged over his forehead, and she knew he'd been running his hands through it again. His neck was red and splotchy above the white collar of his dress shirt; his black bow tie was askew. Richard belonged in muddy hiking boots, flannel shirts, and faded jeans, with a calculator in his shirt pocket and a roll of blueprints under one beefy arm. He always looked uncomfortable in the custom-tailored tux, which he wore only when forced to by social proprieties.

Tonight he looked as if he might split a seam. Lily stood, laid a hand along his jaw, and resisted an urge to ruffle his hair the way she'd ruffled Stephen's. "Take a deep breath, sweetie. You and Frank have gone through hell to make this place what it is, and tonight you ought to enjoy it. Think about your award from the American Institute of Architects. Relax."

"I just want this over with." He bent close to the diamond cluster on her right ear and whispered, "It's been bad enough having Julia Colebrook ranting and raving every minute of the past three years, but tonight we've got the whole goddamned Colebrook tribe. I wouldn't be surprised if Julia takes them on a tour of the men's rest rooms to point out that the urinals are an inch higher than she thinks they ought to be."

Lily frowned. The Colebrook siblings were a clannish group, all six of them—reclusive, infinitely loyal to each other but especially to Artemas, the eldest. They were unpretentious for people who had a famous name and so much money, and every one of them worked in the family businesses. Together they owned an overwhelming majority of the public stock. Together they'd saved a ruined china company from bankruptcy and their family's name from disgrace.

And when Artemas gave one of them a project, impressing him and the rest of the family became an obsession. Julia Colebrook was thus obsessed. She would probably make Richard miserable until the last hurrah. The whole project from its beginning had twisted Lily's own emotions into knots as well.

She gave in and ruffled Richard's hair, then said grimly, "Julia Colebrook just doesn't like to bump her balls when she squats."

Richard managed a wan smile. Lily caught a whiff of his breath. Alarm and surprise scattered goose bumps down her spine. Other than an occasional beer, Richard never drank. He thought her nightly glass of wine with dinner was one step from Baptist hell. "Your breath smells like free-samples day at a package store," she said, casting a glance at Stephen, who, to her relief, was gazing up in distracted wonder at the bridge overhead.

"I'm nervous," Richard answered, ramming his hands through his hair. Lily stared at him. Nervousness in Richard was as rare as hen's teeth. He had always radiated the unshakable serenity of a man who, while not dull-witted or ignorant, embraced life simply. Simple goals guided him—love for her and their son, rigid honesty, hard work.

"I have to go," Richard said. He cupped her face in his hands, looked at her with a brand of anxiety she'd never seen before, and kissed her on the forehead. "Stay right here, all right? I'm coming back as soon as the ceremonies are over. I want to get out and go home. I love you, Red."

"I love you too. And you're going to be great up there."

He swallowed hard. "Your trust is one of the best things that ever happened to me."

He knelt in front of Stephen and hugged him. Stephen wrapped his arms around his father's neck and beamed at him. "I love you, Daddy."

"I love you, too, you little turnip." Richard drew him close, clasped the back of his head, and shut his eyes as he held the boy. As Lily studied Richard's drawn expression, she put a hand on his shoulder. His eyes were full of tears when he looked up at her.

Stunned, she finally said, "You come back as fast as you can. I want to talk to you when we get home. You need a vacation."

He nodded, rose, and set Stephen aside, then disappeared into the crowd. Lily stared after him, worried and confused.

She felt Stephen's hand in hers, breaking her train of thought. "Daddy doesn't like giving talks, does he, Mommy?"

"No, he doesn't. And this is the most important project he's ever worked on. But he'll be all right."

Frank's arrival cut Lily's brooding short. He came through the crowd in a flurry of elegant steps that propelled his dapper, lanky body between the guests without brushing a sequined elbow or tuxedoed arm. Richard's partner had the blue-blooded social training of a prince and the ambition of a mobster. She wondered where he'd been all evening. Usually he and Richard were inseparable.

"She says she wants to start the ceremonies in five minutes," he told her, throwing up both hands in defeat. The *she* was undoubtedly Julia Colebrook. "I told her they're scheduled for eight-thirty, not eight-fifteen. She changed the program. Damn her. I can't find Oliver. And where's Richard?"

"Richard just headed for the bridge. Oliver's probably in hiding. I heard Julia introduce him to her sisters as 'the contractor from hell.' They looked at him as if he'd hidden corpses in the walls. I watched one of the most respected building contractors in this part of the country turn red and mumble like a fool."

"That's what she's reduced us to," Frank said, rubbing a high, elegant forehead with a hand that bore a diamond pinkie ring. "I can't believe she's going to twist the knife right until the end."

"Yes, it's hard to imagine why she'd hate your guts. All you did was break off your affair by sticking a 'Dear Julia' note to a blueprint you sent her."

"Thanks a lot. That was a year ago."

"I wouldn't forget in one year's time if I were Julia."

Frank sighed. "I'll go find Oliver. We'll meet Richard on the bridge."

Stephen grabbed Frank's coattail. "Can I go with you? I think Daddy needs me to hold his hand."

"It's up to your mother." Frank was scanning the crowd. A sheen of perspiration gleamed on his forehead. Frank, as cool as he was brilliant, was no less rattled than Richard tonight.

Stephen tugged on Lily's hand. She looked down into his solemn blue eyes. "Please? I want to be with Daddy when he gives his talk."

"All right. But be a quiet little gentleman, okay? And if you have to go to the bathroom again, tell Daddy the minute you need to." Lily dropped to her heels, hitching her snug gown up a little, and stuck her fingers in her mouth. She combed Stephen's mop of hair with long red nails. "I knew these false fingernails would be good for something besides scratching itches," she teased. "There. You're handsome. Go and tell Daddy we love him."

"I will." They traded hugs, then Frank picked the boy

up and walked wordlessly into the crowd. Lily waved as Stephen twisted over Frank's shoulder and blew her a kiss.

After he faced forward again, she stood in pensive thought, her hand still in the air. A movement high above her caught her eye. Without thinking, she glanced upward, past the willow, the bridge, up the beehive of offices around the atrium. Colebrook had demanded a design more like a hotel than offices, Richard complained. It wasn't practical.

No, it wasn't. It was grand and soaring, a statement, part of a vision. Her gaze rose compulsively, up, up, until it reached him.

Artemas still stood on the balcony, looking down at her. He nodded slightly. She dropped her hand to her side, realizing it appeared as if she were paying homage to him.

Michael was coughing, his inhaler in one hand, when Artemas reached the lobby floor and went to him. "Are you all right?" Artemas asked, laying a hand between his shoulder blades, feeling the ridges of his spine even through his clothes. Michael nodded wearily. "I must be allergic to some of the plants in the garden. My asthma kicked in. No big deal." He shook his head slightly, warning Artemas not to make an issue of it. His allergies and asthma were nothing new, and since the devastation of his wife's death, he'd become even more aware that the family viewed him as frail, which he hated. But the irritation was tempered with a smile, as usual.

"Okay," Artemas said, slapping his shoulder and moving away. Cassandra stood nearby, flicking ashes from a long, slender cigarette into her empty champagne glass and enviously eyeing Elizabeth, who was eating yet another miniature cheesecake she'd taken from a passing tray. "Where's James?" Artemas asked, moving into the central spot his three siblings gave him in their midst.

"Over there near the stairway to the bridge, talking sports with some pompous fart from the Atlanta Braves management," Cassandra answered. "While Alise tries to keep from yawning."

Artemas glanced toward one of the marble stairways that descended from either end of the bridge like down-turned wings. Satisfied when he located James and his wife, he raised his eyes to the bridge, where Julia had commandeered the small dais at its center like a chic blond general in an Adolfo uniform. She was thumping the microphone. No detail, not even these last, minor ones, escaped her. Artemas had asked her to take full charge of the new building shortly after the family had agreed that costs and quality of life made the move from New York to Atlanta a smart business decision. Eager to impress the family with her coup, she'd made it clear that no one, not even Artemas, was going to look over her shoulder.

A grim smile came to his mouth. He'd distanced himself from the project admirably.

Lily had been right to accuse him of maneuvering himself into her life, unwanted, when he'd hired her husband and his partner to design Colebrook International's new headquarters and when he'd made it difficult for her to turn down his request that her small landscaping firm create the interior gardens, but she could never accuse him of any motive except a desire to win her respect again.

Julia turned and spoke to Richard Porter. Artemas watched the husky, broad-faced architect and thought how solid and intelligent and plodding he was, according to Julia's reports. Like a goddamned mule.

Frank Stockman made his way through the crowd on the bridge, carrying Lily's son. Artemas felt a mixture of emotions for the boy—resentment because he was Porter's blood, but affection because he was Lily's. With the curly red hair—just like Lily's hair—tousled on his forehead, he looked as cheerful and sweet as a Raggedy Andy doll.

Artemas watched, surprised, as Richard frowned at his partner. Richard brushed past Julia and took Stephen from the other man's arms.

Elizabeth's soft, startled voice broke Artemas's concentration. "What was *that*?" his sister said. He pivoted and saw her staring at the lobby's white-marble floor.

"I felt it too," Michael said, tucking his inhaler into an inner pocket of his dinner jacket and frowning.

"What?" Cassandra demanded.

Elizabeth looked up at Artemas worriedly. "A tremor."

Alert, instantly aware of his command, Artemas swept a shrewd look around the crowded lobby. Other than a few murmured remarks and quizzical looks, the crowd seemed unfazed. He relaxed. "Probably a sonic boom. Something going on at the Dobbins airfields. A Lockheed test."

Cassandra exhaled a puff of white smoke and crushed her cigarette into her fluted glass. "Are you kidding? With our connections? The United States Air Force had better not rattle a Colebrook party."

When nothing else happened, Artemas fixed his attention on the bridge again, where Julia had just begun her welcoming remarks. Suddenly a hand settled on his arm from behind, the fingers digging rudely through the fine black cloth of his jacket, the grip aggravating and rough. Surprise and anger flooded him. Artemas turned and clenched the offending hand by its wrist.

And met Lily's frozen gaze. "Lily?" he said, his mind blank with confusion. Her complexion was chalky. Her gaze darted past him. In a voice so low only he could hear it, she said, "Look at the tapestry hanging on the wall to your left. Second story. Near the point where the bridge merges with the balcony. Don't say anything. Just look."

He swiveled and followed her gaze. Cold horror slid through him, all other thoughts and emotions evaporating. A vertical crack easily ten feet long had opened in the wall alongside the tapestry.

He raised a hand and signaled Michael, Cass, and Elizabeth with a soft snap of his fingers. They looked at him curiously. "Find the security guards," he said, his tone soft and controlled. "Tell them to very quietly move people away from the bridge and *off* the bridge. We don't want anyone to panic and run. Someone might be hurt."

Startled, they looked in the unwavering direction of his gaze. Elizabeth gasped. Cassandra carefully handed her glass to a passing server. Michael shot a grim look toward the people standing near the bridge's overhanging staircases and said, "James. Alise."

He and his sisters pushed into the crowd—not frantic, but coolly determined. Artemas caught Lily's arm as she angled past him. She whipped around and said in a barely audible but steely voice, "I don't know if that crack means anything serious or not, but I have to get Richard and Stephen down."

"I'll go with you. I'll send Julia down and take her place, as if nothing's wrong."

They moved toward the curving staircase, his hand still latched around her arm. She looked over her shoulder at the dais on the bridge. Stephen saw her and waved from the safety of Richard's arms. Richard was staring straight ahead, as if lost in thought. "Stay here," Artemas told Lily, swinging her to face him. "I'll get them down. I swear it."

"Don't tell me what to do. I'm not one of your people."

The floor trembled again, worse this time. Adrenaline shot through Artemas. People around them staggered. Cries of alarm came from some. Lily jerked her arm free and plowed toward the bridge, cupping both hands around her mouth and yelling up, "Get off the—"

Her voice was lost in the deafening groan of concrete and steel tearing apart. The marble floor shuddered, and the hotel gave a guttural roar, as if in pain. Julia Colebrook shoved the microphone out of her way and latched both hands onto the balcony in front of it. Her eyes were vivid with shock.

Lily's voice died in her throat. Her attention was riveted on Richard and Stephen. Richard stumbled as the bridge swayed, Stephen's expression was a frozen mask of terror, stabbing her, making her reach out to him uselessly. Richard pulled their son's head into the crook of one shoulder and covered it with a hand. Richard's face was brutal with concentration as he tried to keep his balance. People were shrieking and shoving at each other on the bridge and the balcony, which began to sag on both sides. Frank tumbled to his knees, his hands flailing for a hold.

"Richard! Stephen!" She screamed their names repeatedly as she staggered up the first few steps of the staircase, falling, losing one of her shoes, being knocked back by people rushing down from the bridge. Fierce hands lifted her. Artemas.

He circled her waist with one arm, lifted her half off her feet, and dragged her back to the lobby floor. "We'll never get up there in time! Come on!" He wound a hand in the back of her dress and pulled her, staggering, after him. They reached the floor in front of the bridge's collapsing center. "Julia, *jump*," Artemas yelled.

Lily held her arms up. "Richard! Throw Stephen to me! Throw him!"

But the bridge folded in the center like an overburdened paper plate, piling people together in a terrible heap of struggling bodies. A woman in a glittering silver gown tumbled over the balustrade and plunged to the lobby floor dozens of feet below, landing with a sickening thud. Richard and Stephen were being pressed against the sinking balustrade along the bridge's front, the crowd mashing them horribly. Stephen's small arms tightened around his father's neck, and he screamed for Lily.

"Throw him!" she cried, trying to get under the bridge's railing, stopped only by Artemas's grip on her dress. "Julia!" he called again, his deep voice resonating with authority and frustration.

The bridge collapsed, ripping down the balconies of the floor above it, pulling them inward on top of itself, swallowing the crowd trapped on its surface.

Artemas jerked Lily backward as chunks of marble fell in front of them. She sprawled with him on the hard floor, her hands winding into his shirt. Together they twisted, staring back at the bridge.

He saw his sister try to cover her head as she was enveloped in jagged concrete, marble, and steel. He heard Lily's blood-freezing scream of horror and felt her hands convulse into fists against his chest, as Richard and Stephen disappeared into the same hell.

• • •

The rattle of jackhammers. The growl of a crane's engine. Shouts. Sirens. Dust. Blood. Paramedics rushed from the dead to the injured. A dozen bodies lay in a corner of the lobby, covered in blankets. Frank Stockman's body was among them.

Julia's body lay in one of her sibling's arms.

Artemas stood over them, drained of hope, filthy, his fingers raw and bleeding from digging into the jagged debris. She was strange, a horrible and pitiful remnant of herself. A trickle of blood had dried at the corner of her lips. Her torso was oddly distorted, like a doll who'd been crushed by a careless foot.

His baby sister. The loss was so stunning he had no words, no tears, only a lethal sense of fury and determination. He would break down after he sorted through the horror and found the cause. Cassandra and Michael wore shattered expressions. Elizabeth sat by Julia's head, sobbing as she gently stroked both hands over her sister's blond hair.

Artemas moved leadenly. He had given so many orders, directed so many terrified people, tried to organize the chaos. He had to go back to Lily, who was still searching through the debris.

Lily. Julia. James. The rest of his family. All the others who needed his attention, who'd come here at his invitation. He was being torn apart. He could only move from one scene to the next, as if there were some way he could give them equal time, equal heartache. He walked a few feet away, where James lay on a stretcher. Alise was huddled beside him, one hand on his forehead, her gaze fixed with abject terror on his groggy, half-shut eyes and the oxygen cup that covered his mouth. Paramedics were bundling him in blankets and pulling straps tight across his body. James's right leg was bare to the thigh, the trouser leg cut off. Blood seeped onto the stretcher under its twisted wreckage.

The sight of his proud, vigorous younger brother lying maimed and helpless made bile rise in Artemas's throat. He looked down into James's eyes. James raised a hand and, fumbling, pushed the oxygen mask aside. His lips moved faintly. "Why? *How?* Who did this . . . to us?"

Artemas touched James's cheek, leaving a stain of blood. "I'll find out. And destroy them."

"Make them pay . . . forever. . . ." James's voice trailed off. A paramedic slid the oxygen cup back into place.

Artemas found himself back with the others, dazed, not quite knowing how he'd returned. His muscles felt slack. Words came like dream-induced thoughts. "I have to stay here," he said. "One of you should go to the hospital with Alise and James."

He didn't know if they heard him. He walked away, pulled his blood-and-dust-stained jacket off, dropped it on the floor, and continued onward, absently wiping his bleeding fingertips on his shirtsleeves. A policeman ran up to him and asked a question about the building's exits. Artemas's gaze went to Oliver Grant. The contractor sat limply on a chair by one wall, his head in his hands.

Artemas strode to him, lifted him by the lapels of his dinner jacket, and slammed him against the wall. "Why did this happen? I want answers."

Grant was crying. He stared at Artemas blankly, shaking his head. The policeman wedged himself between Artemas and the contractor. "He's in shock, Mr. Colebrook."

Artemas shook Grant, then let him go. The man slid down the wall and sat down limply on the floor. Artemas bent over, wrenched his chin upward with one hand, and looked into his eyes. Grant's expression quickened with horror; he stared up at Artemas's deadly expression in fear. Artemas said, "You help this officer. He has questions about the building. Help him, or by God, you'll be sorry."

Grant finally nodded.

Artemas walked away. *Can Grant tell you why this happened? Who's responsible? Is he the one? Or, God, Stockman and . . . Porter. Lily's husband.*

The terrible idea would have to be dealt with later. Artemas skirted the mountain of steel and concrete in the lobby, sidestepping crying people, police, and paramedics, and workers guiding the crane's claw onto a lopsided boulder.

He was jolted by the sight of Lily and several men halfway up the side of the jagged mound, frantically shoving at the smaller slabs of concrete. Barefoot, her hose ripped to shreds, she was balanced precariously on the uneven surface, her feet braced apart. She'd ripped the skirt of her gown up the front to her knees to free her movements. The ruined skirt trailed across the debris in a ragged train. Long strands of her hair hung down around her neck and over her eyes.

Her hands and arms were streaked with sweat and dust. She clawed at the debris as Artemas had, not caring about the effect on her bare fingers. She shouldered her way in between the men and fitted her hands under a slab bristling with torn steel cable.

Artemas climbed the debris and pushed his way in beside her. "There's a space under here," someone told him. "We caught a glimpse of it."

The slab shifted. With one more shove, it slid away. Lily lunged on her hands and knees to the lip of the dark space it revealed, her face stark with fear and determination. "They're *here,* they're here," she chanted, lying on her stomach and reaching down inside the opening. "Get a flashlight," Artemas said to the others.

He moved to her side and grasped her by the shoulders. "Don't look." She clung to the edge of the hole and refused to let him pull her away. "They're alive." Her voice was ragged, hollow. "Let go of me."

"Lily, you have to move back." He slid an arm under her and pulled her away slightly. Her arm still strained toward the dark pit.

Someone knelt at the edge and angled the flashlight's beam downward.

Richard still had Stephen in his arms, and they were not alive. One glance told Artemas that.

And Lily. Her hand fell limply. He let her go, and she

pulled herself to the edge again, lying absolutely still, looking down into the light. Then she curved her arm under her head and rested her face there, her eyes shut. Silent sobs racked her body.

He bent his head to hers and cried with her. Their legacy that had begun so long ago was doomed.

Two

MacKenzie, Georgia, 1962

Artemas was only seven years old, but he knew a lot of secrets, most of them bewildering and terrible.

Uncle Charles had big balls and a tight ass. That was one secret. Father said so. Artemas must never again ask President Kennedy to arm-wrestle when the president was visiting at Uncle Charles's house, because it embarrassed Uncle Charles. Uncle Charles was the only Colebrook who'd inherited the Family Business Sense, and that was why Grandmother let him run the Colebrook China Company. She owned it but nobody asked her to do any work. That was another secret.

Father had married Mother for her money. Mother was half-Spanish, and Spaniards were Failed Royalty, whatever that was, but Mother was also, as Father put it, a Gold-Plated Philadelphia Hughs. What upset Father was that she'd done some mysterious bad things with money, and that had made Grandfather and Grandmother Hughs mad, so they'd stopped owning her, they'd *Disowned* her, and her money had gone to Aunt Lucille, who'd married a Texas oilman and moved to a ranch, where people said she was raising children and hell.

Artemas loved Mother and Father desperately. That was no secret, but his love couldn't erase their frightening moods or the whispered words he'd heard once among the servants at Port's Heart, the home Grandfather Hughs had given them, by the ocean on Long Island.

The children will be marked for life.

Other secrets were trickier. No one told him they were secrets; he decided on his own. He'd rather die than reveal what he'd seen his parents do once in the gazebo at Port's Heart, after the bank men from New York drove away with boxes full of Father's important papers. Artemas, playing in the roses nearby, had been too frightened and horrified to let his parents know he was there.

Father and Mother had yelled at each other about money. Then Father tore Mother's skirt open and shoved her down on the gazebo's hard marble floor. Mother slapped Father, and Father hit her back until she screamed. Then he opened the front of his pants, got on top of her, and pushed down between her legs so hard that she began crying. He bumped up and down on her. Then he said, "You're as worthless as I am, you spoiled bitch."

The next day Mother cut up all her ball gowns with a pair of garden clippers. Then she bought new ones. There always seemed to be money for what Mother and Father wanted, particularly for clothes, parties, and travel. Father was on the board of Colebrook China, but Uncle Charles didn't ask him to do much, so he had plenty of free time.

The currents swirling around his family frightened Artemas. Only one place was safe from them.

Blue Willow. For the past two years Artemas had spent his holidays and summers there, with grand, dignified Grandmother Colebrook.

Blue Willow was a lost kingdom, with ruined outbuildings, dark forests, and overgrown fields to explore, and in the center was an enormous, echo-filled mansion perfect for a seven-year-old's fantasies, all hidden safely in the wild, watchful mountains of Georgia. Zea MacKenzie, the housekeeper; her husband, Drew, the gardener; and Drew's parents lived on their farm in the hollow beyond the mansion's lake and hills, along the ancient Cherokee trail. They were poor, Grandmother said, but they were MacKenzies, and that would always make them special.

Grandmother was special too. People whispered that when she was young she'd been something called a Ziegfeld Girl, before she became a Golddigger and married Grandfather. Grandfather had slipped and fallen out a window on Wall Street during the Depression, so to help Grandmother after he died, his sisters took Father and Uncle Charles away from her.

They told Grandmother she could stay at Blue Willow, and they'd raise her sons for her, in New York. She'd been at Blue Willow ever since. Which was fine with Artemas, because it meant he could visit her. Grandmother said he was her Consolation Prize, and he liked the sound of that.

But she was too old to keep up with a little boy all the time, so she turned him over to the wonderful MacKenzies. He loved them and felt loved by them in a way that made him feel frantic with guilt and confusion when he thought of his parents. Every day with the MacKenzies was an adventure. If being poor only meant that you had to live on a farm like theirs, he wanted to be their kind of poor.

The Colebrooks were poor now, too, but in a different way. They looked rich enough, but people felt sorry for them behind their backs. That was one of the secrets he must keep, Grandmother said.

Without money, all a Colebrook had was the Right Friends and an Important Name. Mother said that was enough, if you knew who to suck up to.

Artemas decided to avoid learning more family secrets if he could help it.

Mrs. MacKenzie was dusting Colebrook china and telling stories. "When Gabriel comes back to blow his horn, the Colebrooks will probably send their butler out to shoo him off, and the MacKenzies will tell him to hie his fanny away till the crops come in," she told Artemas solemnly.

"Bumfuddled by such an ornery pair of families, old Gabriel won't remember his toot from his toenail."

Artemas liked the way Mrs. MacKenzie put things.

"The MacKenzies and Colebrooks are stuck together like green on a frog's butt," she continued. "They've shared secrets and dreams for more years than you can imagine, Artie. Blue Willow is at the center of their covenant, and always will be."

"What's a covenant?"

"It's like a circle of promises, and as long as nobody breaks the circle, everybody will be safe inside."

Mrs. MacKenzie gave a little gasp of pain and stopped dusting, one hand on the huge stomach straining against the fabric of her uniform and apron, the other letting the duster droop. Beams of September sunlight cast weird shadows over her through the mansion's tall leaded-glass windows. Everything in the enormous upstairs gallery was in shadow except her, and several generations of Colebrooks watched from their portraits on the teak wall. Her red hair, plaited in fat braids around the crown of her head, gleamed like blood.

She hunched over Artemas, who sat on the rug in grubby overalls, barefoot, hugging his knees as he gazed up at her, transfixed. Just a few minutes earlier she'd been telling a story about the time Grandpa MacKenzie drank too much corn liquor and threw up on the preacher. Now, Artemas thought she was going to tell another throwing-up story.

But she shut her eyes and rocked back and forth on the heels of her sturdy work shoes, her face pinched and drained of blood. This wasn't the beginning of a story.

Artemas leaped up. "What's wrong? Is the baby coming?"

She exhaled, chuckled, and opened her eyes. "No, it's just Mother Nature making plans for a few weeks from now." She winked at Artemas, her blue eyes nearly the color of the blue pattern on the china plate she'd been dusting, and brushed a glistening arm over her forehead.

Tears burned like lemon juice in his eyes. Colebrook

boys never cried. They knew what they wanted and how to get it, Father said, so Artemas willed the tears back. "I won't be here then. Grandmother's closing Blue Willow next week. She has to come live with us, in New York."

Mrs. MacKenzie, who was always laughing and teasing, looked sad for the first time. She bent down quickly and kissed his forehead. He threw his strong, suntanned little arms around her neck and hugged her, and she held him protectively. "You're too serious for your age, too full of worry. Let's talk about something happy." She grinned at him. "Drew says when his daddy was young, he made moonshine all the time. And *your* grandpa bought truckloads of it for the parties here. Once, when Fred Astaire was visiting—" She broke off with another sharp gasp. "Lord," she said, and cupped her stomach with trembling hands.

Artemas watched closely. "Did Fred Stare throw up on somebody too?" Then he realized the story had stopped again. Tendrils of fear ran through him. "Is the baby doing something wrong?"

"Oh, I don't think anything's happening. It's a little early—" She gave a strangled yelp. Stepping back and frowning, she studied the dark stain spreading on the threadbare Oriental rug. Artemas, horrified, saw streams of water trickling down her hose and over her sturdy lace-up shoes. Why was she peeing on the rug?

Her rasping breath cut into his embarrassment like a knife. Holding her belly, she staggered to a chaise longue and sat down heavily, straddling one corner. The hem of her uniform sagged between her knees, hiding the source of the terrifying mystery from Artemas's dazed scrutiny. Strange fluids gushed over the velvet upholstery and trickled down one of the chaise's gilded legs. It was a Louis Quinze, whatever that meant. He knew, at least, that people shouldn't pee on it.

"I guess I figured wrong," she said, trying to smile at Artemas. "Go on now, and tell somebody to call Mr. MacKenzie inside. I'm having my baby."

Relief made Artemas's legs weak. Babies! Now he

understood! He knew about female creatures having babies because for the past two summers Mr. and Mrs. MacKenzie had let him watch cows and cats and even a hog give birth.

"I'll get help!" he shouted, and ran to the staircase at the far end of the gallery. He barely touched the steps down two flights to the entrance hall. Running from room to room in the vast main level, he yelled for the butler and the last remaining maid. Minutes ticked by with awful speed. All the big clocks began to chime the half hour. He ducked through a door in the library and hurried down steep narrow stairs to the basement level. His feet echoed eerily on the old tile floor as he searched the laundry rooms and then the row of kitchens, bakeries, and pantries, all sitting empty and quiet.

He threw a stool under the intercom on one wall. Punching buttons, he yelled, "She's having the baby! Come upstairs to the big gallery! Mrs. MacKenzie is having the baby! Get Mr. MacKenzie! Help!" There were so few servants left, and Grandmother had gone out for a drive in her pony cart. Suddenly he remembered that the servants had the afternoon off. They had gone down to Atlanta to shop.

Frantic, he raced to the service elevator, a huge, groaning monster like a jail cell on a pulley. He rode it upstairs and galloped through a maze of hallways to the gallery.

Mrs. MacKenzie was crying on the chaise, her head thrown back, her hands clawing at the cushions. His knees wanted to collapse, but he made himself go to her. "I can't find anybody! What should I do?"

She panted. "You go outdoors and look for Mr. MacKenzie. I'll be all right."

'No, I can't leave you, I can't."

She shuddered and dug her hands into the chaise, her body heaving. "Shit!" she said cheerfully. Artemas was not about to leave her side, held by love and the fear that something terrible would happen if he left.

Mrs. MacKenzie relaxed as if collapsing inward, caught her breath, and grasped his quivering, outstretched hand in both of hers. "This isn't like you watching old Bossy have her calf. You go on now, you hear?"

"I can help. Please, I'm not scared." His teeth chattered, but he stepped closer. "There's nobody else around. I'm not scared, I swear."

"Go on, I said. Mind me!"

She groaned and pushed herself upward on the chaise, until she was propped on the backrest. Dust motes burst into the air as her elbows pumped the old cushions. Her knees drew up spasmodically, and her dress hem slid down to her thighs. Artemas wanted to look away, but he couldn't. Her hose and garter belt and white panties were soaked in pinkish water, and her stomach bulged as if it would pop like a balloon.

"Is the baby coming out?" he asked, frantically patting one of her knees.

Mrs. MacKenzie gave a choked laugh. "Like a freight train through Atlanta!"

"I'll help! I helped with the hog! Please, please, tell me what to do!"

"Me and the hog ought to be grateful, I guess. This is not for a little boy to see. But you're no ordinary little boy, I figure." Grunting and pushing herself upright, she wailed softly. "Stand up by my head, and don't watch."

A little relieved at that idea, he moved close to her and turned his head toward the gallery of his ancestors. A dozen Colebrook men and women watched from tall portraits in gilt frames. He tried to concentrate on them. MacKenzie and Colebrook, sharing again, part of the circle, chasing Gabriel back to heaven . . .

The raw sound of ripping cloth made him jump. He turned and watched Mrs. MacKenzie tear her panties from between her legs. The heat of embarrassment seared his face for a second, then faded in a rush of curiosity.

"It looks just like Bossy's place, but smaller," he said in awe.

Mrs. MacKenzie chortled at his comment, then moaned and cried out "Drew!" as if her husband were there. Artemas's heart thudded painfully in his chest. She struggled to reach over her huge belly again, gasping and sweating, her face unrecognizable with lines of pain.

"Come here, Artie," she commanded. "You've gotta make sure the baby doesn't slide off the couch."

The very idea of a baby bouncing onto the floor made him lurch around to the end of the chaise, his hands splayed out in readiness. His legs nearly collapsed when he saw the gory opening between Mrs. MacKenzie's legs fill with the dome of the baby's head. Sheer willpower pushed him forward as Mrs. MacKenzie dug her thick black shoes into the chaise and threw her head back. In one convulsive shove she slid the baby into his quivering hands.

Warm. She was warm, soft, and covered in sticky blood. A fibrous cord led from her navel back inside Mrs. MacKenzie. Life pulsed through her. Holding her was like holding a beating heart, his heart, because it expanded with sheer wonder at the sight of her. Her eyes were squinted shut. Her arms and legs quivered and seemed to reach toward him. She had a funny, puckered frown on her face. She opened her mouth and wailed for a moment.

He had saved her from bouncing on the floor. He had done something worthwhile, something that made all his shame and family secrets seem unimportant. If he could do this, he could do anything, save everyone and everything who depended on him. He loved her, and he would never be the same.

"I've got her!" he said loudly, and repeated it several times. Tears slid down his face. "I did it! I caught her! She's gooey and funny-looking! Isn't she great?"

"Artie, hold her up, hold her up so I can see if she's all right." Mrs. MacKenzie took long, hoarse breaths of relief. Trembling with worry over every movement, he lifted the baby higher.

Mrs. MacKenzie's eyes gleamed with pleasure. "Look at her, oh look," she crooned. Artie put her in Mrs. MacKenzie's outstretched hands and sat down limply on the bloody chaise. Mrs. MacKenzie laid the baby across one thigh and sat up gingerly, pulling her dress down over her private parts and the long umbilical cord. "Artie, you did just fine," she said, smiling wearily at him. "I tell you what, you're one brave little man. And I'll promise you this—you'll never see a first baby born that fast again. I bet I set a record."

He stared fixedly at the baby. She opened her eyes. "She's looking right at me! Hello, little girl." His lungs were bellows, and he wanted to shout with excitement. He knew he'd never forget this moment. "What's her name?" he whispered.

"I don't know. It's bad luck to name a baby before it comes." They sat in silence for a moment, while Mrs. MacKenzie rubbed the baby dry with the hem of her white cotton slip. Motherly tenderness radiated from her hands and eyes. For a heart-stopping second Artemas wondered if she might bend down and lick the baby, the way animals did. But she only lifted her to her chest, dragging the bloody cord, and cuddled her. The baby mewled softly against the mounds of Mrs. MacKenzie's breasts. Her dried hair was a lighter red than her mother's.

"What do you think her name ought to be?" Mrs. MacKenzie asked.

Artemas, transfixed, almost said "Carrot," then kicked himself for being so stupid. He thought immediately of the flower bulbs he had helped Mr. MacKenzie plant in one of the gardens that morning. On the burlap sack that held them was a color picture of the flowers in bloom, and he'd never seen anything like their soft orangy red until now.

"Lily," he blurted.

"Lily. Lily." The baby mewled again. "I think she likes that." Mrs. MacKenzie looked at him thoughtfully. "Lilies are strong and pretty. They endure. Lily. Yes sir, I like that a lot. I bet Mr. MacKenzie will too."

Artemas thought his chest would burst with happiness. "You mean you'll name her that? Really?"

"Really. Lily MacKenzie. Because you're a special boy, and you helped bring her into the world. See? We MacKenzies and Colebrooks are stuck together like glue. Been that way for one hundred and twenty years. Probably'll be that way forever."

Artemas reached out gently and touched one of the baby's outflung hands. The tiny fingers curled around his. He sighed. Everything was all right. There would always be MacKenzies and Colebrooks here at Blue Willow, and it would always be a place to love. Lily MacKenzie owned him, heart and soul.

The long black car brought him to the MacKenzie farm on the last day. He was dressed in a black jacket, linen shirt, tie, knee-length gray shorts, white socks, and stiff black shoes. His black hair had been brushed by the nanny until his head hurt. He had promised himself he would not cry. He was important now. He had to be strong.

The farm sat in a big hollow surrounded by forested hills. If he had been allowed, he would have climbed them one more time to look at Victory Mountain, miles away. His ancestors had owned the land all the way to that mountain, but Grandmother had to sell that part to the state, for a park. Now, instead of enclosing a kingdom, the Blue Willow estate enclosed only thirty square miles. It was still more land than Artemas could imagine.

The driver opened the car door, and Artemas got out slowly. The MacKenzies were waiting for him on the porch of their farmhouse—Mr. MacKenzie, tall and strong, one arm ending in a nifty metal hook, his tanned face and brown hair making him the same color as a long stretch of earth. Grandfather and Grandmother MacKenzie, both old and hunched but full of great stories about bears and wildcats and Colebrooks, and Mrs. Mackenzie, holding Lily.

Artemas measured his step across the sandy yard, stepping with dignity past the flower beds and under the big oaks, ignoring the fat yellow dog licking his hand and the purring cats coming out to meet him. Inside he was an empty ache.

The thick grove of willows along the creek moved gracefully, waving good-bye to him. Their history was tied up in the mysterious circle of MacKenzies and Colebrooks. There was even a huge willow in the park at the estate's entrance, given to his family by the MacKenzies. That was *his* tree. He thought he'd die if he never got to climb it again.

"How do, Artie," Mr. MacKenzie said kindly, then came down the porch steps and scooped Artemas up in his good arm. Startled, Artemas choked up, hating the way his lower lip trembled. Drew MacKenzie was the opposite of his own father. Without the least embarrassment he gave Artemas a deep hug and kissed him on the forehead. "You be good now, you hear? You grow up to be the kind of man your grandmother wants you to be, all right?"

The store of confusion and heartbreak and shame inside his chest burst up through Artemas's throat and couldn't be contained any longer. He said brokenly, "Grandmother says it's all up to me. But I try to make things better, and I never can. I try and try until it hurts so much I can't breathe. I *know* I can fix things some way. But how can I figure it out by myself?"

He heard Mrs. MacKenzie make a soft sound, like a cat searching for its kittens. "You helped bring Lily into the world. You caught her and kept her from fallin'. If you care that way for everybody who needs you, you won't go far wrong."

Artemas pondered that clear-cut idea and clung to it. "Catch people and keep them from falling. I can do that."

Mr. MacKenzie patted his leg approvingly. "Always do what's right, not just what's easiest. Listen to the wise voice inside you. Don't ever stop listenin', and it'll tell you exactly."

Artemas nodded, gripping one of the suspenders that kept the old brown trousers from sliding down Mr. MacKenzie's long legs. "I'll miss you," he finally managed.

Mr. MacKenzie nodded, swallowed again, and carried him up to the porch. He set him down in front of the grandfolks. Their warm, gnarled hands patted Artemas as if he were a beloved puppy, and Grandmother MacKenzie said a prayer for his future. Then he went to Zea MacKenzie and Lily.

His chest was tight with memories—all the days and nights he'd spent here with Mrs. MacKenzie, wearing soft overalls and going barefoot, eating fresh peaches and homemade ice cream, working in the fields, playing with the animals. She knelt down in front of him, her big blue eyes full of tears, and swept him to her while she cradled Lily in her other arm. The baby, dressed in a diaper and tiny white T-shirt, seemed to look straight at him.

"We'll take care of Blue Willow for you," Mrs. MacKenzie whispered.

Tears crept down Artemas's cheeks then, and he couldn't stop them. "I'll come back. I promise." He looked at the baby, cleared his throat, and said what he wanted to say most. "I'll come back and marry Lily, and then you'll really be my family."

Mrs. MacKenzie hugged him tighter and made a soft chuckling sound. "You come back when you're grown and talk to Lily about it."

"I will. Promise you won't move away."

"I can't picture this farm without a MacKenzie on it," she said vaguely. "We'll see."

"I'll come back."

Mrs. MacKenzie searched his firm, tear-streaked face silently. She looked sad. "Good-bye, Artie. Stay this sweet, and you'll do fine."

"I will come back, I swear." He bent over and kissed Lily's red hair. "I caught you," he whispered to her. "You're mine."

Before he got into the car, he turned and looked at them all one last time. Confusion, love, and grief hollowed him. They didn't believe he'd never forget them. But they didn't know how stubborn he was, or how possessive of the people he loved. Lily was his. They had a covenant.

Three

Mama said the Old Brook Prince had helped her get born and named her and promised to come back and marry her someday, and that he'd left his home in her keeping, and that made Lily the only bona fide princess-in-waiting in the town of MacKenzie.

Not that Lily cared about boys or getting married, but she supposed that after she got rich and important and old she might want a boy as strong and sweet as Daddy around to help do the farm chores. She'd heard the only way a girl could get a boy for good was to marry him.

The girls in her Sunday school class said nobody else would want to marry her anyway, because her daddy had a hook for a hand and her mama came from white trash, and even if the MacKenzies had a town named after them, she was too big and ugly and mean. The Old Brook Prince wouldn't mind though. He'd promised.

So there it was. When she needed to get a boy, she'd marry the Old Brook Prince.

Flat on her stomach, Lily hugged the thick willow limb and stared, wide-eyed and fascinated, through the drooping blue-gray leaves. *A stranger was coming.* Sassafras, mired in the weedy grass far below her, her shaggy yellow coat dotted in runny brown splotches from the rotten crab apples Lily had dropped on her, sucked her dripping pink tongue in and woofed softly, watching him too.

Didn't he know this was the main driveway through Blue Willow? How had he gotten past the giant old gate? Only MacKenzies could walk on this road or play in this big tree.

The tall, unsmiling boy sidestepped cracks in the pavement, where weeds jutted up. He wore a green uniform like the soldiers on TV, and it looked just as dirty and rumpled. Maybe he'd been fighting Vietcong too.

Lily crept like an inchworm farther along the limb, her bare toes digging into the crevices of the rough bark, her overalls snagging on a twig. It was hard to move; she had the last of the mushy crab apples in her hands. She'd gotten them from the bottom of the barrel stored in the barn since last fall. Their slimy juice squeezed between her fingers.

Who was he? His hair was black and short as a scrub brush. He had a pack on his back. Below one eye was a big, ugly bruise.

The hackles rose on Sassafras's ruff. Her good ear—the one that the bobcat hadn't chewed on—flattened against her head. She ran out from under the tree, roo-roo-rooing at him. He stopped and frowned at her. He didn't know that Sassafras hadn't ever bitten anything but fleas.

"Nice dog," he said. "I remember you. Big, dumb, nice dog." He had a voice like the boys in high school. It cracked from up to down in two words. But it wasn't like their voices, or Lily's. It was fast even when it was slow.

But Sassafras wagged at him and sat down, convinced. He walked past, his near eye squinting at her over the bruise. Then he looked at the huge willow, and Lily bunched up, hoping he wouldn't see her. He walked into the weedy old park around it, sighed, took off his backpack, then dropped it on the ground. He patted the rusty sign on the stone post there, the one that had a lot of words she was just beginning to learn on it. MacKenzie. Colebrook. Blue Willow. One-nine-oh-oh. Rubbing a long, skinny arm across his forehead, he ducked under the low-hanging limbs.

Directly under her bomb path.

Because he was trespassing on the land the Old Brook Prince had put in her keeping, and because a bad little girl had taken over her hand, she dropped one of the apples on him. It burst right on the top of his head.

"Christ almighty goddamn!" He jumped to one side, all arms and legs, like Scarecrow in *The Wizard of Oz*, dragging his hands over his head and staring up into the tree. "You little shit!"

She was five-and-a-half, but she knew the hottest brand of hellfire when she heard it. The blast of shock made her toes let go and her knees turn weak. She slid sideways, screamed, clawed at the limb, and fell.

Lily landed in his outstretched arms. What was left of her breath exploded out of her in a *whump* that caved her chest into her backbone, and stars shot across her eyes.

She moaned and gulped. The stars turned into fireflies. He laid her on the soft earth. His sweaty, bruised, open-mouthed face appeared in the middle of the stars, and his bony knees settled against her side. Syrupy brown apple juice slid down one side of his face like blood.

Halfman. He could be Halfman, the haint who kept watch over MacKenzies and might float down from the mountains to eat little girls who'd been bad. He was staring at her with big gray eyes like a wolf's.

"Breathe, for God's sake!" he said.

She inhaled raggedly. "Don't eat me!"

"I'm not going to eat you!" He moved his hands over her face. They smelled like jonquils and gasoline. He was pulling aside one of the long red braids that was draped across her chin. He patted her head. Halfman probably wouldn't have done that.

A little reassured, her air coming back, she dug her elbows and heels into the ground, scooted away, and sat up. Sassafras licked her cheek. Lily's eyes burned from staring at the stranger without a blink. "What were you doing up there?" he demanded.

"Playing."

"Where'd you get apples in my willow tree?"

"I brought 'em with me."

"Where do you live?"

She jerked her shivering head toward the woods. "Way over yonder."

"How'd you get here?"

"My daddy left me while he went to the big house to fix a window."

"Whose house?"

"Down yonder. The prince's house." She pointed a trembling finger over her shoulder, toward the cracked road disappearing into the forest.

His mouth was beginning to turn up at the corners. "What prince?"

"The Old Brook Prince. He named me."

"You mean the Colebrook . . . prince?"

She nodded. "But he went away when I was born."

"And you live way across the woods over there?" He lifted a long, wolfish arm and pointed.

"Yeah. On a farm."

Now, he was staring at *her* without blinking. He took the end of one of her braids between his fingers and tugged it gently. "Lily? Is your name Lily MacKenzie?"

She nodded, stunned.

His wild gray eyes became tame, his horrible-looking face smiled, and he suddenly became the handsomest boy she'd ever seen. "Well, I'm the Old Brook Prince."

Artemas had a mission. He'd told Mrs. MacKenzie he'd come back, and this might be his only chance. He was thirteen, old enough to see that he couldn't control much about his life. But he listened to the voice inside him, the one that always had a MacKenzie drawl to it. It said keep your promises and do what was right.

Before the future closed in on him, he'd say his good-byes.

So he'd run away from the military school in Connecticut, taken a bus as far as his money held out, which was

Memphis, then started hitchhiking. On a lonely country road south of the city a pair of black boys with arms like stone posts had climbed out of their pickup truck and jumped him. His face throbbed and one side ached as if their fists were still in it.

But he was here, finally. With the MacKenzies. When Mrs. MacKenzie came out on the porch and saw him riding behind Mr. MacKenzie and Lily on the tractor, she screamed and laughed and ran to him with her arms out. He jumped down and hugged her like a kid, but he didn't cry. He was thirteen years old, after all. And he felt even older. The farm looked run-down, paint peeling, fences leaning like toothpicks. Only the willows along the creek were as wonderful as his memories. They, and the love he felt around him.

"Grandmother knows where I am," he told them, when they were all sitting on the porch. "I sent her a letter. My parents are somewhere in Europe." *Sponging off their friends.*

"My Lord, my Lord," Mrs. Mackenzie said, sinking into a chair and pulling at the apron over her jeans. "Artie, what were you thinking?"

He shrugged, embarrassed. "I hate school." *I hate everything,* he added to himself.

"Me too," Lily chirped. "I'm in kindergarten, and I'm bigger than everybody else. Even the boys."

He looked down at her in wonder. She sat by his feet at the base of a rocking chair and watched him with wide blue eyes. She was plump and freckled, missing a front tooth, and fuzzy bits of red hair stuck out of her braids. Apple slime was smeared on the white T-shirt inside her overalls.

It would be a long time before she'd turn into anything he might want to marry. She was only three years older than his youngest sister, Julia. Besides, he'd decided a long time ago that he wouldn't get married. Not if it made him act like his parents.

Yet he reached over and pretended to thump her head,

and a feeling of protectiveness stole over him. "I'm sorry I scared you out of my tree."

"It's *my* tree. I take care of it."

"You'll have to be the 'Old Brook Princess' to own my tree."

Her face became solemn. She looked up at him the way she had under the willow, when he'd smiled at her. Mrs. MacKenzie grinned down at her. "Lily doesn't want to be a princess, she wants to be a farmer."

Lily blushed red from the hair down. "And a princess," she whispered, then got up and ran into the house.

Mr. MacKenzie drove him to Aunt Maude's house, in town. Drew MacKenzie couldn't work the farm very well with one good hand and only Mrs. MacKenzie to help him. Artemas was shocked to realize Mr. MacKenzie had brought him to Aunt Maude's because the farm had no phone. Then he remembered it hadn't ever had one. That merely curious fact from Artemas's childhood now became a grim one as he understood: The MacKenzies couldn't afford a phone.

During the ride to town he cast pensive glances at Mr. MacKenzie, who was still a strong giant with a smile for everyone. But he looked grim and tired, and his brown hair had thinned so much that Artemas could glimpse the freckled tan scalp of his crown. He wasn't old, but his shoulders were stooped. He'd lost his left hand in a hunting accident as a boy, and the metal hook he wore had fascinated Artemas. Now, he saw that the hook was tarnished and dented, ugly, pitiful.

Artemas called his grandmother in New York. She lectured him about his responsibilities and said she'd arrange a plane ticket for him. She'd negotiate with the school about his punishment.

Grandmother said he'd only end up bitter and small, like Uncle Charles, if he didn't stay at school. A military career was her dream for him; a Colebrook could redeem the family's name with discipline and service. She'd use her connections to have him nominated to West Point after he graduated from prep school.

After all, he was a top student, a leader, and a Colebrook. That might not mean much to the rest of the world anymore, but it meant everything to her. The whole world sat on Artemas's shoulders.

Humbled and depressed, Artemas barely touched his dinner of peas and corn bread with the MacKenzies that night. Grandpa MacKenzie had died a year ago. Grandma MacKenzie had heart trouble and stayed in bed all day, knitting and reading her Bible. They helped her to the table. As she gummed corn bread and buttermilk, she watched him with bright little eyes.

"You've got to go back, boy," she said. "You're too old to run off from responsibility."

Responsibility. Artemas hung his head. All grandmothers had that word welded to their dentures. They didn't know just how much responsibility he had. His parents had lost Port's Heart to the bank. They'd moved the family to Uncle Charles's shabby but still respectable estate, where Charles disdainfully refused to share the main house. Instead, he gave them an old ten-room cottage that had served as the estate manager's home in the glory years long before Artemas's birth. Dismayed by the ignominy, Artemas's parents cultivated their far-flung friends and were always visiting somewhere, often for weeks or even months at a time. They left Artemas's brother and sisters in the care of governesses.

Grandmother, who lived in the main house, was constantly fighting and scheming to evade Uncle Charles's control. Charles's wife snubbed the entire Colebrook clan and paraded their college-age daughters in society, telling everyone that she'd get them safely married to money and a better name.

Grandmother told Artemas that neither Uncle Charles nor Father were the men she would have raised them to be, if she'd had the power to keep them with her at Blue Willow, but at least Uncle Charles was bright enough to keep Colebrook China out of bankruptcy. She put up with him.

Artemas tried to set an example for his brothers and sisters and make certain they were treated decently. He tried to live up to Grandmother's expectations. He tried manfully to ignore his uncle's nasty comments and petty humiliations.

He was filled up to the throat with trying, and he knew how it felt to strangle.

Mrs. MacKenzie clucked at his lack of appetite, then rose and came to him. "I'll put some more liniment on you after I've washed the dishes," she said, smoothing her warm, callused hands over his throbbing face. "You rest now, you hear? You have to go back to New York, but you sure don't have to worry about it until tomorrow."

He was shocked at how her touch embarrassed him. He wanted to stare at the large breasts making mounds under her short-sleeved flannel shirt. He'd never thought of her that way, almost six years ago. He flushed from the inside out, filling with strange, discomforting sensations he'd begun suffering lately around the opposite sex. Guilty and confused, he looked away. Nothing was the same.

But Mrs. MacKenzie ruffled his crew cut as if he were still a child. "I think it's time Lily heard the bear story. I bet you don't even remember me tellin' it to you when you were little, do you, Artie?"

"I remember." He shot a grateful look at her, warming to the memory. Cutting his eyes across the table at Lily, he added, "But I bet it's too scary for a little girl."

"Is not," she chirped. "I saw a baby bear in the back pasture last year. And I didn't run."

"I bet *it* ran," he countered, arching a brow. "I bet it said, 'There's that monkey with the rotten apples.'"

"I'm not a monkey!"

Mrs. MacKenzie put her hands up. "Hush, both of you. Do you want me to tell the story, or not?"

"Yes!" they answered in unison.

After the dishes were washed and put away, and they'd helped Grandma MacKenzie back to bed, and Mr.

MacKenzie had gone out to check on the livestock for the night, Mrs. MacKenzie took Artemas and Lily to the plain little front parlor, switched on a small ceramic lamp on a claw-footed table in one corner, and told them to sit on the couch. Lily curled up beside Artemas, cheerfully elbowing him in the ribs. He thumbed his nose at her, and her mouth popped open in shock. "Mama, he—"

"Tattletale," he interjected.

She clamped her mouth shut and gave him a slit-eyed stare, but said no more.

Suddenly Mrs. MacKenzie crouched and growled, capturing their attention. The lamp cast spooky shadows on her. She crooked her hands into ferocious bear paws and growled again. "This is the story of how the MacKenzies and the Colebrooks met. It's about Old Artemas"—she pointed to Artemas—"who was your great-great-great-grandpa, and Elspeth MacKenzie"— she pointed to Lily— "who was your great-great-great-grandma."

Lily couldn't figure out why people who weren't even around anymore were called *great,* but as long as her relatives were as great as Artemas's, she wouldn't protest.

"Old Artemas came straight off a ship from England and traveled through these woods looking for a place to settle. Elspeth had come here a few years before that, from Scotland. She lived right here, in a cabin where this very house stands today. Her husband died, and she had two half-grown sons to raise."

Mama growled and clawed the air. "Old Artemas was young and strong, but he didn't know these woods. There came a bear!" Lily jumped, then slid closer to Artemas. Her mother leaned over them, her hands hooked, glaring at Artemas, who smiled in anticipation.

"The bear, he rose up over your great-great-great-grandpa, with his fangs dripping slobber—the bear, not your grandpa—and then, then, that big black bear, he drew back one big paw and ripped your grandpa's arm right to the bone!"

Her arms waved wildly as she pawed the air inches

from their faces. Lily was breathless with excitement. "What happened then?"

"Old Artemas whipped out his hunting knife with his good hand, and he quick-like cut that bear's heart out!" She snatched a piece of kindling from the hearth and carved an imaginary bear. "And he ate it!"

"Agh! Neat!"

"Then he staggered off through the woods, dripping blood—Old Artemas, not the bear—with his arm hanging half off." She let her right arm dangle as she staggered dramatically. "And finally he fell down, and he crawled, and he crawled, and he crawled, because he was a big, tough Englishman, and he wasn't about to give up and die when he'd only been in America a few months."

"And then Elspeth MacKenzie found him," Artemas said, leaning forward eagerly.

"That's right. The Widow MacKenzie, with her two half-grown sons, took in that wild-looking stranger, all torn and bloody where the bear had clawed him. There weren't any doctors in these mountains then. The widow Elspeth sewed his arm up and nursed him while he healed, and he fell in love with her, because she was so smart and strong and pretty."

"Like you!" Lily said.

"Elspeth's two half-grown sons became like kin to Old Artemas, and they even forgave him for being an Englishman and city-born and a terrible farmer, what with the MacKenzies being Scots and lovers of the land."

She clasped her hands over her heart dramatically. "Elspeth told Artemas he'd never make a farmer, and he had to do what God had gifted him to do, just like all his people before, back in England. She helped him find the white clay the Indians had told her about, right down here in the creek bottom over at Blue Willow."

"Where the big lake is now," Artemas said.

"Right there, yessir. Down where the bass swim now, at the bottom of Clay Lake, that's right where old Artemas dug the clay and set up his china business."

"Is the building still there?" Lily wanted to know. "If I held my nose and sat on the bottom, could I see it?"

"No, no, the MacKenzies burned it all down right before the war. But that's another story. Now, where was I?"

"About Old Artemas's clay," Artemas told her.

"Yes. Well, he knew this clay was special, just as fine and creamy as the clay the Chinamen had used to make the most beautiful china in the world. So Artemas built himself a potter's wheel, and a furnace, and he went to work. And in a year he was sending white china down to Marthasville by wagon to be sold and shipped. He and Elspeth were so happy over it all."

Lily nodded drolly. "And then he got rich, because he was a Colebrook."

"Hold your horses, that wasn't till lots later. Anyhow, everything was fine until the next spring, when Old Halfman came through."

Lily huddled closer to Artemas but looked up at him slyly. "I know what *he* looks like." Artemas put an arm around her. Her sly expression dissolved into red-faced delight.

Mama drew herself up and waved her kindling like a wand. "He was half—Cherokee Indian and half colored, and everybody was scared of him, not only because of him being different, but because he was a preacher, and a peddler, and a soothsayer."

Lily dragged her attention back to her mother. "What's a soot sayer?"

"A sort of witch. Halfman would look at people's spit and blood, and tell their futures."

"Their *spit and blood*? Ugh!"

"Halfman was sickly, and Elspeth let him stay in her barn. She fed him and took care of him. And when he got ready to leave, Elspeth called on him to tell her future. She drew a sharp knife across her forefinger." Mama pretended to slash her finger with the stick of kindling. "*Drip, drip, drip.* Her red blood fell into Halfman's palm. Then she spit on top of it."

"Into his hand? Ugh!"

"But that's the way it had to be done. Halfman, he looked at his palm, and he shook his head. Then he reached into his big ol' peddler's bag and pulled out a pair of little-bitty willow saplings, all wrapped in dirt and paper. And their leaves were *blue*, not like any other willows in the whole world. He smeared Elspeth's spit and blood on them. 'You're the blue willow,' he said, looking straight at Elspeth. And she stared back in horror—because she knew he meant she was going to die."

"How did she know? How?"

"Because willows are women. That's what the ancients said. And blue women are sad women. And the only thing that would make Elspeth sad would be to leave her land and her sons—and Artemas, her new husband."

"Wow!"

"Then Halfman said, 'These here are magic trees, not like any others. For love of you they and all that grow from their seed will keep your loved ones safe, them and theirs and all that cometh from their blood.'"

"Neat!"

"So she planted those little saplings down by the creek, right out there"—Mama pointed to a window, making Lily crane her head in fascination, as if the original trees were right outside—"and they grew tall and beautiful."

Lily hugged her knees. "And Elspeth went to heaven?"

"Yes, she went to heaven having Old Artemas's baby, and the baby went with her."

Lily looked at Artemas ruefully. "I guess God put you here to make up for that. You're supposed to do what I tell you to do."

"Hmmm." He hooked his arm around her neck and jostled her as if she were a small wrestler. "I think I was put here to catch you. You don't bounce very well."

Her face broke into a puckish grin. Turning back to her mother, she waited for more with wide eyes. Mama was watching the two of them with a soft little smile. "Anyway, when Elspeth was being buried, Halfman showed up. No one knew how he'd heard she'd died. He just came, like some kind of all-seeing mountain spirit, to pay his respects to Elspeth and her blue willows. People said he was never seen again, after that day."

"But he still lives in the mountains?"

"Could be."

"And what happened to Old Artemas?"

"Oh, it was terrible. Elspeth's sons turned away from him. They said he'd killed their mother. Old Artemas had to leave their farm and live in the back of his potter's shop."

"Under the lake!"

She nodded patiently. "Under the lake now. And he grieved and grieved. He wanted to tell the whole world about his Elspeth, his blue willow. He thought about an old, old Chinese china pattern called Blue Willow, and he decided he'd make his own pattern from it, in dark blue cobalt from the iron mines over in Birmingham. And he did. And his work was so special that people couldn't mistake any other Chinese willow pattern for the Colebrook Blue Willow, and it became famous, and Marthasville became Atlanta, and Artemas became a rich man, with a big house over by the Toqua, and a corn mill, and of course, his china factory."

"Under the lake!"

"Under the lake, that's right. But his money couldn't buy love from Elspeth's sons, who never stopped blaming him for what happened to her. To make matters worse, Artemas married a Yankee woman visiting from New York and turned to supporting the northern cause."

Lily frowned. "Artemas isn't a Yankee 'cause he's from New York, is he?"

"No, I'm sure the shame's worn off by now," Mama said. "Anyway, Elspeth's sons were grown men then, important farmers with wives and children of their own, and they had duties to the town they'd started."

"MacKenzie? Just like now?"

"Uh-huh. So they had stronger roots here than Old Artemas, and besides, there's no accounting for people's politics. Anyway, the war made the MacKenzies and

Colebrooks enemies. Bad times, bad blood. Elspeth's sons got a big gang of men together and rode over the Smoky Hollow Trail late one night when the moon was dark, and they set fire to Old Artemas's house, and his china factory, and everything else he owned, 'cept his corn mill, which folks around here needed."

"That was mean."

"I guess that's where you get your temper from," Artemas quipped. Lily elbowed him again.

"Yes, it sure was mean," Mama continued. "And Old Artemas, he came over to their farm the next Sunday, when they were at church in town, and he brought his own gang of men, and they kept the field hands back while Artemas cut Elspeth's trees down. He burned them—burned them to the roots. It was his way of saying her boys had broken the bond between him and them."

"What did they do then?"

"Nothing. There was no mending the terrible breach between them and Old Artemas. He said he'd leave and not come back until he could lord it over every MacKenzie in the county. So he took his money and his Yankee wife, and he went to New York. And he bought clay quarries, and that led to buying iron mines to get the blue cobalt from, and pretty soon he and that woman had grown sons who knew how to buy things and make money, and the Colebrooks sold the best china in the country besides owning all sorts of businesses. And in those thirty years they became rich as Midas and began struttin' like bantam roosters." Mama's eyes became wide with drama. "But you know what? *The willows grew back.* They couldn't be killed, because Elspeth's love was too strong!"

Lily squealed and clapped her hands. "Because they're *magic.*"

"Yes."

Artemas had grown silent and withdrawn. Now, he took his arm from around Lily's neck and, propping his arms on his legs, stared at the floor. Lily worriedly poked him on one knee. "I like you anyway, you rich rooster."

"Thanks for nothing."

"Hmmmph." Mama scowled. "Well, the MacKenzies never got rich, not by Colebrook standards, but they were always the best farmers in north Georgia, and on top of that they became county-court judges, and sheriffs, and preachers—and moonshiners, but that's another story."

Lily bounced. "Tell me, please!"

"No, no. I only meant to tell the bear story. It's gettin' late."

"Can't you tell her how the Colebrooks came back?" Artemas said, raising his head slowly, his eyes somber. Mama looked down at him for a minute, then sighed. "Oh, well, all right." Sitting down on the floor by Lily, who gazed from her to Artemas with puzzled sympathy, she said, "You know that sign under the big willow up on the estate road?"

"Yes, ma'am?"

"Well, your great-grandparents gave that tree to Artemas's great-grandparents, when they came here in 1895. Johnathan Colebrook was rich, richer than all the other Colebrooks, because he inherited most of the family money. He came down here from New York to build Blue Willow and reclaim his grandfather's—Old Artemas's—home."

Mrs. MacKenzie cleared her throat. "But when ol' Johnathan said, 'Why, I think I'll buy everything for miles around here and build one of the biggest houses in America,' the grandsons of Elspeth's boys said, 'You're not lording it over us. Have at it, but we're not selling.' Johnathan saw there wasn't any getting around the MacKenzies—except to buy the land around 'em. So that's how Blue Willow came to be, and the MacKenzie farm came to be in the middle of it."

Lily studied Artemas. "But how come you left?" She leaned in and peered at his face. "Aren't you a rooster anymore?"

"Stop making fun of me."

"I'm *not*. I think you ought to stay. I want you to stay. You promised to come back and stay."

"Shut up." He bounded up from the couch. "I'm going to sit in the pasture a little while." The front door screen slammed loudly as he stomped onto the porch. Lily scrambled after him. "Artemas, Artemas," she called plaintively. Her mother grabbed her by the back of her overalls and swung her into her arms. "Shush, Lily," she whispered. "He's sad. He needs to be alone for a little while."

"Why is he sad?"

"Because his family isn't what it started out to be, and he's ashamed. Don't you ever tell him I said that. He's a fine boy."

Lily swiveled her head and looked out the window, tracking Artemas's tall, rigid form as he walked through the distant pasture in the moonlight, her small heart throbbing with bewilderment and compassion.

Late that night he sat by Grandma Mackenzie's bed in a narrow room smelling of old wood and spring air and read her Bible to her, feeling awkward because no one in his family had ever expected him to do anything more religious than sleep in church. His ancestors had built one of the biggest Episcopalian churches in New York. Father said they'd bought all the blessings they needed.

Mr. and Mrs. MacKenzie went to their bedroom upstairs. Lily slept on a cot in her grandmother's room, but she crept out of it and snuggled on the bed beside the old lady, her mop of curly red hair brushed to a smooth mane, a big T-shirt of her father's swallowing her to her skinned knees. She curled up with her head on the soft lap covered in quilts, watching Artemas with gentle, curious eyes.

Grandma MacKenzie fell asleep. Artemas put the Bible on her nightstand and told Lily with all the big-brother firmness he used on his siblings, "You go to sleep too."

"I play on the loggie at the big house," she told him.

"You mean the loggia?"

"Uh-huh. The big porch. I wish I could see inside. Will you take the boards off the windows?"

"I can't." He looked away sadly. "I would, though, if it was up to me."

"What's inside?"

"Nothing. It's all empty. Everything was sold."

"Mama says it's like a castle in a fairy tale."

"I guess. I liked it."

"How many brothers and sisters do you have?"

He frowned at her change of subject. She wasn't predictable. He liked for people to be predictable. "Yeah. Five."

"I wish I did."

"Why don't you?"

"The doctor says Mama can't. She tried." Lily yawned. "One came out last year, but it was dead as a rock."

"Geez! What a way to say it!"

"Well, sometimes animals have trouble, and they die. I've seen 'em. The cat ate her kitten. I found its tail." She shut her eyes and sighed.

Artemas got up, feeling miserable and lonely. "Shit."

She gasped. Her head wobbled up. "You're going to hell."

"Good."

He burrowed his hands under her, then carried her to the cot. She snuggled into the soft old mattress but opened her eyes as he put the sheet and quilt over her. "I won't let you go to hell. I'm strong. I can look out for you."

"That's good. I'll leave it up to you."

"But you gotta stay here and live with us."

"I can't do that. Could *you* run away and leave your family?"

"No, 'cause *my* family's not mean to me."

"Parts of my family aren't mean either. That's why I have to go back."

"Make them come here."

Tears stung his eyes. "You just don't understand *anything,* do you? Go to sleep, you little apple-throwing monkey."

He left the room, flicking the light switch on the faded rose-papered wall. She lay in the darkness, wrestling with her conscience and her sorrow. Mama and Daddy said family matters were private, that the family was something to be proud of—to fight for. And that meant holding the truth close to your heart and keeping your head up when stupid girls in kindergarten teased you.

So she never told anyone how ashamed and angry their teasing made her.

But Artemas needed to know he wasn't alone.

She scooted out of bed and tiptoed through the house, into the living room, where he lay on the couch in the darkness with one of Grandma's quilts over him and a pillow jammed under his head. Lily crept to his side, sat down cross-legged in the floor, and poked him on the shoulder.

"Go back to bed, for God's sake," he muttered.

Tears slid down her face. In a small, choked voice she said, "Don't feel sad, Artemas. At kindergarten they call me Monster Head, because I'm so big. I bet it'll be even worse in first grade."

He turned on his side. She could feel him looking at her. "They just wish they were like you." His voice was soft, friendly.

She sniffed in surprise. "Why?"

"Because you're a MacKenzie, and MacKenzies are special."

That was too easy. She persisted. "And a boy in Sunday School said Daddy is . . . is *a cripple*. And that Mama is . . . *a nobody*, because she was poor and nobody wanted her when she was little." She bowed her head, tears falling freely on the undershirt wadded in her lap. "I hit him with a rock."

Artemas gave her a kind little shove on the shoulder, to get her attention. "Listen to me. Don't *ever* let anybody make you feel bad. I wish my mother and father were just like yours."

She stared at him, her tears evaporating. "You do?"

"I do." He tugged lightly on a strand of her hair. "We'll make everybody sorry they made us feel bad, won't we?"

"Yeah!"

"And as long as we know what's right, it doesn't matter what anybody else thinks, does it?"

"No!" This was startling. He *understood*. Nobody else would ever understand better. Lily crossed her arms on the couch and pillowed her head on them, close to his side. He draped his arm around her shoulders, awkwardly at first, then relaxing. She gave a peaceful little sigh, and was asleep within a minute.

Mr. MacKenzie cranked the truck and sat in the driver's seat, waiting. He wasn't one for long good-byes, he said. Neither was Artemas.

"Here's my address at school," he said, drawing a slip of paper from his knapsack and handing it to Mrs. MacKenzie. "I thought, maybe, sometimes—"

"We'll write to you," Mrs. MacKenzie answered softly.

Lily, still wearing her nightshirt, whimpered, ran forward, and threw her arms around his knees. Looking up at him, she cried, "I want you to stay!"

Shaken, he dropped to his heels and gripped her shoulders. "I can't stay, and I can't come back. When you're as old as I am, you'll understand."

"Why did you come if you won't stay?" she insisted, tears sliding between the freckles on her round cheeks.

"Because I promised. Now, be a big girl and behave."

"I love you!" She wiggled out of his grip and put her arms around his neck. Mortified, he sat rigidly still. Then, awkwardly, he put his arms around her for a quick squeeze. "Good-bye, Lily," he said against her hair. "I love you too. Remember what I said last night. And if you ever need help, you write and tell me. Promise?"

"I don't need help! I'm a *MacKenzie*!"

He gently pushed her away and stood, but held one of her hands. She bit her lip and looked up at him tenaciously. "You will come back. You *will*. Christ almighty goddamn."

"Lily!" Mrs. MacKenzie said. Pulling her aside, she swatted her on the rump. "Where did you learn talk like that?"

"From *him*, the big shit."

Mrs. MacKenzie gasped. "I'll deal with you later, miss."

"I love you all," Artemas said gruffly. His voice cracked. He turned and stomped out of the house. Lily ran behind him and stood on the porch's edge, gripping the rail as he went to the truck. "You will come back!" she called. "I'm the Old Brook Princess, and I say so!"

He turned and bowed to her. Mrs. MacKenzie came out and took her by the shoulders, holding her shaking, furious little body against her legs. "Take care, Artie," Mrs. MacKenzie called, crying now herself.

He sat straight-backed on the truck's passenger side and stared at nothing, his jaw clenched, as Mr. MacKenzie drove out of the yard.

"I don't need your help, I don't need your help," Lily muttered brokenly, her voice trailing off to a defeated whimper. "Come back."

The neat brown box arrived in the mail a month later. Lily stared with avid excitement as Mama put it on the scarred old kitchen table. Daddy sat down and pulled Lily onto his lap. She curled her fingers around his metal hook, playing absently with the wire tendons. Mama stood over the box, clipping its tape with her sewing shears. "It's from Artemas."

She pulled a bulky object wrapped in thick white paper out of the box, set it on the table, and unfolded the paper slowly. She covered her mouth and stared at a small, perfect teapot. "Oh, Artie." She drew a trembling finger over the rich blue design on creamy white. "See this, Lily? It's the Blue Willow pattern. The pattern came all the way from China. See the willow and the bridge, and the little sparrows kissing each other? See how clean and pretty the blue color is, and all the little details in the pictures? Nobody made Blue Willow china as pretty as the Colebrooks. That's how they became famous." Picking up the delicate lid, she saw a piece of paper inside. She laid the lid down reverently and unfolded it.

Clearing her throat, she read, " 'This is old. It's worth a lot of money. I took it for you when I went home for a weekend. Grandmother knows. You can sell it.' "

Mama sank into a chair and put her head in her hands. Daddy sighed. "The boy means well."

Lily scowled at the teapot, a horrible realization growing inside her. "He thinks we're *poor*? He thinks we're trashy?"

"No, no, hush," Mama said sternly.

Mortified, Lily was still stunned. Mama and Daddy looked upset, but they didn't seem angry. "MacKenzies don't take *welfare*," she chirped, mouthing the terrible word she'd heard her parents use often, with so much loathing.

"It's not welfare, because we're never going to sell it," Daddy said. Mama nodded. But she pulled the teapot against her breasts and hugged it. "It's a gift of friendship. Artie was only trying to show us how much we mean to him."

That night, after Daddy had gone to bed and Grandma was snoring in her room, Mama took a pen and piece of notebook paper and called Lily into the parlor. They sat on the couch, Mama balancing the paper on one of the old encyclopedias that were stored in a glass-doored bookcase by the window. "What do you want to say to Artie?" she asked.

"That we're not poor."

"Don't you want to write to him—nice things, not things that will only confuse him?"

Lily sighed, confused herself. "Say, 'I'll take care of the teapot for you. Come back.' "

Mama wrote diligently for several minutes, then placed the encyclopedia and its paper on Lily's lap and handed her the pen. "Put your name at the bottom."

Lily bit her lip in concentration and wrote it in large, blocky letters, as big as her pride, as filled with emotion as a scratchy pen on rough paper could make it.

Artemas lay on his bunk in a bare little room with nothing but khaki-green walls and hard furniture, a place of such unremitting ugliness that every day he realized more of his own emptiness. He opened the plain little envelope reverently, touching it with fingers made callused from the chores and duties of a cadet. Mrs. Mackenzie's neat, looping handwriting was so pretty, in contrast to his surroundings.

There will always be a place for you here. When you are feeling bad and don't know that anyone loves you, don't forget that we do. You will be fine if you remember that you can make yourself whatever you want to be, no matter what people do to you. Your gift will always be part of our family, and so will you.

Lily's childishly exuberant name was scrawled at the bottom.

From then on he wrote to her, short, simple notes on the school's stationery or his own notepaper, a nice card when he had a chance to buy one. Mrs. MacKenzie wrote back, telling him about ordinary, funny things that happened on the farm, always with Lily's signature at the bottom, and never hinted that their life was anything but the fantasy he wanted it to be.

four

The Schulhorns had made their money in newspapers, but the fortune was so old that the last Schulhorn who'd actually worked in the business was a forgotten twig in the family tree. Now, the Schulhorns lived off their investments. *Never touch your principal,* Mr. Schulhorn said to Father. Artemas doubted Mr. Schulhorn had been near a principle in years.

He and Mother had been in college together, though Mother had been kicked out for some mysterious dishonor no one discussed. The Schulhorns lived on one of their family estates outside Philadelphia. Artemas detested spending part of his summer vacation with them, but it was better than staying at home, where Uncle Charles found ways to badger him and humiliate the younger ones. Uncle had nosed around at school and learned about Artemas running away last year. *You'll never be anything but a loser,* he told Artemas smugly. *Just like your father.*

The walls of the Schulhorns' downstairs gallery were full of animal heads and stuffed birds. Father and Mr. Schulhorn were both hunters; Hemingway's bastard clones, Mother called them. Mother liked to hunt, too, but she preferred to do it on horseback, chasing rabbits and foxes with her hounds. Shooting things was no challenge, she said. She enjoyed a good fight.

Across the garden terrace, Mrs. Schulhorn shrieked with laughter. Artemas forgot his brooding thoughts in a rush of confusion and loathing. She was Mr. Schulhorn's third wife, and he probably hadn't picked her for her personality. Father and Mother were always putting their hands on her, rubbing her shoulders, patting her lower back.

Once, in a hallway with no one else around, she'd cornered Artemas. "You're uptight to be such a good-looking kid," she said. "Always so righteous and quiet, always judging people behind those gray eyes, aren't you? I'm twenty-three, but you look at me as if I'm some snotty brat."

Slit-eyed with amusement, she grasped him between the legs. Her breath, sweet with mint and liquor, had warmed his mouth, though she never kissed him. He stood there quivering in disgust and blinding arousal while she rubbed him with the palm of her hand. His knees buckled a little, his lungs strained for air, and it only took a few seconds for him to realize that he was going to come right there, in his tailored shorts. The rush of heat and moisture was humiliating but irresistible, and he felt trapped. He opened his mouth to say something—"Stop" and "Please," with garbled meaning—but it was over before he could sort the two thoughts out.

"You aren't a saint, kid," she said with a laugh, and walked away.

Out on the long veranda at the back of the house, the servants had set up a buffet for dinner. Mother, Father, and the Schulhorns had been playing tennis and bridge all day, and now they lounged on heavy teak Adirondack chairs with cigarettes and the first of their evening drinks in hand. Mr. Schulhorn's children by his first two marriages were away at riding camp.

Artemas had spent the day watching over his brothers and sisters. He'd taken them on a picnic at the Japanese teahouse in the woods beyond the rolling, manicured lawn, supervised them while they played in the Schulhorns' giant pool, bullied them all into taking an afternoon nap, broken up fights, and cleaned Michael's face when the squabbles made him vomit.

Father and Mother had dismissed the governess months ago. Whenever servants were let go, one of Father's gambling debts must be due, or another of his careless investments had failed, or he'd simply spent too much money on someone or something that had temporarily caught his fancy.

Artemas was tired of playing parent to his siblings. James, twelve, was old enough to help, but James's temper made him unpredictable. Besides, James always hung back and waited for Artemas to tell him what to do. James had wet the bed until he was eight, and all those years of Father's scorn and Mother's embarrassment had taken a toll on his confidence.

The long, full day had worn the younger ones out, finally, and they were eating quietly at a special table set aside from the adults. Artemas cut Julia's roast beef, coaxed Elizabeth to put down the doll that seemed constantly welded under one arm, wiped mashed potatoes off of Michael's T-shirt, and kept a watchful eye on Cassandra's mean-spirited game of stealing food from James's plate. James chewed his fruit salad in contented ignorance.

Artemas didn't want to upset the temporary peace by reprimanding Cass, who suffered enough scolding from Mother. Cass was probably the fattest ten-year-old in America, and she wore her fat like an armor. Her bright, wary hazel eyes were beacons of misery above chipmunk cheeks. The more Mother, who was reed-thin and obsessive about image, humiliated her, the more she ate.

Elizabeth, on the other hand, was slender and lanky, like Michael, her fraternal twin. Now, she edged closer to the side of her chair nearest Artemas, and when he looked down at her, she leaned against him and sighed like a weary old woman, not a pampered eight-year-old. She lived in a secretive little world, peopled by invisible friends who would never threaten her timid nature.

"You okay, bug?" he asked.

She blushed and turned her head against his arm. He patted her head awkwardly. Artemas didn't understand her shyness. She was Father's favorite, with hair the color of sunshine and deep-set, thickly lashed eyes, a ringer for Mother's Hughs relatives. Artemas and Cassandra had black hair, like their Spanish grandmother; James's was dark brown, like Father's; Michael's was sandy. Julia's hair was yellow-white and stringy. Like cheap butter, Mother said.

Father openly doted on Elizabeth, always cuddling her and stroking her hair. He never subjected her to careless taunts or, almost as bad, his nonchalant apathy.

But in the past year she'd begun sneaking into Artemas's bed at night, crying, shivering, clinging to him wordlessly. At first he'd been alarmed—he was too old to have his kid sister climb into his bed when she had nightmares.

No matter what calming things he said or how often he carried her back to her own room, she continued to come. Desperate, he'd told the governess, who'd questioned Elizabeth rigorously about her nightmares. But she'd only say that monsters were after her, and that Artemas kept the monsters away. The governess had locked her in her room at night. But now, with the governess gone, she was showing up in Artemas's bed regularly. Defeated, he simply turned his back and let her huddle against it.

Michael watched everything with merry distraction. Pale and thin, he was always suffering from an allergy or with his asthma. But he had an elfin smile and a vivid imagination that made them all laugh. Already he had a way with words. Grandmother Colebrook's oft-repeated phrase, *Noblesse oblige*, became *No less, oh, please* when Michael said it. He might not know the meaning, Mother said with one of her elegant snorts, but he had the right idea.

Julia kicked an unceasing tattoo on her chair legs and rocked from side to side as she ate. The nannies said they'd never seen a four-year-old with more nervous energy. Julia's favorite pastime was running in small circles until she careened into the nearest piece of furniture and fell down.

"A deer," Mrs. Schulhorn squealed, leaping up and going to the stone balustrade along the terrace. "Come look! It's grazing on the far end of the lawn!"

"We haven't seen a deer in months," Mr. Schulhorn added.

"Bring me a gun," Father yelled to the butler.

Everyone hurried to the balustrade. Artemas led Michael and Elizabeth by the hands. His mouth tasted brassy with anxiety. He knew Father's bloodlust. Father had taken him hunting and fishing many times. When he was younger, he'd wanted to please Father and had been in awe of his big, brawny, fearless attack on life—and on living things.

Now, watching Father yell for the butler, Artemas recoiled. Father's face looked fleshy and evil in the setting sun. Though his forearms, showing under the rolled-up sleeves of a safari shirt, were hard and sinewy, a fleshy paunch hung over his belt. He caught Artemas looking at him, and sarcasm flashed across his expression. "Come here, Art. See if you can kill it cleanly from this distance."

Julia began butting her head against the balustrade. Elizabeth whimpered and hugged her doll. Michael chirped worriedly, "I *like* the deer, Daddy. Don't hurt it." James stuck his fists in his shorts pockets and glowered at the floor. Cassandra headed for a plate of cookies on the buffet. "Don't you dare, you fat little toad," Mother ordered, rolling her eyes. Cassandra slunk back to Artemas's side.

The butler arrived with a powerful rifle cradled in his hands. "Give it to my boy," Father told him.

Artemas shook his head. "Why kill the deer? It's not worth anything as a trophy, and we're not going to eat it."

"Don't question me. Get over here."

Artemas linked Michael's and Elizabeth's hands to Julia's. "Stay together, you three. Go inside with James and Cass."

"No, no," Mother countered, pulling the younger ones

close and ruffling their hair. "It won't harm them to watch. The huntmaster gave me bloody foxtails to play with when I was no older than they."

Artemas took the rifle and stood beside his father. The deer, a small doe, grazed at the edge of the lawn, a hundred yards away. He aimed at a spot in the grass behind it and fired. "Goddamn!" Father yelled, as the doe sprang toward the woods. He snatched the rifle from Artemas and threw it against his shoulder, then pounded out several quick shots. Blood exploded from several places on the doe's side, and she fell. But she struggled to her feet again and staggered into the woods before Father could finish her.

"Artie, how could you?" Mother snapped. "What poor sportsmanship."

Artemas shrugged, so angry he couldn't speak without risking a fight. Father's temper was nasty and could result in a hard slap with little provocation. Father was cursing now, as he shoved the rifle back at the butler. The Schulhorns were laughing. "It's only a deer, Creighton," Mrs. Schulhorn said. "Who cares if your kid's got a soft streak?"

"He's going to be queer, if I'm not careful," Father answered.

"Oh, he won't be a fag," she assured everyone. "He's his father's son, no doubt about it."

Artemas clenched his fists. "We can't just let the doe bleed to death."

"Don't be a fucking sissy," Father retorted. Jabbing a fresh cigar into his mouth, he stalked back to his chair.

Artemas turned toward the butler and took the rifle. "I'm going to find it."

Mother sighed. "Go on, if you want to be silly. But take the others with you. They need to see what life's all about."

"They're too young, Mother."

"I was only five when I went on my first fox hunt. Either you take your brothers and sisters, or you don't go."

Artemas flipped the safety catch on the rifle and handed it to James. "Come on." Carrying Julia on his back, leading Michael, who led Elizabeth, with Cass waddling along behind, they left the terrace via a flight of marble stairs, went through a formal garden, then followed the lawn's edge under the long shadows of the trees.

When they reached the edge of the lawn and turned toward the woods, where they were out of sight of their parents and the Schulhorns, Artemas put Julia down and gathered the others around him. "Stay here."·

"Shit, no," Cassandra blurted. He turned to her sternly, scowling, all big brother, his nerves frayed. One look like that and she was reduced to tears. "Don't kill the deer, Artie. Don't be like Father and Mother."

"I'm not like them." He squatted down and looked at her apologetically. "It's hurt and probably dying. It would be wrong to let it suffer."

She sobbed. Julia jumped from one foot to another in a manic little dance. Michael and Elizabeth started to cry too. James stood by, the gun weighing him down, his mouth set in a hard line but his chin quivering. "Kill it," he said. "It's us against them." Artemas took the rifle. "You make sure the others stay right here."

"I will." James turned toward the others and spit, "Shut up, you stupid crybabies."

His throat burning, Artemas walked into the woods. He found the trail of blood easily. A hundred yards into the forest he discovered the doe, collapsed in the underbrush, blood bubbling from her mouth and nose. He knelt beside her, then carefully stroked her hot, delicate neck. "I'm sorry," he whispered, and tears slid down his face.

He stood abruptly, knowing that sentiment wouldn't get the job done. He put the rifle's muzzle in the soft hollow behind her trembling ear. His hands shook. *I'm better than this. My family's better than this.* The trigger was slick and smooth against his sweating finger. Bitterness soured his stomach. He pulled the trigger.

When he returned to the others, he tried to be calm for their sake. Every muscle in his face strained to hold back his tears. But Michael shrieked when he saw the gore spattered on Artemas's bare legs beneath his walking shorts. "You killed Bambi's mother!"

"Shut up, you little turd," James growled. "Father made him do it."

Artemas handed the rifle back to James, then cleared his throat and sat down in the center of his huddled, crying siblings. "I don't get to do what I want. None of us do, okay? But we have to stick together, no matter what. We have to take care of each other. All right? Be quiet. We're not going to let anybody see us cry. We're going to be better than they are."

Elizabeth, Cassandra, and Michael snuffled and nodded. Julia jerked at a tuft of her ragged blond hair. James saluted. Artemas led them back to the house. He vowed to be the best, the strongest, the most powerful, and the most noble. He would eclipse his parents' dark legacy until there was only a faint outline of their ugliness around him and his brothers and sisters.

Mama and Daddy had more money now; there was a shiny black wall phone on the kitchen wall, and they'd bought a special glass cabinet to display Artemas's teapot. Grandma had died a year ago, and now the room she and Lily had shared was Lily's alone, with a bright white bedstead and matching dresser and desk, and bookcases filled with books on one wall. The other walls were covered in paper printed with trees and flowers. Lily had picked it out because it made her think of being outdoors.

But she missed Grandma terribly. And she missed being a farmer. Mama and Daddy had more money, but they weren't free anymore, and Lily knew it.

A farmer was free. A farmer had to answer only to the land, Daddy said, and the land was a partner, not a boss. But a farmer with only one hand wasn't equal to the land, so Mama and Daddy took jobs at a pet-food plant. They came home each night looking tired and smelling like hot cereal. Sometimes the foreman let them bring home burst bags of feed, for Sassy and the four cats. It all seemed ugly and like welfare to Lily, but she'd never hurt their feelings by saying so.

The afternoons Lily had spent roaming the woods and fields with Sassy were over. After school each day she slunk unhappily off the bus at Aunt Maude's grand white gingerbread house in town, and the only rambling she could do there was in the yards and rose garden out back. Not that Aunt Maude let her ramble much.

Aunt Maude said Lily's mind could wander like an Indian, but her fanny had to stay at the kitchen table, doing homework. And when the homework was done, Aunt Maude read to Lily from encyclopedias or the latest issue of *Newsweek,* or made Lily read out loud from books in Aunt Maude's library. The reading was fun, because Lily loved books, and Aunt Maude approved of that.

And even if it was no fun to be trapped in town, Lily began to take Aunt Maude's favorite saying to heart, once she figured out what it meant. *The only helpless female is an ignorant one.*

Maude Johnson MacKenzie Butler was a general in a girdle, Daddy said. She owned half the buildings around the town square and ran for mayor every two years. Most times, she won. She wasn't kin to Lily by blood, because she was a MacKenzie from marrying Daddy's much older brother, Lawrence, and Daddy said Lawrence had gotten blown up by a mine in Korea before he and Aunt Maude had any children.

Aunt Maude married Mr. Wesley Butler not long after, and they had twin boys, who were freshmen at the University of Georgia now. Wesley must be a lot older than Aunt Maude, because he had thin all-gray hair and hers was a big brown helmet with little sprinkles of gray at the sides. Uncle Wesley used to own grocery stores, but now he went fishing and hunting all the time, so Lily rarely saw him.

Sometimes Aunt Maude's two sisters drove up from Atlanta to visit, and then things livened up, because Little Sis—who was married to an important man who worked in a bank and had two girls in college—wore love beads and read palms, and Big Sis—who was a widow, with grandchildren Lily's age—spit chewing tobacco and worked as a volunteer for something called the Republican party.

So when Aunt Maude and her sisters got together there was a lot of palm reading and spitting and arguments about whether or not the country was going to hell. Lily loved it.

Lily was spending Saturday at Aunt Maude's. Mama and Daddy had been called to work overtime at the plant. Springtime was in full bloom, putting clouds of white on the dogwoods and red on the giant azaleas along Aunt Maude's front walk. Aunt Maude and the sisters were in the parlor, sipping whiskey and fussing at each other.

Lily sat on the front steps by the sidewalk, letting Sassy lick chocolate-cupcake icing from her knees. Her knees were always skinned from climbing the willows at home or falling off the old bicycle Daddy had bought secondhand for her eighth birthday. Sassy's tongue felt good on them. Lily curled her bare toes under Sassy and rubbed her stomach, which Sassy liked.

Lily wiped chocolate-smeared fingers on her T-shirt, then drew a handful of dry dog food from the front pocket of her cutoffs. Somewhere in the distance she heard a car coming up the side street that turned onto Aunt Maude's. She ignored it, because people drove slow in the neighborhoods. There were more and more cars on the main streets, and they went too fast, but Mama said those cars were driven by fools, not local folks.

"Here you go," she told Sassy, scattering the round chunks on the sidewalk. Sassy went over to them and neatly swallowed each one. A few had rolled off the curb. She ambled into the street and began picking them from the gutter, her yellow tail wagging contentedly.

The car's engine became a powerful rumble. The vehicle had turned onto Aunt Maude's street.

Lily propped her elbows on her knees and idly watched Sassy roll the last piece of dog food out of the gutter with her nose and catch it on her tongue. Suddenly the car swooped by. The front bumper caught Sassy in the side and tossed her. Sassy gave a high-pitched yelp, like a scream.

Lily leaped to her feet, staring in openmouthed horror as Sassy landed in a heap in the road. The car angled around her and slid to a stop. It was a big red mirror-shiny car with dark windows. Lily ran to Sassy, who raised her head and tried to drag herself with her front legs.

Falling to her knees beside her, Lily stroked her muzzle and called her name. She heard the car's door open. "You oughta keep your dog out of the road!" a man yelled. Lily looked over at him. He had on a red coat with a patch sewn over the breast pocket. She knew what he was, then, because Daddy had pointed out people like him lots of times. He was a real-estate man with one of the big Atlanta companies, the ones Aunt Maude and Daddy blamed for coming up here and making the land cost more because they sold it to rich people, the kind who came into the grocery store asking for some kind of French water in bottles.

"Your dog shouldn't have been in the road," the man said again, with a nasty look on his face. "It's not my fault I hit the thing."

"She's not a thing, she's Sassy," Lily yelled. "And you're a damned reeler-state agent!"

He snorted and got back in his car, slamming the door. Lily looked around furiously, grabbed a rock from the gutter, vaulted to her feet, and threw it with an aim much respected in MacKenzie's girls' softball league.

It struck the passenger door on her side of the car. The man bolted out and began yelling at her. Sassy writhed and whimpered on the pavement. Lily got another rock and hurled it. It caught the man on one cheek.

Aunt Maude and the sisters came running out of the house. "This goddamned brat almost put my eye out!" the man bellowed. Lily sat down in the road and, her hands shaking, cuddled Sassy's head. It felt heavy and limp. Sassy's eyes looked empty. Looking into them was like staring into a windowpane and seeing only yourself. She wasn't moving anymore. Her bad ear, the one the bobcat had chewed on, hung the way the flag at school did when there wasn't any wind.

Aunt Maude clamped a hand on Lily's shoulder. "What happened?"

"He hit Sassy. And then he said it was her fault, for being in the street. He called her a *thing*."

"This wild little white-trash kid ought to be in a cage!" the man said, jabbing a finger at Lily.

Big Sis hawked a stream of tobacco juice on the car's hood. Little Sis bolted over to the car, grabbed the radio antenna, and bent it double. Aunt Maude advanced around the car with a deadly look on her face. "You *get* your fat, red-coated, piss-headed self into that car before I call the sheriff," she said. "Because he's a cousin of mine, and he doesn't think much of shit-birds like you."

"You're all crazy, you hillbilly bitches!"

Little Sis lifted a foot clad in hard platform shoes and began kicking dents in the shiny front fender. "Your karma is bad," she said, still kicking. Big Sis opened the passenger door and spit onto the seat.

"The longer you stay," Aunt Maude said evenly, "the more hell you'll catch."

The man clamped his mouth shut, got into his car, and roared away.

The street was suddenly silent, except for the hushed murmur of Lily's sobs. Aunt Maude and the sisters squatted around her and Sassy. Aunt Maude put a hand under Sassy's chest and the other over her nose. After a second she said softly, "Sassy's gone to sleep, honey."

Lily drew a breath. "No," she answered as calmly as she could. "She's *dead*. She's dead, and it isn't fair. That man took her away, and there's nothing I can do about it."

Little Sis pulled a long string of her wooden love beads from under her scoop-necked blouse then put them around Lily's neck. "You fought back, little war-woman. That's what you did about it."

Big Sis patted Lily's cheek with a cool, blue-veined hand. "Sometimes that's all the victory you get—the knowledge that you fought back."

Aunt Maude added, "But that's a great victory."

Lily bent her head to Sassy's and slid her arms around the dog's soft, quiet body. "Then I'll always fight back," she whispered.

When Mama and Daddy came to get her and found out what had happened, they cried over Sassy. Next to the time when they'd cried over Grandpa MacKenzie's death, it was the most frightening thing Lily had ever seen. The grown people she loved and trusted more than anyone else were just as helpless as she was. She would have to fight back for them too.

They put Sassy in the back of the truck and took her home. After Daddy pulled in the yard under the deepening shade of the willows, Lily asked in a small voice, "Can we bury her next to our people? She always liked people better than she liked other dogs."

She was breathless with the bravery of her question. The family graveyard was sacred; Elspeth, the first MacKenzie, was buried there, and the baby she'd had with Old Artemas, and Elspeth's sons, their wives, and too many other MacKenzies to remember. MacKenzies weren't buried there anymore; it just wasn't done that way in modern times, Mama had explained once. The last few, including Grandpa and Grandma, were at the Methodist church's graveyard in town.

"I think old Sassy was special," Mama said, giving Daddy one of the sideways, prodding looks she used when she wanted him to agree with her. Daddy thought for a minute, then nodded.

They put Sassy on a piece of plywood and carried her over the creek. Lily dragged a shovel in each hand. A dusty foot trail wound around the edge of the cornfield there. Beyond the creek, where the field ended, the land rose up into the hills that climbed toward the distant blue peak of Victory Mountain. The MacKenzie graveyard was in a little hollow at the base of a hill, as if the hill were holding it carefully in its lap.

They opened the gate of the black iron fence and

carried Sassy to a corner. Faded old gravestones seemed to stand guard, some tall and grand, others that looked like no more than melting, oddly shaped rocks.

Daddy pulled her against his warm, broad chest and spoke to her a long time, telling her how God wanted hurt things to be at rest, and how it took strength to do what was right, not just what was easy. She listened through a haze of heartache, one thought settling in her mind. *Do what was right, not just what was easiest.*

When he finished, she got down on the ground and kissed Sassy's nose. Sobbing, Lily ran to Mama and buried her face in her middle, clinging to her inside the circle of Mama's petting hands.

They sat down around her while Lily stroked her unmoving side. Mama said a little prayer and helped Daddy dig a grave. When Sassy's limp, broken body lay in the bottom of it, Lily stretched out on her stomach and placed leaves over Sassy's face.

Silent tears ran down her cheeks as she watched Sassy's much-loved yellow form disappear under soft shovelfuls of dirt.

That evening she lay despondently in her bed, thinking about Grandma and Sassy, and how strange and lonely life became as a person grew up. "Look what came in the mail," Mama said from the doorway. She brought a small brown package to Lily and laid it beside her huddled body. "It's from Artemas."

Lily bolted upright. *How did he know exactly when she needed him? It must be magic, just like the blue willows.*

Mama opened the package. " 'Dear Lily,' " she read " 'I have a part-time job in the warehouse near the academy. I saw this in a shop and thought of our bear story. Love, Artemas.' "

It was the longest letter he'd ever written. Lily looked at the small stuffed bear Mama took from its wrapping. She reached for it with a burst of welcome and hugged it to her chest. "See how good things show up just when you're feeling awful?" Mama said softly.

Lily wrote back to him that night, the bear cuddled in

her lap. *I wish you would come back. I still miss you.* She tore that up, thinking. *Do what's right, not what's easiest,* and wrote instead, *I am grown up now. I am learning how to fight. You do that too. Nobody can hurt you and me then, okay? Thank you for the bear. Lily. P.S. It told me to say it loves you a lot.*

Five

The fist landed between James's shoulder blades as he left Evertide's gym through a rear door of the locker rooms. It drove the breath from him in a painful burst. He staggered and fell to his knees on the sidewalk. A second blow struck his temple. He sprawled to his side, dazed, dimly aware of puddled rainwater seeping into his khaki trousers and the cold, rough concrete stinging the palms of his hands.

"You're not tough enough to start on the varsity squad," a voice taunted. A different one added, "You screwed me out of my place in the lineup, you shithead."

James's thoughts swam in dizzy confusion, but he recognized the voices. They belonged to junior classmen, a year older than James. But not better on the basketball court. Not taller, or faster. Not more determined. No one was more determined.

He tried to get up, but a sneakered foot lashed his side, sending shock waves of pain through his rib cage. He gasped for breath. Through half-shut eyes he saw their feet in front of him. His pulse roared in his ears. But then dark, brilliant fury began to clear his mind. *Wait,* it said. *Think.*

They began a round of taunts.

"You don't belong here, Colebrook. You and the rest of

your family aren't good enough to be at Evertide. Why
don't you go to public school, with the niggers and the
wops?"

"Your father got kicked out of the country club. They
couldn't get him to pay his bills. My father said he's a
cheat. You're a fucking cheat too."

"We heard you're screwing one of the senior girls,
Colebrook. You're out of your league."

"Takes after his old man."

"Your mother's a whore. Can't keep her legs together.
Everybody knows that."

Adrenaline ran through James's muscles like an electric
charge. He vaulted upward, catching one of the boys in the
stomach with his head. He reveled in the boy's yell of pain
and the way his body tumbled backward.

Instantly James swung toward the other one and
rammed a knee into his groin. The boy doubled over.
James slammed his fist upward and felt the victorious
crunch against his knuckles. Blood cascaded from the
older boy's nose, and his legs collapsed.

The other one had gotten to his feet again. He rushed
James, who sidestepped him. James caught him by the hair
and smashed a fist into his temple. He fell face-forward,
groaning.

James stood over them, feet braced apart, fists raised.
Waiting calmly. He knew why Grandmother had sent
Artemas away to military school and why Uncle Charles
wanted to keep him there. Artemas was a threat—the eldest son of the eldest son, the wise and strong exiled
prince, already a better man than either Uncle Charles and
Father would ever be. James loved his brother and paid
homage to him like a medieval baron in the history books
that James consumed with fervent interest.

Artemas would be this family's king. But James was
preparing to be its minister of war.

"They said you started it," the headmaster told James.
James stood rigidly among the office's rich antiques and
brocaded walls. "They're lying," he replied calmly.

The headmaster, a small, effete man, flipped through James's records. "You're a good student, an excellent athlete—but you have your family's predisposition toward irresponsible behavior. There have been fights and confrontations between other students and every one of your siblings."

"We're only defending ourselves."

The headmaster threw the file on his desk. His eyes narrowed. "You left one of those boys with a broken nose and the other with a concussion. Yet your only injuries are a few bruises."

"I'm smarter than they are."

"Or just inherently vicious." The man pounded his desktop. "I want to know every word that was exchanged. And I want you to admit that you started it."

"No."

"I could suspend you. I could have you and your whole defensive little tribe of brothers and sisters suspended."

"You won't. My grandmother has connections. Senator DeWitt arranged for us to enroll here. You won't do anything to upset the senator."

The man's face turned pink with helpless fury. James smiled.

The others showed up in the entrance hall that afternoon. The buildings for the younger grades were across campus. The four of them were out of breath from the long, illicit trek. James stood in the center of the lobby, where he'd been ordered to stay. They surrounded him: Cass, a roly-poly sentry with food stains on the blazer of her uniform; Michael, pale, thin, but rigid with dignity; Elizabeth, a dainty, terrified-looking accomplice; and seven-year-old Julia staring up at him with solemn love while she chewed the end of her braided hair. "Go back to class," James commanded, staring straight ahead.

"It's not fair," Michael said. "It wasn't your fault."

"Do you have to stand here forever?" Elizabeth asked, her lower lip trembling.

Cass snorted. "No, stupid, just until he tells them what they want to hear."

"Forever," Julia concluded, nodding.

Michael squared his shoulders and aligned himself beside James, looking up at him firmly. "Then we're staying with you."

"I said *get out of here*."

"It's what Artemas would want us to do," Elizabeth said. "He's always telling us to stick together."

That was true. James didn't have an argument for it. They took up their defiant places.

The headmistress of the lower grades, her body quivering with frustration, shook a stiff finger at them. Dislodging the younger ones from James's side would take physical force, and she knew it. "I don't have any more patience for any of you *or* your parents, and I'm calling them immediately."

James gave her a scalding look, while he died inside. "My parents are visiting friends in Hawaii. They won't be back for a month."

"As usual," the headmistress said, disgust blossoming on her face. "All right, then all of you can stand right here and be humiliated together."

She marched away, leaving them in a forbidding, echoing hall of paneled wood and somber marble floors. Michael wobbled and coughed. "I hate them all," Cassandra noted, chewing her fingernails.

"Shut up and act like you don't care." James looked at his huddled army. He wished he had the gentle brand of authority that Artemas used, but he didn't. He could only stand there in stony silence, while other students and teachers walked by, staring. He felt angry from the top of his clipped brown hair to the soles of his polished loafers. His navy blazer was skewed aside by Julia, who had wrapped her arms around his waist.

Elizabeth leaned wearily against him on the other side. Michael stood at attention, his hands clasped behind his back, coughing but looking dedicated. Cass shifted from side to side and occasionally gave the finger to the older students walking by.

James loved his strange little aides-de-camp with a pride that made his chest ache.

Hours passed. Michael was eleven years old, but his face had the pasty color of an old man's. James began to feel weary and defeated. He couldn't let Michael and the others suffer. "I'll say the fight was my fault," he told them.

Michael shook his head violently. "If you tell stuff that isn't true, I'll knock your head off. I'll tell Artemas, and he'll knock your head off too."

"I'll hang you up by your scrawny thumbs, you little asshole. You look like you're going to faint."

"Nobody's moving," Cass announced. She pulled a half-eaten candy bar from her blazer's pocket and shoved it at Michael. "There. That'll make you feel better."

"Cassie gave away a *candy bar*," Julia said in shock.

At lunchtime the front door opened, and a lanky little girl came running in, her dark hair flying back from a serious, wide-eyed face. "I came to see you," she said, stopping in front of them all and staring up at James as if his predicament made her want to die.

He gazed at her grimly. Alise Wyndham was in Michael and Elizabeth's grade. The fact that she was their most devoted—and probably only—friend made her special. The fact that she had a crush on James made her an embarrassment.

"It's okay," Michael told her with dignity. "We're Colebrooks. We're used to being in trouble."

Alise sidled up to James, looking up at him with sad adoration. It made him uncomfortable, because it was so bewildering—and besides, he didn't want anyone to find him adorable, he wanted them to be frightened and impressed. "I believe you. It wasn't your fault," she said softly.

"Go back before the teachers notice you're missing and you get in trouble."

"I don't care what the others say, I'm going to talk to you."

"Go away."

When she looked terribly wounded, he grew confused and remorseful. Her parents were dead, and she lived with an aging great-aunt. Grandmother said the old lady was missing more than a few marbles and gave more attention to a horde of pet cats than to Alise. James bent down to her and whispered, "I don't want you to get in trouble because of us. Okay?"

"*Alise,*" the headmistress called, striding into the hall. She took Alise by one arm. "I'm shocked at you, Alise. Now, you've let these children get you in trouble too. What would your great-aunt think if you had to stay here with them?"

"Leave her alone," James said slowly, gritting his teeth.

"I'm staying here," Alise said.

"All right, you do that. If you're going to let them shame you, you stay here and pay the price."

"Yes, ma'am." As the headmistress walked away, Cassandra looked over her shoulder at Alise. "You idiot."

"Shut up," James told her. He put a hand on Alise's small, bowed head. She lifted it and gazed at him with plaintive appreciation. "I'd rather stay with you anyway," she said, so bravely that he wished he could tear the whole damned school and all its elite, hateful people down for her sake as well as for himself and his family's. But he couldn't. He wished he were Artemas.

The afternoon passed with agonizing slowness. They hadn't sat down all day. They hadn't eaten.

The entrance hall's large doors swung open with a crash. Artemas strode down the hall, his cadet's cap tucked formally under one arm, his bearing as straight and dignified as a general's in the academy's gray uniform. He was so tall and his expression so solemn that James felt threatened and worried, but at the same time his chest swelled with love.

The younger ones ran to Artemas desperately, throwing their arms around his waist as he came to a halt. His face softened, and he put one long arm around them. He nodded at James approvingly. "You did the right thing."

"Grandmother called you?"

"Yes. Come on." He picked up Julia. Michael tugged at his sleeve. "We can't just *leave,* can we?"

"Grandmother and I will deal with the school," Artemas said.

Alise murmured from behind the others, "I can't go."

James took her hand. "Yes, you can. I'll explain to your aunt for you." She smiled up at him.

Artemas steered them out the front doors and into a lumbering old sedan that belonged to Uncle Charles's gardener. Artemas did everything with the calmness of a grown man, not a seventeen-year-old boy. He drove them to a restaurant and bought hamburgers. "What will Uncle Charles say?" Elizabeth whispered.

"I'm in charge of this family, not Uncle Charles," Artemas replied.

James nodded to himself and smiled. Artemas would never let them down.

Lily had a new letter from Artemas in one back pocket of her dungarees, a hardbound library copy of *Charlotte's Web* in the other, and a mind to sit in the palm court at Blue Willow while she looked at them.

She climbed along a stone ledge at the base of the looming old mansion, brushing against the plywood that covered the palm court's glass sides at the bottom level. Above her the hulking mint-green structure rose to a peaked roof. There were jagged holes in the upper panes of glass, where uncaring trespassers had heaved bricks. She reached the spot where the plywood had rotted and fallen away. Someone had knocked out the whole window.

She climbed in and stood on the dirty tile floor, letting her eyes adjust. Autumn sun filled the huge room with soft green light, spotted with white where the sun came through the holes. At the right end the giant glass doors into the mansion were covered with sheets of steel.

The palms' fallen, decayed trunks lay jumbled across

the tile pathways. Sunk into the ground, like ships settling in a sea of clay, were big ceramic pots with chunks broken out of their sides. Spiderwebs big enough to catch a horse hung from the corners of the ceiling.

In the court's center stood a fountain, with a pretty little stone girl pouring empty air from a vase. A decade of rain had drawn dark rivulets down her and her pedestal. Even the fountain seemed to be melting into the ground.

The first time Lily had discovered the open window and explored here, she'd shaken with dread. It was a forgotten fairyland, and who knew what might be hiding in the shadows at the walls' bottoms, where the plywood hid her view of blue sky and mountains? But there was nothing, only the whisper of the wind through the broken panes overhead.

She sat down with her back against the fountain's base and her legs crossed on the dusty tiles. They were white with blue willows on them. She rubbed one with the sleeve of her flannel shirt, cleaning up her special place a bit, paying the mansion back for letting her come here. Taking care of it, for Artemas.

She pulled her book and the letter from her pockets. She'd been such a baby when he'd come to visit. Now, she was ten. She wrote to him about everything she did, and he wrote back to encourage her. The letter was on his school's paper, with an important-looking gold crest at the top.

She read avidly. His handwriting was dark and beautiful. *Keep making good grades in school, and don't believe the teacher who said you're too smart for your own good. You're just too smart for her, that's all. Tell that boy who called you a "giant red goober" that he has a small mind. Someday, he'll be sorry. And keep remembering, I wouldn't trust just any little girl to take care of Blue Willow for me. You're the only one.*

Lily sighed with delight and pressed the letter to her chest. She had a mission in life, a mission that made everything right.

A gunshot echoed through the woods outside. Lily raced to the broken window. Crouching, she peered out.

Down the hill, where the forest opened onto the old lawn, she spied Joe Estes among the weedy grass and little pine trees. He was dressed in his hunting clothes, and he carried a rifle. A little ol' squirrel rifle. Lily sniffed in disdain.

He was a grown boy, and his folks owned Estes Hardware and Feed, in town. They were nice, solid people, Mama said.

But Joe raced stock cars like a fool, and he'd been in trouble with the law for things Mama and Daddy would only whisper about, and he liked to hunt. He could hunt from now till the cows came home, but he'd better get off Blue Willow. Furious, Lily stuffed her book and letters back into her pockets, then slipped out the window. She tiptoed down the hill, hiding behind the tree trunks, her heart racing.

When she reached the bushes along the edge of the forest, she hunkered down and began growling. She'd scare him off, make him think a bear was after him. There were still some around these woods. He couldn't kill a bear with a squirrel rifle.

She rattled the bushes, made the most terrible, low-pitched noises in her throat, growling louder and louder, and peeped at him, wanting to see him run. He turned, staring in her direction.

Then he put the rifle to his shoulder and fired.

An invisible hand slapped her backward. She lay on the ground, blinking in amazement. A pain like fire ran down her right arm. She could hear Joe tromping toward her. Dazed, she looked at her arm and saw blood everywhere. Her shirtsleeve was torn near the top. It revealed a long, deep gouge on her shoulder.

"Oh, my God," Joe said, when he parted the bushes and looked down at her. "It was your fault, you stupid little shit. I oughta leave you here, but it'd just cause a stink."

Lily glared up woozily, pointed at him with her good arm, and intoned, "This is *my* land. If I was a bear, I'd bite your head off." Then she fainted.

*   *   *

Aunt Maude and the sisters' faces appeared over her like angels. Mama and Daddy were looking down at her too. Lily gazed up at them from a dreamy mist, smiled, and shut her eyes again. She was in the guest bedroom at Aunt Maude's, she remembered. Her bandaged arm was cushioned on a pillow.

"She'll sleep all afternoon, doped up on those pain pills the doctor gave her," Lily heard Aunt Maude whisper. "Leave her here till you get through talking to the sheriff."

"I'd like to kill that damned Joe for hunting on the estate," Daddy answered, his voice sounding tired and worried. "But I can see how him shooting Lily was just an accident. Good Lord, who expects to find a ten-year-old girl hiding in the middle of nowhere and growling at him?"

"What are we goin' to do with her?" That was Mama, Lily knew. She sounded upset. "She thinks that old estate belongs to her. She thinks she has to take care of it for Artemas Colebrook."

Little Sis. Her voice was high and squeaky. "Can't fault that kind of loyalty, Zea."

"But I worry about her. She's not like other little girls. She keeps to herself, reads all the time, hangs out at the old mansion. I can't keep her away from it."

Big Sis. Her voice was gravelly. "She's as tough as a mustang and twice as stubborn. She'll never get by on dainty temperament or dainty looks—not with her size and that cap of orange hair. But that doesn't matter. She's smart. You might as well get used to the fact that she's odd. It's a remarkable kind of odd."

Odd? Tears pooled behind Lily's eyelids. What could be good about being odd? When an old man who lived down the street from Aunt Maude had started going outside with no pants on, people said it was because he'd gotten *odd.* His wife sent him off to a home for crazy people.

"She thinks Artemas Colebrook is coming back someday to marry her." That was Mama again. Lily's heart jerked at the tone of disbelief in Mama's voice.

"Well, you don't know," Daddy said slowly. "Stranger things have happened."

"Oh, *Drew*, don't you dare encourage her notions. She'll outgrow 'em. When she's older, she'll figure out that the world doesn't work like something out of 'Cinderella.' "

"Let her daydream," Little Sis whispered. "Maybe it'll keep her away from the bull-necked dimwits around here. You want her to go to college, don't you? And you *sure* don't want her pregnant or married before she's old enough to know her head from a hole in the ground."

Lily listened in stark despair as they tiptoed from the room. She opened her eyes and let the tears roll out the corners. She wasn't going to marry anyone, not Artemas, or dimwits, or anybody else.

She wrote to Artemas about getting shot. By return mail he sent a large package. Inside neatly folded tissue paper was his beautiful gray academy jacket, with gold piping at the stiff, stand-up collar, ornate brass buttons down the center, four gold stars pinned in a perfect horizontal line across one breast, and under them, a shiny little nameplate with ARTEMAS COLEBROOK, SENIOR CADET COMMANDER in etched black letters.

On a piece of academy stationery he had written, *I wore this to graduation. Now, I want you to have it. What you did was very brave but you have to promise not to get shot again.*

She wrote back, *I promise. It wasn't much fun.*

Lily modeled the jacket for Mama and Daddy. Artemas's jacket swallowed her. "He must be as big as Daddy," she said in awe. So big and sweet that *he* wouldn't mind that she was wild as a mustang, with fuzzy red hair, big hands, big feet, knobby knees, and a long bullet scar on her shoulder.

Artemas would come back someday. He already knew she was *odd*, and it didn't seem to bother him.

Six

These were Artemas's last few weeks of freedom before he entered West Point, and the summer sun splaying down through the trees was warm as life on his naked body, and Susan de Gude was his first girl.

"Yes, like that," she whispered against his ear, bare and golden beside him on the soft forest floor. Even though the air rolling in from the sound was tepid, he burned, sinking into a blinding need to learn what a girl felt like inside. But this was her first time, too, and he didn't want to hurt her, or God help him, do anything that would make her want to stop.

They'd spent what seemed like hours reaching this point, touching each other with awe and, for a while, embarrassment, until the fire of excitement erased everything but sensation. Now, she was writhing under his hand, and he was exploring the moist recesses between her legs with a restraint that made him light-headed. "You're so smooth inside," he murmured, taking her mouth as she tilted her head up to his again. She moaned into his lips, then broke away, her green eyes smoldering, her hair, dark red and tangled, catching on bits of grass as she twisted her head from side to side.

He felt as if the ache between his legs would consume

him. There was no longer any way of knowing where it ended and the limits of his skin began. She and he had managed to get a condom in place only seconds ago, snickering over it, nearly shooting it across his belly a time or two before the laughter faded into desperate intensity, and her fingers, trembling but incredible, had stroked it down firmly.

"Now, okay?" she begged, her narrow hips grinding upward into his palm. Her face and breasts turned a brighter shade of pink, her small nipples becoming as dark as roses. Her lashes quivered and lowered shyly. "I'm going to do it, you know, *come,* any second."

Those were the most erotic words in the world. Shaking, Artemas tried to say something coherent but only managed "Me too" before he carefully moved over her, frantically aware that she was much smaller and softer than his brutally muscled body. There was a painfully awkward moment in which their legs became entwined and he jabbed her upper thigh with his jutting arousal, but then he instinctively slid his hands under her and lifted her legs around him, and they were dignified again.

Then, suddenly, he was pressing into the edge of her sex, feeling it stretch, holding back so hard that every muscle in his back and buttocks quivered. They inched closer, her eyes wide on his. "Does it hurt?" he asked desperately. "Is it all right?"

A smile broke across her damp lips. "Yes. It's perfect."

They wrapped their arms around each other and huddled together. He began to move. It was amazing, wonderful, the sliding and tug of her flesh and the grip of her hard thighs on his hips. She gasped and burrowed her face into the crook of his neck, then shuddered and began struggling under him. "Susie?" he said with alarm. He could barely think, but he forced himself with the iron willpower he'd spent his whole life developing.

"Don't stop *now,*" she ordered, whimpering.

He arched against her slowly, staring down at her face, his heart merging with love until he knew he'd die with happiness. The swelling throb in his body was suddenly being stroked by waves of tiny contractions inside her. None of his friends' descriptions of their own exploits had done this feeling justice. Artemas had never suspected that Susie's body would hold on to him the same as her mouth had, earlier, but with a thousand small lips.

She made a soft, throaty sound that sank all the way through him. He pounded against her, forgetting restraint, feeling her fingers digging into his back, her voice saying urgent little encouragements and thank-you's, then her body relaxing only a little. That signal broke him, and he surged inside her, dragging his lips back and forth across her cheeks as she clung to his rigid, arching spine.

"Oh, Artemas, Artemas," she was moaning, as his head began to clear. "It was great. You were great. Everybody said it'd be awful the first time. But it wasn't."

He lifted his head to look at her ecstatically. She raised a hand and stroked his jaw. "You're clenching your teeth. Are you okay?"

Surprised, he realized she was right. "Sure. I just do that sometimes." In the very second when he felt the most pleasure, he'd also felt a dark frisson of fear. He couldn't let himself lose control completely. Who knew what might come out? All those terrible weaknesses Uncle Charles said he'd inherited from his parents—the ones they kept proving—might be lurking inside.

"I just . . . didn't know what to say." He looked at her apologetically. Dismayed and bewildered, he smiled at her quickly. She stroked a hand through his hair. "You're a clam, but I don't mind." She drew a finger to his face and tickled the tiny brown mole at the edge of his right eye.

She began grinning at him, and he forgot the strange moment. He kissed her, and the grin became another sweet invitation to enjoy the rest of their time together.

Much later, when the woods were filling with shadows, they rose and dressed. He held her hard and listened to her cry. "I'll write to you," she whispered.

"I'll write back."

"I'll die before Christmas gets here, I just know it."

"No, we'll have a great time.'

"But it'll be so cold then. Where will we go?"

"I'll think of something. I'll save my money and rent a motel room for us."

"Yes! Of course!" She looked up at him with dawning enthusiasm. "I'll put aside half my clothing allowance at school. We'll get a suite, with a Jacuzzi, and we'll keep it the whole holiday! We can meet there all through Christmas."

"See?" He forced himself to smile down at her as if Christmas didn't seem years away. "All we have to do is use our imagination."

"And a lot more of the other parts." They clung together, absorbing each other in a kiss filled with sadness. "I'll walk you home," he said.

"No, it would only look suspicious, me coming out of the woods by the beach house at dark with you. Mummy has an eye for these things. And Daddy would think the worst."

"What, that you're in love with your terrible Colebrook neighbor?"

She chucked him under the chin and shook her head. "You're the best Colebrook around."

"Keep that in mind when all those guys from Yale are chasing you."

Her eyes glistened with new tears. She took his face between her hands. "No one can stop me from seeing you. You are so gentle and romantic."

She drew away, gave him a wistful smile, then turned and ran up the path toward her estate.

Artemas watched her with an ecstatic sense of pride. Today he'd proved—in the most intimate way—that he was not like Father.

Susan slowed to a walk halfway through the woods. Wiping her face, her head down, she didn't hear the soft rustle of horse's hooves behind her until the animal's breath was almost on her back. Whirling, she looked up at Artemas's father.

Big, powerful, but his spongy middle hanging over the tops of his riding britches, he swung down from the hunt saddle and walked up to her, drawing the reins over his horse's head and flicking the plaited center between his fingers. He had a sly smile on his face.

"Hello, Mr. Colebrook," she said nervously, starting to back up.

"I saw you and my son together. I've been watching. Quite an exciting show."

Sick horror rose in her throat. "Oh, God."

"You don't want me to tell your parents, do you?"

"You go to hell." Terrified of his smile, she whipped around and tried to run. His arms snaked around her neck, and one hand clamped over her mouth.

Screaming uselessly, she was dragged down.

Artemas was preparing to come home for Christmas. Her last letter reached him the same day her body was discovered in the bathroom of the apartment she shared with several other girls. She had tried to abort the baby with a knitting needle sterilized in liquor.

He raped me, Artemas. I'm pregnant. I love you. I don't know what to do. I'll never get over this.

He found his parents at a lavish Christmas party at the apartment of a film producer in the city. Before the irate butler could stop him, he was shoving his way through the entrance hall and running into the midst of the glittering crowd. His father's tall form, lounging by a baby grand with a drink in one hand, was easy to spot.

Artemas had his hands around his throat in an instant. They went down in a fierce jumble, scattering a silver candelabra and an arrangement of poinsettias in a crystal vase. People were screaming. Somewhere among them was Mother's voice, a shriek of disbelief.

His father slammed a fist into his face, and Artemas fell back, blood from his mouth spattering the jacket of his cadet's uniform. Deadly silent and blind with fury, Artemas felt the base of the candelabra against his hand and swung the implement viciously. Blood spurted from his father's nose as they both struggled to rise. Artemas hit him again, and there was the sharp crunch of a heavy jawbone breaking. His father's knees buckled. Artemas half stood and drew back his arm once more, but men were clawing at him, falling on top of him and knocking him backward.

In the stunned silence following the halt of violence, his arms held by grown men struggling to keep his wild fury still, Artemas stared into his father's shocked, broken face. "I'll kill you," he told his father softly. "I should have done it a long time ago."

His mother appeared between them, falling to her knees with a long red gown bunched around her. "Artemas, how *could* you?" she cried.

"He raped Susan de Gude. She killed herself because of *him*."

Mother's mouth opened in a wail of shock. There was chaos around them—people gasping and talking excitedly—but his father's eyes only flickered with hatred and denial. Mother turned to him and leaned delicately against his bloody dinner jacket, collapsing with her head on his shoulder. She pierced Artemas with a look of disgust. "I'll *never* forgive you for accusing your father this way. And in public!"

The New York courts ordered Artemas's younger siblings placed in state custody until their father's trial. Mother complained mildly, protesting a judge's opinion of her competence, then withdrew into her parasitic circle of friends. Only the lingering influence of the Colebrook name, combined with Grandmother's shrewd lawyers and Uncle Charles's grudging bribes, circumvented the court order. For the first time since coming to their uncle's estate, they were allowed to move from the cottage into the shabby Tudor mansion.

Artemas refused his grandmother's entreaty that he go to Aunt Lucille's ranch in Texas. He stayed with his distraught brothers and sisters, who cloaked him in their loyalty. Father was released on bail. He and Mother went to the Schulhorns'.

Susan's parents were moneyed and respected in the ways the Colebrooks no longer were. They barred outsiders, including Artemas, from their daughter's funeral, and when he stood in silent honor and grief outside the sanctuary on a crowded New York sidewalk, he was hounded by reporters. They fed greedily on the lurid drama between the well-known old families, and the rest of New York fed with them.

He went to the De Gudes' house repeatedly but was turned away by the hired guards, until finally Susan's father came out to meet him in the courtyard. A big, sturdy man with Susan's auburn hair, he spit on Artemas and backhanded him across the face. "Between you and that animal who fathered you, you killed my little girl. That murdering S.O.B. will pay for it. And you'll never escape the shame." Artemas murmured an agonized apology and left.

January crawled by in a maddening haze of grief and frustration. He withdrew from West Point. A career in the military had no meaning for him anymore; he had loved the order and discipline of West Point, not the prestige. He lived for revenge and spent hours with his stunned siblings trying to make them believe that their lives had not come to some terrible end.

Grandmother, queenly in her blue dressing gown, her white hair knotted, crownlike, around the top of her head, called him to the parlor in her suite every day. He stood by a window, pretending to listen as she talked vaguely of fate and the future.

One day he came at her request to find two unfamiliar men in her company. Both were well dressed in dark business suits; both carried themselves with formal, straight-backed dignity. Both had the first featherings of gray hair at their temples.

But one was tall and stocky, with a short Afro and skin the color of dark mahogany; the other was small and lithe, fair-skinned, with sandy, thinning hair combed sideways over a high forehead. Grandmother gestured toward them gracefully. "I'd like you to meet Edward Tamberlaine and

Leson LaMieux. Gentlemen, this is my grandson. The young man for whom you'll be working someday."

Artemas was too stunned to say anything. Tamberlaine came to him and held out a broad, dark hand; LaMieux, a slender, pale one. Artemas shook their hands and looked at his grandmother for an explanation. She nodded. "Mr. Tamberlaine is an accounts manager for the company. Mr. LaMieux is your uncle's secretary. Both are highly qualified and quite trustworthy." She paused, her bright little eyes boring into Artemas's bewildered ones. "Quite trustworthy in *my* service, that is."

The implications of her conspiracy against Uncle Charles sank into Artemas with a resounding sense of the inevitable. His future had always been an unspoken assumption between Grandmother and him. His surprise faded quickly, replaced by a stark feeling of having reached a destination he'd always expected. And wanted.

Studying his face, Grandmother smiled. "There will come a day when their knowledge of Colebrook China will be invaluable to you."

He looked at Tamberlaine and LaMieux with a composure that drew respect to their shrewd, assessing eyes. "You'll never regret being associated with my family's name. I can't say that's true now, but it will be. I swear to you."

"I take you at your word," Tamberlaine answered.

"Myself as well," LaMieux added.

Grandmother came into his room as he was working at the desk there, reading company reports Tamberlaine and LaMieux had given him. Artemas stood and carefully helped her into a thickly upholstered chair across from the desk, then sat on the desk's edge. She looked up at him somberly. "The time for you to take your rightful place will come soon enough. Until then, you must do everything you can to prepare."

"In what way?"

"College. Ceramic engineering would be appropriate, don't you think?"

He and she shared a look filled with portent. "What will you tell Uncle Charles about our plans?"

She smiled grimly. "Whatever inventive lies will best soothe his fear of you. When he eventually realizes the cold truth, there won't be anything he can do to change it." She took Artemas's hands in hers. "I've waited so many years—decades—to see your grandfather's pride restored."

"I *will* do that, Grandmother."

Tears came to her eyes. "Then all my sorrow and loneliness will have been worth it. But there's one other thing. The old estate, Blue Willow, meant so much to him—"

"It won't be forgotten. It won't be lost. Someday it will be as wonderful as it was when you and he lived there together." Artemas knelt by her chair and put an arm around her. He'd never told anyone about the correspondence between him and Lily. He'd always felt a little awkward about it—admitting that he'd been, God, a *pen pal* to a child all these years. And that her whimsical adoration and encouragement meant so much to him.

"Let me tell you about Lily MacKenzie," he said now. "Believe me, Grandmother, Blue Willow has been in *very* good hands."

There came a frigid February day when Father returned from Philadelphia and came to the house. Uncle Charles was in New York, at the company offices. Artemas sat in his room, poring over company files. His brothers and sisters were at school.

He heard Father yelling obscenities at the housekeeper. As he sprang to his feet, Grandmother came to his door, leaning heavily on her cane but as unmovable as a force of nature. "If you go down, who knows what will happen?"

"I have to go. Sooner or later, we have to finish it."

She hissed derisively. "Do you want to ruin the rest of your life? Or do you want to survive this for the sake of your brothers and sisters? Be a better man than your father. Be better than your frivolous, foolish mother. You're only eighteen years old—you have your life ahead of you.

All my hopes are set on you. I can't change what my sons are, but I can make certain you don't become like them."

"Then please don't ask me to hide like a coward, because that would be very much like them."

Her frail shoulders slumped. She reached into a brocaded pocket of her gown. A small silver revolver emerged in her gnarled hand. She offered it to Artemas on her palm. "Take it. I won't have you killed or maimed as a result of Creighton's rage. But you won't be at peace until you decide whether your future—this family's future—is worth more than your revenge."

Artemas tucked the gun into the belt of his trousers and covered it with the tail of his white sweater, then stepped past her. He went downstairs. Father was pacing in the library. His black overcoat hung open to reveal a rumpled suit. His dark hair was disheveled, his face florid. Artemas walked in and shut the doors. Father wheeled to face him. "You vindictive young bastard. How dare you agree to testify against me at the trial?"

With calculated and swift certainty Artemas slipped the pistol from his belt, clicked the safety off with his thumb, and raised the gun at arm's length. He sighted unerringly at a point on his father's forehead. His father's expression stiffened in shock. "This is the only way I can live with what you did and what you are," Artemas said softly.

He held his father's astonished gaze. He saw uncertainty, disgust, but also fear. Artemas continued in the same low, deadly tone. "Why does Mother love you? That's the strangest part, to me. She's as sick as you are. How could anyone love you? How could anyone bring children into the world knowing that you're their father? *Six* of us. When neither of you is capable of caring about anyone but yourselves."

"Don't do this," Father said, his voice cracking. "You're our son."

"I can't change that fact. I can only try to forget it."

"What do you want from me? An admission that I'm selfish? Hell, boy, that's a right people such as we have *earned*. The fortune this family created helped build this country. We made it what it is. We deserve the status and the power. Don't you understand that ordinary rules don't apply to us?"

"You never built anything."

"I inherited power. It's in my blood. And yours. And girls like that one we screwed—they don't mean anything. We can have a thousand like her. Don't you understand? *If we can have anything we want, why shouldn't we take it?*"

Contempt made an acrid taste in Artemas's mouth. He trembled from the black hatred rising up inside his chest. Between gritted teeth he said, "If you have to take what you want that way, it doesn't belong to you. You don't deserve it." He latched his thumb on the revolver's hammer and slowly pulled it back.

His father gaped at him. "You want me to beg for mercy? Hell, I don't mind." He sank to his knees; he was trembling. Artemas tracked him with the pistol, lowering it, keeping the sight on the ashen, mottled skin between his father's dark eyes. Grandmother's words rang in his ears: *You're better than this.*

Here was the proof he'd needed. Domination. Superiority. In form as well as spirit. Artemas dropped his hand to his side. "I don't need to kill you. You're dead to me already. Get out."

Creighton Colebrook staggered to his feet. "I knew you couldn't do it," he said, his voice shaking. "You haven't got the guts."

Artemas smiled and went to the doors. "You haven't got the guts," his father called bitterly. "Your mother will agree with me." Artemas opened the doors and walked out. He was free.

The next day, a cold weekend morning with the sun glinting on a fresh layer of snow outside, they had the house to themselves. With Uncle Charles, his mousy little wife, and their two taunting daughters away in the city, life seemed almost peaceful.

James secluded himself in Uncle Charles's gym, forbidden to him ordinarily, punching a boxing bag with endless anger. Elizabeth was tucked into a corner of the tiny bed-room she shared with Cassandra and Julia, playing with dolls she called "my poor babies." They were always being threatened by imaginary monsters from whom she pro-tected them. Her favorite warning to the monsters, deliv-ered in a soft, fervent voice when she thought no one was listening, was, "I'll go get Artemas."

Cassandra was hidden somewhere, feeding on a gallon of ice cream she'd stolen from the kitchen. Julia stood in front of a television set in the housekeeper's office down-stairs, jumping up and down to a cartoon-show theme song. Artemas began rounding his siblings up for lunch. He couldn't find Michael.

When the other four were gathered in the dining room, Artemas held out a copy of *Swiss Family Robinson*. They stared at it dolefully. "Do we have to take turns reading again?" James demanded.

"Yes."

"Why?"

"Because this book is about a happy family, dammit." Softening, he added, "Because it's good for us to do things together. Where's Michael?"

"I saw him go outside an hour ago," Elizabeth volun-teered timidly. "He said he was going to find fairy icicles in the woods."

Artemas threw the book on a table and went to get a jacket. For a sickly twelve-year-old, Michael and his whim-sies could be a strong pair. But he enjoyed the excuse to go outside. His uncle's house was oppressive—filled with brooding English antiques and grotesque Victorian sculp-tures. He preferred the lawn and woodland stretching into the distance around it. Even though this part of Long Is-land was filling up with shopping centers and subdivi-sions, there was still open space and magnificent estates hidden among the trees, and the aura of gentrified, care-free ghosts riding tall thoroughbreds to the sound of the hunt horn.

Artemas reached the doors that spanned the old Tu-dor's back terrace but then saw Michael staggering across the snowy lawn from the woods, his jacket hanging open. His unnatural gait and splayed, stiff hands sent Artemas running through the light snow in barely concealed alarm. When he reached Michael, he slid to a stop, staring.

Dark stains covered the insides of Michael's brown trousers from groin to knee. He gazed blankly at Artemas and murmured, "I went on myself. I s-saw . . . and I couldn't help it—" He slumped to the snowy ground. Artemas scooped him into his arms and said gently, "What, Mikey? What did you see?"

"F-Father." Michael's head lolled.

"*Where?*"

"In a t-tree. The b-big tree by the b-bench."

Artemas curled the fragile body close to his chest and started back to the house at a swift walk. His heart threatened to explode. "What was he doing?"

Michael's eyes glazed over. "Hanging." He fainted.

Artemas gave him to James with instructions to call a doctor, warned the others to stay behind, and ran to the woods. When he found Father, he gagged and sank to the ground.

The bloody corpse hanging by a chain in the tree had been gutted.

There was no bare lightbulb swinging over Artemas's head, no beefy men wearing shoulder holsters and chewing cigars. He sat at a table beside his attorney, in a claustrophobic interview room with smooth green walls, while a pair of clean-cut detectives paced in front of him. Exhausted and emotionally drained, he found himself idly keeping count each time one of them passed in front of him. The flickering of a fluorescent light fixture on one wall made him think of the way sunlight had dappled the horrible thing he'd found hanging in the tree.

"Come on, son, talk to us," one of the men said, bending over the table and meeting Artemas's unwavering gaze. "You hated him. A couple months ago you tried to beat the hell out of him in front of dozens of people. Yesterday you threatened to kill him—even pointed a gun at his head. Your mother says he told her about it on the phone."

"If I'd intended to kill him, I would have done it then."

The other detective sat down across from him. "You were too smart to kill him at the house. So you waited. You went to your father's hotel this morning. No one saw your father leave the hotel. But we know from the room-service records that he ate breakfast at eight and was out of the suite by eleven, when the maid came in. I think you asked your father to meet you somewhere. I think you shot him in the back of the head—not with your grand-mother's revolver, which wouldn't have blown his brains out quite so delicately—but with a different gun, one we'll find, eventually."

The first detective draped a leg over the corner of the table and settled near Artemas's shoulder. "He was dead when you dragged him into the woods between your un-cle's estate and the De Gudes' place. You wouldn't have any trouble doing that. You're what, six-three, six-four? Your school records show that you do some serious weight lift-ing and run track. Even as large as your father's body was, you had the physical strength to pull it several hundred yards along a path through the woods."

The attorney interjected, "There's not one speck of physical evidence to link this young man to the death."

"But there's a helluva lot else. Enough to bring down formal charges, when we get the case together."

The attorney snorted. "What about De Gude? The fa-ther of the dead girl had every reason to want Mr. Colebrook dead."

"Don't bring him into this," Artemas said, leveling a hard gaze at his counsel. "I won't accuse anyone else the way I'm being accused."

The words Susan's father had spoken to him pounded in his brain. *I'll make you and your father pay.* But the thought of using De Gude to draw suspicion away from himself made a bitter taste in Artemas's mouth.

"Oh, we're going to be questioning De Gude," one of the detectives said. "We'll be talking to a lot of people."

His partner sighed. "But let's get back to our interesting little scenario here." He leaned on the table and propped his chin on one hand. Looking at Artemas through narrowed eyes, he said, "You dragged your old man's corpse to the tree, threw fifteen feet of heavy chain over a limb, then made a little necklace for dear ol' Dad and hung him up like a trophy buck."

"Please, this is sickening," the attorney said. "This young man's been through hell—"

The detective continued, "Then you took a knife and unzipped him from breastbone to testicles. To add insult to injury, you cut those off and stuffed them in his coat pocket."

The attorney choked and reached for a glass of water near his briefcase. Artemas stared at the detective without flinching, while nausea clenched his stomach and beads of sick perspiration slid down his temples.

"You need some air?" one of the detectives asked, not unkindly. Artemas shook his head. "I'll see his body like that as long as I live. My younger brother will never forget it either. That's the worst part. But I didn't kill my father."

"Look, after what he did to your girl, who's to say you didn't have good reasons?" The detective's eyes were sly, coaxing. His voice dropped to a consoling tone. "I mean, he raped her right after she'd been with you, she got pregnant—who knows, it might have been *your* baby? She was too ashamed and frightened to ask anyone for help, so she took a knitting needle—" the detective stuck a rigid finger into the air—"went into the bathroom in her apartment, and—" he jammed his finger upward—"tried to fix the problem. Only thing was, she punctured an artery. She must have lain there a long time—alone, afraid, dying, maybe calling your name—"

"Stop it," the attorney hissed.

The detective shook his head somberly. "I can understand why you'd want to leave your old man hanging inside out in a tree."

Artemas bent his head in his hands. He could feel the detectives watching him eagerly, waiting. But the emotions washing over him were turning doubts into cold serenity. He had wanted his father dead. He should have killed him. It would have been an act of justice. But he'd chosen the family's future over personal revenge. The welfare of the family—its preservation, its restoration, its ambitions—would always override his own desires. He had been green before, like fine clay molded into a shape but still too easily broken. Now, the form had hardened beyond delicacy, had been fired and finished.

The detectives leaned closer. "What do you want to say to us?"

Artemas raised his head and looked at them with a self-assured calm that dismissed their threats and petty theatrics. "He got what he deserved. I wish I'd killed him," he said, bringing a gasp from his attorney. "But I have more important things to do."

Mother returned to New York from the Schulhorns' estate in a stupor of tranquilizers, accompanied by her maid, a private nurse, and her chauffeur. She settled in a suite at the Plaza. When Artemas visited her, he found her curled on a divan in the suite's living room, wearing a beautiful white silk robe over a lace-drenched nightgown, her bright blond hair elegantly tousled, her eyes swollen from crying. The chauffeur—a young, pretty-faced man with a muscular build—stood behind the divan, massaging her shoulders.

"Leave us, Bernard," she said, waving him toward an inner door. Artemas stood in the room's center, tracking the man's departure with loathing. The jumble of sympathy and resigned pity he'd felt toward his mother swiftly became stoic disgust. She was someone to endure, not to love.

When they were alone in the room, she clasped her hands to her chest. "Why won't you let the others visit me? I need my children."

"They don't want to see you. It was their decision. They're hurt because you came here instead of to Uncle Charles's. If you want to see them, make an effort."

"I *can't* go there. Not so close to where your father— oh, I can't even bear to go to the funeral home. I'll never survive the funeral if I think of—of . . ." Her voice trailed off.

Artemas looked at her wearily. "Take *Bernard* with you—I'm sure he'll give you all the help you need. Just remember something—James is old enough to take one look at your chauffeur and know you hired him for something besides his driving record. If you don't want him to despise you, tell *Bernard* to keep his hands off you in front of the family."

She leaned forward, her face contorting with fury. "Don't you dare judge me. Don't you *dare* make Bernard feel unwelcome at your father's funeral."

"I won't be at the funeral. I don't have any respects to pay. But the others will go—if they want to."

"You turned your brothers and sisters against us!"

"No, the two of you did that without my help."

"Get out!" Artemas turned and started for the suite's doors. His mother screamed after him. "You killed him! I know you did it! And if they charge you with doing it, I'll never be able to hold my head up in public again!"

His back stiff with pride, he stepped into the hall without answering, shut the doors calmly, then jerked the top of an ash stand and retched into its canister.

"What did Mother say?" James asked, when Artemas walked into Uncle Charles's house several hours later. The others were gathered around him, their faces pale, their eyes hollow. They looked up at Artemas hopefully.

Artemas choked for a moment, then got his voice under control and lied as gently as he could. "She misses all of you, and if she weren't sick right now, she'd come to see you."

They straggled out, except for James, who waited until the rest were out of earshot, then whispered "Bullshit" to

Artemas. Artemas gave him a level, uncompromising look, then went to a chair and sat down, his head bowed. James awkwardly patted his shoulder. "She doesn't matter any-more," he said. "We believe in each other."

Dear Lily. Artemas paused, looking out the window beyond the desk in his bedroom, lost in the whipping snow and darkness. The small pool of light from the desk lamp made him feel secure in a safe moment of memories and hope. He looked down at the sheet of paper and the pen standing immobile in his hand. What should he say about the past two months to an eleven-year-old girl who admired him?

Nothing about the truth. Just the hopes.

He asked about her schoolwork, her rambles in the woods, the pet squirrel she'd nurtured after finding it in a nest ruined by predators, the beef cattle her parents were raising to make extra money. He asked her to have her father write down everything he could remember about the gardens at Blue Willow, reminding her that someday he'd be back to open the house and restore the gardens around it. But he warned that it might be a long time before he could do that.

A week after his father's funeral Artemas received her reply, on a note card printed with flowers. *Okay. I'll wait for you,* she said. *You'll be back. You promised.*

One morning Grandmother called him to her room. Tamberlaine and LaMieux were there. Chilling anticipation slid through Artemas.

When she saw him, his grandmother's face dissolved in wistful affection and sorrow. But her eyes gleamed. "Susan's father killed himself last night. With the gun he used to kill Creighton. It's all over, my dear. Your father's death is behind you."

Artemas thought of Susan and her ruined family, then of his own. Unable to speak, torn by too many different emotions, he simply nodded. Tears burned the backs of his eyes. He went to a window and stood rigidly, his fists in his trouser pockets, his head bowed.

Behind him, Tamberlaine said quietly, in a voice of deep, epic resonance, "The king is dead."

And LaMieux added, "Long live the king."

Seven

Mama lay in the big four-poster bed, crying. Lily heard Daddy rattling pans downstairs in the kitchen. Early-morning sunshine streamed through the upstairs window, promising a hot, muggy day even though it was only May. "Take it easy, Mama," she begged, sitting beside her and stroking the tangled red hair back from her face. "Your back's gonna be just fine. It'll take a few weeks to heal, that's all."

Biting her lower lip, Mama got herself under control and said, "I hope the doctor's right. I feel useless."

Lily had never seen her mother disabled by pain before. Worse, she had never seen her look defeated. The managers at the pet-food plant said Mama didn't qualify for full insurance, because she couldn't prove her back problem came from her job. As if lifting twenty-pound sacks of dog food eight hours a day wasn't good evidence.

Lily raged silently against the unfairness, but only said to Mama, "You're not useless, because I'm gonna help you get dressed and go downstairs, and get you set up at your quilting rack, and by the time your back's well, you'll have a queen-sized double-wedding-ring quilt to show."

Mama snorted. "Quilting's for old ladies with rheumatism and bad dentures. They sew and click their teeth for fun." But she pushed herself upright, her mouth set in a grim line. "At least I've still got my own teeth."

"That's right. As long as you can bite and chew, you're not too bad off." Lily helped her out of bed and braced an arm under her shoulders. As they shuffled toward the bathroom, Lily glimpsed the two of them in the long mirror standing in one corner. The sight made her throat ache—they looked like two scruffy, redheaded angels in their long cotton nightgowns. Mama was hunched and pale next to Lily's towering height and ruddy complexion.

When she got her mother settled in front of the bathroom mirror, Mama waved her away. "Go on downstairs and make sure your daddy isn't scramblin' eggs with his hook. I've got to do things for myself, so I won't get weaker."

Lily read the stubbornness in her face and left her reluctantly. Down in the kitchen, her father, already dressed for work, held a glass bowl filled with eggs in one hand. He was stirring the eggs with his hook. Lily kissed his cheek and took the bowl away from him. "You'll rust," she teased gruffly. She wiped his hook with a dish towel.

He tried to smile, but his face was haggard. He went to the big table in the room's center and sat down, staring into space over a mug of coffee. Lily busied herself at the stove, while worry crawled into her stomach and chased her appetite away. "I'm gettin' a job," she told him. "Aunt Maude says the Friedmans will hire me at their greenhouse after school's out for the summer."

"You're only fourteen," Daddy said.

"That's why I have to have your permission." She went to him, her hands trembling, and sat down across the table. "Please. You can drop me off on your way to work each morning and pick me up on your way home. Aunt Maude and I've got it all figured out. And it's five dollars an hour, Daddy. Tax-free. They'll pay me in cash, because Mr. Friedman doesn't want me on his books."

"That's not right, keeping money you ought to pay the government."

"Daddy, the government wastes more money than we'll

ever see in our whole lives. It's not fair. This family needs every penny. We don't waste it."

"You've been listening to Maude and the sisters talk politics too much." He sighed. "I don't want you working the way your mother and I had to when we were your age. Besides, you're set to study art and music at the community center this summer."

"Aunt Maude'll get my registration fee back for me. I'll take the classes next summer." She leaned forward, her hands clenched on the table. "I want to help out around here. This is my home too." She hesitated, cast a furtive glance toward the door to the hall, listening for Mama's steps on the stairs, then whispered, "It's gonna take a lot longer for Mama's back to heal than she thinks. I heard you tellin' Aunt Maude. And I heard you say you've got to take out a loan to pay the doctor's bills. There's no way we can pay all those bills and the loan, too, unless I get a job."

Her father's lined, leathery face stiffened with pride, but there was resignation in his eyes. Lily continued quickly, her tone passionate. "Nothing's more important than keeping this place. Someday it'll belong to me, and if I ever have kids, I want 'em to grow up here. And I'm no good at waitin' for miracles, Daddy."

He tried to smile, but the little lines around his eyes made it look painful. "I remember when you daydreamed that Artemas Colebrook would come back and make you a princess."

She blushed but raised her head proudly. "Oh, that was kid stuff. Women aren't meant to wait around for some man to rescue them. That's a myth of the male-dominated social structure."

"You've been reading Little Sis's books on women's lib again."

"It's all true, what those books say." She was silent, thinking wistfully of the letters Artemas still sent, and the ones she wrote back. They were a cherished part of her life, but only a dummy would sit around fantasizing about a boy she'd last seen when she was six. "He's off in college," she said slowly. "I expect he's got about a dozen girlfriends." She dropped her gaze to the old wooden table and scrubbed her fingertips over imaginary stains, as if too busy with important work to care about Artemas. "I'm going to college too. I want a good job and lots of money. Something I can do outdoors, working with plants. I think I'll start my own business." She raised her eyes and met her father's somber, affectionate gaze. "If there's any rescuing to be done around here, *I'll* do it."

He exhaled, then nodded. "I've raised me a tough little bird."

She went to him and hugged his neck. "A big bird, Daddy, a big one."

Uncle Charles interred Grandmother in a marble mausoleum in the private Colebrook Cemetery, surrounded by high, thick walls to keep out the less fortunate dead people. Artemas came back to the mausoleum afterward, alone, and said his good-bye. His father's and mother's names loomed in the dim light near Grandmother's crypt.

Mother, drunk, had driven her car into a tree the year before. The young man with her had died also. His wife told everyone who would listen that Mother had killed him in a jealous rage.

James and the others copied Artemas's relentless determination to move ahead. He wanted them to see, through everything he did and said, that shame could be erased by hard work and rigid scruples. He drilled it into them—discipline, goals, integrity, honesty. He'd graduated with honors and got an engineering degree; he expected each of them to be just as dedicated.

James was a junior majoring in business, achieving the Dean's List every semester. His love for sports had come to a grim crossroads when he'd entered college. He loved baseball and played on the collegiate team, and Artemas knew he dreamed of reaching the pros. But Artemas told him to consider his options—he might never be good enough, and a baseball player was of no use to the family business. James brooded and suffered, then quietly devoted himself to academics.

Cass had graduated from Evertide with honors and had entered college this year, majoring in art. Her weight had dropped dramatically, and she'd become compulsive about dieting. Michael, Elizabeth, and Julia were straight-A students. All knew that their futures were with Artemas and Colebrook China, and they had a mission.

He wrote to Lily about his grandmother's death. There had always been two constants in his life—his family and the simple little notes that slipped back and forth through the miles and the memories between him and a girl he hadn't seen in nine years. He kept his strange hobby a secret, feeling odd and protective that someone his age, with his dark, serious nature, should enjoy writing to a child. He couldn't picture her as anything else, and she'd never sent a photograph of herself.

He received a neat little box from her, containing a check for twenty-five dollars. *Please donate this to some charity your grandmother loved. Mama and Daddy say she was noble and kind. I cleared a spot in the old gardens behind the estate house and planted a willow there, in her honor.* Lily's handwriting was sweeping and confident, not a child's anymore.

Uncle Charles had always said he would put Blue Willow up for sale the day it passed into his hands. When Grandmother's carefully hidden will was produced by her new lawyers, the ones she'd hired after Father's death, Uncle Charles vowed to fight the will in court.

Grandmother had left both the old Georgia estate and her controlling interest in Colebrook China to Artemas.

"You won't fight it," Artemas told him calmly. "And when I have the money to buy you out, you'll very quietly sell me the remaining stock." Artemas handed him a packet containing photographs of his wife with two naked, drunken female friends from her bridge club. When Grandmother's detective had shown her and Artemas the photographs, Grandmother had said, with all the aplomb of an elderly Ziegfeld Girl who'd seen a bit of everything during her life, "I suppose they're practicing a new type of trump trick."

Standing triumphantly in the lawyers' offices in a rumpled black suit with threadbare elbows, Artemas said to his apoplectic uncle with a smile of contempt, *"I own this family's future, and if you try to interfere, I'll ruin you."*

He took his brothers and sisters from Uncle Charles's control and moved everyone into an old brownstone not far from the company's run-down offices in New York. James and Cass would live at home to help with the younger ones and save money.

When he went over the company's assets with Tamberlaine and LaMieux, he saw that it could be kept from bankruptcy only by hoarding every dollar and sacrificing everything else in his life—his personal time, except for parenting his younger siblings, would be owned by the company for years to come.

There would be no glamour, no luxuries, no playing at corporate lifestyles. He was the head of a failing business that clung to respectability with famous but outmoded china designs that had little appeal for younger customers. There was a whole world of affluent young buyers eager for innovative designs, but Uncle Charles had never bothered to cultivate them.

Management was disorganized, inefficient, and apathetic. The handful of china factories scattered from New York to the Carolinas were dilapidated, the employees poorly paid and unmotivated. Salvaging and rebuilding the company would take more than his good intentions and slavish hard work. Somewhere along the way, he'd have to sacrifice more. What that might be, he couldn't tell. But he knew he'd do it.

Artemas wrote to Lily about his takeover of Blue Willow and the family business. She wrote back, *Good for you. This is what you were meant to do. But now that you're the head pooh-bah, don't get cocky and forget us. I'll have to come after you with some rotten apples if you do.*

There would always be Lily. Now that he was in charge of his life—such as it was—he had to find a way to see her again.

•   •   •

Lily stuck another tiny begonia in a plastic pot and worried about the algebra test tomorrow, the one for which she'd barely studied. She glanced wearily down the rows of bedding plants on long wooden tables. Her shoulders ached from potting begonias. Summer had stretched into fall. December sunshine slipped through the greenhouse's long expanse and beckoned to her hopelessly—her weekday afternoons and every weekend belonged to Friedman's Nursery and Greenhouses.

Mama's back would never be strong enough for her to go back to work at the plant. They accepted that now. She couldn't even stand up at home for long stretches without her back aching, so she spent her time making quilts to sell at the tourist shops.

Quilts didn't pay the bills.

Lily tried not to think about the straight-A average slipping downward or what the school counselor had said about college scholarships going only to the best students. She dug her fingers into the potting soil and sighed.

"Hello, gorgeous," Andy Holcomb said, as he passed her with a sack of fertilizer on one shoulder. "Are you just about done?"

"Yep." She gave him a half-smile and succumbed to a rush of awkward pleasure. Big, blond Andy Holcomb was the son of a local minister. He was leaving for college after Christmas. He wore nice khaki trousers and tight pullover sweaters, usually with a thick gold cross hanging over his collar on a gold chain, and the cross gleamed almost as much as his mouthful of braces. The Friedmans went home at dark most nights, leaving Andy and Lily to close up. Mama and Daddy thought the world of him. They let him give her a ride home in his Camaro sometimes, after work.

When she finished, she washed her hands at a spigot, went into the shop attached to the main greenhouse, and pulled Artemas's cadet jacket over her sweater and jeans. She'd carefully stored the insignia in the Colebrook teapot, and had worn the jacket so much that it had little bare spots at the elbows. She'd grown into the jacket enough that her fingertips stuck out of the sleeves instead of being swallowed by miles of extra cuff.

She got her baggy cloth tote stuffed with paperbacks from behind the counter and waited for Andy. He turned out the lights, donned a leather aviator jacket, and locked the front door behind them. The night was clear and crisp, and the buildings were outlined by a white half-moon above the rim of the mountains. The lights from town stretched out on the black ridge in the distance, and the road in front of the greenhouses was a soft gray stripe.

"Pretty night," Andy commented as they walked to his car. "I'll miss driving you home at night."

Overcome with this sudden admission of interest, Lily mumbled something about missing his company at work. She settled in the low-slung passenger seat and sat in fluttery silence as he drove. They crossed through town, where the sidewalks were already empty and the shop windows dark except for a few small restaurants, then into the countryside again.

When they turned off on Blue Willow Road, Lily distracted her churning thoughts by studying the forlorn clocktower standing in a field at the intersection. It was the Colebrooks' estate clocktower, and it looked like a Gothic pillar in the moonlight. The clock face was broken, and the hands stood at 2:15. Daddy could remember when its bells had rung every hour, keeping the Colebrooks' time. The estate began there.

They crossed the Toqua River over an old steel bridge. Inky forest closed in on both sides of the narrow road, hemmed in on one side by a crumbling wall of gray stone interspersed with iron fence.

They passed the looming main gates at the estate, sagging in the middle, where their matching wrought-iron willows met, locked by a chain as thick as her wrist. Beside the gate was the gatekeeper's house, a ghostly stone cottage with broken windows. The remnants of rotten shutters hung from them. The kids at school thought the gatehouse and the massive gate beside it looked like the entrance to a haunted world, but Lily loved them.

Farther down the road the estate wall parted. A big mailbox on a stub of black railroad tie marked the MacKenzie driveway. Andy pulled into the graveled road. The forest closed in even more. He stopped the car and cut the engine but left the radio playing on a rock station. Lily squinted at him in the faint green light from the dash.

"I wish you were older," Andy said, leaning toward her. "Because you're too pretty to just be fifteen."

Lily's heart jerked in an excited little rhythm. "I think you've been eating fertilizer."

He laughed softly. "In a few years maybe I'll ask you out on a date. Have you ever been out on a date?"

"Noooo. But I've been out in groups after the football games."

"I mean a real date. Would you like that?"

Lily considered the enormous shock of being asked this question by an older boy, a respected and good-looking boy, one who was almost as tall as she was. "Sure."

"Want to test it?"

"How?"

"By giving me a kiss?"

She'd never been one to resist an adventure, even if her adventures had been limited to the world inside her books and her solitary explorations in the woods. "Okay." She leaned over to him and planted a small kiss on his mouth. Except for the embarrassment of knocking her teeth against his braces, it was an enthralling experience.

"Not like that," he said. "Like *this*." He pulled her to him and ground his mouth on hers. At first the shock excited her—all the heat and taste and sloppy wet contact—but then his braces began scrubbing painfully into her lower lip.

She kept kissing him, or trying to, wondering if the act was supposed to be this gooey and awkward. His tongue poked into her mouth like a wet fish. *Don't be a nerd,* she told herself. Except for obese Myrna Simpson and a few other outcasts at school, she was probably the only girl old enough to tote tampons who'd never been kissed. Most of them had done considerably more than *that*.

So she persisted, holding the front of his sweater because she didn't quite know what else to do with her hands, while he draped his arms around her neck like a vise. She began to get a cramp in her neck, and her mouth started to burn unpleasantly. Each time she tried to pull away and plant a kiss on some part of his face not covered by wire mesh, he intercepted her mouth and began mashing it again. Her lips were stinging now, and the excitement turned to disappointment.

If this was standard procedure, she'd just as soon stop. Her heart was pounding with dread, not enjoyment. "Relax. You'll get the hang of it," he said, when she drew back and pushed at his chest.

"I've got the hang of it," she replied. "Stop."

"You started it. Just cooperate, okay? But, listen, you can't tell anybody about this. Nobody'd believe you anyway."

He slid his hands down her coat and pushed it open, then jammed a hand inside and grabbed one of her breasts. Lily recoiled, grabbing his wrist, confused. She *had* started it, hadn't she? Did that mistake give him the right to maul her? Andy looked as serious as doomsday. "What a set," he said breathlessly.

He put a hand on her upper thigh, his fingers digging and massaging roughly through her jeans. Then he lurched at her again, out of his seat and half into hers, pinning her against the door. His mouth slammed into hers. Pain scalded her lips.

Her confusion evaporated in a burst of fury. She rammed a hand downward and grabbed him between the legs—low, beneath the hardness, right to the soft, round testicles. Lily snapped her fingers tight and wrenched them. He jerked back, gasping, clawing at her hand, then trying to slap her.

The slap grazed her bruised lips. She let go of his crotch, balled her hand into a fist, and punched him in the mouth. He fell back into his seat, groaning, one hand over his crotch, the other over his braces. Lily was dimly aware of the pain in her knuckles. She considered hitting him again, but he was already shrinking against his side of the car and drawing his knees up to ward her off.

Lily grabbed her bag, shoved the door open, and got out. Shaking, she looked back at him and said evenly, "You'd better not tell anybody about this. Nobody'd believe you."

She slammed the door and walked up the driveway. She wanted to run, but pride kept her at a fast walk. The darkness closed in. She heard his car engine, and her courage broke. She darted into the woods and plastered herself against a broad tree trunk, then looked back toward the main road. He backed out without turning on the headlights. Rubber squealed as he hit the paved road. Lily watched as the Camaro's black shape fled back toward town.

The road to the farm was nearly a mile long, twisting up and down along the hollows and hills. She knew every step of it by heart and wasn't afraid of the dark forest. Forcing herself to walk slowly and calm down, she touched her lower lip and shivered. It was already swollen. God, what would Mama and Daddy say? What would they do?

Once, years ago, Mama had looked up from a chair at the Laundromat to find herself staring at a half-naked man who was playing with himself in the doorway. The man had run off. When she'd come home and told Daddy about it, he'd gone to town with his revolver and a deadly look in his eyes. Mama had called the sheriff frantically, and the man was caught before Daddy could find him.

Lily hung her head and walked slower, thinking. If she told Mama and Daddy what had happened, Daddy would get his big revolver from the table by the front door and hunt Andy down at his parents' house. If he didn't shoot him, he'd at least threaten to, and maybe end up in jail.

All other thoughts fled but fear and embarrassment. She felt betrayed, violated, guilty, as if she'd lost a layer of skin and become a new person, one she didn't understand. Since she'd taken Andy's dare at first, she was partly to blame, wasn't she? Did this kind of thing happen to other girls? No, the ones she knew had never talked about it.

She mashed on her puffy lip, desperately wishing she could force it back into a normal shape. Mama and Daddy would *know;* they'd take one look at her and know she'd done something awful, and she'd have to admit the truth. She thought of having to tell them every detail—having her boob grabbed and everything—and she stopped in the middle of the road and threw up. *Never.*

By the time she reached the fenced pastures and the short driveway between them to the farm, her mind was blank with misery. She cut across the fields, dragging her feet, ignoring the red-and-white Herefords who shuffled toward her curiously, expecting to have their heads scratched. When she raised her troubled gaze to the house, she halted in astonishment.

A strange car was parked in the yard. The porch light shimmered on it; it was a late-model sedan. She climbed through the barbed-wire fence, crossed the driveway, ducked through the fence on the other side, and angled to the far side of the pasture, where the fence ran along the forest. Staying just inside the shadows, she made her way to the barn, dumped her purse on the firewood stacked beside it, then crept toward the car. It had a rental-car license plate. Bent double so no one could see her out the front windows, she tiptoed to the house and edged along one side. A yellow rectangle of light came from the living-room window. The window was open at the bottom— Mama liked fresh air even in the coldest weather.

Lily stopped beside it, listening.

"Lily should be home in a little while," Mama said. "I don't like her working, but it's only a few hours a week. She loves the Friedmans' greenhouses. And they say she's got a good eye for arranging gardens. She makes a little spending money."

Lily frowned. *A few hours a week? A little spending money?* Why did Mama care so much about this visitor's opinion—care enough to bend the truth?

"I should have called to tell you I was coming," some-one said. His voice was deep, resonant, and unfamiliar, a handsome voice with no identifiable accent. "But when I realized my flight had been changed, I knew I'd only have a few hours. I couldn't miss the opportunity to see you all. I wish I had more time."

"You've got business in Atlanta?" Daddy asked.

"No, I'm going to Los Angeles. I had to change planes in Atlanta."

"You'll spend the night on a plane to Los Angeles?"

"Yes. I'm meeting with an artist there in the morning. Someone I'm hoping to hire to do some design work."

Mama said, with obvious wonder in her voice, "This is wonderful. I'm so proud of you. I know you'll do fine."

The stranger laughed, a tired sound, but warm and compelling. Lily inched closer to the window, dying to peek inside. "Do you know what I wish? I wish I could fall asleep on your couch with one of your quilts over me."

Lily frowned. Who was he? She felt like a fool, hiding outside the window. Touching her bruised lip, she cringed. It felt even larger.

"You're mighty tall to stretch out on our couch now," Daddy said. "But you'd be welcome. It's good to see you again. I wish Lily would get here."

"I don't want to miss her," the stranger said.

"Can't miss her," Mama answered, laughing. "She's six feet high, and her hair's still just as red." Lily heard move-ment, sounds like a drawer being opened and shut. "Here," Mama said. "Take this. It's her yearbook picture."

Not that, Lily thought, knotting her hands. Her hair had exploded under the photographer's lights, and she'd felt so awkward that she'd stared belligerently into the lens with her mouth clamped shut.

For what seemed like forever, the visitor said nothing. Then he said softly, "She's everything I pictured her being."

Was that good, or bad, and who was he? Lily pressed the heels of her hands to her forehead. She felt raw inside. Next she heard him say, "I shouldn't have brought her an-other stuffed bear. She's not a child anymore."

Her hands dropped to her sides. Her heart threatened to explode. Dazed, she dimly heard Daddy say, "She still has the other ones. And I think she has every letter you ever wrote to her too, Artemas."

Artemas. Her knees buckled, and she sat down on the ground beneath the window. Her hands shook. She realized she was stroking the hem of his old academy jacket. *He'd come back to see her.* She had to go inside. She had to know what he looked like, and hug him, and—and she couldn't.

Lily cupped a hand over her mouth and bent her head. She couldn't walk in the house like *this*—disfigured, smelling of vomit, filled with shame, fear, and bewilderment. But she wanted to see him so badly that her chest seemed to be caving in with emotion.

She sat there in silent misery, tears sliding down her face, while he continued to talk with Mama and Daddy. She didn't know how much time passed, or even what he said, exactly. She was caught up in the sound of his voice, the depth and richness of it, the tone of authority and the gentleness.

Chairs scraped on the hardwood floor. She heard the movement of feet. Her mind cleared a little, and she realized he was telling them good-bye, that he had to leave now or he'd miss his flight. Lily slipped into the darkness beyond the back of the house. She stood around the corner of the porch there, hidden, looking toward the front yard through the porch's screens.

She heard the front door open and footsteps on the front porch's creaking boards. She splayed her hands on the screen and strained her eyes.

He stepped into view with Mama and Daddy. The sight of him brought a low moan of recognition from Lily, and she bit her injured lip to stifle it. He was perfect. He hugged Daddy, then Mama, then stood with his head tilted back, taking in the sky, shifting his gaze slowly to the creek beyond the house, the willows, then to the house, and finally to her parents again. His expression was troubled; the night breeze lifted his dark hair from his forehead, and he ran a hand over it wearily. A long black overcoat was pushed back from his chest, revealing a rumpled white shirt with the collar unbuttoned and black trousers. He shoved his hands into his trouser pockets, and his big shoulders hunched. He was saying something to her parents. Mama's face took on a wistful, sympathetic expression, and she rose on tiptoe, putting both arms around him and hugging him again.

He walked to his car. Lily cried against the screen, her face mashed to it, her fingers forming claws on the mesh. As he drove away, she stepped away from the house and stood in motionless despair, watching, her hands limp by her sides.

Stumbling blindly to the creek, she knelt there and rinsed her mouth. The icy water numbed her face but only made her more aware of the ache of shame and loss inside her chest. He was gone, and it was her fault she hadn't gotten to speak to him. She picked her way back to the barn, retrieved her purse, brushed her hair, then approached the house with halting steps. She would have to lie.

When she entered, Mama and Daddy turned from the hearth and stared at her. "You'll never guess—what in the world happened to your mouth?" Mama asked.

Lily shook her head and feigned disgust. "I was feeding scrap wood into the mulching machine, and it flipped a chunk back at me."

Mama moved gingerly, bracing her back with one hand, coming to Lily and laying the other hand along her chin. "You've been crying! Oh, sweetie, are you hurt that bad? Are you all right?"

"Yeah. I stopped on the way to wash my face in the creek up near the road."

Daddy frowned in bewilderment. "You were walking? Why?"

"Andy was in a hurry to get home. Had a Bible-study meeting tonight. I told him to let me off at the paved road. I like the woods at night."

Daddy's face relaxed. "You and your rambling. I swear."

Mama gazed at her worriedly. "I'll get you some ice. But we've got something to tell you first. Sweetie, I'm sorry you weren't here. I'm so sorry. *Artemas* came to see us."

Lily listened, struggling to keep her face impassive, as Mama talked about Artemas's visit. "He wanted to see you," Mama finished, gazing at her sadly. "And I know you would have loved seeing him. Lily, he's absolutely handsome. Way over six feet tall and solemn as a banker, but just as nice as he could be."

"Aw, I look awful. He'd have run."

"Oh, *Lily*," Mama said. She put her arms around her and pulled her head to one shoulder. "He wouldn't have minded. He took your picture with him. He thinks you're beautiful."

Lily's control shattered. She pulled away, went to her bedroom, and stood with her back against the shut door, crying harshly into her balled hands. Through the glaze of tears she saw the posters of mountains and flowers on the walls, the books jumbled on the nightstand, and the neatly made bed. The new bear propped against her pillows brought a ragged sound from her. Beside it was a spray of red roses wrapped in gold paper. She sat down on the bed, held the roses and the childish bear to her face, and kissed them.

She felt as if she'd broken some vow to Artemas, lost some precious chance, and that she'd never see him again.

Eight

Despite the glitter of a massive chandelier overhead, the potent scent of gardenias in the ornate centerpieces, the clink of crystal wineglasses, the inviting plate of poached salmon in front of him, and the high-powered chatter of more than a dozen of New York's most elite political couples, Artemas was trying not to fall asleep. The struggle had become a habit over the four years since he'd taken over Colebrook China. Given any moment of relative peace without a calculator or a computer or a sheaf of notes in front of him, his thoughts wandered and his eyelids filled with sand. He wanted to excuse himself and step outside on the room's balcony for a reviving minute in the frigid air, but the new year's first snow was falling.

Marketing reports, management analyses, inventory outlines, and interoffice memos swam lazily in his mind. Senator DeWitt's oratorical bass voice droned pleasantly from the head of the table, as the senator held forth on the attributes of the recently inaugurated Ronald Reagan. Artemas focused on the heavily engraved sterling fork in his hand and willed it to slice a section from the salmon. A set of delicate, pale fingers appeared on the sleeve of his black dinner jacket. A soft, feminine voice whispered nearby, with lilting humor, "I'll have someone bring you a cup of coffee."

Decorum and willpower overcame drowsiness. He straightened and looked gratefully at the delicate dark-haired young woman beside him, her solemn, pleasant little face coming into clear focus. Glenda DeWitt, the senator's only offspring, looked demure, even frail, in a frothy red gown cut high on her thin shoulders. Her unpretentiousness and her intelligence were shown in large pale green eyes that watched him shyly. Her small hand withdrew and settled gracefully on a glass of mineral water beside her plate. The slice of salmon there was plain, dry, and unappetizing. Glenda never complained about her severe diabetes or the regimen it imposed on her life, or the multitude of related health problems that kept her sheltered in the doting senator's care even now, though she was several years out of an elite women's college, where she'd majored in French literature.

"I'll have to learn more about ceramics and china," she said, tilting her head at Artemas and watching him with open affection. "So we'll have something to discuss that will keep you awake."

"It's not your fault. In fact, I let myself doze because I feel so comfortable with you." He smiled at her gallantly. A blush crept up her thin cheeks. They'd known each other for years, meeting at social functions hosted by the senator, talking easily, finding shared ground in her interest in fine china and his appreciation for her unspoiled nobility. She said with a light laugh, "I doubt the other females you know would consider that a compliment."

"I don't know that many—not in the way you mean. I don't have time."

"I enjoy talking with you. I look forward to it." She cast a rueful gaze at her spartan dinner and glass of water. "It's one of my few reckless pleasures."

"Tell me about your work with the library foundation."

"Really? It's not nearly as exciting as what you're doing—the new company you bought."

"Industrial ceramics are much less interesting than

literature, I assure you. Especially when my main concern is whether adding a small, unknown company to Colebrook China is the first foolish thing I've done."

"That's not what Father says. He thinks venturing into industrial ceramics is the *smartest* thing you've done. He's so pragmatic. You *know* he judges everything by its usefulness." Her expression became pensive. "Except me. I'm the only frivolous thing he loves."

"You're not frivolous. The world would be a very dull, narrow-minded place without people who love and preserve books."

Her face brightened. She called for the waiter to bring a cup of coffee. When it arrived at Artemas's place, she bent her head close to his and whispered, "Please stay awake and talk to me. You're the only reason I'm not falling face-forward into the salmon myself."

He laughed and saluted her with a raised cup. She clinked her glass of water to it. Artemas caught the senator watching the two of them shrewdly.

After dinner, when the other guests were having drinks in the living room, the senator beckoned Artemas into his darkly paneled office and shut the doors. "My daughter adores you," he said, fitting a pipe into his mouth and flicking a gold lighter over the bowl. As he sucked the flame into the tobacco, he studied Artemas over the blue-gray smoke rising from the pipe's bowl.

Senator DeWitt was the perfect media image of a stately politician—white-haired, dignified, tanned, with a jowly, rugged face. A widower for many years, he maintained wily discretion over his personal life, and the only rumors that surfaced about him added to his charm with the public. It was said that he was a favorite with the older women in his gentrified social tribe. It was also said, with fearful awe, that he was the most powerful senator on the Armed Services Committee.

Artemas suspected that there had been a time, decades ago, when his grandmother and the senator had been more than friends. His loyalty to her in the later years—a platonic loyalty by then, Artemas thought—had never flagged.

Artemas measured his response carefully. "I think Glenda is one of the most courageous and principled people I've ever met."

The senator arched a bushy white brow at him and settled in a leather armchair. "That's a diplomatic answer. You've been very kind to her." He gestured to the chair across from his. Artemas sat down slowly, alert and wary. "I consider her a friend. I don't pity her, if that's what you mean."

"Good." The senator laid his pipe on an ash stand and leaned forward, his shrewd gaze boring into Artemas. "You've done a remarkable job of salvaging Colebrook China from complete ruin, but its future is far from secure. The smallest setback could destroy all you've worked for in the past few years. Industrial ceramics are your only hope of building a solid financial base."

"Yes." The strange segue from Glenda to his struggles to save Colebrook China perplexed Artemas. "I realize I have to expand beyond the china business."

"Your youth and your family's reputation are against you. The competition for military contracts is ferocious. I can make certain that you have the edge you need to survive. It is a question of ruthless survival, Artemas, and if you don't face that fact, you'll lose everything."

"In time I can—"

"Work yourself to death and see very little in return for it." The senator gave Artemas a look filled with deep weariness. "I've circumvented the schemes of at least a dozen men who'd like to marry a senator's daughter. Now, I find myself in the odd position of having discovered one man who's worthy of her but who isn't interested."

"I like Glenda too much to disappoint her—or to imply a commitment I can't make."

The senator savored his pipe for a moment, his eyes narrowing in thought. "You've had your share of women. I know—I've checked. A few months here, a year there—

faithful devotions, from what I've heard, each monogamous, as long as each lasted. You break things off when the women become too serious. It's not a record that reveals any urge for stability, but nothing that condemns you either. At least you're honest.

"I have all the permanent responsibilities I want, with my work and my brothers and sisters. And now, with the new company—"

"Typlex Ceramics." The senator smiled, stroking his pipe stem. "A less scrupulous young man would have no reservations about cultivating my influence over military contracts. Or about using my daughter to win it."

"I know that. That's one reason I've avoided Glenda."

"My daughter has been deprived of so much she deserves." The senator stood, clasped his hands behind his back, and went to the fireplace. He scowled down into the flames, looking haggard. "She was only nine years old when we lost her mother. She's always been restricted and sheltered because of her diabetes. The doctors have told her she's too frail to bear children."

He faced Artemas, and his expression hardened. "I want her to have everything she wants, before—before her health fails completely. And if that includes you, I'll do whatever is necessary to get you for her." He paused, watching Artemas closely. "Don't look so shocked, my boy. I was a good friend to your grandmother. I helped her as best I could, and she knew there'd come a time when the favor would be repaid. Now is that time."

"You're asking me to deceive Glenda? To treat her like a fool?"

"As long as you make her happy, and she never learns the truth. You'll be faithful to her, and gentle. You'll treat her the way I want her treated."

"My God."

"You say you care about her. You imply that you have great respect for her. And certainly, though she's no beauty and she's not the most robust young woman in the world, she's not unappealing to you—physically."

"But that's not enough. It's not fair to her for you to—"

"It's heinous of me to provide my daughter with happiness? Even at your expense?" He shook his head. "What have you got to lose—a haphazard sex life with women who don't mean very much to you? And in return, I'm offering you the kind of opportunities you *cannot* turn down. A respected, admired, devoted wife. An influential father-in-law. Most important, a future for your business. Security for your brothers and sisters. A chance to build the dreams your grandmother drilled into you from the time you were a child. *Her* dreams—the only ones your father and your uncle didn't ruin for her." He paused, his eyes becoming colder. "I'm offering you a chance to make a powerful friend, instead of a powerful enemy."

Artemas stood, his thoughts jagged, anger and pride battling with the cold determination that had driven him for years. The senator added softly, "You owe me a debt. Pay that debt and you won't be sorry. I don't really think you have a choice. If you think you can achieve all you want without sacrifice, then it's time you learned a lesson about reality. You're not selling your soul, my boy. You're only pawning it. Someday you'll have all the money and power you need to buy it back."

Artemas returned late that night to the old warehouse he'd bought and refurbished for Colebrook's new headquarters. A cold January moon hung over the riverfront. The area was seedy, but developers were moving in to restore it. He'd bought ahead of the rush. Always thinking of the future. He had a large apartment upstairs, above the maze of offices and meeting rooms. James had his own apartment not far from the offices. At twenty-four, only two years younger than Artemas, he was already deeply involved in duties for Colebrook. Cass and the rest still lived at the old brownstone close by. Cass was getting a master's in art, and the twins were in college—Michael majoring in psychology, Elizabeth in business. Julia was still in high school. Artemas kept tabs on all of them. In time, they'd take their places in his plans. He'd never tell them what he'd done tonight.

The apartment was spartan, with soaring, steel-girdered ceilings and creaking wood floors. The furnishings were old pieces gleaned from salvage shops—not only because he was frugal, but because he liked them. He lay, fully clothed, on his bed, which was no more than a mattress and springs set on a plain metal frame in the middle of the vast space. A year ago he'd begun smoking to alleviate the boredom of endless paperwork. A full ashtray lay on his chest, a carton of filtered cigarettes beside it. He drank from a bottle of bourbon he'd bought at a package store on the way home.

When he was sufficiently drunk, he crushed his last cigarette into the crammed ashtray and reached for the stack of mail LaMieux had placed on his nightstand.

The letter from Lily lay on top. He held it up to the light of the metal desk lamp bolted to the nightstand, staring at it, letting the light shine through it, illuminating her bold handwriting. She was eighteen years old now, saving money to enter college, planning to study botany. He remembered from her last letter.

He'd return to Blue Willow someday and enjoy seeing how she'd grown up, whom she'd married—if anyone; he knew Lily's streak of independence—and what kind of plans she had for her beloved old farm. And if she ever asked for advice, or money, he'd give generously.

So he shouldn't be feeling guilty. What he held in his hand were just polite words on paper from someone whose childhood fantasies had merged with his, someone who had admired and encouraged him ever since, as he had her.

He crumpled the letter in his fist and dropped it into a trash can under the nightstand. She had lost her Old Brook Prince, and he didn't know how to tell her so.

They had on their best clothes. For once, Zea's back didn't ache. It was a sunny Saturday afternoon, and there was a hint of spring in the air that curled into the old truck when Zea rolled the window down a crack. She drove because Drew had trouble negotiating traffic on the busy interstate with only one good hand. She smiled at him. He looked so handsome sitting next to her, like Gary Cooper, she thought, in his brown suit with the new tie she'd given him for their anniversary. He draped his hand on her knee, his big, blunt fingers tickling her through the skirt of her new dress. Flirting with her like he always did. Zea shoved his hand away, and he put it back. She smiled as she drove.

Lily teased them about their games sometimes, when she caught them necking in front of the fireplace or saw one slap the other on the fanny in passing. But she was proud of her parents, and said so. Proud that after twenty years of marriage they still wanted to flirt with each other. When she'd heard that they wanted to go to Atlanta for the day and have dinner, she'd presented them with a registration slip for a downtown hotel. She'd given them a room for the night, with a hot tub.

"You better save that for the hot tub," Zea said now, as Drew edged her skirt up and tickled her inner thigh. "We haven't even had dinner yet."

"We could go to the hotel first, then go to dinner."

She cut her eyes at him, flashed him a coy look, and caught his sly grin in response. When she returned her attention to the crowded highway, he withdrew his hand and turned the radio on. He found Merle Haggard on a station and settled back happily. "One of these years," he said, his voice low and thoughtful, "after we've helped Lily go off to college, I'm gonna build us a hot tub on the back porch. Every night you and me'll strip all our clothes off and sit in it and drink some wine."

"I'd like that."

The car in the lane beside theirs, an old sedan, swerved a little. Zea frowned and watched the driver carefully. Burly-looking and disheveled, he lifted a can to his mouth and took a drink. The car's back end was barely clearing the truck's front bumper. "Pull back from that character," Drew said. "I think he's drinking a beer."

She stepped lightly on the clutch and then the brake. The sedan lurched in front of them, moving into their lane too quickly. Zea gasped and stomped the brake to the floor. The sedan's fender caught them.

She gripped the wheel fiercely as the truck careened sideways. Drew's hand gripped her shoulder. "You've got it, you've got it, just hold on," he yelled, as the truck began to fishtail.

But suddenly the truck was twisting, slamming into a car on the other side. The impact slung her hands off the wheel. She twisted toward Drew, screaming. They had always survived together. It couldn't be over.

Then the world was in chaos, spinning, collapsing, breaking apart.

"I'll put a hedge of forsythia along the side of the yard," Lily told the sporty young matron, who chewed the end of a gold fountain pen and traced Lily's crude sketch with a manicured nail. Lily planted her callused forefinger next to the client's and balanced the sketch pad in her other hand. She squinted in the bright February sunlight coming through the Friedmans' shop window and continued, "Then some smaller shrubs in front of the forsythia, and in front of *those,* a wide bed of perennials. I'll finish the edge in liriope or hostas."

"And all of it will be easy to take care of?" The woman poked at the designer glasses sliding down her tanned nose. "My husband and I want to come up from Atlanta and *enjoy* our vacation home, not spend our time diddling with the landscaping."

"Oh, everything I've outlined is hardy and pretty much self-sufficient."

"All right then. Go ahead."

Lily closed the sketchbook and laid it on Mr. Friedman's desk. She dusted pieces of mulch from the front of her jeans and tucked a gnawed pencil into the pocket of her flannel shirt. "Good. I'll figure out the budget and give you a call tomorrow—no, let's see, tomorrow's Sunday. Monday morning then. If the budget's okay by you, I'll start working at your place with my crew on Tuesday."

The woman nodded, buttoned her white cashmere

coat, and eyed Lily curiously. "I'm impressed. When the Friedmans told me their landscaper was only eighteen years old, I was a little concerned, frankly. But you're very talented and confident."

"Thank you."

"Why aren't you in college?"

Lily shoved her long hair under a floppy felt hat and tried not to show her discomfort with the question. "I'm saving money to go. Maybe next year."

"A young woman as bright as you should have gotten a scholarship."

"Didn't have quite the grade-point for it." Lily didn't feel like explaining that working all these years to help pay her family's bills had made it difficult to be an honor student. She shrugged lightly.

After the client left, she sat down at the desk and tried to concentrate on the budget she'd promised her. She heard Mrs. Friedman talking to customers in the nursery shop beyond the office's open door. Checking the tarnished watch latched on one arm with a cracked leather band, she realized she'd have to take the paperwork home with her.

Pulling a nursery catalog toward her, she bent her head over a pad of paper and began making notes. Landscaping came easy to her—she had a lifetime's experience with growing plants and trees, a natural understanding for what made them flourish or die, and as for the artistry of drawing designs, well, she'd studied every book she could find, poring over pictures of everything from cozy, free-form country gardens to formal masterpieces.

Lost in concentration, Lily looked up blankly when Mrs. Friedman stuck her head in the door and spoke to her. "Your aunt's here to see you," Mrs. Friedman said again.

Bewildered, Lily leaped up and strode into the shop. Aunt Maude stood there in a raincoat and her work dress—a baggy blue wool jumper with one of Uncle Wesley's big sweaters underneath. Her favorite apron with the permanent blueberry stains on the bib and the patched spot on the white skirt hung crookedly on her stout body. Her graying hair was mashed, with the teased sections poking out like lumps in Cream of Wheat. Her face was ashen, and her red-rimmed eyes met Lily's without blinking, as if frozen in the moment.

Lily gestured toward her strange, unkempt appearance. "What's going on? . . ."

"Get your things and come with me." Aunt Maude's voice was low and hard. "Don't ask questions. Just come with me."

When Lily stared at her without moving, tendrils of fear crawling up her spine, Mrs. Friedman nudged her shoulder. "Go on. *Go.*"

A minute later Lily was striding into the parking lot beside Aunt Maude, her coat over one arm and her purse clutched in one sweaty hand. "Maudy?" she said, but the older woman shook her head violently. Lily halted in shock when she saw the sheriff standing beside his red-and-white patrol car. Sheriff Mullins, Aunt Maude's cousin, was short and beefy and half-Cherokee, with kind, dark eyes in a dusky, hawkish face. His thin black hair swept back from a high forehead. He held his tan broad-brimmed hat in both hands, clenching the brim. The sick little smile he gave Lily turned her stomach over.

"What'd I do?" she joked limply, peering down at him.

"Not a thing." He opened the patrol car's front passenger door, then the back one. "Maudy, you sit in the back, okay?"

Lily took a tentative step forward. Her nerves were screaming for answers. "What is it?" She looked from him to Maude. "I don't like mysteries. You know, us MacKenzies like to have everything out in the open, no coddling, no favors, no . . ." Her voice faded. She wavered, her knees loosening. "Is something wrong with my folks?"

She felt Aunt Maude's arm go around her shoulders. "They've been in an accident on the highway, sweetie. A drunk ran into them."

Lily backed away. Her aunt's face became blurred. Cold

horror and denial stiffened Lily's back. "How bad is it?" she asked, hearing her voice from a distance.

Aunt Maude didn't answer. Her stoic, fleshy face crumpled around the edges, and tears crept down her cheeks. Lily turned blindly, searching, not knowing for what, sweeping the empty sky and the road and the parking lot surrounded by greenhouses and nursery beds. Instinctively searching for something—some sign. The whisper of Mama's and Daddy's voices, assuring her they were all right.

She heard nothing but the shriek inside her own mind and the echo of emptiness.

Nine

The girl was bad off. Hopewell Estes could see that, in her hollow eyes and gaunt face, in the way her fingers picked a piece of lint to shreds, her shoulders slumped under a loose black dress. But she sat up straight in her chair in Maude's parlor, surrounded by Maude and the sisters, and him. He cleared his throat, stared at the knees of his black trousers, and thought of his son, Joe, ten years older than she but not half as tough or admirable. Joe was an embarrassment, a bad seed, some might say. Hopewell sighed. His and Ducie's son hadn't turned out very well. It was killing his wife, giving her heart trouble.

"This ain't real good timin'," Hopewell said, planting his hands on his knees. "I know that, Lily, with your folks only gone a month. But you gotta think about the future. There's no way you can pay all the bills you've got. Not even with your aunt Maude's help."

Lily stirred, raising vacant eyes to his. She blinked as if regathering her thoughts, then said, "I know that. I'll think of something."

"I need a place for Joe to live. With him, hmmm, with him needin' a good, quiet place, after—" Hopewell stopped, unable to form the rest of the sentence. *After he gets out of jail,* he didn't say. They all knew what he meant.

Everyone knew. Joe had been caught growing and selling marijuana, and it had been the most shaming thing Hopewell had ever endured. And more than his wife could endure. He had to get the boy straightened out.

Or at least get him out of the law's sight, deep in the wilderness that surrounded the MacKenzie farm, where his illegal crop could be hidden next time. "Your old farm is just right for him," Hopewell continued, his throat raw. "I'm thinking that I'll add to the cattle, maybe help him get started in the beef business."

"I can't sell it," Lily answered. "That'd be like selling my own bones."

Big Sis leaned on her cane and spit brown tobacco juice into a ceramic pot between her feet. Her lined old face worked with emotion. "Your folks wanted you to go to college. They wouldn't want you to hang on to the old place until you were broke and it had to be sold at auction."

Lily said softly, "They'd want me to fight to keep it. It's mine. It's all I have."

"How are you going to keep it?" Little Sis asked, patting Lily's shoulder. She waved the long-stemmed rose she'd brought to the meeting for memory and luck—what a strange, feisty floozy she was, Hopewell thought—and stroked the red hair hanging down Lily's back in limp waves. "You'll work yourself to death and still lose it. No, honey, it's just not in your destiny." She picked up one of Lily's hands and studied it. "Your palm says right here that you're going to, well, it's odd, it says you're going to break with the past, but then *this* line makes a circle, and goes way up there—meaning there's a long period of time involved—but then it comes back, so certainly, someday—"

"Oh, shut up," Big Sis said. "Go read a cereal box. It'd make more sense."

Maude stood impatiently and took command. "Lily needs time to think this over, Hopewell."

He stood, too, glad the offer had been made, and that

he'd done all he could, for the moment. "Joe won't be back for a couple of months."

Lily looked up at him. The expression in her eyes was wrenching, but strong. "I've still got the scar where he shot me."

Hopewell nodded, too depressed to respond. His son's irresponsible nature had been obvious, even back then. "You call me at home or my store, whichever. I'll be waitin'."

After he left, Lily sat dully, raw inside, her mind fuzzy. "Get her some tea with a shot of bourbon in it," she heard Aunt Maude tell Little Sis. Aunt Maude sat down in a chair next to hers and said, "Mr. Estes has got plenty of money and a good business in hardware and farm supplies, Lily. He's a respectable man. His family came here over a hundred years ago. It wouldn't dishonor you to sell the farm to him. Even if he wants it for Joe."

Lily stood. "I've got to go feed the cattle. And I'm going to spend the night there. Alone."

Aunt Maude frowned. "We agreed that you'd stay here for a while longer."

"I've got to go. I've got to look at it all by myself and think. I've got to think."

"But, honey—"

"Let her go," Big Sis said. "She's grown now."

Lily went out and climbed in the old Jeep parked along the street. Daddy and Mama had gotten it for her birthday last year. The dull brown finish had splotches of red where they'd painted over the rust marks, and the vinyl seats had bandages of duct tape over the torn places. But it ran like a fine watch. Substance over looks, Daddy had said. She cranked the engine. She knew what she had to do, and appearances didn't matter in that case either.

His flight had been delayed by fog, and the unwelcome wait gave Artemas time to think. He was about to board a plane for England, to iron out the details of a partnership with a firm that used ceramics in state-of-the-art medical applications. Ceramic scalpels.

A cocktail lounge at LaGuardia was a bad place for soul-searching. Leaning over a drink, a cigarette in one hand, his tie loosened, he felt like a youthful caricature of a world-weary business hack.

Glenda was happy. He'd made her bloom with appreciation, had begun taking her to bed a few weeks ago with gentle restraint, had encouraged her to trust him. He cared deeply about her; it was possible to love her, in a way— the way he could love anything or anyone of rare quality. He hid the fact that he would never love her the way she thought he did. He was trapped by her father's devotion to her. He'd made his choice—his family's future over his own. His decision was part of the price. He thought he'd reconciled himself to it.

But each time one of Lily's letters arrived and he threw it away, unopened, he knew he would never resolve what he'd done. Perhaps there would be some means to tell her, to explain, eventually. Perhaps someday he'd secure everything he wanted for his family, and then be free. His brooding was interrupted when he heard his name being paged. Frowning, he went to a phone. Tamberlaine was searching for him.

Elizabeth had tried to kill herself.

Elizabeth was asleep in a private hospital room, and Artemas could only wait through the night, until she woke and he could ask her why she'd swallowed a handful of sleeping pills. Why she'd tried to end her life at twenty. How he and the others had failed her.

Anger, bewilderment, and anxiety summed up the emotions he felt, and saw on his siblings' faces also. They had gathered in the visitors' lounge near her room. Artemas leaned by a window, cigarette ashes falling, unheeded, on his black trousers and shoes. He jammed his cigarette into the ashtray he held in one hand and cursed silently. All he'd had on his mind while Elizabeth was overdosing on pills and lying unconscious on the floor of her college dorm room were his own problems.

James paced leadenly across the open space where the

lounge opened into a corridor near the nurses' station. He'd been at the Colebrook offices when word had reached him from Elizabeth's college upstate. He'd arrived here at the hospital before anyone else. He looked angry, stalking back and forth with his hands shoved into the pockets of his dress slacks, his tie thrown on a table somewhere and forgotten, his large shoulders hunched in misery. James always wanted to know who was responsible, who deserved to be punished or rewarded. He treated their business associates that way, with a cool, threatening demeanor that concerned Artemas. Yes, James was an effective, even ruthless agent, doggedly loyal to the family, devoted to the business, proud to a fault. But he was a loose cannon also. He was already talking of suing the college, a venture Artemas would block.

Artemas lit another cigarette. His throat was raw; his eyes ached with fatigue. He felt much older than twenty-six. Elizabeth's college wasn't to blame for her problem. He, Artemas, was. It was his duty to be her parent—father and mother—and somehow, though he'd tried to make time for the family as well as the business, he'd failed. She was still shy and fearful of the world and completely lacking in self-confidence. Her sweet, dark blond prettiness and solemn intelligence drew people to her despite her timidness, but she never recognized her appeal.

He didn't understand. Neither he nor the others reacted to the world as passive victims, the way Elizabeth did. Artemas swept his tired gaze around the lounge. Cass was in the hallway, talking to an intern, her head tilted back coyly so that her dark hair slid smoothly along the scooped neck of her snug coatdress, one slender hand occasionally toying with the lapels of the doctor's white coat. The bedazzled-looking young man probably had no idea that the elegant, stylishly lanky Cass considered him a fool and was prying information about Elizabeth's condition from him.

Michael sat cross-legged on a sofa, looking collegiate and intellectual, as befitted a psychology major, in faded jeans and a bulky pullover, holding hands with a delicate brown-haired young woman wearing glasses and looking just as solemn. He was already completely in love with Kathy Goldberg, a fellow psychology major, and she adored him as well. They were planning to marry next year.

Julia sat on the floor flipping through a schoolbook and pretending to study, while she chewed the top of a highlighter pen and darted worried glances toward the hall. Her pale blond hair was askew in a short ponytail, and a long print skirt was tucked between her legs. Occasionally she wound a hand in the hem of her matching blouse, which she'd pulled from the skirt's waistband.

Artemas surveyed the group worriedly, his nerves on edge. James vented his self-doubts in aggressiveness, Cass had a compulsive need to remain reed-thin and dominate every man who crossed her path, Michael viewed the world with unrealistic expectations of its kindness, and Julia approached every task with manic energy. Artemas saw the world as something he could make over and control through rigid personal honor. He and they had found imperfect but strong ways to deal with their past. Why was Elizabeth so different, so self-destructive?

Glenda rounded the corner of the lounge area with a large paper cup in one hand, gazed at Artemas with fine lines of worry pulling at the center of her small dark brows, and picked her way to him through his siblings, smiling at them sympathetically. "Drink this milk," she told him with mild authority.

She leaned against the wall, facing him while he sipped from the cup, her thin body sheathed in a simple blue dress and low pumps, her shoulder-length hair tucked behind her ears and shimmering under the low lights, which caught the fine gold necklace at her throat. He welcomed her affection while fighting the familiar sense of betrayal in his chest.

"Is there any new information?" Glenda asked.

"No, she'll probably sleep for hours."

"I called Father. He says he's contacted Dr. Bolin. Bolin

will come by in the morning to meet with her, if you want him to."

"I want her to have the best therapist. If that's Bolin, then I agree. But I have to talk to her myself first."

Glenda slid an arm through his and clasped his hand. "This may be one problem you can't fix for your family without help. Please don't feel so responsible."

"I do. I've been too busy in the past few years. Away too much on business. If I'd talked to her more, spent more time with her—"

"Ssshh. The whole family feels awful. But none of you could have seen this coming. You're so close to each other, so protective. You're not to blame."

Alise's arrival cut the conversation short. Artemas watched as she ran up the hallway and halted in front of James, who stopped pacing and stared down at her in surprise. They hadn't seen each other often in the past two years. Alise was attending college out of state—driven to leave by James's refusal to see her as anything but the young girl who'd dogged his steps adoringly for years. He'd been right, in his way, because Alise was four years younger than he. But his involvement with a series of women his own age had wounded her so much that she couldn't remain where she might encounter him with one of them at his side.

But now he studied her slender beauty and somber, concerned eyes with obvious shock, his stern face slowly relaxing into an expression of tenderness. "I came as soon as I heard," Artemas heard her tell him. "Is Elizabeth all right?"

James wavered. He pulled his fists from his pockets. They unfurled and met her outflung hands. "She'll be fine. She's just sleeping."

"You look so tired and upset. Is there anything I can do?"

His fingers slid through hers. Her face brightened with amazement and pleasure. "Walk downstairs with me. I need some fresh air." He paused, then added gruffly, "I'm glad to see you. Just having you here makes me—makes all of us—feel better."

His gaze was riveted to her face, as if he was just discovering her. Slipping an arm around her back, he walked with her down the hall, disappearing beyond the lounge's wall. Cass deserted the intern and came over to Artemas, one black brow arched meaningfully. "She's not a sappy kid anymore. I think James just realized it. She'll have him tagged and bagged before very long. I'm taking bets."

Artemas eyed his sister grimly. "Maybe he'll set a good example."

"For *me*? Shit. I'm only getting started in the game. You won't find me mooning over anyone in particular." Her strained, cocky attitude faded. Shadows of fatigue and worry clung to her eyes like bruises. She looked in the direction of Elizabeth's room. "I've got to spend my time giving Lizbeth some lessons in survival."

Artemas put an arm around her shoulders. She brushed tears from her eyes. "How could she do this to us? Why didn't she say something, if she had problems?"

"We're going to help her. I'll make sure nothing gets in the way."

Tamberlaine and LaMieux walked around the corner. Artemas had told them they weren't expected to stand this vigil, but both men had become so close to the family that they were part of it. Dawn was making pink stains on the cityscape beyond the lounge's window. Artemas stood with them, looking out at the first glint of sunrise. "I have to concentrate on my sister's problems right now," he told them. "I'll send James to England in my place, if one of you will go with him."

"I'll go," LaMieux said.

Artemas looked at Tamberlaine. "Then you manage things at the office. Try to clear as much as you can from my schedule. I need all the free time I can get."

Tamberlaine nodded sagely. "No one and nothing of less than vital importance will get past me."

●   ●   ●

The silence was bone-chilling. The house seemed to have died, too, and every little sound made Lily look up and listen, expecting to see Mama or Daddy walk in the door, to hear them moving around in the other rooms. She couldn't bear to think of them the way she'd seen their bodies, first at the hospital, then at the funeral home. She couldn't bear to think of them buried in the ground at the church cemetery in town.

Her desperation to have them back made her understand insanity; her thoughts ran in strange patterns. Sometimes in the past month she'd felt giddy, as if excited about the adventure and the challenge of being alone. Then her mood plunged into abject grief and fury. Aunt Maude and the sisters said it was normal to shift emotions like that, and that eventually she'd level out. They told her patience would get her through each day, and that she should indulge the odd, harmless notions but ignore the foolhardy ones. It was acceptable, then, to stay up all night hanging new wallpaper in Aunt Maude's parlor or spend hours walking around town without speaking to anyone.

But what she was trying to do now wasn't harmless, and she knew it.

She hadn't received a letter from Artemas since January. She'd written to him right after the funeral. He hadn't written back. When she needed him most, he hadn't even sent a card. Why?

She had to believe it was an accident. Her letters were getting lost. Or he was out of town, or out of the country.

For the past few days she'd been trying to call him on the phone. Lily had gotten his office number from long-distance information. Every time she called, the receptionist took her name and number and said she'd pass it along.

There had been no answer from Artemas.

Her hand trembling, she dialed the New York number again. A woman answered formally, "Colebrook International. Good afternoon." Lily always thought the name sounded alien. When had it changed from Colebrook China? Her heart pounding, she said as evenly as she could, "I need to speak with Mr. Colebrook, please. I've been calling you for days, and this time I can't just leave a message. Nobody calls me back."

"One moment, please."

A deep masculine voice came over the line. "Mr. Colebrook's office."

"I need to speak with Artemas, please."

"He's not available at the moment," the man answered politely. "Can I take a message?"

"Not if you're just going to ignore it, the same as everyone else."

"Perhaps I can help you."

"No, just tell him, please. It's really important that I talk to him."

"He can't be disturbed right now. I don't know when he'll be able to talk with you. Could you tell me the nature of your business?"

"If you tell him Lily called and it's important, he'll know what that means."

"I'm afraid I can't give him such a vague message. Is it personal?"

"Yes." *Yes, calling to tell him Mama and Daddy died and I need a loan to pay bills is pretty personal.*

"I'm Edward Tamberlaine, Mr. Colebrook's assistant. Anything you wish to tell me will be held in strict confidence."

"Won't you just ask him to call me?"

"Your messages have reached him. I'm afraid that's all I can tell you."

Her head swam. It wasn't possible that he'd known she'd called but hadn't bothered to call her back. "Is he in town? Is he there? Couldn't you buzz his desk real quick and say that Lily MacKenzie's on the phone?"

"I can't give you Mr. Colebrook's schedule. I'm not familiar with your name, Ms. MacKenzie. Mr. Colebrook accepts very few personal calls at the office."

"I'm a friend. An old, old friend. I'm calling from Georgia."

"Mr. Colebrook has given his staff a list of friends who are allowed to speak with him at the office. I'm sorry, but your name isn't on it. But I *will* check with him and make certain he knows you've been calling."

Lily clenched the receiver until her fingers ached. *Colebrook International* kept playing in her mind. It sounded more important and sophisticated than anything she'd imagined, and so did Edward Tamberlaine's voice. She suddenly felt foolish, humiliated, naive—and that made her angry.

"If Mr. Colebrook has to talk to me through other people, then he's in a sorry state," she said. "Thank you, but I'll think of some other way to get in touch with him."

She hung up and turned away, hollow inside, desperate and disappointed. She had to know if Artemas no longer cared about her or her family. Like the farm, his friendship was all that kept the emptiness from closing in on her.

"Elizabeth?" Artemas sat down on the edge of her bed. Her face looked small and forlorn against the white pillow; her wavy blond hair was matted to her head. Her blue eyes were hazy and tormented, and when he took her hand, her fingers curled limply inside his.

"I'm sorry I upset everyone," she whispered, tears sliding from the corners of her eyes.

"Ssshh. You're going to be all right. That's all that matters to us." He held her hand tighter.

Her mouth trembled, and her flushed, swollen face became a tragic mask of self-control. In a barely audible voice she said, "I don't know if I really wanted to die."

"Of course you didn't want to die. You need help, and you were asking for it. I blame myself for not being the kind of brother you could come to."

"Oh, Artie, it's not your fault."

"I don't want you to hurt yourself again. We have to work this out. We all love you, and we want you to be happy. That's all that matters. Listen to me." He took her chin as if she were still a child who needed a milk mustache wiped off her mouth, and turned her face toward him. "Nothing could be worse than what the six of us have survived together. We don't want to lose you."

She stared at him in anguished consideration and began trembling. "I won't do it again. I swear."

"Tell me why you felt so desperate."

"No. It's my problem. I won't talk about it."

"Elizabeth," he said with mild warning.

"*No.*" She jerked away from him, turned on her side, and put her hands over her face. "Leave me alone. I'm never going to talk about it."

Artemas stared at her in desperation. "A psychiatrist is coming by this morning to see you. Will you talk to him?"

"No. Don't hate me for being stubborn. Just leave me alone. I won't try to kill myself again. I told you."

At a loss for options, Artemas said sternly, "I could have you committed to a hospital if you won't cooperate."

Elizabeth jerked in alarm and twisted in the bed, staring at him in horror and disbelief.

"You've changed. You never could have threatened me before. I don't understand what's happening to you."

He bent his head and shut his eyes. Through gritted teeth he said, "I want the best for you. For the whole family. Goddammit, try to help me."

"I will," she said, her voice breaking. "But don't scare me."

"Then talk to this doctor when he gets here. Promise me."

Her face crumpled. "All right. But just to him."

His hands were clenched. He hadn't realized until that moment how much rage and frustration were trapped inside him. He forced himself to relax, or to give the appearance of it, at least. "You have my word that I'll do everything I can to help you, and I won't ask questions that upset you. And neither will anyone else in the family. But this family is going to survive. If I have to be a bastard to make certain of that, I can do it. You hear me? *Survive and win.* And that includes you. Don't ever doubt that I'll do whatever it takes."

She looked relieved but frightened. Artemas gripped her shoulder reassuringly. His word had power because he never broke it. Not to his brothers and sisters, not to the senator, not to business associates, not to Glenda. The guiding voice he listened to still had a sweet southern drawl. It had never deserted him.

Lily stepped from a fat yellow cab, paid the driver, then stood on the sidewalk, looking at the building in front of her. It was not what she'd expected. She'd pictured all of New York as a postcard scene from Manhattan, with sleek, modern skyscrapers making canyons along wide streets filled with people. Instead, she found herself on a narrow street lined with blocky, aging warehouse buildings of dingy brick and rusty steel. Their parking lots jutted out to the sides behind tall security fences. A cold March wind whipped down the street, carrying bits of trash. The rumble of heavy construction equipment came from gaps where buildings were being demolished. Large signs in front of the sites indicated that some kind of expensive redevelopment was under way.

Her pulse was thready as she returned her scrutiny to the looming old edifice fronted by a small brown lawn and severely clipped boxwoods. The bottom level was as welcoming as a bunker, with no windows and only a huge, simple set of glass doors set in the middle of a brick stoop. The upper level contained enormous windows, but rows of pale blinds covered them. Only the cars that filled the small parking lot and the glimpse of light inside the front doors gave a clue of human occupation. A small sign on the lawn said COLEBROOK INTERNATIONAL in stern white letters on a black background.

It wasn't grand in the way she'd expected, but it was no less formidable. She had a sense of its purpose and practicality, of mysterious labyrinths behind the solid brick walls, where large sums of money and important deals were negotiated. Where she'd find Artemas.

Her head throbbed with tense anticipation. So much was confusing and painful these days; she felt lost. Glancing down wearily, she unbuttoned her bulky, quilted jacket and smoothed the wrinkles in the white sweater and long gray skirt she'd donned in the rest rooms of the Port

Authority bus terminal. The wind bit through the pale hose on her legs. Her feet looked too large in their flat black shoes. They looked rooted to the pavement, afraid to move.

But she could only move forward. Hitching her tote bag and the long strap of a black purse over her shoulder, she advanced on the wide glass doors.

Inside was a small, pleasant lobby with philodendrons sprawling out of tall white ceramic planters in each corner. On one side, heavy tan couches and overstuffed chairs were arranged around a gleaming black coffee table. On the other was the small half-moon of a receptionist's booth, a forbidding obstacle staffed by a uniformed security guard with a spiky crown of short dreadlocks and a grandmotherly little woman in a business suit. They marshaled their position near a wall dominated by double doors painted an unfriendly steel gray. Her destination.

Lily eyed the doors, then the people, as she approached the booth.

"Can I help you?" the woman asked.

"I'm here to see Mr. Colebrook. Artemas Colebrook."

"Do you have an appointment?"

"No. I'll just wait until he has a free minute. I'm a friend of his. Lily MacKenzie. From Georgia." She straightened her back rigidly as they scrutinized her with skeptical expressions. "You're the one who's been calling, aren't you?" the receptionist asked.

"Yeah."

"Then you've come a long way for nothing. You'll have to leave a message. He'll receive it when he comes in. He's not here today."

"Will he be here tomorrow?"

"You'll have to leave a message," the guard interjected.

Lily glanced toward the seating area. "I'm not trying to be a problem, but I have to see Artemas. So I believe I'll wait for him." Her knees were shaking, but she walked calmly to a couch and sat down. Casting another look at the slack-jawed stares of the duo watching her, she added,

"Don't worry. When he sees me, everything'll be all right. If not today, then tomorrow. I'm patient."

The guard shifted, frowning. He and the receptionist traded an ominous look. "I'd better call Mr. Tamberlaine," the receptionist said briskly.

A few minutes later a large man in a crisp suit walked through the double doors. The suit was black. He was black. She thought of Othello, and was almost unnerved. He glided toward her with elegant grace, his regal face composed politely. Fronds of gray hair highlighted his temples. He was the most distinguished-looking and forbidding person she'd ever seen. She stood, determined to face whatever harassment anyone offered, even his. He halted in front of her and introduced himself. He gave a slight nod—a hint of a bow. "Ms. MacKenzie, I grant you points for persistence and ingenuity."

"All right, so I got on a bus and came to New York. If that effort's so impressive, then please get me in to see Mr. Colebrook. I don't believe he knows I've been trying to reach him. He couldn't know. He wouldn't ignore me if he did."

"I can't speak for Mr. Colebrook. If you'll tell me *why* you want to see him, I'll pass the information along. Perhaps he doesn't realize your message is urgent."

Her shoulders sagged. She hadn't come all this way to be stopped by pride now. He gestured toward the couch. They sat, she facing him, frowning over her shoulder at the pair at the desk, who were pretending to be busy. She turned her back to them and spoke to Mr. Tamberlaine in a hushed voice, trying to compress nearly 140 years of MacKenzie and Colebrook history into a concise story, telling him that she and Artemas had written to each other since she was six years old, that he'd always promised to help her if she needed him, and why she needed that help now.

About halfway through her speech his patient expression had begun to stiffen. By the time she finished, it had become an unreadable mask. "So you've come to ask for money," he said.

"I came to ask for a *loan*. But even if Artemas—if Mr. Colebrook—can't give me one, I'd like to see him." Her throat tightened, and tears stung her eyes. She willed them back. "He's the only one who understands. I can ask him for advice."

"Frankly, I find your story dubious. You say he hasn't seen you since you were a child. Yet you expect him to solve your problems for you."

Lily gritted her teeth. "I expect him to be my friend, because he always has been."

"The letters you mentioned—do you have any of them with you?"

"No."

"Do you have *any* proof that your story is true?"

"No."

"Then I suggest you come back when you have some."

"I don't have the money to go home and come back. Or to stay in New York a couple of days while I wait for my aunt to send the letters."

"I'm sorry then." He stood. "Go home, photocopy one of the letters Mr. Colebrook allegedly wrote to you, and mail it to me with a letter explaining your request for money. I'll make certain he receives it."

Lily clenched her hands in her lap and stared up at him. "All right. Thank you."

"Would you like to have the receptionist call a cab for you?"

"Yes. Thank you."

He said good-bye and left the lobby the way he'd arrived. She stood by the front doors, watching for the taxi. When it came, she got into the backseat and sat silently, lost in thought. The driver glanced back at her. "Where ya going?"

"Take me to the nearest hardware store."

He shot her a puzzled frown but put the car in gear. As they moved up the street, Lily stared fixedly out the window.

•   •   •

"Hello again," she said calmly the next morning, when Tamberlaine ran into the lobby after the receptionist's frantic phone call. He halted, staring at her. Lily tilted her head back and held his stunned gaze without blinking. The guard and the receptionist stood nearby, their faces angry and shocked.

Seated, cross-legged, on the carpeted floor by the building's front doors, Lily set aside the coat she held in her lap, then latched one hand in the chain that was padlocked around her waist and shifted a little so Mr. Tamberlaine could see that the other end of the chain was looped and padlocked through one of the doors' metal handles.

"She walked in, said, 'Good morning,' and did it before I knew what was happening," the receptionist moaned.

The composed and unflappable-looking Tamberlaine scowled at her so fiercely that she thought he might explode. She wound a clumsy hand around the tote bag beside her and pulled it to her chest, like a shield. "I want to see Artemas."

"Go outside and don't let employees or visitors try to enter the building through these doors," Tamberlaine told the guard. "Send them around back. And don't say why."

The guard bolted past her, swinging the other door open and disappearing outside. The blast of chilled air felt icy on Lily's flushed face. But she never took her gaze from the tall, dignified Tamberlaine. He turned toward the receptionist, whose hands seemed perpetually lodged at her throat in astonishment. "Call a locksmith."

She ran to her desk and snatched a phone book from a drawer. Tamberlaine pivoted to glare down at Lily again. Her stomach twisted. This wasn't going as she'd hoped. She'd thought once they saw her determination, they'd call Artemas. Instead, it looked as if they'd keep him and everyone else from knowing she was here again, and get rid of her immediately.

But she said evenly, "I spent the night moving from one diner to another and buying sandwiches so nobody'd chase me off. I was pestered by men who asked how much

I charged—you know what I mean—and somebody even tried to sell me cocaine. After all that, nothing you can say or do can shake me."

"Oh?" Tamberlaine pulled a chair in front of her, sat down, and casually crossed one leg over the other. "If you don't get on a bus today and return to Georgia, I'll have you arrested for trespassing."

The threat hit her like a slap. "Arrested?"

"Think about that—being taken to a police station, fingerprinted, questioned, searched, locked in a cell with strangers. Think about being humiliated in court and having to pay a fine. Can you afford to pay a fine?"

Hope was falling away, leaving her exhausted and uncertain. As he studied her face, he frowned. "I don't want to do that to you, but I assure you, I will. I can't have you wasting Mr. Colebrook's time."

"I wouldn't be wasting it."

"Oh? What if I told you he's received your message and asked me to handle it? That he doesn't want to see you?"

Yesterday she would have rejected that idea. Today, seeing that her persistence meant nothing to the people Artemas trusted, that he had put a shield around himself that excluded her, made her wonder if she'd been a fool. "Did he say why he doesn't want anything to do with me?" she asked finally.

Tamberlaine pursed his lips and scrutinized her shrewdly. "You said you'd already written to him about your dilemma, and he didn't answer you. Why would he want to see you now?"

"I thought my letters got lost. Or that he was out of town and hadn't read them yet."

The slow, negative shaking of Mr. Tamberlaine's regal head sent aftershocks through her. Lily trembled with anger and a sense of betrayal. "He *promised*." The words made a desperate hiss between her teeth. "He promised he'd help if I ever needed him."

A flicker of dismay showed in Tamberlaine's eyes. "Did he write that in a letter recently?"

"Not in so many words, but—"

"No written agreement, you're saying? No discussion of personal commitment, no promise to give you money for any reason?"

She choked. This man thought she was some kind of con artist. "No, it wasn't like that. We just always encouraged each other, like friends—"

"This was a very odd correspondence you had. I can't picture Mr. Colebrook writing to a child that way."

"He was just a kid himself when it started!"

Tamberlaine shifted forward, piercing her with an assessing look. "When *what* started? Exactly what are you alleging?"

"*Nothing.*" She felt sick. "You think I'm saying this is about *sex*? What do you think he was—a pervert?"

"Hardly. I just wanted to be clear on your allegations."

"I don't *have* allegations! I have—I *had*—trust in him. I always thought, I *knew*—" She was fumbling, coming apart. She took a deep breath and crashed to a stop. "I was wrong."

"Yes, obviously. Perhaps you don't fully realize that Mr. Colebrook is a grown man, a very important man, and not the sentimental boy you claimed to have known. To be frank, he's also very deeply involved with a young woman here in New York, who's likely to become his wife."

Lily stared at him in silent despair. Was that why Artemas had stopped writing to her? He didn't want some woman to know he had a female friend?

"Go home," Mr. Tamberlaine said, not unkindly. "If Mr. Colebrook wants to get in touch with you again, I'm sure he will."

She pulled a key from the pocket of her coat and opened the padlock at the chain around her waist. Unwinding it, she rose wearily to her feet. "I'll go."

"Not alone, you won't. I'm going to make certain you don't come back." She watched in humiliation as he opened the door and called to the guard. He looked back at her sternly. "I'm sending him with you to the bus station. He'll make certain you leave."

"No. Hell no."

"You don't have any choice. Either do this my way, or I'll call the police."

When she saw that she had no choice, she straightened proudly, chewing the inside of her mouth and saying nothing. The guard brought a car from the parking lot. Tamberlaine grasped her by one arm and gently but firmly pushed her ahead of him out the front doors. Shame flooded her, but she decided that jerking her arm away from him would only make matters worse.

He guided her into the car's front seat, while the guard held the door. "I'm sorry you were so misguided," Tamberlaine said. "If it means anything to you, I admire your courage."

She settled fierce, shaken eyes on him. "Nothing means anything to me right now. I've lost it all."

A long, late-model sedan pulled up along the curb behind the guard's car. Lily twisted to stare at it, ignited by one last inkling of hope. Two women about her age and a young man got out, gazing curiously at Tamberlaine. They were tall, handsome people, one of the women blond and sturdy, the other dark and slender, the young man too thin but kind-looking, with sandy-brown hair falling over his forehead. They were well dressed and moved with confidence.

Tamberlaine shook his head at them and waved them inside. They went past, casting curious looks at each other and at Lily. She sank back in the seat. "Good-bye," Mr. Tamberlaine said to her. "And good luck."

He watched the car pull away, exhaled with relief, then walked into the building. Michael, Cass, and Julia were waiting in the lobby. "What was *that* about?" Cass asked. "Who was she?"

"Someone of no consequence. Don't mention it to your brother. He doesn't need the distraction. Not a word. All right?"

"All right, Tammy," Julia said. "Whatever you say."

Michael asked, "Has he come down yet?"

"No, he's still in his apartment. Making arrangements

to bring Elizabeth home from the hospital. We've all got to work together now. Come along."

As they went through the doors to the offices and the private stairs that led up to Artemas's rooms, Tamberlaine glanced back toward the lobby and the empty street beyond the entrance. He hoped he'd saved Artemas some unwanted trouble. But Lily MacKenzie stuck in his mind. Yes, he had to give her points for trying. Whatever she'd really wanted, he'd never met anyone quite so willing to suffer for it.

Ten

James woke slowly, enjoying the rare sense of contentment, but then suddenly aware that he was alone in bed. Muted sounds came from the kitchen—the oven door opening and shutting, water running in the sink. He raised his head from the pillow and listened, satisfied, relaxing. He'd never cared whether a woman stayed with him afterward, but now he did.

His bare back was cold without Alise's lithe, snuggling body molded to it. He enjoyed recalling the warmth of her breasts and belly against him, and didn't pull the jumbled sheet and blanket upward. The sheets, the pillow, the whole bed, smelled of sex. Usually he found the scent more annoying than exciting—a stranger's imprint on his territory—but this time he reveled in it. The faint scent of Alise's perfume mingled with the musk. Feeling foolish but indulgent, he reached behind him, brought her pillow to his face, and sighed.

This was a side of his personality he'd never exposed to anyone else, and barely to Alise. Smiling, he looked across the bedroom at stacks of military histories and books on medieval pageantry along the empty walls. Her white lace panties were draped on one mound of books, her bra on another. Just looking at them made him hard.

He tossed the pillow and sheets aside and left the room, padding, naked and aroused, through a living room dominated by a high ceiling with ornate molding at the top. The room contained little besides a heavy couch, a desk, and various computers in one corner, and a massive, baroque sideboard where he'd set a television and stereo components. A mixture of rain and snow drizzled on tall windows with no curtains. It was a wonderful afternoon for staying inside and in bed.

James slipped into a spartan kitchen with white-tiled floors and steel appliances. She stood at a counter with her back to him, the twin curves of her small buttocks peeping from under the waistband of the white sports shirt he'd slung off hours ago, her dark hair tangled along the collar.

Before she realized it, he was behind her with his hands under the shirt. She yelped softly, twisted inside his embrace on her hips, and looked up at him with gleaming, troubled eyes. "I was trying to fix us something to eat from the empty cave of your refrigerator."

He glanced over her shoulder at the bologna, bread, and mayonnaise sitting on the counter. "Not much luck there, I'm afraid. I'm not very domestic." His eyes returned to hers. She searched his expression anxiously. "I know. I guess I'm not either." Her gaze dropped slowly down his hairy chest, and she inhaled with amazement at the jutting penis that prodded her inner thighs.

James shoved her sandwich supplies aside, lifted her to the countertop so that her legs were spread on either side of him, and pressed himself between them, nudging the silky hair at the center. Her eyes flickered with appreciation. His blunt sexuality didn't threaten her, he'd realized, any more than his brusque, antagonistic nature did. She caressed his face, dissolved the urgent lust in him a little, and quieted him with that simple touch. Her effect continued to astonish him.

"Would you pose for me sometime?" she asked. "Let me sculpt a torso of you?"

"Like this? I don't know if I want this captured for posterity."

"I do. I promise not to show it to my professors. Most of them are gay. They'd be envious." She gave him an impish look. "On the other hand, I might finally get some decent grades and feel as if I have some talent."

James kissed her forehead. Alise loved art but admitted she lacked the aptitude to be more than a hack. She dabbled in jewelry, making funny little ceramic pins to give away to friends. "I think you have talent," he said gallantly.

She draped her arms around his neck and gazed at him with pensive regard. "No, after I graduate I'll take my puny little inheritance from my great-aunt and probably use it to open a gallery where real artists can display their work. I should copy Cassandra and treat art like a business asset."

"Cass sees getting a master's in art as a way to learn enough about design to be of use to Colebrook China. She and Michael and Elizabeth and Julia will all have their places in the company, eventually. Cass knows that. She's driven by it. Don't judge yourself by her."

"I'd like to be useful too." When he smiled slyly and pulled her pelvis against his, sliding his erection up her belly, Alise laid her head on his shoulder and sighed. "Okay, so I'm useful in one way."

James's teasing mood faded. He felt awkward, unaccustomed to tenderness, as wary as he was drawn to it. "You think I coaxed you to come here today because I needed someone—anyone—to fill up a rainy weekend afternoon?"

"You didn't coax me. I wrapped my ankles around your foot in the restaurant, and you couldn't leave without promising to take me with you. I wanted you to know that I'm not a child anymore."

"I don't remember it quite that way. I remember sitting at the table and sticking myself in the mouth with my fork because I was too intent on seducing you."

"I thought you were distracted by the woman at the next table. She kept pursing her lips at you. I noticed."

She lifted her head and looked at him with wistful devotion and hope. "There's been a boy at school. I slept with him because he reminded me of you. Because you were too much older to be bothered with me. I couldn't have you, so I took him." She hesitated, her face flushing at the admission. "Does that annoy you?"

James stared down at her with unfurling adoration but also possessiveness. "Only if you're disappointed now."

"Oh, no." She shook her head. Her eyes were somber and painfully intense. "I wish today could go on forever." When he didn't answer, she scrutinized his frowning expression and added, "I shouldn't have said that. I promised myself I wouldn't make you feel like a shark with a sucker fish attached to your fin."

"You think I'm a shark?"

Her olive complexion blossomed into full redness. "I *love* sharks. I only meant that you're a loner, and you don't want me the way I want—oh dammit." She clamped her mouth shut and closed her eyes, then finally looked him straight in the face and said, "I should have known I'd say too much, or the wrong thing. I had to bite my lip when we were in bed together to keep from crying and saying that I love you." Her dignity crumpled, and tears came to her eyes. "But I've always loved you. And I think you've always known it. You don't have to say anything, or apologize."

He wouldn't. He *couldn't,* though the need welled up inside his chest. He distrusted emotional confessions. Melodramas were lurid and pointless—he always thought of his parents' excesses. Outside of his brothers and sisters, Alise was the one person who understood and accepted him the way he was. Maybe he could give her just enough of himself to keep her with him. Losing her suddenly seemed unthinkable.

"If you're not happy at college, you ought to leave," he said. She looked forlorn but not surprised at his abrupt change of subject. "Come home," he continued. "Enter a college here in New York. You could stay with Cassandra and Elizabeth and Julia until you find an apartment. Elizabeth needs your friendship more than ever, and the brownstone has plenty of room now that Michael has moved to his girl's place."

"No," she said, her voice weary but firm. "I'm not coming back to *fuck* you occasionally and wonder how many other women are doing the same thing." The choice of sharp, obscene words was unlike her, and cast an ugly shadow on what they'd done together all afternoon.

He moved away, leaned on the counter adjacent to her sitting place, and studied her through narrowed eyes. His heart raced. "All right. You could live here with me. If it doesn't work out, then"—he shrugged—"no harm done."

Shock, then delight, glimmered in her eyes. She dipped her head and scrutinized him from under the wings of slender dark brows, the assessment adoring and deadly accurate. James turned away, flicked a handle on the sink, and scooped cold water into his hands. He splashed it on his face and reached for a towel. The silence grated on him. He felt exposed and cornered. He played by his own rules, and if she wanted to stay, she'd have to accept them. She *would* stay. He'd do anything to keep her here. Anything except wallow in emotion.

She slipped off the counter, reached around him, and shut the water off. Taking his hand, she led him back to the bedroom.

The low droning of the building's air-filtering system made a constant hum in Artemas's ears. Whenever he spent several days at the Typlex plant outside Chicago without a break, the low *shushing* sound crept unpleasantly into his sleep, masked in his dreams as the breath of a faceless monster or the buzzing of a wasp—what some might see as a symbol of threat, unhappiness, or doubt. He preferred to believe the restless dreams came from his concern for the success of Colebrook's new venture.

He walked through the ceramics plant beside James, who seemed unfazed by the droning or the loud rumble of huge ball mills grinding clay and other ingredients into a fine dust for mixing into ceramic compounds. The heat radiating from giant kilns wilted their clothes and made beads of sweat on Artemas's forearms below his rolled-up shirtsleeves. Ties and jackets were ridiculous accessories here; by the end of a long day the plant's sweat and fine dust gave him and whatever he wore a patina of grime.

They moved past slurry-mixing vats, stacks of casting molds, and stopped at an enormous rack filled with greenware waiting to be pushed into the kilns for firing. "There they are—the first shipment," Artemas said, speaking loudly to overcome the noise. James stepped closer, his hands sunk in the front pockets of his black trousers, and studied the rack with a somber, satisfied expression. It was filled with hollow ceramic nose cones, slender and starkly handsome objects for their size. Each was no more than two feet wide and three feet tall—a small masterpiece of high-tech ceramic science capable of withstanding intense heat and pressure at the tip of a missile while letting the missile's radar penetrate to track a target.

Artemas watched his brother's face closely, wondering if James ever brooded over the ethics. They were helping to create devices of destruction. The missiles that would be sheathed in these nose cones would take lives. But they would also help preserve the peace and balance of power in a chaotic, complicated world. Artemas hated them, but he couldn't dismiss their necessity.

"They're goddamned wonderful," James called to him proudly. "We're going to make a fortune."

Artemas wasn't surprised by his brother's pragmatic attitude. James saw the world in black-and-white terms, a place in which diplomats were less important than generals. Artemas saw it as a maze of contradictions and compromises, filled with sidetracks and dead ends, where pride and principles were always in danger of being lost, and where the maze too often became a prison.

"I don't want the others involved in this," he said abruptly, walking onward. James fell in beside him. "Why not?"

"Because military applications aren't what I want our name associated with. This investment is a means to an end. We'll expand into ceramic components for electronic circuitry and medical hardware. We'll concentrate on building a secure financial base for Colebrook China. And philanthropy—I want the Colebrook name to be known for humanitarian work—that's where Michael and Elizabeth belong after they graduate. Cass will always care more about the china company than anything else. Good. That's where she'll shine."

"And Julia?"

Artemas almost smiled. "Julia's a tornado looking for a place to touch down. With her interest in management, it's just a matter of steering her on the right course. God help anyone who gets in her way."

James was silent, his head bowed in thought as they walked. "And me? Where do I fit in?"

"Here." Artemas led the way up a flight of steel stairs. They entered the complex of offices on the upper level and halted in an unoccupied hallway there. James faced him. Artemas gestured, indicating the industrial plant below. "If you want this to be your project, then it will be."

"I want it. But you're the one with the connections."

"You handle the details. I'll take care of the politics. I have the patience for negotiations. You don't."

James's eyes gleamed. "If you can pull in the influence we need to get larger contracts, I'll make damn sure the rest is a success." He hesitated, searching Artemas's face. "You already have it. The senator. He has something to do with this."

Artemas turned away, went to a window that looked down on the factory floor, and stood without answering. Behind him, James said carefully, "Are you going to marry Glenda DeWitt?"

Artemas stiffened. "Probably."

"Are you happy with her?"

"Yes."

"Would you consider marrying her if you had a choice?"

Artemas slammed a fist against the window, pivoted, and stared at James fiercely. He'd never disclosed his conversation with Senator DeWitt to any of his brothers and sisters, and he never would. "What are you implying?"

"That you're willing to sacrifice your personal life if you have to, for our family's future."

"Don't ever bring this subject up again. And I'd better not hear questions about it from the others. It's my business, and doubting my motives isn't fair to Glenda. She deserves the family's affection and support. I won't have any of you resent her or voice doubts about her place in my life."

James came to him and put a hand on his shoulder. Stark admiration and acceptance glittered in James's eyes. "You don't understand. I'm not questioning your integrity, I'm giving you my support. What's best for Colebrook International's future is all that counts. I've never doubted that you put the family first. That you'll never let us down, and therefore we'll never let you down."

"Drop it, I said."

James nodded, withdrawing gracefully under the searing threat in Artemas's voice, but looking no less proud.

"Sign it," Aunt Maude whispered, patting Lily's back in unspoken sympathy.

Lily's hand shook. The lawyer's paneled office loomed around her, dark, too small, too confining. She couldn't breathe. The stack of contracts and copies on his conference table blurred as she stared at the top page, with its blank line awaiting her signature. She felt Mr. Estes and his lawyer urging her silently, watching her. As if 140 years of MacKenzie history could be sold with an easy movement of the pen in her clammy fingers.

She shut her eyes. In her mind she saw herself neatly tearing the contract in half, tossing the pen down, and walking out. On the sidewalk Artemas would be waiting, and he'd say his not coming sooner was due to some innocent misunderstanding, that he'd come to give her a loan and grieve with her for Mama and Daddy. She'd throw her arms around him and be held in return.

But she opened her eyes, and the contract was still in front of her on the table. Artemas had forgotten her—

worse, he'd deliberately ignored her. There was no hope, no more time to stall.

Her stomach was squeezing into a tight knot. Dazed, she knew she'd humiliate herself by throwing up if she didn't wrench some willpower together. *I'm going to get my home back, someday. And I'll make Artemas pay for deserting me.*

She stabbed the pen into the thick document, signed it, flipped the page, signed another, then another, until all the copies bore her name.

"You won't have to leave for a couple of months," Mr. Estes said, sounding relieved. "Joe won't get back here before May."

Aunt Maude patted her back. "Then she'll come and spend the summer with me. And this fall, she'll start college down in Atlanta. Think about it, Lily—you'll have all the money you need, after the farm's debts are paid. Think about that, honey."

Lily left the office, ran down a creaking staircase to the door at street level, and burst onto the sidewalk. Gulping air, she swept a gaze around the town her ancestors had founded and named—the small brick courthouse Elspeth's sons had helped raise the money to build, the library Great-grandmother MacKenzie had fought to secure for the town, the dogwoods around the square, planted by her grandparents.

She sat down on a wooden bench in front of some shops, absorbing the scene while desolation ached inside her. *I sold my family's history, and it's Artemas Colebrook's fault.*

Artemas slipped from bed, walked naked to one of the apartment's large windows, and opened the blinds, letting the first rays of May sunlight cascade into the dark, vast space. He stood with the stripes of sun and shadow across his chest and face, looking out on the wide, slate-gray river. Stretching before him was a panorama of tugboats, arching steel bridges, and, far across on the opposite banks, industrial buildings and offices spreading in a maze cut by narrow streets.

Today Elizabeth was moving into an apartment with several friends of hers. Her doctor said she was progressing well enough to leave Cass and Julia. She would return to college during the summer and finish getting her bachelor's degree. Artemas lit the day's first cigarette. Elizabeth still refused to discuss the reasons behind the incident with him or anyone else in the family. He had to trust the psychiatrist's opinion of her emotional health.

All he could do now was return to a full schedule at the office and try to keep track of Elizabeth as best he could.

A soft sound came from his bed. He turned and watched Glenda stir sleepily, murmur something, then pull the black coverlet higher on her thin shoulders and settle down again. She looked pale and small in the large bed, a frail companion floating in the center of the large, spartan room.

There was little raw excitement in their careful couplings; she loved being held and cuddled, she loved talking and listening, and they had long conversations in bed, but her appetites were as delicate as her health. His life with her had the appeal of collecting fragile porcelain figurines. There was undeniable appreciation, but no surprises, no challenge, no sense of the exquisite obsession he wanted to feel for a woman.

He took a shower and dressed in a dark double-breasted suit, then went back to the bed and sat beside her on the edge, smoothing her fine hair back from her forehead. She smiled, opened her eyes, and cradled his hand to her throat. "I'm going down to the office," he told her. "Do you mind having breakfast alone?"

She kissed his hand. "I'll manage. But I've gotten used to having more of your time. I'm a little sorry you're going back to a full schedule—but glad Elizabeth is doing so well. I'll go by this morning and see her at the new apartment."

"Tell her I'll come by tonight." He bent and kissed her lightly. "Don't forget to take your insulin."

"I won't. I love you for taking care of me. You take care of everyone. I wish I could do as much for you."

"You're my island of peace in the middle of chaos."

"Hmmm. Sounds nice."

He kissed her again, left her dozing, and exited the apartment through an elevator to the ground floor. Tamberlaine was waiting for him in the hushed, empty offices below. They always started the day with a meeting before any of the employees arrived. LaMieux would be the first, hurrying into the building in an hour or so, charging through stacks of mail and flipping on all the lights. Artemas nodded to Tamberlaine, and they went into Artemas's office, a room along the back, crowded with bookcases overflowing with technical manuals and marketing reports, a bulky old desk, and several leather chairs. A pot of coffee, two mugs, and a plate of bagels waited on the desk. Tamberlaine always provided this morning ritual.

"It's good to have you back at full throttle," Tamberlaine noted, as he settled in a chair across the desk from Artemas. On his knees he balanced a thick notepad and pen atop a folder bulging with memos. Tamberlaine's expression was uneasy, a rare sight. "What's wrong?" Artemas asked.

"I have something to discuss with you. Something I put off since March, because I thought I'd made the right decision at a time when you needed to be isolated from petty concerns. I was certain I had done what you wanted. Then, a few days ago—well, let me bring in the box I received in Monday's mail, before I begin."

Artemas frowned in bewilderment as Tamberlaine suddenly dumped his paperwork on the desk, then leaped up and walked from the office. When he returned, he carried a bulky cardboard box with packaging tape dangling from the open lid. He sat down with the box on his lap and looked at Artemas somberly. "Have you been writing to someone all these years—a young woman named Lily MacKenzie?"

Artemas went very still, one hand tightening around the mug he'd been filling. He shoved the mug and coffeepot aside. "Yes. But how—"

"In recent months have you stopped answering her letters?"

After a stunned moment Artemas nodded. "I stopped reading them or answering them." He leaned forward, his eyes glued to the box. Tamberlaine was studying him intently. "Was I right to assume, then, that you don't want any further contact with her?"

Artemas raised his gaze to the older man's. "God, don't tell me she needed to talk to me but couldn't get through."

Tamberlaine looked dismayed. His answer was obvious. In a low, apologetic voice he said, "If I'd known, if I'd had any idea you didn't intend to avoid her—"

What did you do? He listened in growing alarm as Tamberlaine told him that Lily had tried repeatedly to contact him, and had even come to New York to see him in person. And had been sent away in humiliation. Tamberlaine told him the story she'd given about her parents' dying, about needing a loan. "She *chained* herself to a front door," Tamberlaine finished, his dark face strained with regret. "I thought she was a remarkable but outrageous young woman. I'm sorry. I'm very sorry."

"She needed money? Her parents died?" He put his head in his hands. Zea and Drew, gone. Lily in grief, alone, desperate for the help he'd always promised to give. "They were killed in a car accident, I believe she said," Tamberlaine told him in an awkward tone. "I dismissed her story as a dubious invention." He set the box on Artemas's desk. "But when this arrived. I felt I had to tell you about it."

He opened the box, moved thick wads of newspaper aside, and lifted the antique Colebrook teapot out. Its delicate blue Oriental pattern—the old Blue Willow pattern that had been the foundation of Colebrook China's early success—stood out in sharp relief against the white porcelain. "There was no message with it," Tamberlaine added, then said gruffly, "I suppose she decided this was message enough. Do you know what it means?"

Artemas took the old vessel carefully. "It means good-bye."

"Is there anything I can do, anything to help—"

"Get me the first flight available to Atlanta."

Eleven

Lily shoved another bale of hay atop the stack that was slowly filling the barn's loft. Cracks between the barn's weathered old boards let sunlight inside. The cows and their new calves could be heard shuffling around in the hallway before. They'd come in from the pastures in the hope of getting handouts. The loft was warm and pungent with the scents of the hay, the old wood, and the sweet spring air curling in through the open door at the front. It was a place she knew as well as her own bedroom, a place where she'd played and worked and daydreamed since she was old enough to climb the creaking ladder from the dirt floor of the hallway below.

She wasn't going to turn the farm over to Joe Estes next week with the hay sitting outside as if it didn't matter. His father owned the farm now—the fields, the house, the barn, the cemetery, the creek, the willows, the cattle, the hay.

Daddy had ordered the load of hay months ago. When it had arrived this morning in the midst of her packing, she'd stared at it in despair. How could he and Mama be gone if their plans were still in motion? She'd sat on the porch for a while, her head in her hands, unable to overcome the grief. Then she'd laced ankle-high work boots to

her feet, stuck a pair of gloves on her hands, and gone
to work.

If she had to leave, she'd leave with pride. Neither Joe
nor anyone else would say the MacKenzies had given up
their pride when they'd lost this place.

Dust and sweat streaked her face. Bits of hay were
caught in the braid of hair pinned loosely at the nape of
her neck. Her hands were sore inside their leather gloves
from gripping the coarse twine around the bales. Red
blotches and scratch marks from the hay dotted her bare
arms and legs. *I should have put on jeans and a long-sleeved
shirt. Daddy will fuss at me for not—*

She halted, frightened and hurt by the way her
thoughts slipped backward. Daddy wasn't here to mumble
at her in his benign, lovable way. She'd never hear his
voice again, just as she'd never hear Mama's. Her vision
blurred. Scrubbing her eyes with the back of a gloved
hand, she cursed loudly, then went back to the open door.
Two dozen bales of hay remained on the ground below.
She dropped a thick rope attached to the pulley set on a
thick wooden arm above the loft's hatch, then climbed
down the ladder along the barn's outer wall. Working furiously and trying not to think, she picked up the large
iron hook attached to the rope's end and snagged the tip
under the parallel bands of twine around another bale.

She climbed back up, pulled the bale up to the door, and
wrestled it inside. Constant, backbreaking work was all that
kept her from brooding about the future. She hadn't slept
much in the past two weeks. She'd spent the time packing
household belongings into boxes and hauling them to Aunt
Maude's attic. Joe would get the house's furniture, but not its
heart—the knickknacks, the books, the heavy iron pots and
skillets Mama and Daddy had used in the kitchen, the quilts
she'd made, Daddy's hand tools, his guns, his collection of
agricultural magazines dating back to Grandpa's youth—she'd
keep all of it, and someday, someday—

She shoved a dusty, sagging cardboard box aside on the
loft's bed of old hay, put the bale down, then stood over
the box, breathing hard with fatigue, her hands on her

hips. The box was something she didn't want to open, and she'd been pushing it aside for hours.

She ought to just throw it out—take it to the burn pile in the field beyond the creek. In the past few days she'd watched the fire consume so much that agonized her. She'd given most of her parents' clothes and shoes to the church, because Mama and Daddy would want it that way—nothing wasted when it could help others.

But there were things no one needed or wanted, and she'd burned them. She'd sorted through Mama's old nightgowns, keeping a couple for herself because she needed to feel them on her skin. She'd kept a few of Daddy's old work shirts, soft, comforting pieces she would wear. But there was so much else—socks, underwear, torn old sweaters, the yellowed suit Mama had worn when she married Daddy, then used over and over for special occasions, until it was so shabby and out of style that she'd put it away.

Lily sank to her knees and ripped the box open, then tugged her gloves off and undid the twist-tie on the black plastic garbage bag inside. Pushing the top open, she looked at the jumble of stuffed bears and the neatly folded cadet jacket Artemas had given her. She'd stored everything up here years ago, after the terrible night when he'd come to visit. She'd felt so ashamed and blamed herself for causing that hypocritical son of a bitch Andy Holcomb to think he could paw her.

Boys weren't worth the trouble, even if she admitted to an urgent curiosity about their bodies. They either made crude remarks about her height or treated her like something they could own if they just made the right noises. She hadn't wasted much time on them since then. And she didn't owe Artemas any childish loyalty. The humiliating scene in New York two months ago had made that obvious.

Still, seeing the musty bears and gray jacket opened a hollow spot in her chest. She gathered them to her, sat down limply on the loft's floor, and rocked a little. Bone-aching weariness overcame her, and she lay down. Her eyes grew heavy with a kind of numb relief. Her mind floated, and she dozed. This was the crazy way she operated—hustling around like a maniac for hours on end, then collapsing and falling asleep.

The sound of a car door slamming jerked her awake.

Lily lurched to her feet and brushed at herself groggily. If Joe Estes had come to wander around his new home again, she'd get the big .45 revolver from her bedroom and offer to give him a scar like the one he'd given her. Joe was a hulking redneck in designer jeans and expensive cowboy boots, with a pasty face from his jail time. He always looked at the farm with a little shit-eating smile, as if he was slightly disgusted at the idea of his father's conservative little plans for him.

She hurried to the loft door. And froze, her hands knotted by her sides, her mouth open in shock.

Artemas.

He stood in the yard beside one of those plain late-model sedans the rental-car agencies loved. There was nothing plain about *him*.

He hadn't noticed her looking down at him yet. He was taking in the place, his large, handsome head tilted back, the dark hair feathered by the breeze, his eyes narrowed in concentration. A clinging white pullover covered his thick chest and was tucked into rumpled tan trousers cinched with a brown belt. His feet, encased in heavy-soled hiking boots, were braced apart. He radiated compressed energy, scanning the surroundings with an expression of intense concentration on a face so roughly constructed that only the large eyes saved it from being too harsh. His face was even more mesmerizing than she remembered.

Lily felt helpless—hypnotized against her will. He looked so confident. His height and the physical power enclosed in the broad shoulders and pantherlike cleanness of his body weren't daunted by her high vantage point; she could stand on a mountaintop and look down on this man, but he'd still seem bigger than life.

He owned her thoughts. He owned her emotions. He

even owned her body, the core of heat spreading through her breasts and between her legs, a heedless feminine reaction to something very primitive and beyond reason. The loss of control terrified and angered her. She couldn't move. She waited for him to come to her—as she'd waited all her life—but hated him for it.

Artemas studied the boxes stacked on the porch of the old whitewashed house, and his pulse surged at the sight of the front door standing open. Through the screen he saw the dim interior, the hall that opened immediately into a central room, with a rough-stone fireplace on one side. The blue-green willows towered a few dozen yards behind the house, at the creek, making the majestic backdrop he remembered so well. The wind stroked the treetops with a low murmur, and frogs chorused along the creek banks. The small sounds made the greater silence and stillness feel lonely, as if nature were taking the place back, its covenant with the MacKenzies broken.

A vague premonition made him hold his breath without knowing why. Where was she? He had to find her and make everything right again. Something in his subconscious overcame rational thought and offered up excitement, along with sorrow. *I'll always come back here. Again and again. To Lily.* The idea presented itself effortlessly.

He turned slowly, absorbing the yards and fields, feeling dazed and a little wary of the sentimental effect. But he couldn't shake the languor. He found himself thinking that he'd stepped into a compelling shadow outside the real world, or come to a turning point. Indefinable longing and anticipation made his throat ache.

His attention moved slowly to the old barn with its peaked tin roof, sitting on a knoll in the pasture behind the house. His gaze rose. His strange torment came into focus vividly.

Lily.

He'd only seen the one photograph of her since childhood, the picture of a startlingly vibrant and compelling adolescent girl that her parents had given him. But he knew the tall young woman standing defiantly, feet apart and one hand braced on the frame of the barn's open loft door. He walked toward her swiftly, almost running, his eyes never leaving her. From the motionless set of her head he knew she was watching him just as intently.

Astonished details clicked into place in his mind, a new one with each hurried step. Her hair, still the fantastic color of the flower that was her namesake, hung in a thick, loose braid over one shoulder. Her body was full at the breasts and hips, with long, muscular arms and legs. The loose shorts she wore with a plain T-shirt jammed into them only called attention to the vigorous combination of sexual ripeness and unapologetic strength.

She tracked his approach with the poised, searing scrutiny of a hawk—watching, waiting, brilliant blue eyes glittering at him from a strong face with a flamboyant, tightly clamped mouth. Everything about her expression and stance whispered danger.

Stunned, he halted underneath the loft door and looked up at her. She was magnificent. Nothing he'd expected had prepared him for this hopeless torture.

Artemas held her condemning gaze. "You were six years old the last time you looked at me that way," he said, his voice rough with emotion.

When she didn't answer but only continued to stare down at him bitterly, he struggled against an urge to shout, to vent his frustration at the tragedy that embroiled them. "You were furious at me for leaving, because you couldn't understand it, and I didn't know how to explain it to you very well. You were a child—so was I. But we're not children anymore, and we have to talk rationally. I didn't deserve your disappointment then, and I don't now. Come down here and *talk* to me."

She calmly reached for the heavy hook dangling in front of her from the loft's winch, pulled it inside, then wedged a foot into it and jerked the rope taut. Artemas's breath stalled as she stepped out into space. The winch creaked as she quickly lowered herself to the ground, settling less than an arm's length from him. The sudden closeness electrified the air between them. She was only a few

inches shorter than he, delicate in comparison but not by
any other standards. Her face was ashen except for ruddy
splashes of color on her cheeks. She slung the rope aside
and faced him, motionless, trembling.

They looked at each other without speaking, the emotions and the blatant adult sexuality too dangerous, so
jumbled that no words existed to express them. There was
one split second of intuition, as he realized the tension was
about to explode.

She slapped him across the face with the speed and ferocity of a coiled snake. The heavy leather glove she wore
deadened the sting but not the force. He had braced himself the instant her hand flashed out and didn't flinch, but
the blow rocketed through his skull. Her face convulsed
with sorrow. She hit him again.

This time shock impelled him to action. Artemas
grabbed her by the shoulders. He shook her—just once,
but with a restrained power that flung her head back and
made her gasp. Then he jerked her to him and trapped
her, one arm around her waist, pinning her arms to her
sides, the other around her shoulders. He caught her hair
where the braid met the back of her skull and held her
head still. She tried to wrench herself away from him,
making hoarse, broken sounds of fury, kicking him in the
ankles.

Artemas lifted her to her toes and tightened his hold.
His face was almost touching hers, and her wild eyes
stared into his without blinking. "I didn't know," he said
through gritted teeth. "I didn't know you needed me. I would
never have turned you away."

"Liar! You goddamned liar! You didn't care!"

They struggled together, swaying. He was trying not to
hurt her, but she seemed intent on the opposite. "Stop it!"
he shouted. "Listen to me." Their furious battle quieted.
His shins throbbed where she'd slammed the toes of her
heavy boots into them. Her expression was startled, disbelieving, disgusted.

He drew a sharp breath. "The man you spoke with in
New York—Tamberlaine—had instructions to sidetrack

people who might be a nuisance to me. That's why he told you I wouldn't see you. It was a mistake."

Her eyes narrowed in accusation. "But I *wrote* to you, and you never answered. I told you my parents died. I needed your friendship even more than I needed money."

"I stopped reading your letters. I didn't know your parents had died or that you needed money. I had no idea that you came to New York two months ago to see me. I just found out this morning. Believe me."

He was still holding her on her toes, as if by brute physical contact he could break through her resistance. She was rigid inside his embrace, but he couldn't make himself let go of her. Her eyes glittered with warning, but there was pain in them, too, and the combination struck a chord inside him. "You'd have known if you'd wanted to," she insisted. Her voice rose. "Why didn't you read my letters?"

The truth about his coldblooded bargain with Senator DeWitt might damn him forever in her eyes. He could only give her vague explanations, and he knew they'd sound cruel. "Someone is living with me now. I planned to write to you about her, eventually."

"You couldn't read my letters because your ladyfriend might be jealous?" She twisted violently, and when his hold didn't loosen, groaned with defeat. "Do you think I've been sitting here all these years waiting for you to come back and marry me because of some bullshit promise you made when we were kids?" The breath was raging out of her, her chest rising and falling convulsively. Her mouth curled in disgust. "You have bad taste in women if you picked one who doesn't trust you enough to let you keep your friends. Or you must be the most pussy-whipped man in New York."

"You have a vocabulary like a garbage dump."

"I picked it up from you, when I was six. It stuck."

"You haven't seen me face-to-face in twelve years, and that's all you remember?"

"I remember everything," she replied, her voice a low snarl. "How I thought you were wonderful. How your letters always came just when I needed them most, and how you made me feel special when no one else could. That's why I can't accept some stupid excuse now."

He set her down but kept his arms around her. "I'm so goddamned sorry I hurt you," he told her. "I'm not the white knight you thought I was. I make mistakes. I make compromises. But I came here because I *do* care, and I want to help you."

Suspicion curved her mouth into a hard line. Artemas despaired of ever gaining her respect again. He asked grimly, "Does it matter if you don't understand why I've changed or what my life is like now?"

"Yes," she said, drawling the word with a bitter lilt. "Because I still want to believe you're the 'Old Brook Prince.'" She flushed at the sound of that. "Because you were worth believing in. Like my parents"—her voice faltered—"after they died, I thought, There's still Artemas. *God,* what a fool I was."

"Lily." Her name came out like a gruff plea. His hand relaxed on her hair but stayed there, cupping the back of her head. Her fists were trapped against his thighs. She unfurled her hands and flattened them to her own thighs, drawing back from the contact. The violence faded, but the undercurrent of tension was barely dormant. "I came here as soon as I learned what had happened," he repeated hoarsely. "Why would I want to help you now, if I'd deliberately avoided you before?"

He watched that logic sink in. Her eyes glazed with confusion. Artemas bent his head to hers, lightly resting his cheek against her hair. "I can't change anything," he whispered. "I wish I could."

She gave a low groan of despair. "If wishes were dollars, beggars would be rich. I'd be a millionaire."

"I'll do whatever I can. Tell me what happened to your parents."

She didn't answer. He felt the resentment and doubt in every rigid muscle of her body. *"Tell me,"* he ordered softly.

"A drunk clipped them on the expressway." The agony in her voice made him shiver. He stroked the back of her bowed head. "Mama was driving," she continued, each word hesitant, welling with pain. "Daddy could never handle a steering wheel very well, with his—with only one good hand. They were going down to Atlanta to celebrate their twentieth anniversary. I gave them a room for the night at a nice hotel."

"When did it happen?"

"February."

He felt the tremors in her body. She'd been through hell, and had barely had time yet to deal with the raw grief. "You came to New York only a few weeks later?"

"Yeah. I must have been out of my mind. That explains why I thought it made sense to chain myself to your office door."

His heart was bursting. "No. You're the bravest person I've ever known." Her courage was formidable, and he connected with it. The scrappy little girl had become a woman of steely willpower.

"Daddy had to be cut out of the truck," she continued, her voice shaking. The horror sank into Artemas. "They said he never had a chance. Mama, she—she was thrown out of the cab. She died in the ambulance." She choked, then added, "When I went to see them, they looked like—like they'd been broken by a pair of big hands."

"Lily, I'm sorry. I've never forgotten them. They were wonderful to me."

She searched his face, swallowing harshly. "I do believe *that*," she said, and a little more of the antagonism melted.

"What happened to the driver who caused the accident?" he asked.

She struggled for control, her face working, then said, "Goddamn him, he only lived a few days. I was really crazy then, I know. Because I kept thinking that if he didn't die, I'd find a way to kill him."

Artemas was silent, fighting the ache in his throat. Finally he said, "I'll do whatever it takes to help you keep this place. I swear it."

She stiffened. "You're too late. I've already sold it."

"*When?*"

"Not long after I went to New York. The new owner takes over next week." Her voice faded miserably.

"You had to sell it so quickly?"

"I had bills to pay."

"Then we'll buy it back."

Her eyes widened with amazement. Artemas looked at her in silent torment. He wanted to do everything for her, wanted to win not just her understanding but *her*. That realization slammed into him and broke on the hard reality of his other commitments. His family. The business's future. Glenda's loyalty, and his agreement with her ruthless father.

He cleared his throat and stepped back. "I can't stay here more than a couple of days. If you want my help, then let's get started. There's no more time to debate my fall from grace."

For a relentless eternity she looked up at him as if weighing need against pride. "I don't want to believe you fell," she answered finally. "I think you were pushed."

The pensive tone in her voice nearly destroyed him. Her willingness to expect the best about him crystallized the dark force that he'd been trying not to analyze.

He wanted to take her in his arms again, and tell her the damning details of his life, and why nothing was more important than the fight to rise from his family's legacy of *disgrace*. He wanted to close up the gaps in all the years since a troubled little boy had devoted himself to a newborn baby girl and vowed that she belonged to him. He wanted to learn everything about her that she'd never said in her letters, and know all that she'd become.

But he could only look at her without softening and say, "Either way, I'm your only hope."

"I don't want any more sympathy from you," she told him. "I don't want to waste time looking for miracles."

"Lily, dammit—"

"I just want you to stay with me until I have to move to Aunt Maude's." Shock filled the silence. She felt his gaze on her and returned it. His eyes narrowed; he seemed capable of piercing her facade with the intensity. Sorrow and wariness were stamped on his face. "Why?" he asked in a low voice.

He hates being asked to stay. Humiliation stabbed her. She looked at him with merciless demand. "So I'll have something to remember. So I'll get to know you, really know you. That's something I've wanted all these years. I won't write to you anymore. I'll never ask you for help again. I'm not going to count on anyone but myself from now on. But when you go back to New York, to the people who are really important to you and to all the important responsibilities you have, I'll have this little piece of your life nobody else can ever own."

His expression slowly softened. There was a kind of harsh tenderness in it. "All right."

She had what she'd wished for. It was both frightening and satisfying, like realizing she had the courage to jump off a cliff without knowing whether she'd survive. Lily covered her confusion by giving him a brusque nod. She tried to think what to do next. "We'll go see Aunt Maude," Lily announced. "So she won't hear someone's at the farm and think I've taken up with a stranger."

Artemas arched a black brow in rueful acceptance. The masculine scent, the size, the dangerous *feel* of his presence sent chills up her spine. They had been together less than ten minutes.

She had taken up with a stranger.

Twelve

Aunt Maude and her sisters were playing croquet on the front lawn—Little Sis traipsing around in a tank top and tight jeans, with her graying hair stuck up in a ponytail, Big Sis leaning on her mallet like a cane, with a print dress billowing around her bony knees, Aunt Maude kneeling on the ground to line up a shot, her big hips and stocky torso draped in a brightly colored caftan. A bottle of Jack Daniel's and three full glasses adorned a white wrought-iron lawn table they'd brought from the backyard. A dozen odd-looking tan balloons drifted above it, tied to pieces of string.

Lily cut the Jeep's engine along the sidewalk. The yard was fronted in beds of purple irises, a cheerful spring place with shadowy trees and green grass. "You remember my Aunt Maude and the sisters?" she asked Artemas, snapping the words off like brittle tree branches. "I've written you about them a few times."

Little Sis saw Lily, raised her mallet in salute, and staggered drunkenly. Big Sis spit a stream of tobacco. Aunt Maude sat back on her heels, her caftan making a tent around her. She looked like a large, flowering shrub.

"How could I forget?" Artemas said dryly.

When he and she walked into the middle of the staring

trio—mostly they were staring at Artemas—Lily introduced them. They gaped at him, as motionless as hens laying eggs. Lily felt bleak victory. *See? He did come back.*

He went to each and shook hands. Maude pushed herself to her feet, clasped him by the shoulders, and scrutinized him. "I remember the day you came here to use my phone. I thought you were the most solemn youngster I'd ever seen. You still look solemn as a judge."

"I came here to help Lily get her farm back."

Aunt Maude lowered her hands, shot a slit-eyed look at Lily, and a mask dropped over her expression. It was the same poker face she used when she presided at city council meetings. The sisters gaped at him. "You been to see Mr. Estes yet?" she asked.

Lily shook her head.

"It won't do any good."

"Money talks," Artemas interjected.

Little Sis snorted. "Not to him. He's an Aquarius. I asked him about his birth date when he offered to buy Lily's place. Had to know if he was worthy." She went to the table and downed a glass of amber bourbon in one long swallow. She wandered back to them with a few loose steps and added, "Aquarius men are high-strung and stubborn. Of course, men in general are that way." She sat down, cross-legged, on the lawn. "What are you?" she asked Artemas.

"An Aquarius."

"Oh, goddammit to shit."

Aunt Maude looked at Lily apologetically. "She's divorcing Marshall."

Lily knelt in front of Little Sis and put her arms around her. "I know things weren't going real well, but I'm sorry."

Little Sis waved a hand in the air. "He's sleeping with one of his bank tellers. I found out yesterday. The slut's no older than our daughters." She tilted her head back and gazed up at Artemas, who looked too distressed by everything to be amused. Little Sis scrutinized him shrewdly. "Gimme your palm, boy."

He came to her, knelt down on one knee, and held his

hand out. She grasped it and squinted at the lines. "Yes, yes," she said finally, patting his hand and giving it back to him. She looked at Lily, grabbed her hand, and studied it, swaying in place as she did. "Yes, yes."

Big Sis hobbled over and poked her younger sister with the business end of a mallet. "Leave 'em alone, you drunken fool."

"It's fate," Little Sis answered belligerently. "Can't change it."

Lily rose quickly, tugging at Artemas's arm. He stood also, frowning from Little Sis to her. Lily shook her head. "Don't pay any attention."

"You know what those are?" Little Sis said, swinging an arm toward the table festooned with balloons. "Condoms. We're using 'em the way they do the most good. Full of hot air."

Big Sis made a strangled sound of embarrassment and tottered to the table, then pulled a penknife from a big pocket on her dress and began puncturing the obscene decorations.

The loud popping made Lily's nerves jump. Artemas had an expression of benign amazement on his rugged face. Aunt Maude stepped between them and Little Sis, who was scowling at Big Sis, distracted. "Stay for dinner," she said, shaking her head in defeat. "It's almost ready. We were just having Little Sis's divorce party first."

"Mr. Estes—" Lily began.

"His son is tearing his folks' hearts out. I don't know what it's all about, but I suspect Hopewell and Ducie are desperate to keep him out of trouble. I've heard he's already running with a bad crowd again."

"He can't have Lily's home," Artemas said.

Aunt Maude leveled a hard but sympathetic gaze at him. "He already owns it."

Lily's anguish reached new heights. "You can't talk to Mr. Estes for me? Try to change his mind?"

"Oh, I'll talk to him. But I already know he sees your old place as a godsend. I don't understand why, but that's the way it is." She put an arm around Lily's shoulders and shook her gently. "You're going to college this fall, honey. Even if you could get the farm back, what would you do with it?"

Lily's head drooped. "That's like asking why someone wants to breathe. It's part of me."

Artemas had been watching them in strained silence. Now, he said, "I'm sure I can convince him to sell. If Lily wants to live there, she can find a local college to attend."

Aunt Maude's stony expression became even harder. "Lily's not going to sit in the shadow of your old estate and daydream about you coming back to stay for good. She's done that all her life, and you encouraged her, and that's *wrong.*"

Lily wanted to sink into the ground with shame. "This has nothing to do with Artemas."

Little Sis snorted loudly and staggered to her feet. She came to him, reached up and patted him on the jaw, then wagged a finger at him. "Your life course lies in another direction." She held up her other forefinger, making a partner to the first. "Parallel to Lily's, but separate. But not always separate. *Click.*" She pressed her fingers together. "Like this, someday. But not now."

Lily pressed her hands to her head. "Oh, God, y'all are twisting everything."

"Where were you a few months ago?" Big Sis demanded, tottering up to Artemas and shaking her cane.

He scanned the sisters with frowning, polite restraint, a muscle popping in his jaw. "I didn't know Lily needed me. That was my mistake. I'm here to fix it."

Aunt Maude sighed. "She doesn't need you. She's been half-crazy with grieving, and she's *still* reckless. I don't want her confused and hurt any more."

"I'm not a croquet ball," Lily protested. "Stop talking about me like you can knock me around the lawn anywhere you want. I know what I'm doing."

Tense silence closed in. Little Sis leaned over to Aunt Maude and whispered at the top of her voice, "She has to get burned so she'll learn to stay away from the fire."

Aunt Maude exhaled and flung up her hands. "I won't say any more."

Big Sis spit tobacco juice violently. "Thank God. You and Sissy shut up. Both of you."

"Stay for dinner," Aunt Maude repeated. It was an order. "Come on. Artemas, you get Little Sis by the arm. Let's take this scraggly group inside."

Lily looked at him as he looped a broad hand under Little Sis's elbow. He'd been shell-shocked.

Dinner was an awful masquerade of Little Sis's slurred speeches about the uselessness of men, Big Sis's blunt sarcasm, Aunt Maude's baleful staring at Artemas and Lily's attempt to eat when all she wanted to do was crawl into a hole where Artemas couldn't watch her suffer.

He sat beside her, pushing food around on a delicate china plate of pure white porcelain with raised scrollwork on the edges. "Colebrook," Big Sis announced, leaning over from the end of the table and rapping her fork on the piece. "Maude gave it to me for my forty-fifth birthday. Twenty years ago. Holds up nice. You ought to be proud."

"I knew it was a Colebrook setting," Artemas answered, giving her a pensive smile. "We have a new one coming out—an updated version, with a contemporary design on the rim."

"Good. Good." Big Sis chewed on a piece of creamed chicken and studied him. "How long are you going to be in town?"

"A few days."

Lily took a deep breath. "He's staying with me. At the farm."

Silence descended. She glanced around the table, noting Big Sis's beady, intrigued glower, Little Sis's groggy stare, and Aunt Maude's frown. Artemas said carefully, "If I ever hurt Lily deliberately, you all have permission to put a curse on me."

"Maybe we already have," Little Sis answered. "And we're waiting to see how well it works."

•   •   •

Little Sis ambushed Lily as she was returning from the hall bathroom, where she'd gone after dinner to soak her face in cold water. They were alone in the hall. "Here," Little Sis hissed, and thrust a small package into Lily's hands. "If you need 'em, use 'em. If you don't know how—read the instructions."

Lily stared at the open box of condoms. Her head swam. "I don't need any balloons," she joked numbly.

Artemas stepped into the hallway from the parlor, where she'd left him to fend for himself between Big Sis's questions about china and Aunt Maude's baleful silence. He looked at Lily with the kind of exasperated relief that made the condoms suddenly feel like a red-hot brick in her hand. She clamped her fingers over the logo and furtively shoved them back at Little Sis.

Little Sis pursed her lips like Mick Jagger in concert, stuffed the box into the hip pocket of Lily's shorts, then darted away, leaving the lure of disaster firmly in place.

The old farmhouse was pitifully empty of the small trinkets and personal touches that had made it so warm, so inviting. Artemas walked through the downstairs room brushing his fingers over the furniture, looking at the bare walls, the empty bookcases, the packed cardboard boxes stacked in corners. The soft light from aged white wall sconces gave false promises of the comfort he remembered.

He heard Lily moving around in the downstairs bedroom. She'd disappeared in there to ready the place for him. The idea of sleeping in her bed made him restless, gnawing at the fragile barricade between what he wanted to feel for her and the intimacy he could never indulge. He went into the main room, leaned on the fireplace mantel, and stared at the empty, cold grate.

A door opened from the room off the back hall. He listened to her footsteps on the bare wooden floor, his senses strained with awareness of every movement. "I put an extra pillow on the bed," she said, coming to the hearth and sitting on its edge, her elbows propped on her bare knees. Her throaty, drawling voice curled through his blood.

"You'll probably have to lay it across the foot rail, because your feet'll stick over. Mine hit the rail when I stretch out, and you're taller. You could have Mama and Daddy's queen-sized bed upstairs, but I've got boxes stacked all over it."

"Where do you sleep?"

"In the barn loft." When he shot her a surprised look, she shrugged. "I slept out there on hot summer nights when I was growing up. I like it." Her eyes held a stark, wounded aura he'd noticed before. Beneath all the bluster and determination was a shattered, lonely soul. "I can't sleep in this house now. I go out to the barn every night. I tried not to, at first. But I'd hear little sounds when I was half-awake and think everything was the same as before, that my folks were still here."

Artemas watched with wordless sympathy as her shoulders hunched. She dropped her forehead to her hands and massaged the pale, tightly drawn skin. Her misery was like his own—a self-contained burden, not easily displayed to anyone else. When others might give up, pity themselves, or become bitter, she trudged on. He shivered because he understood that brand of pride so well. It was, in many ways, a prison as well as a savior, a merciless drive.

And he was dangerously drawn to her because of it. He sat down beside her and took her hands in his. The contact was stunning, a swift merging of touch and emotion. Fighting the urge to pull her to him, he turned her hands over and pretended to study the callused palms. Her hands were blunt and strong, with graceful fingers. He rubbed his thumbs over the marks of hard work. "I've always thought I could have whatever I wanted," he told her. "That it's only a matter of *knowing* what I want and learning how to get it. But that's not true. Because I can't bring your parents back for you."

Her fingers curled over his and held tightly. "Don't want what's impossible," she whispered. "You'll always be disappointed."

The wistful despair in her voice sent shivers through

him. He met her somber, troubled eyes. "It isn't always easy to know the difference. Or to accept it."

They were talking about something else now—the future and the magnetic current between them that touch only intensified. She searched his face for a moment, and he struggled to keep his expression unpromising. The glimmer of hope that had come into her eyes faded just as quickly. She dropped her gaze to his hands. Slowly she drew hers away. It was as if life were being drained from his skin.

Artemas forced himself to move away from her before regret overcame reason. Going to the old chintz couch across from the fireplace, he sank back in one corner and stretched his legs in front of him, a show of nonchalance that took all his willpower. "In the morning we'll see Mr. Estes. We have to try."

Lily studied him in silent sorrow. The past had charged into her life and taken over, but not the way she'd dreamed of when she was little. It was full of contradictions—a war between pride and need, a threat that filled her with confusion. The Old Brook Prince was no boyish romantic, eager to carry her to his gilded castle; there was no castle, only a dilapidated old mansion sinking into ruins, and she was no demure, patiently waiting princess.

She got up and went to a box on a pine sideboard along one wall. Searching through the contents, she found the bundle of photos in a cigar box and sat back down. She felt his gaze on her as she sorted through them. When she found the one she wanted, she set the box aside and came to him, holding it out.

Artemas straightened and took the wrinkled black-and-white picture, and his heart sank. "I couldn't have been more than six," he said, studying the boy standing beside a spindly calf, barefoot and wearing only baggy cutoff jeans, with one arm draped around the calf's neck. He turned the picture over and looked at the inscription on the back. "Artemas and Fred," he read, and realized he was smiling sadly. "I named him Fred. Yes. That was one

of the happiest summers of my life. I asked your father if
I could take Fred home with me when I left. But Fred had
to stay here. I envied him."

Lily stood over him, watching "I'm glad you didn't
name *me* Fred."

He laughed. The awkward tension between them, and
the sorrow, broke into shreds. She began to laugh with
him, then sank down on the couch and put her face in her
hands. The laughter died. Her shoulders shook.

"*Lily*," he said with gruff anguish. He pulled her to him.
She tucked her feet under her and hunched into a tight
ball of misery next to his side. "I miss them so much," she
whispered.

Trembling, Artemas kissed her hair. It was a harmless
gesture of sympathy; self-restraint was his proudest asset,
and he trusted it, even when the contact quickly fogged
his mind with tenderness and greed. "I know you do. You
don't have to hide that from me."

She knuckled her hands to her mouth and bent her
head to his shoulder. Deep, agonized sobs tore from her
throat; her whole body convulsed with them. Artemas
stroked her hair and the side of her face, murmuring low,
anxious sounds meant to soothe but sounding tragic even
to himself. He lifted her face into the crook of his neck,
then rocked her. Tears burned his eyes and finally slid free.
He hurt for her, for the people and dreams they had both
lost at such young ages, for what they would probably
never have together.

When she felt the moisture against her temple, she
raised her head quickly. Her face was wet with grief; sympathy broke from her in a low moan. "Oh, no, *no*," she
said desperately. He shut his eyes and shook his head
slightly. She put her arms around him and rested her
cheek against his. He gave in, holding her tighter, trying to
melt into her and diffuse the pain. His stiff and soundless
anguish made her stroke the back of his head gently.

"You don't know how to cry very well," she said, her
voice barely audible, breaking on each word. "But you
don't have to hide it from *me*."

Despite her urging, he suppressed the hollow grief pounding behind his eyelids and said through clenched teeth, "You're the only person in my life who knows I'm even capable of it."

"I can't believe that. They can't *do* that to you. It's too much to expect."

"It's what I've taught them to expect. To rely on."

"Even *her*?" Lily asked without condemnation. It was clear who she meant.

His loyalty to Glenda would only let him answer, "It's not her fault."

The note of careful allegiance in his tone was enough to distance Lily from him. She exhaled wearily. She continued to hold him, but her hand stilled on his hair, and she angled her face away, resting her cheek on his shoulder. "You must love her very much."

"She deserves to be loved."

The vagueness of his answer was no escape route to Lily. "Then you love her," she prompted.

Artemas knew the truth wouldn't help either of them. A lie would be appropriate, even wise, because it would help keep Lily away from him. The dilemma raged in his chest. *I don't want to hurt her. Whatever I say, it will hurt her.*

He took her by the shoulders, held her back from him a little, and looked at her without saying anything. She studied him, her blue eyes piercing, provoking, but failing to find what they wanted. Her ravaged face settled into a mask of resignation. "She's *important* to you," she said carefully.

"Yes. Very."

Artemas felt the deadened acceptance. She had handed him a way out. God, she was able to sacrifice that, because she knew she'd lost. Her courage was everything he'd ever dreamed about, and something he would never stop wanting to celebrate and protect.

Lifting a hand to his face, she smoothed a trembling finger over the fading dampness on one of his cheeks. His breath caught. One more second and he'd be catching her hand to his mouth and kissing the palm. She saved him from that disaster by suddenly dropping her hand to his chest and pushing lightly. He let go of her, and she moved to the middle of the couch.

Artemas faced forward and brusquely rubbed a hand across his face. She did the same. Their charade of dignity was as pathetic as tornado survivors picking through the ruins of a house. As if there were any way to make the effort look noble.

"You never wrote much about your parents," she said. "You mentioned they died, but you never said what happened to them."

"I don't miss them."

"Not ever?"

He glanced at her. "No."

Her face paled at his brutal tone. "Why?"

Telling her would tear away more of her idealistic expectations about him and keep her at a distance. He started with Susan de Gude, softening the details but leaving nothing out. As he talked, horror crept into Lily's expression. The questions she interjected held a note of sick regret, as if she were compelled against her will. And by the time he finished with a few terse words about his mother's drunken death, she was hugging herself.

Artemas sat back, exhausted and defenseless. He felt dirty, as if the words had stained his mouth and skin. "That's what I come from," he said. He jerked a pack of cigarettes from his trouser's front pocket and fumbled with the cheap lighter he'd tucked into the cellophane sheath. Lily lurched forward and grasped his wrists. His startled scowl only made her look at him sadly. "You think you can go back and change what they were. Isn't that what pushes you? Believin' that everything they did wrong will disappear if you make enough money and impress enough people?"

"Yes."

"You could lose the whole point of your life that way. Lose yourself."

His skin felt feverish where her fingers clamped it.

"Just the opposite," he told her with growing dismay. "I know who I am and what I have to do."

"For *them*." Her voice rose, became a plea. "But what do you want for yourself?"

She was tearing him apart, making it impossible to think clearly. "This. I'm saving this." He felt reckless, bursting with the half-realized desires that suddenly crowded his mind with vivid recognition. He jerked his head toward their surroundings, then looked at her. "And you. And the estate at Blue Willow. All of it's mine."

The words were hardly out of his mouth before he realized how possessive and intimate they sounded. In one thoughtless, vulnerable moment, he'd revealed too much, not only to her but to himself.

"Sentimental memories," he explained quickly. "Friendship. A sanctuary."

She whispered his name in awe, leaned over, and kissed him on the mouth. The sweet, hot pressure made a clean thrust into an unguarded part of his shield, a wound that felt mortal. She could take his life, if he let her. It would be so easy to let her.

Artemas pulled his hands away from her powerful grip and grasped her chin. He was kissing her back blindly, his only thought to make her lips damp and luscious and open to him, and she was urging him on. Nothing had ever felt so right, so complete. If they continued, he would forget every duty but the one to her. He could not.

Artemas broke the contact and held her apart from him. She lunged forward, trying to kiss him again. Her eyes were shut. She seemed dazed, wild. He groaned bitterly and grabbed her arms. When she finally realized his harsh resistance, her eyes flew open. Shame and regret seeped into them.

She stared at him from the dangerous space of a harsh breath, then slid away. Her hands quivered as she covered her flushed face. "I better go." She strode to a pile of blankets and pillows on a chair near the front door. Artemas followed, cursing silently. Gathering her bedding, she turned and flashed a shattering, anguished look at him.

"Relax. I'm not goin' to do that again. Don't lecture me about your live-in ladyfriend. If you cheated on her, I wouldn't have much respect for you. And I'm not some fool who thinks going to bed with you would change anything."

His hands were clenched by his sides. He was dying. "Good," he forced himself to say. "You summed the situation up nicely."

She blanched at his uncompromising answer. He trailed her to the porch and watched her hurry out into the pasture. A full moon made a silver mist on the knoll where the barn sat, a low, dark form with a peaked roof against the night sky. She tied the winch rope around her things and climbed the ladder to the open loft door, disappearing into its blackness. The bedding rose slowly, pulled upward by her expert hands, with the eerie effect of floating, until it was absorbed in the dark loft with her.

Artemas turned and went into her bedroom, pulled the neat patchwork quilt from her bed, then strode through the house turning off lights. When the darkness matched the barn's, he went to the front porch and sat on the edge, the blanket thrown loosely around his shoulders, his eyes on the barn's loft entrance.

A boy's childish vow had become a grown man's passion. Unfettered desire and possessiveness overwhelmed him. He had never wanted anything or anyone with such vivid, painful certainty.

Insects sang in the small grove of peach and apple trees beyond the yard, as if the morning were peaceful. Artemas stood in the open door of the screened back porch, brooding over a charmed world washed in the last pink shadows of dawn. The budding vines of old-fashioned roses draped a remnant of wooden fence that had been left as a border for an herb bed. Huge ferns were beginning to unfurl along the creek banks, shaded by the willows. Crepe myrtles and hydrangeas dotted the yard's edge, and trellises held muscadine vines. He remembered popping their fat, sweet grapes into his mouth when he was a child, and the smell they made simmering in huge pots on Mrs. MacKenzie's big gas stove.

His restless attention moved to the pasture beyond the shrubbery, then to the barn. Lily obsessed him. Wanting her was like walking into a dark, unfamiliar room and immediately, without rational explanation, knowing how to find the light.

Artemas stepped into the yard, dropped to his heels by a spigot, and filled his hands with frigid well water. He scrubbed his face roughly, wishing the icy sting would jolt his good sense.

To throw away the alliance he'd made with Glenda's father meant ruin for all his hopes of building the Colebrook businesses. It meant ruin for his family's future. Yes, his commitment to Glenda DeWitt had been conceived in necessity rather than choice, but he'd promised himself he'd never hurt her, and that vow was all that had saved his self-respect.

You could have Lily too, a rebellious inner voice whispered. *Who would blame you for rewarding yourself?*

Bile rose in his throat. That was an option his father would have chosen without a qualm. An arrangement that would degrade Lily, even if she agreed to it, which Artemas doubted she ever would. He thought about their seven-year age difference. He hadn't been naive at eighteen, and neither was she. She'd see his dilemma for what it was—a coldblooded choice. He'd chosen to build something for his family, and he would never sacrifice that.

Artemas slammed a fist onto his knee. He had spent the night weighing his options against reality, and reality had won.

He left the yard at a fast walk. When he reached the barn, he climbed the weathered ladder to the loft without any attempt at being quiet. *Wake up, we have a lot to do,* he'd tell her, as if she were just an accessory to his day's schedule.

But he hoisted himself over the top rung and halted, looking at her still asleep on the loft's golden mat of hay. She was curled up on her side, colorful quilts jumbled over her, her bright red hair splayed across a pillow. One arm was curled around some kind of gray coat; the other was flung out on the hay, the hand unfurled and vulnerable, as if reaching toward him. Her face was poignantly relaxed. For the first time he could imagine how she must look with a carefree smile, or laughing.

The sight of her unleashed an ache of loss and longing in his chest. He glanced around the loft, trying to distract the feeling. To his left, beside a mountain of neatly stacked bales of hay, sat a large open box. He pulled it to him, hoping the rustling sounds would make her wake up. She stirred, hugged the odd coat closer to her chest, but continued sleeping.

Artemas exhaled in defeat. Without caring, he glanced down into the box. The stuffed toy bears brought a vague sense of recognition. He pulled them out one by one, piling them on the floor by his knees, and when his hand touched the box's bottom, he felt a small bag filled with sharp edges. He lifted it out and stared in astonishment.

Through the clear plastic he saw his insignia from the military academy. The nameplate, the cadet-commander emblem, even the gold braid from the collar and cuffs. Suddenly he realized that the stuffed bears were the ones he'd given her over the years. Staring at her again, he studied the faded gray coat and knew what it was—his academy jacket.

A mouse scurried along a rafter overhead, dislodging the brittle clay remnant of an insect's home. The crumbled bits fell on her face, and she jerked upright, disheveled and looking around wildly. Hay clung to her hair and the T-shirt she still wore from yesterday.

When she saw him, she flinched in surprise. Her cheeks were flushed, her eyes unguarded as they swept over him. It was a provocative examination, taking in a new image of him in jogging shoes and old jeans with a faded football jersey tucked into them. They were all he'd brought with him in the rush to catch a flight out of New York.

Finally she noticed the items in front of him on the

floor, darted a horrified gaze at him, then bounded over. Sitting on her bare feet with her wrinkled shorts hiked high around her thighs—a view that did his simmering frustration no good—she scooped the bears into her lap and began shoving them back into the box. "Old things," she muttered, her voice high. "I meant to get rid of 'em."

She grimaced at the packet of insignia he still held in one hand. Artemas dropped it into the box. "I didn't mean to pry. I'm sorry." He hesitated. His life was a maze of hidden needs, small human wishes and dreams he couldn't indulge. He wanted this time with her to be his, just his, with as little deception as possible. "I'm not sorry," he corrected. Her astonished gaze flashed up to his somber one. "I like knowing that you kept all of it."

"Oh, Artemas." Her voice was soft, but more distressed than pleased. Rubbing her hands over her face, she sighed and shook her head. "I put it all away after the night you came to visit."

"Why?"

Her chin jutted forward. He recognized that lockjawed, stubborn look. It was as familiar to him as his own. She wasn't about to tell him, unless he pressed. When she moved as if starting to rise, he reached out and tugged gently on her hand. She stared at his hold on her for a moment, flexed her fingers around his careful grip, then settled down again, looking defeated. Artemas casually let go of her, as if it were easy, and draped his arm over one updrawn knee.

She told him what had happened to her that night, how a boy she'd trusted had mauled her, how ashamed she'd been, how she'd hidden outside the house, listening miserably as her parents and Artemas had talked, then watching him leave. Artemas studied her reddening cheeks and deceptively shuttered eyes. She might not realize it, but she radiated guilt, even now. Guilt because she thought her story would disgust him, that she'd been foolish and gullible, deserving some blame.

Humiliating memories of his own flooded back. A haze of fury misted his vision and made him light-headed. He moved next to her without a second thought, and put both arms around her. "I'm just going to hold you," he said. Self-restraint coiled inside him, choking off all possibility that he'd do more.

She gave a fervent little nod, as if she couldn't bear to hope otherwise. Slowly she leaned against him, curled her legs to one side, and shut her eyes. He kept his head up, staring fixedly at the beautiful morning outside the loft door. Then he told her what had happened to him when he was fourteen.

As he described how Mrs. Schulhorn had confused and shamed him with her drunken groping, he felt Lily stiffening with shock. He glanced at her anxiously. She wrenched back from him a little, her face tilting up to his gaze, livid. Her teeth were bared. "That *bitch*." Her voice was low and deadly serious. "I wish she were here. I wish I could beat the ever-lovin' *shit* out of her."

Her fury on his behalf had a strange effect. It voided the ugly memory, the feeling of having been used, victimized. Because Lily really would have beat the shit out of Mrs. Schulhorn.

Before he knew why he needed to, he was laughing. Throwing back his head and laughing—with relief, with delight, with lurid disdain for people who thought they had the power to humiliate him, or Lily.

"You think I'm *kidding*?" Lily asked in a low, strained voice. Glowing with pleasure, he looked down at her and shook his head. She scrutinized him. "That's not a smile on your face," she said. "It's exposed fangs."

He exhaled. It was a soft hiss of threat. His lips barely moved. "I want that boy's throat between my hands. I want to break his neck."

Her face lit up. "Really?"

"The last thing I'd let him do is gurgle an apology to you. So there'd be no doubt in your mind that you weren't to blame for what happened."

He saw his own brand of giddy relief rising in her eyes. Tentatively at first, then with a snap of certainty. "You'd

crack his neck like a wishbone?" she inquired, arching one
brow expectantly.

"He'd look like an accordion." Her absurdity captivated
him. He asked slyly, "And you'd punch her until she
squealed?"

"I'd give her more dents than an old Chevy."

"I'd break all his fingers."

"I'd stomp on her head."

On some unspoken cue they scrambled to their knees,
grasped each other by the shoulders, and swayed, pushing
and pulling vigorously. "Kick his ass black and blue." *"Twist
her nipples off!"* They were shoving at each other, as joyous
as wild children. "Rip his stomach open and spit in his
guts!" *"Slap her till her eyes popped!"* "Jerk his arms into
pretzels!" *"Pull out her eyelashes one by one!"* "I can't think
of any more!" *"Neither can I! And I'm gettin' seasick!"*

Shouting with elation like battle-fatigued soldiers, they
leaned against each other and sat down limply. The laughter trickled away, punctuated by a spontaneous new outburst here and there, as they leaned against each other.
Artemas wiped his eyes. Lily patted her stomach and took
deep breaths.

The fragile mood settled and darkened, until they were
both silent. A soft, heated breeze curled inside the barn.
Artemas turned his face into it gratefully, glancing at Lily
as he did. She looked both pensive and peaceful, which
was how he felt too. "Thank you," she said, keeping her
eyes straight ahead.

"Thank you."

One sleeve of her shirt was jammed up to her shoulder. His closeness to her let him notice the thin white scar
there. It made a horizontal stripe along the smooth, tanned
skin dusted with freckles. A jolt of recognition made him
grimace. Artemas twisted toward her a little and touched
his fingertips to it. "Is this where you were shot?" he asked
gruffly.

She followed his intense gaze. "War wound," she said,
and jerked the sleeve over it.

"It *is* where you were shot. When you pretended to be

a bear to chase someone out of the woods around the estate."

"You remember." She smiled sadly.

"Lily, I loved your letters."

He had done the wrong thing, bringing that subject up. Her face became grim. "Until you stopped readin' them."

"That was a mistake. Maybe I thought . . . I'm not what you want me to be. You were writing to someone you believed in, and it wasn't fair to you."

"Because you have a lover."

"Because there isn't much innocence in my life anymore."

"I don't understand."

"Just believe this—I care about you. I always have. I always will."

She started to say something, but it seemed to catch in her throat. Her face softened, not forgiving, but resigned. "I believe you," she said, swallowing hard. She got to her feet and went to the forgotten cardboard box. Kneeling beside it, she shoved the flaps down and wrestled them shut. Her mouth was set; her hands moved swiftly.

She pushed the box aside as if afraid he'd ask more questions about her reasons for keeping everything he'd ever sent her, then settled her hands in her lap and leveled a somber gaze at him. "The man who shot me is going to live here now."

When he didn't say anything, her shoulders sagged, and she looked away. Artemas fought the emotion rusting his throat. "I'll do everything I can to prevent that," he told her.

"You can't stand losing, can you?"

"No. And I doubt you can either."

"Maybe we're two of a kind. Maybe that's our worst problem." She rose and hurried past him, then climbed swiftly down the ladder.

Artemas moved to the edge of the loft door and watched her walk to the house. *Two of a kind* echoed in his thoughts.

Thirteen

Lily stood beside him in the shallow parking lot in front of a line of businesses in town, looking up grimly at the large, handsome old building that was Mr. Estes's hardware and feed store.

The vast whitewashed front porch was lined with gleaming new lawn mowers and wheelbarrows for sale. The pair of shallow steps that led up to the porch were made of gleaming marble blocks. Row after row of bedding plants—tomatoes, peppers, squash, cucumbers, and much more—were stacked on big bleachers at either end of the porch.

The store's shingled roof came to a peak above a pristine red-and-white sign that said, ESTES FARM AND HARDWARE SUPPLIES, ESTABLISHED 1946.

The double wooden doors were shut. A large, hand-lettered sign hung on the screened doors in front of them: CLOSED—ILLNESS.

Lily's shoulders sagged with disappointment. Artemas had gotten her psyched up for victory, not this. He frowned at the sign, cursed under his breath, but squeezed her arm in reassurance. They looked at the half-dozen empty parking spaces on either side of her old Jeep. "We'll try again tomorrow," he said.

Lily spotted Little Sis coming out of a small vacant shop up the street. Her brindled hair was done in a French braid. A brooch snugged a funky red-velvet jacket to her waist. A long print skirt billowed around her legs, and she tapped one earth-shoe-clad foot impatiently as she stopped to converse with her companion. Pudgy Mr. Ledbetter, the placid little man who'd owned the block of buildings as long as Lily could remember, shook Little Sis's hand.

"She's making some kind of deal," Lily said.

"How can you tell?"

"That's how she dresses when she's serious."

"My God."

"Come on. Maybe she knows what happened to Mr. Estes."

When they walked up, Little Sis squinted from Lily to Artemas and distractedly waved good-bye to Mr. Ledbetter, who drove off in an old yellow Cadillac. "I'm renting this shop," she announced. "And I'm moving in with Maude and Big Sis."

Lily explained to Artemas. "Big Sis started living with Aunt Maude this past winter. Uncle Wesley died last year, and Aunt Maude was lonely."

"Wesley was never home anyway," Little Sis interjected tartly. "He had a stroke and fell off his bass boat. Drowned with the bass swimming around him. I say it was poetic justice." Little Sis tilted her head back and eyed Artemas.

"Good morning," he said politely.

"May the Force be with you," she shot back.

Lily intervened quickly. "What are you going to do with this shop?"

"Sell books and such. New Age. This town needs an alternative to reality. There are a lot of tourists now. They'll buy." Little Sis waved her hands, dismissing the subject as if it were beside the point. "You came to town to see Mr. Estes?"

"Yes. But his store's closed. Do you know what's going on?"

Little Sis looked dejected. "He went home to take his wife to the doctor. She was having chest pains. He's a stiff-lipped old stud—I feel sorry for him. Frail wife. Lousy son." Gently laying a hand on Lily's arm, Little Sis added, "Maude talked to him this morning, honey. He said he won't sell."

Lily was unprepared for that sudden crash of hope. She stood there numbly, the morning sunlight stabbing her eyes. Suddenly Artemas's arm was around her shoulder, and his deep voice was near her ear. "We'll talk to him again. Don't you dare give up."

She raised her chin and looked at him gratefully. She wasn't giving up on *anything*, him included.

The mansion at Blue Willow was sinking into a green ocean of greedy pines and young hardwoods, hemmed in a web of thorny vines. Ragged ivy climbed the walls. The gabled roofs of weathered blue slate rose bravely against a dark blue sky. Gothic and Victorian, the house had a cathedral-like dignity. It whispered of the gilded age when Gatsbyesque industrial barons made outlandish fortunes and spent them building estates to rival those of Europe's landed gentry.

To Artemas, it was a proud symbol of dreams that had been too good to last. Reality had returned with the Depression, overextended investments, modern taxation, and the mismanagement of a fortune and a legacy by Artemas's ancestors. Blue Willow had been their victim.

All the lower windows and doors were covered in large sheets of tin anchored by bolts in the stone. Rust marks streaked them. The upper windows, with their peaked cornices and delicate little panes of glass, reflected silver light from the afternoon sun. In places the panes were broken—a whole set missing in several—and they made dark holes in the light, like a gap-toothed smile.

Shadows engulfed the vast, empty spaces under a loggia that anchored the mansion's base. He'd spent countless hours on that windswept veranda, sailing balsa-wood airplanes Mrs. MacKenzie helped him construct. If he closed his eyes, he could see himself dodging among islands of white wicker furniture as he chased them.

Below the loggia was a terrace bounded in a stone balustrade. The spires of three tall fountains peeked over the pines that had taken over where Mr. MacKenzie had kept a neat lawn and flower beds. Artemas had never seen the fountains work; their plumbing had fallen into disrepair before his birth.

The house's pearl-gray stone walls were softened by the overgrown patches of ivy; the majesty and solemn grandeur were, somehow, unforbidding. To Artemas the house was a part of the mountains beyond, and just as majestic.

He stood beside Lily at the edge of the lake below, filled with the disastrous sense that he was sharing this view with the only person beside himself who appreciated it.

Their clothes were damp with the sweet, muggy air. She was close enough to bump against him, something they both avoided awkwardly. Standing with her head thrown back, she latched her hands in the back pockets of loose jeans. A faded blue T-shirt clung to the rise and fall of her breasts. Her sturdy work shoes sank into the soft soil as she braced her feet apart. Her attitude said she was strong enough to endure his company without saying any more about past or future, hopes or disappointments.

But the unspoken tension was there, a bleak force between them.

"To me, the house always looks friendly," she said, her voice mingling with the soft lapping of the lake. "Every kid in the county grows up telling ghost stories about it. I made some up myself. I decided if people were scared of it, they'd leave it alone. You can see from the broken windows that a lot of them prowled around."

She pointed to the palm court jutting from the left end of the house. Its soaring green-glass structure was banded with sheets of plywood at the bottom. "When I was little, someone tore off some of the plywood and broke a big hole in the glass. I used to climb inside and sit by the fountain, with a book to read. After I got shot wandering around up there, Daddy covered the hole. I thought I'd never forgive him. I lost my private hideaway."

Artemas wanted to tell her that he'd restore the place

someday. He wanted to say she'd be welcome to visit. And that he'd buy her land back for her, even if it took years of patient assaults on Mr. Estes's strange stubbornness. But she wouldn't believe him right now.

He walked past her, following a narrow path that curved around the lake's northern end, then up the ridge to the house. She hurried after him.

They made their way up the hill through pine thickets where a vast lawn had stretched from the back terrace to the lake. Sunlight dappled the ground, and the only sounds were the soft rustle of their feet on a mat of pine needles. The sensation of entering a lost, enchanted world enveloped him.

A set of stone steps, nearly submerged in the soil, marked the rise to the terrace. They grew out of the ground, becoming steeper, until they ended at an entrance in the terrace's balustrade. It was unsettling to walk in a forest where he remembered open lawn. The terrace fountains loomed in the thicket, looking eerie and displaced.

Suddenly he and Lily emerged at the grand stone steps to the loggia. They were several dozen feet wide, and tall stone urns marked each side. Artemas halted on the lowest step, and Lily moved up beside him. Her arm brushed his, moist and hot, a kiss of skin on skin. She seemed oblivious to the startling contact, or determined to ignore it.

Gazing up at the cavernous veranda and its tall stone columns, she said softly, "My grandmother told stories about the Christmas pageants that were held here. She said your grandparents invited everyone for miles. They brought in a choir—at least a hundred singers, she said—and if the weather was warm that year, the choir would stand outdoors on these stairs. She said it felt as if they were singing to the mountains."

She bounded up the stairs and turned. Artemas watched her look out over the pines, her head held up proudly. For a moment the sorrow that always hovered in her expression was replaced by contentment.

He followed quickly and stood beside her. His vivid

memory of the view had not been a child's fantasy; the panorama of rounded mountains and deep sky was breathtaking. "I envy you," he said gruffly. "You've had so many years to enjoy this. I only had a few."

"But you have the rest of your life. This all belongs to you." Her temporary enchantment faded; her face became somber, and a little angry. Artemas grasped her hand and pulled her up the rest of the steps. "Show me how you got to the opening in the palm court."

She shot a startled glance at him. "I climbed up on the foundation. A ledge runs along the bottom of the glass walls."

"Lead the way."

They strode across the loggia's echoing marble floor, leaving footprints in the thick dust. At the far end a narrow set of stone stairs led down to what had been rose gardens, now a jungle of pines capped in wisteria. The house loomed over them as they pushed through the undergrowth. The stone wall gave way to the palm-court wing. Soaring glass panels rose out of the girdle of warped gray plywood. The mansion's foundation formed a ledge, just as she'd said.

Her head back, she searched for something midway down the long expanse. "Here it is." They stopped under a sheet of wood that was less colored with age. Artemas studied the vertical rows of corroded nailheads sinking into the dilapidated wood. "I think we can pull that sheet off," he said.

She looked at him with glowing eyes. "All right."

Before he could help her—as if she needed or wanted it—she lodged a toe into the deep crevices between the blocks of stone and boosted herself onto the wide lip at their top. By the time Artemas climbed up beside her, she was standing by the plywood panel and eagerly tugging at its edge. He took the other side.

The wood groaned as they jerked outward, caving in around the heavy nails. "Let go of it, old girl," Lily said under her breath, talking to the mansion with comfortable intimacy. "We'll put your patch back on when we leave."

Earthy-smelling air gusted from the palm court's interior as the sheet came loose. Artemas glimpsed a shadowy world of genteel ruin inside, and his heart twisted with recognition as a ray of sunlight fell on the fountain at its center. They set the wooden panel aside. The missing section of glass left an entrance easily large enough for them to step through without bending.

"It looks almost like I remember," Lily said, as the soft greenish light surrounded them. She nodded in satisfaction at the ruins of palm trunks scattered around the floor, the fountain with its girlish cherub stained with years of rainwater from the broken panes overhead, and the huge, cracked ceramic containers leaning haphazardly on the floor. She dropped to her heels and brushed dirt from white tiles decorated with delicate blue willows.

Artemas looked at the place with a dull ache rising in his chest. "I remember it filled with plants and wrought-iron garden furniture, and the palms reaching the ceiling, and the fountain—it was the only one that still worked. My grandmother kept goldfish in it. And she had parakeets. They were tame, and they'd light on my hands. It was heaven."

"I wish I could have seen it. But I love it even the way it looks now."

He knelt beside her and brushed his fingertips over the tiles. One of them wobbled under the pressure; he pried it loose. "Would you like to keep this?"

She looked at him with tenderness darkening her eyes, as blue as the color on the tile. In that second the invisible distance between them faded; they were close in a way they hadn't been before. "No, it belongs here," she answered softly.

So do you, he wanted to say. But she took the tile from him and carefully put it back in its place. "Do you remember the story my mother told about the willows? About how things started?"

"Of course."

"I've read all about Colebrook Blue Willow. I got books about china makers from the library. They said the Blue

Willow pattern was well known. The great English potters had been adapting it and other designs from the Orient for years. Old Artemas must have known that Americans couldn't get enough of it."

Artemas shrugged. "By all accounts, he was ambitious and smart."

"He was *real* ambitious," Lily corrected. "He saw that Americans wanted 'imported' Blue Willow because that sounded fancier, so he stamped 'England' under his trademark and worked out a scheme to have his china carried by English ship captains up north, where it was sold at prices that undercut the real McCoy. He fooled people for years."

Artemas frowned at her accusing tone. "The public thought it was buying fine English china at a reasonable price. He was English. It was fine china. That's not much of a deception."

"I've always wanted to believe that Old Artemas got the inspiration to make the Blue Willow pattern from my great-great-great-grandmother and her willow trees. But maybe he was just looking for a smart business opportunity. Maybe it wasn't sentimental at all."

"No," Artemas said firmly. "They were married. She died having their child. Those are historical facts. If he loved her, he must have wanted to honor her. My grandmother always said that Colebrook China owed its beginnings to Elspeth MacKenzie's influence."

"But it's just legend. Like believing that the willow trees were a gift from a dangerous mountain spirit disguised as an old man. They're botanical mutants, and Elspeth probably bartered with some scruffy peddler to get 'em."

"I prefer your mother's version of the story."

"Why? It's pretty corny for a tough character like you."

He stood, angry and restless, glaring down at her. "I have my fantasies." Striding to the fountain, he stepped up on the basin's wide rim, then turned slowly, taking everything in, finally including her again. She had risen to her feet and was watching him with uncertain, melancholy admiration. "This place needs a caretaker," he said slowly. "Someone to keep the ghosts in line. There used to be some guest cottages on the front side, beyond the old stables and greenhouses. Are any of them still standing?"

"The roofs have fallen in, and all the windows are gone. The stone walls are still there though."

"I should have one of them restored. Lily, I could give it to you. You could live there. It would be yours—I'd deed it to you. And some land—"

"No." She ran over and halted at the fountain's base with her head tilted back. Her cheeks flushed darkly, and her eyes gleamed with tears. "That would make me feel like a servant here. My parents were Colebrook servants, but I won't ever be."

"I swear I didn't mean it that way."

"I know." She sank to the fountain's rim, staring into space, her back rigid with pride. Artemas dropped down beside her. "I only want to make things right for you," he said. "For everything our families have shared, for what you've lost, for what our friendship means to me."

She glanced at him, then studied the toe of her shoe, stirring up the years of fine dust that had settled in her private sanctuary. "Maybe you already have, just by coming back."

Artemas cleared his throat. "I want you here—I want you to live here. Somehow."

"Even if I have to leave, I'll come back for good someday. To my place. And you will too. To yours."

Always separate. With other people in their lives. She would find someone, love someone, marry. There was nothing he could do to change that. The words he wanted to say were locked inside him. He massaged his temples, trying to drive away the frustration pounding there. He imagined himself snatching her into his arms. *Stay here for me. I'll hide what we have together. I'll come to see you every chance I get. No one has to know.*

Except Lily. Lily would know. He'd tell her why he wasn't free, and she might understand, but she'd despise him for it too. "Are you all right?" she asked, touching his arm. "You look like you feel awful."

He stood, dropping his hands to his side in fists. "I'll get your fucking place back for you. I'll do that if it takes the rest of my life. You'll never forgive me if I don't."

Lily slapped a hand on the fountain. The eerie echo underscored her furious voice. "I don't blame you. I did before, but not now. You're not responsible for what happens to me."

He flung his hands out. "I held you before your own mother did. I named you."

"You named Fred the calf too. Fred grew up and became somebody's steak dinner."

She had a way of coloring things in the most absurd way. He stared at her. A sharp, disgusted laugh burst from him. Artemas exhaled wearily and shook his head. Lily's angry attention darted to the floor near his feet. She lunged down, scooped something into her hands, then straightened and held out her cupped palms. A tiny green lizard sat there, frozen in fear. "I thought you might want to name it," she said sarcastically. "So you can own it."

No one but Lily could provoke him this way. Artemas picked the lizard up by its tail. "Bob," he said. Then he dropped it on her shoulder. It fled under the neck of her T-shirt.

Her mouth dropped open. She didn't scream—a lizard was just a lizard, and she'd had dozens of them for pets. But it was scurrying into the valley between her breasts. She snatched at the front of her shirt, flapping the material. The lizard's tickling path continued along the inner curve of her right breast and came to stop near her nipple. She shivered in defeat. "He's in my bra. Thanks a *lot*."

The look that came over Artemas's face was priceless—he wanted to laugh or curse, she couldn't tell which. He looked painfully amused. Lily hissed at him and turned her back. Her face burned. Embarrassment, but also the tingling fire of his gaze on her back, made her muscles suddenly feel limp. She pulled her shirt up as demurely as she could and felt underneath. The lizard made a ridge under the tight pink rayon cup. Her underwear was plain and sturdy, nothing she thought Artemas would enjoy catching a glimpse of.

She edged her fingertips under the cup. The lizard crept on top of her nipple and sat there, as if clinging to the stub of a tree branch. Cursing silently, mortified, she jerked the cup above her breast and tried to catch him. He skittered down her bare stomach, heading straight for the escape path between her skin and the waistband of her jeans.

Dilemma overcame decorum. *"Catch him,"* she ordered, swinging toward Artemas, clutching her T-shirt over her breasts, her stomach exposed. "I'm not taking my jeans off!"

Artemas cupped a hand over the lizard as it reached her navel. Everything came to a stop. The lizard was trapped in her navel. Artemas's broad, rugged hand lay intimately on her stomach, riding the unstable surface, which flexed rhythmically with her short, shallow breaths.

He was bent beside her, his cheeks ruddy, his expression tense. There was no shyness in *him,* though, because he looked at her drolly and said, "I don't have time to check. Are you an innie or an outie?"

She wanted to strangle him. But she wanted the pressure of his fingers, the fire on her skin, to stay. "Just catch the lizard. Try not to hurt him. I *like* lizards."

He curled his fingers inward. They drew lines of sensation, meeting over the center of her body. He pulled his hand away. "Got him." His voice was ragged. Lily couldn't look at him. From the corner of her eye she saw him stoop and release the lizard. "Good-bye, *Bob,"* he said dryly. "You'll have a helluva story to tell your grandchildren."

He straightened. The silence and the tension were a tangible force. Her hands were still clenched over her breasts. She couldn't breathe. Wanting his touch made her drunk and angry. She faced him, tugging her shirt and the bra up to her armpits. Cool air kissed her naked breasts. "Look at me," she urged huskily. She met his eyes. They glowed like silver above the flat, warning line of his mouth. "You can't tell me I'm not a grown woman, or that I don't know what I want." His gaze moved down slowly, an explicit, dangerous caress.

"You're beautiful. You deserve the best. I didn't have to see your body to know that. I knew it before I ever saw a picture of you." He turned and walked swiftly toward the opening in the court's wall, his shoulders squared and back straight.

Lily bit her lip. Her head dropped. She rearranged her clothes and followed him.

The afternoon sun cast long shadows by the time they emerged from the woods at the end of the MacKenzie road. Lily glanced back sadly at the rutted Jeep trail disappearing into the old-growth forest. It ran for nearly two miles through enormous oaks and sourwoods and maples, and it had always linked the estate's main grounds and her family's land. Before the MacKenzies and Colebrooks had arrived, it had been part of a Cherokee hunting path. Grandpa had given her a collection of arrowheads he'd found along the creek.

"Tell me what you're thinking about," Artemas said, and she realized he'd been watching her face. "History," she answered, her throat aching. The raw throb of grief surfaced, and she couldn't say anything else. She halted in the middle of the gravel road, frantically noticing everything, bombarded by vivid details. The tiny blue violets growing along the road's ditches, the hog-wire fences and rolling pasture opening up on the other side of the road, the meandering red-clay driveway cutting through them, and farther away, the willows and orchards clustered around the house.

I'll die without it. I'll die without Artemas, she thought. Those were cowardly ideas, and she kicked them out. Her people had endurance and courage and faith—everything she was looking at proclaimed it. Artemas would leave soon. She would pack her things and leave here herself a few days from now. She'd survive, learn, prosper. And she'd hope for a future when he wouldn't choose his other life over this one, and her.

They stayed up most of the night, talking. About quiet, innocent things that wove a gentler fabric between them—music, books, movies, food. The way it felt to watch a sunset. The taste of the air after a rain. He played the old upright, out-of-tune piano in the living room. Lily had never known that his grandmother had taught him. He was an encyclopedia of the music from her heyday as a Ziegfeld Girl. Funny old songs, most of them familiar—"Tea for Two" and "My Blue Heaven." "Ol' Man River" and "Stardust."

Later they sat in darkness on the porch, listening to screech owls, catching a glimpse of a deer, watching a raccoon steal across the edge of the flower beds. She told him how to judge good garden soil from bad, how to coax a hen to set, and how to find ginseng in the forest. He was interested. Not just faking it to be polite either.

"I know how to do a lot of things that aren't very important outside these hills," she said pensively. "The kind of stuff only the old-timers care about—them and the back-to-nature types who move up here from Atlanta with their collections of *Mother Earth* magazines and electric woks."

Artemas said with a low riff of amusement in his voice, "You don't have any patience for outsiders."

"Most of them think they're coming to save us from our own backwardness. They think they're gonna find a bunch of Daisy Maes and Li'l Abners—or else something that's a cross between *Deliverance* and a Norman Rockwell painting."

"How do you want them to see you?"

He might as well have asked, *How do you want me to see you?*—because she realized she was trying to make some small connection between his life and hers. When she'd gone to New York, she'd seen the differences. They made a gap as wide as the moon.

"Remember that mushy-mouthed saint Sandra Dee

played in those *Tammy* movies? And all that southern-belle crap you see on TV shows? Well, that's not me. I've been known to drink a few beers. I smoked pot once at a party, and it made me feel stupid, so I won't do that again. I've never met a boy around here I couldn't do without, so I've . . . done without. So far. I started working at Friedman's Nursery and Greenhouses when I was fourteen—after school and on weekends, summers, holidays—I've worked every spare minute. I've got a knack for landscaping, and I know more about fertilizer than anybody'd care to hear. That's my life." She snapped a slight nod at him, for emphasis.

"That's a good life. I mean it."

Not good enough to keep you here, she thought. "Aw, let's talk about something else," she said, leaning back on a porch post and staring at his large, dark silhouette with an empty throb of longing. *That woman of yours. Let's talk about her.*

And ruin everything. No. "Your parents," he said softly. "Do you want to talk about them?"

"No." She curled a hand over her chest. Chills ran up her spine. "They're inside me, all the time. If I try to say anything, it feels like they're easing out of me, that I'm losing them. I know that doesn't make any sense, but—"

"I understand." Artemas was glad she couldn't see his face. *I understand because that's how I feel when I try to talk about the bond between you and me.* He suspected the way he was looking at her right now would have drawn her to him.

He got up and went back inside, to the piano. She followed and lay down on the couch behind him. Shortly before dawn Lily fell asleep on the couch, listening to him play the piano again, some haunting, bittersweet old tune. Her last awareness was of him easing a quilt over her, then the light caress of his hand on her hair.

Maybe Little Sis's prediction was right. It was only a matter of time.

fourteen

He smelled coffee. Right under his nose, steaming, pungent, like sharp chocolate. Artemas woke to find Lily sitting on the porch steps near his head, wafting the aroma toward him from the mug in her hand. He had taken a pillow and quilt from her bedroom and lain down outside, where he could look in the screened door to the living room and watch her sleep on the couch.

"It's late morning," she said, studying him with her head tilted to one side and her bright red hair streaming over one shoulder. She wore a pretty shirtwaist dress with tiny blue stripes on a white background and flat white shoes. He'd never seen her in a dress before, and he rose to one elbow, somberly enjoying the graceful sight. She glanced down at herself with a scowl. "I figured I'd shock you. And maybe impress Mr. Estes. I called Aunt Maude. She says he's back at his store."

Artemas nodded and took the mug as she held it out. His stomach was raw; he had no appetite for anything but getting this place back for her.

Negotiating with the man who'd bought Lily's farm would just be a matter of sweetening the original deal. No one could turn down an easy profit. Money would solve the problem.

After that he'd help Lily unpack and return the house to order, and talk to her about her plans for college. He'd set up a fund for her—of course, he'd have to call it a loan, because otherwise she'd never agree. And after he returned to New York he'd work out some discreet way to make certain she was safe here, alone. Perhaps hiring a caretaker for the old estate would be wisest—someone who would have an excuse to visit her, make certain she was all right, and report on her progress to Artemas.

She'd be all right. He'd make certain. And somehow, he'd get on with his life, his goals. Artemas sipped the coffee, letting it burn his mouth, the sharp heat unnoticed, lost in the specter of a future he couldn't control.

Lily inhaled raggedly and tried to think. She was glad they'd arrived at Mr. Estes's place during a lull in business. The parking spaces were empty. One wooden door stood open behind its screen. Her heart was rattling in her chest.

"Mr. Estes has plenty of money," she told Artemas. "He won't be persuaded by offering him more than he paid. He's got a big house and land outside town, and the rumor is that he made a bundle years ago running an auction house for farm machinery. He's probably the richest man in MacKenzie."

"Then there's no good reason for him to keep your farm," Artemas said, opening to door to her old Jeep and stabbing a cigarette into the ashtray. "He can take his money back and find another one for his son."

Lily watched him with grim fascination. His tone was brusque, confident. The cigarette smoking was something he'd never mentioned in his letters. His face was already rugged for someone who was only twenty-six. The jeans and athletic jersey did not make him look like a college student, because he carried himself with a straight-backed, purposeful command that must have been hammered into him in military school. Mr. Estes's status seemed of little consequence to him. He slammed the Jeep's door and faced her. His face softened. "It'll work out. You'll see."

"You better let me do the talking," she said. "He won't deal with an outsider."

She caught the swift flash of Artemas's smile. It was predatory, but admiring. "All right."

They went inside. The store was huge, with tall, beamed ceilings dotted with slowly whirling fans. Merchandise filled a maze of freestanding shelves along wide aisles. There was a potbellied stove on a hearth along one side. Big windows festooned with advertisements let weird, unsymmetrical shadows fall on the floors. Toward the back were pallets stacked with bags of livestock feed. Bins lined the wall, neatly labeled to show their contents. Seeds of all kinds. Nails. Screws. Hinges.

Behind a big counter with a cash register was a towering door to the back storage rooms. Lily led the way to it and range the bell sitting next to a case displaying pocket-knives.

Footsteps sounded on the wooden floor. Mr. Estes appeared, a notepad in one hand. He was neatly dressed in slacks and a plaid sports shirt, with pencils protruding from the breast pocket. But his peppery gray hair was ruffled and his jowly face had a pallor. He scowled from her to Artemas and back to her, his eyes hollow, red-rimmed, and impatient.

"Mr. Estes, are you okay?" Lily asked. She'd never seen him like this before. "I was sorry to hear from Aunt Maude that your wife's in the hospital again."

"Yeah. What can I do for you? Has Joe been pestering you to move faster? I told him to leave you alone till next week."

"No, that's not it." She gestured toward Artemas, introduced him, and watched Mr. Estes's brindled eyebrows flatten in scrutiny, as Artemas held out a hand. Mr. Estes knew who the Colebrooks were. All the old-timers knew about the Blue Willow estate and the Colebrooks. "You got a problem with my boy living in the middle of your woods?" he snapped, ignoring the proffered handshake.

Artemas looked unfazed, but his eyes narrowed. He dropped his hand to his side. "I've got a problem with anyone except a MacKenzie living there. It's nothing personal. But that land has always belonged to the MacKenzies, and it should remain in their hands."

Lily interjected quickly, "Mr. Estes, I've come to ask you if you'll sell it back to me. I can return your down payment. Please. You can find another place for Joe."

Mr. Estes stared at her, his mouth working silently. "How'd you get the money to do that?" he retorted.

"I'm helping her," Artemas said.

"You? Why? You want to add the MacKenzie place to your land? Yeah, that's it. You just want to close up the peephole in a Colebrook door, have miles of land without a little clan of strangers in the middle of it."

"He's going to *loan* me the money," Lily said. "He's not trying to buy the place back for himself."

"I don't care what he's aimin' to do. Joe wants your place, and I got it for him. I can't sell it back. I'm sorry, but I can't, and that's all there is to it."

"You're a friend of my family's," she said, dragging her hands toward her chest. "This isn't some stranger asking you to do what's right. You know how much the place means to me."

"Yes, I do," he said, nodding, his face set in hard lines. "But I've got Joe to think about, and his mother"—his mouth trembled—"she's dyin' by slow inches." Suddenly his voice rose. "And I don't have time to waste on this! You made a deal, and now it can't be undone! We have to make do the best way we can, with what life gives us! That's a hard lesson, but you might as well learn it like the rest of us!"

Artemas stepped forward. His expression had a kind of restrained deadliness to it. "I'll give you twice what you paid. In cash. By tomorrow. And I'll have a real estate broker find your son a new place."

Lily gasped. The deal he was offering was so reckless, so heedless of good sense, that she felt like crying in surprise and gratitude. He hadn't become head of his family's businesses because of wild decisions like this one. He was doing this for her sake.

She flung an arm across him as he started forward again. He halted, his jaw clenched, looking as if he might strike Mr. Estes at any second. "People call you a good, decent man, Mr. Estes," she said, turning, blocking Artemas with her body. "I know you are. My folks respected you."

Mr. Estes craned his head and looked from her to Artemas proudly. He was shaking with emotion. "You get this straight. I'm keeping your place for Joe." He slung a leathery hand toward Artemas. "I don't care if this young, cocky bull offers me a dozen times the price and a herd of real estate people." Slamming his notepad on the counter, he added, "That's all I've got to say about it."

Lily held out her hands, beseeching him, despair creeping into her voice. "You can't keep it. Please. *Please.* This doesn't make any sense."

Artemas gripped her shoulders and pushed her aside. Leaning toward Mr. Estes, he said, "I won't let you reduce Lily to begging for what's hers. I'm sorry if I made you angry. If I can apologize, if there's anything I can do—"

"Get out." Mr. Estes advanced on them, shaking his fists. "I don't want *nobody* begging me. It won't do any good." Tears slid down his craggy face. "I know how useless beggin' is. I've done plenty of it with Joe, trying to get him to stay out of trouble and settle down. Now, I've got him a good piece of land and a good house to live in, and he's excited about it, and I'm not goin' to ruin it for him. I said *git.* And don't come back with more offers. It's over. I've done what I had to. Go on."

The sight of him crying astonished Lily. There was no way around his decision. "This isn't fair," she said desperately.

"Nothin's fair!"

She pivoted and walked out of the building, her vision blurring with tears. She dimly heard Artemas following her. Outside on the steps he grasped her arm gently. She halted and turned her head away, knowing that she'd sob if she looked at him. Crying wasn't worth a damn.

"It's not over," he told her.

"That's your sense of guilt talking. Forget it. You've

done everything you could. You came back to help me. You offered him a lot more money than my place could ever be worth to him." She pulled away from him and went to the Jeep. Her hands were shaking. She climbed into the driver's seat and gripped the steering wheel, staring blindly ahead as he threw himself into the seat beside her. "It is over," she said, her shoulders squared.

"Lily, goddammit, I—"

"There are things I want from you that you don't want to give. That's just bare bad luck on my part, like what happened to the farm. So don't give me any lectures, and don't tell me to keep hoping."

"*Listen* to me." He took her by the shoulders and pulled her half out of her seat. She braced her hands against his chest. His face was flushed; his gray eyes glittered. "I'm not free. *Understand?* I made a decision a long time ago to do whatever it took to give my family something to be proud of again. Without that, I'm no good to you or anyone else. I'm no good to myself."

"And there's no room for somebody who doesn't help your plans? People have to be useful to you, or they're a waste of time?"

"Not a waste—a luxury I can't afford right now."

The sordid suspicion she'd harbored all along now chilled her. "That woman you're going to marry—*she* must be useful."

"Don't try to analyze a part of my life you know nothing about."

"What's her place in your plans? She's got connections? An important name?"

"There are different ways to love someone. It doesn't have to be as sentimental as the poem on a goddamned Hallmark card."

"You're going to marry her because you're *obligated* to."

"Don't throw wild accusations at me."

"A second ago I practically announced to your face that I'm crazy about you. If you're really in love with your woman, you'd have said so then. You wouldn't have gone off on a tangent about not being free, or about what you have to do for your family. You've got yourself chained to some kind of promise, but it's *not* love."

"I think you're one step away from calling me a whore."

"Closer than that. I'm right on top of it. You *are* a whore."

He slapped her. It was only a slight clap on the chin with his fingertips, a shock rather than painful, but she drew back in alarm, for once in her life too stunned to hit back. Artemas lowered his hands slowly. She watched the anger drain out of his face and an expression of agonized disbelief replace it. "That's a first," he said. "And it makes me sick." The raw whisper destroyed her defenses.

She sagged back on the seat. "I'd hate any other man who did it." She bent her head to her splayed hands. "But all I want is for you to say I have a place in your plans too. There's nothing left for me here. I'd go to New York with you. I'd share you with *her*. That's how crazy I am."

His portentous silence throbbed in her ears. "If I had the morals of a whore, I'd ask you to go," he said in a low, tortured tone. "Eventually you *would* hate me for it."

Dignity crawled into her shattered thoughts. He did want her. That was a jewel she could keep. But he was right about the outcome. She lifted her head and studied him with a sense of defeat and loss so deep it robbed her of the ability to tell him. "You better get yourself on a plane this afternoon," she told him. "The longer we spend together, the worse this is going to be."

"I'll leave tomorrow morning. We don't have to pretend this is easy, but I want something good to remember, just as you do. Will you try to make peace with me?"

The answer shimmered in her mind before she realized what she intended. The fragment of thought running through her mind suddenly became clear.

Artemas was hers, until tomorrow. He wasn't the gallant fantasy she'd cultivated, but a complicated, driven, brutally fallible young man. The last vestige of her childhood daydreams disappeared. He and she had one last day. And one last night. "I'll do it," she told him.

He didn't have to know exactly what she meant.

Night had closed in with a moonless, cloudless sky. "I'd forgotten that the stars were so bright," Artemas said. He hadn't spoken for a long time, and his voice startled Lily. His effect on her had an ebb and flow; she would calm down a little, the pain and hunger and unforgiving anger at him temporarily ignored, then suddenly vivid again.

Sitting beside him on the creek bank, she pretended to study the sky too. The Big Dipper could have been upside down and backward, but she wouldn't have noticed. Her mind whirled with secret anticipation and fear.

He'd tried to talk to her all day about her future. College. Guilt and anger over what had happened with Mr. Estes was eating him up. She didn't tell him not to blame himself; she let him suffer. Her losing the farm wasn't his fault, not directly. But she was hurt and angry about so much else, she couldn't let go of the feeling.

They'd spent the past few hours out here. Peanut-butter-and-banana sandwiches had passed for dinner.

He told her more about his parents, brutal stories that made her frantic with confusion. There was so much he'd never written about—ugly, demeaning episodes that had changed him. She decided he told her those stories to repulse her, so she'd be relieved when he left.

But the stories only showed her why he'd become so merciless about getting what he wanted. She had to accept that fact. He did what was best for his family's future. He always would.

He didn't tell her—and she didn't want to know—about that creature she now thought of as *the woman*. Lily despised her and dismissed her as unimportant. There was no way she'd believe she'd been wrong about her intuition—he needed that woman for some reason, but he didn't love her. She wished she could believe that he'd change, but she couldn't.

Absolute loyalty. That was Artemas. He made up his

mind, and he stuck to it. She loved him for that, but she'd never forgive him for it.

Lily gave up on pretending to look at the stars. It was time. He owed her for what he'd done, and she wanted him to pay. She wanted him. Confused, her nerves crackling with a need to fight and win, she got up and slapped at bits of dirt on her jeans. "It's gettin' late," she told him. "Why won't you sleep in my bed at night? What's wrong with it?"

He rose slowly, a dark, large form in the starlight. She had the feeling he was surprised and wary. "Nothing."

"It's too short for your long legs, I know. Put the mattress on the floor, if you want to."

"I will." He stepped toward her. "Don't go yet." It sounded like more of an order than a request. "I've done most of the talking. I don't usually."

"Yeah, you're not exactly a chatterbox. But I like hearing you talk about yourself. You ought to practice more."

"I want to talk to you about your future. About college. I have so many questions—"

"I've already told you all there is. I got accepted at Agnes Scott a couple of weeks ago. It's a private college for women. Aunt Maude's cousin is a professor there. Great academics. I'll study biology, major in botany. I'll work with plants. What else is there to say?"

"That you believe me when I tell you I'll buy this place back for you."

"I believe you."

"Don't say it like that—just to end the discussion. *Mean* it."

"I know you'll try. I'll try too. But it's water under the bridge for now."

Even in the dark she could feel his gaze piercing her. "I'm not going back to New York and forget about you, Lily. I want to be part of your life—be the friend I've always been."

"Then you will be. Good." She touched his cheek. He flinched, and she dropped her hand quickly. What else could she say that hadn't been said before, and foolishly?

If she tried to tell him how bereft she felt, it would only make him feel worse. "You better try to get some sleep," she said. She turned and walked up the hill to the barn. Her heart was pounding, and she felt disoriented. She wasn't done with him tonight, and he'd see that soon enough.

Artemas stood in her dark bedroom, looking at the mattress he'd thrown on the floor. He was filled with unquenchable anger—at himself, at the circumstances he couldn't change, at Lily for knowing how to push every button. She could do it better than anyone he'd ever known.

He stripped to his briefs and lay down, jerking a quilt over his legs and belly. Her scent was everywhere—the feminine subtleties of makeup and some brand of light perfume sitting in a small basket on the otherwise cleared dresser, the faint fragrance of her clothes. The first night, when she'd left him alone in the house, he'd roamed into her bedroom and belligerently opened her closet door, brushing his fingers over print dresses, a blazer, a straight skirt. He had wondered about the textures and colors of her lingerie, too, but the idea of opening a dresser drawer in search of such things made him feel like an addict looking for a fix.

His mouth was dry; ordinarily he would have smoked a cigarette, but tonight even that distraction seemed hopeless. What he needed couldn't be had, not tonight, probably not ever.

The distinct rattle of the front door opening made him rise to one elbow and listen. He'd left the door to Lily's bedroom half-open, and he stared into the dark hall beyond. The front door closed, and the floor of the main room spoke in soft, rhythmic groans as feet crossed it at a measured pace, growing louder and headed in his direction.

Not expecting Lily and unwilling to let surprises creep up on him in the darkness, he vaulted to his feet and slung the bedroom door open. Lily halted. He could barely see her. Without saying a word, she stood there, watching him in the blackness. His body reacted with wariness coiled around the raw current between them, shooting heat through him and bringing a primal thrust between his thighs.

He held the quilt in a fist. Pulling it in front of himself, he reached outside the door and found a light switch. The dim illumination of a low wall sconce brought her into stunning clarity.

Her eyes were locked on his, somber and defensive. Her face was flushed, and her hair hung over her shoulders in a curly red mane. She wore only a long white T-shirt, and it stopped high on her legs. She was barefoot. In one hand she clutched a tiny box.

"I don't want promises or sympathy from you," she said. Her voice shook a little, but her accusing stare didn't flinch. "I just want tonight." She stepped forward, her chest rising and falling roughly, and held out her strange gift.

When he saw she'd brought a box of condoms, alarm merged with the sharp streak of hunger. He couldn't do what she wanted. Fury grew out of the dilemma. "Get out of here," he ordered. He heard the thread of desperation in his voice. "Right now."

Her hand trembled but remained out, the arm rigid, her fingers clenched in a fist around the package. "I'm not going to hang on to you in the morning. I won't cry and beg and expect you to change your mind. Yeah, I'm asking you to forget about *her* tonight. But you and I had something between us a long time before anybody else laid a claim on you. We were just kids, and it doesn't mean much now, but it was real." She shook her hand at him. "You owe me."

Her manipulation was outrageous but imbued with deadly logic. Artemas tried to intimidate her with a sardonic glare. "Sex won't help matters. It complicates them."

"I thought men kept it simple. When you're hungry, you eat. When you're horny, you *fuck*."

The breath rushed out of him with a vicious sound. "I doubt I'm listening to the voice of experience."

"So teach me."

"What makes you think I want to?"

Her hand wavered, and for the first time painful uncertainty clouded her eyes. Then she stiffened and said, "I don't care if you want to or not."

His patience snapped. He dropped the quilt, leaped forward, and grasped her wrist. "I said *leave*." He bullied her up the hall, crowding her, his nearly naked body slamming into hers. She dug her heels in and drew back her free hand in a fist. Artemas caught it and shoved her against a wall. The contact was instant and damning—their bodies sealed together from chest to thighs, her wrists pinned by her shoulders, making her breasts thrust outward, scalding him with their pressure and the electric scrubbing of the soft T-shirt covering them.

They stared at each other in blank desperation. He was hard against her belly, and recognition flashed through her eyes. She cried out—a low, strident moan of relief or fear. His mind was too fogged to know which—he only knew that he couldn't stand having her feel more fear, hate, or desperation because of him. His head sank against hers. She sighed near his cheek, then kissed the spot. He was lost. Defeated.

"You can say no, or stop, whenever you want to," he whispered through clenched teeth. "But if you don't say either one, you'll have to take what you get."

Her breath shuddered against his face. "All right."

He released her wrists with a caustic little shove, then snatched the box of condoms from her. He turned and walked back into her bedroom. The hall light cast the room in a faint glow, leaving deep shadows in the corners. After a second he heard her step in after him and stopped. His back to her, he tossed the box on the mattress's white sheets, then shoved his briefs down to his feet and kicked them aside. His actions were as graceful as he could make them, but hardly delicate.

He turned to face her. "This is what you think you want. Take it or leave it."

Even the dim light couldn't cloak the stark expression of panic on her face, but she quickly shuttered it behind a grim nod. "It's big enough, I guess. Plenty. I guess I'm lucky. Or unlucky, if it hurts." She paused. "But nothing could hurt worse than the way I already feel."

That plaintive remark nearly broke him, but a terrible brand of self-defense had taken over. He dropped to the mattress and sat with one leg jackknifed against the other, waiting. She stood motionless, her hands hanging at her sides, staring down at him. He expected her to turn and walk out at any second. He prayed she would. His body, hard and virile, rejected that prayer.

Instead, she reached under her shirt and pushed her panties down. The strip of white material slipped to her feet, a dull flag of surrender. He wanted to console her, to tell her he didn't want this charade of uncaring sex. But her pride returned with the sudden, brusque lifting of her chin. She grabbed the bottom of her T-shirt and dragged it over her head. Without hesitating, she dropped it by her feet. Soft and strong, as defenseless as he was, she was devastating.

The torment had been savage before. Now, it became a throbbing menace, a rupture in his self-protective cruelty. "Lesson number one," he said, sarcasm hammering the words, "my cock doesn't reach far enough for you to stay by the door."

She inhaled sharply and shot back, "Maybe I ought to get a pair of heavy pliers and stretch it for you."

She took two long strides and sank down on the mattress's foot, her eyes fixed on some point over his shoulder. Her breasts swayed slightly, and he watched her arms tighten along the sides of them. She started to curl her legs beside her, a demure little movement, while one of her hands moved awkwardly from one thigh to the other, obviously fighting an urge to cover the delicate patch of hair between them.

"No. Lie down," he ordered, scrutinizing her with

unrelenting challenge. She shot him a fierce look but stretched out on her side, her back to him. "For God's sake, you know what I mean." The ugly instruction came out sounding hoarse and tortured, not what he'd intended. She flung herself over on her back, clamped her mouth in a tight line, and defiantly laced her hands behind her head, as if to prove that being naked didn't embarrass her.

"Don't order me around," she whispered fiercely. "At least have the guts to *touch* me."

Touch her. He couldn't resist the one lovely gift that had always belonged just to him. In one smooth movement Artemas came down on her, snagging her waist with both hands, sinking his mouth onto hers, pulling her to meet the weight of his torso. She quickly challenged the rough kiss, catching his lower lip between her teeth and biting. The sting of it cleared his senses; he wasn't capable of humiliating her, not even to make a point.

Jerking his head back, he looked down at her narrowed eyes and gritted teeth. The ragged cadence of her breath roared in his ears. He lowered his mouth to hers again, slower, softer, calculating. It wasn't a surrender, but she wouldn't know that.

Her heart beat wildly against his ribs; her lips were tight and unforgiving, but her hands faltered, then rose to his shoulders, digging into them. The taste of her mouth shot through him. He touched her teeth with his tongue, then dragged gently at her lips. He felt her first, tiny concession, as they pursed a fraction, searching.

Losing himself in that pursuit, he coaxed her more, barely touching his mouth to hers for a moment, then sealing it, nudging her with almost imperceptible movements of his jaw. Her heat rushed into him, a backwash of intensity, building, returning, surging outward again. A silent sigh went through her body, and her fingers spread on his arms, feathering across the fevered skin.

Lily felt her anger and humiliation changing to astonishment. His seductive power could erase everything. The surrender worked both ways; he was apologizing—that must be it, because he was suddenly so gentle. The deep, drugging force of his mouth traveled into her blood like the pulse of a drum. His smoky male scent invaded her; the careful thrusting of his tongue stroked chords of agreement inside her, and a kind of exquisite lethargy radiated from it.

One of his hands smoothed upward, catching her breast. There was the first thrill of fingers other than her own stroking the hot skin, moving in maddeningly small degrees to the nipple, the coarse pad of his thumb scrubbing that peak. And the shudder of his breath in reaction to touching her.

This was too much to think about at once. His leg, a delicious heaviness on her thighs. The moistness on his skin, and hers. The progression of his hand to her other breast, then down the center of her stomach, riding the slight arching of her body. His fingers slid lower, flooded her with a path of heat, pushed into the damp, curly hair between her thighs. Her thoughts focused like a beam of light on them. Distracted pleasures converged on a single small destination.

She rolled against the pressure of his fingers, urging them, showing him with the greed of her kisses that she wanted more. And that she wanted to please him, in return. Her hands slid to his face, touching it gently, telling him she'd never doubted that he was still what he'd always been to her—special, someone to cherish.

Abruptly he took everything away—his mouth, his hand, the weight of his chest and belly, the clamp of his leg. Her eyes flew open, and she watched him sit up. His expression was carved in hard angles, his mouth set in judgment.

Without looking at her or speaking a word, he snatched a packet from the box crushed between them on the mattress, ripped it open, and fitted the filmy sheath over his erection. Chills scattered over her skin, trust fled again, muscles tightened into a shield. His tenderness had been a tactic, not an apology.

He rolled toward her and rose over her—long, powerful arms stabbing down on either side of her shoulders, his knees spreading hers. With the face of a tyrant he loomed over her, a large-shouldered male animal no longer cloaked in fantasy.

"Say 'Stop,'" he ordered, his voice lower than a whisper, strutted with emotions she couldn't analyze.

"No." Her legs flexed, anxious to press inward and keep him out; she willed them apart and drew her knees up slightly. "Hell, no. You come here." She hesitated. "Please."

"You don't want me like this. You don't want me anymore. Admit it."

"I want you," she retorted. "You owe me."

He said something indecipherable but obscene just by the sound of it, then levered himself into her gently. Still, it was like a wedge driving inch by inch into living wood. Her vision clouded. A willow could feel its fibers ripping, she was certain. The wedge stabbed deeper. Her mind was glazed with the image of the tormented willow. She heard it moan with pain and betrayal, felt it shivering violently.

But she was the willow.

He flexed into her again, but the pressure was collapsing, softening, then slipping away. His head and shoulders sagged; the fierce, unpliable pillar of his back relaxed. Her mind cleared; sight returned. She was looking up into Artemas's tortured eyes. He raised a fist and slammed it into the mattress. Sinking back on his knees, his chest heaving, he gave her a look of weary defeat.

Lily felt as if her lungs were flattened. She tried to take a deep breath, but it hinged on what he would do next. He lay down beside her, on his back. The mattress was too narrow for privacy; they were joined from shoulder to hip. Lily darted a glance at him. He stared upward, his face, in profile, carved with unhappiness. He drew short, sharp breaths. Intuition too vague to define made her turn on her side and ease her cheek against his shoulder. His hand moved against hers; their fingers intertwined.

She trembled with sympathy as he brought her hand to his chest and continued to hold it. The muscles convulsed under her fingertips. "My God, Lily." Slowly he turned his head to look at her. Bittersweet. Troubled. Resigned. "*Lily,*" he said again, and this time it was a caress. They lay still, finally seeing each other for the first time, the battle lost on both sides.

"Could we start over?" she asked. "Could we pretend— just tonight—that nothing else matters, and not talk about anything except what's happening right now?"

"It would be better if you left."

She clamped her lips together against an urge to plead with him, squeezed his hand tightly, released it, and sat up, facing forward. Her bare back felt like a freshly turned field exposed to the sun. She knew his eyes were on her.

Artemas couldn't breathe. *Let her go. It's for her sake, not yours.*

Lily slid to the end of the mattress and started to rise. There was a soft rustle as he lurched upright. His hand latched on her arm from behind. "Don't," he told her hoarsely. "Don't go."

Tears slid down her cheeks. She twisted around on her knees and met his outstretched hands, sank into his embrace, and wrapped her arms around his neck. Bending her head beside his, she held him tightly. He pressed his face into the crook of her neck. His fingers dug into her back, quivering. She whispered his name.

Time had no meaning. Hours might be passing, drugged with the slow progression of caresses. They eased down on the mattress, facing each other, kissing, exploring, breathing in each other's low sighs, sounds like a cat's purr or a wordless plea. The fearful pleasure she'd felt before was gone; now it was urgent and trusting. He touched her with so much tenderness that everything before was erased; she was bathed in his caring.

His erection was no longer a weapon; it pulsed with welcome inside her awkward, eager hand. He showed her how to remove the sheath over it, and when, marveling at the silky skin, she naively scrubbed the tip too hard, he gave a sharp, gallant laugh as he flinched.

She frantically curled herself over him and kissed it. He

flinched again but not with discomfort, and it was the most natural thing in the world to taste him with her tongue. The musky flavor excited her, and she closed her lips around him, just a bit of him, every nerve tuned to his reaction. His body flexed and rose; she thrilled at the way he wanted more.

"Too much," he whispered, sinking one hand into her hair and the other beneath her chin. He guided her upward again, held her face between his hot palms, and kissed her deeply. "Too good. I'll show you why."

He rolled her onto her back with exquisite roughness and dropped quick, sucking kisses over her breasts, feeding on them, as she gasped and arched her back. His attention moved to her stomach, then the taut plane of her belly, as his hands curved over her legs and eased them apart. Suddenly the fevered core of her womanhood was sealed to his mouth, and unimaginable pleasure streaked through her blood. She cried out, latching her hands in his dark hair, struggling, exploding.

Coarse and elegant demand opened her, an instinctive knowledge that she needed him to fill her from the inside out. She lunged at him as he lifted his head, catching his mouth with hers and petting him wildly with her hands. They fell back together, bending and curving like one body. "This time it won't hurt," she said.

"I won't let it," he promised, his voice aching with tenderness. His hands shook as he prepared himself again; this time she was all over him, kissing his chest, pulling him down to her, winding her legs around him.

He swept both arms under her. His face over hers, his eyes holding her gaze, he eased his hips forward. It was a smooth entry, and he measured it slowly, scrutinizing her expression for any sign of pain or fear. There was none.

The rhythm didn't control them at first. It was restrained, testing. He knew what he expected to feel, and she didn't. He seemed to recognize that and experimented for her curiosity's sake—with slow movements, then a fast burst, then halting—nearly motionless, watching her as she carefully flexed upward, gauging the unfamiliar male flesh that connected them so intimately.

"Go on," she whispered, satisfied. He kissed her. "Go on," she said again, holding him tightly, her head falling back, eyes half-shut.

Artemas was caught between lust and concern, grinding into her fiercely, yet always holding back, afraid he'd add too much shock to the newness. But even in the dim light he read ecstasy in the dark flush on her face, watched her head loll to the side, saw the dazed concentration in her smoldering, half-shut eyes. Her hands clutched at his hips, then went limp, while her body stiffened, shuddering around him, driving him crazy with the tightness, the sight of her, the scent, and finally over the edge with the deep-throated moan that cascaded from her throat. He had never wanted anyone so much, never wanted to please someone so much, and most of all, had never felt that anyone cared so unselfishly about his own pleasure.

He called out something—it wasn't clear to him what, but she gave a soft shout of happiness and took his face between her hands—then all he could think about was being lost inside her and never wanting to leave.

They took a long time getting to the point where words made sense again or seemed necessary.

"What did I say?" he asked finally. His head was pillowed on her breasts, and one arm curved possessively over her thighs. She traced the line of his jaw, his brow, stroking the damp hair back from his temple. "You said, 'I wish, I wish to God.' And then my name."

Her hand lay still on his cheek. He felt the spasm in her breath. Artemas moved upward and took her in his arms. Her eyes bored into him accusingly, then filled with tears. She bowed her head against his. "I hate some things about you," she said in a ragged tone. "And I always will."

He shut his eyes. "I know."

The dreamworld between half-sleep and awareness was filled with sorrow and erotic desperation. They touched

and held each other even like that. The night was almost
gone. She was bending over him, her hands smoothing
over his chest, his nipples, his belly, the hardness that
surged there immediately, then along his thighs, pushing
the quilt aside, moving inside and out on his legs, even to
his feet, then returning along the same path, until her
touch lingered on his sex.

He opened his eyes. Her breasts were silhouetted in the
faint light; her hair hung in a thick screen over one shoulder, shielding her face, her thoughts. She stroked her fingertip over the tiny drop of liquid on him. Artemas rose to
one elbow and reached for her. He pushed her hair aside.

She looked at him. Breathless tension hung in the air.
She put her fingertip to her lips, tasted it. He thought his
chest would explode.

"I wanted a little of your body for keeps," she said.
There was nothing coy about it, nothing deliberately flat-
tering or provocative. She meant what she said.

Nothing he could answer would do justice to her. He
drew the backs of his fingers over her cheek. Tears burned
his eyes. She searched wearily on the mattress, found one
of the packets scattered around their bodies, opened it, fitted it over him. "Like that?" she asked. He nodded.

She knelt over him and guided herself down on top of
it, her eyes squinted shut, concentrating. She was sore.
She'd told him so, some time ago. Artemas clasped her
shoulders and folded her down. She burrowed her face
against his neck and slid her arms under him.

He didn't have to move. The rush was immediate and
involuntary. A soft groan and the swift tightening of their
arms in unison encompassed it. The drowsiness that followed was a sanctuary. Eventually her breathing slowed,
her arms relaxed. He gave way enough to let her slip sideways, lying half on top of him, and he fumbled with the
quilt until he pulled it over her, smoothing the edges,
tucking them around her shoulders. His fingers felt thick
and clumsy with emotion, but they were unable to give
her his message. Spreading them on the side of her neck,

he absorbed the soft throb of her pulse. It drew the heart out of him.

Lily stood by the door, watching him sleep. The room was filling with the silver mist just before dawn. She clutched her T-shirt and panties in a bundle against her stomach. If she let herself hope, she'd lose her mind. She didn't want to spend their last few hours fighting.

Trembling, she held out one hand, palm down, as if she could touch him. She had to hurry and be very quiet, or he'd wake up. *Good-bye* echoed repeatedly in her mind.

She backed out of the room, hunching over, trying to hold the ache inside. Out in the hall she leaned against the cool old paper and plaster of the wall, crying silently. Self-preservation saved her, forced her to move. She slipped away.

He woke to bright sunlight glowing through the thin white curtains on the window beyond the bedstead. She was gone.

Artemas sat up, staring despairingly at the empty space beside him. He strained to listen, praying to hear some sound of her in the house. The silence mocked him.

He jerked his jeans on and his jogging shoes, searched the rooms quickly, upstairs and down, then bolted outside and trotted to the barn. She wasn't in the loft. He'd suspected she wouldn't be, but hadn't wanted to believe it.

His feet leaden, he climbed back down and stood in the pasture, sweeping a dull gaze around the dewy, peaceful morning. Birds sang. The hum of cicadas rose and fell in a chorus. Not searching for her was impossible. He had to say—what? That he could change his life? Or that he would, at least, visit her at college and sleep with her—in secret—whenever he could? God.

He dropped his head in his hands. The rage and frustration she'd shattered last night came roaring back, now clouded with more grief than before.

He walked dully back to the house. As he passed

through the kitchen he saw the sheet of notepaper positioned in the center of the old Formica table, with his shirt folded neatly beside it. His hands were cold with dread as he picked it up.

I won't come back until you leave. You can't find me. Saying good-bye would only hurt us both.

He staggered outside again, the note crumpled in one fist. Turning, he scanned the woods. She was there, watching. He felt it. "I love you, Lily," he shouted, his head thrown back, the words torn from his throat.

Nothing moved, no one answered.

Lily stood among a towering grove of laurels high on the ridge. Her body shook. She made a low mewling sound. The curtain of dark green leaves let her catch only glimpses of him as he left the house for the last time. He stood by the rental car, his eyes searching the hills. He looked defeated.

When he got in the car, her knees buckled, and she sat down, hugging her legs, her head up and eyes shut. The rumble of the car's engine streaked through her. When it finally faded, she said aloud, "I love you too."

Part Two

Family is everything. It defines you—the heart of your spirit, the heritage of your smile, not only the color of your eyes but also how they see the world. You are bound by kinship. You add your own link to the chain, and that's where you strengthen or weaken what you've been blessed—or burdened—with. That's where you use the indefinable quality that belongs to you, alone, the bit of uniqueness you pass on to your children for good or bad, the part of you that will always be separate from those who share your name, your blood, and your past.

Lola Shiner

Fifteen

Almost twelve years had passed since Artemas Colebrook had come to Georgia to visit Lily. Almost twelve years since he'd left Lily heartbroken. Maude wasn't going to miss this opportunity to study the man for herself again. Since the tragedy, he was more dangerous to Lily than ever.

Huddled around the television screen in a darkened room, Maude and her sisters listened carefully for Lily's movements upstairs.

"This is pure trash," Big Sis whispered, stabbing a finger at the television. "If Lily knew we were watching it, she'd be sick."

"Lily's already sick," Maude retorted. "Sick with grief and fear, half-crazy, probably upstairs right now talking to one of Stephen's teddy bears again, telling it how much she misses little Stevie and Richard. We've got to keep track of what's being said about the Colebrooks and her, so we can help ward off more trouble."

Little Sis waved the remote control. "Besides, if she comes down here, we can just switch the channel."

Maude nodded. They traded stoic glances, wise and protective, like owls around a damaged nest, then leaned closer to the television.

The reporter clutched a microphone and looked at her

viewers as though this were serious journalism no matter what the critics said, then continued to intone with lurid emphasis, "The decade of the eighties and the first few years of the nineties were one long *fabulous* success story for the six Colebrook brothers and sisters. They built an empire in industrial ceramics. But are they destined to suffer for their fortune? Has the legacy of the Colebrook *curse* descended once again?"

The camera panned to the Colebrook office building. "The newest chapter in the curse that has plagued the Colebrooks for decades. That's what some are calling the tragedy that ended the lives of a dozen people at this magnificent new office complex in Atlanta. Was it *destiny* that doomed a glittering crowd of several hundred guests in the midst of a gala celebration of this building's opening?" The reporter paused for effect, turning to gaze across brown lawns and winter gardens toward the majestic stone tower.

Snow feathered down, casting the building and grounds in melodramatic patinas of January silver and white. "Many experts called the soaring bridge inside the lobby of this building a *masterpiece* of architecture. Now it's a crumpled *tomb* of steel and concrete—a *Frankenstein* that destroyed even the two men who designed it. Inside the terrible debris rescuers found architect Richard Porter holding the body of his young son. Also among the *crushed* bodies pulled from the rubble was that of blond, beautiful Julia Colebrook, the youngest sister of the powerful and close-knit Colebrook family. Her brother James lies brutally injured in an Atlanta hospital, where doctors are attempting to save his mangled leg."

The scene changed to the memorial service—the Colebrooks leaving a church in New York among a crowd of their employees and the families of the Colebrook executives who'd been killed. Despite dark sunglasses and bodyguards, they seemed vulnerable and exposed to the prying camera, which gravitated to Artemas's harshly set face. He was guiding his sisters and the younger brother, Michael, into a long black limousine.

"Look at the power in him," Little Sis whispered. "The

sexual energy is still there. It's had over ten years to ripen. We have to warn Lily."

Big Sis gave her a scalding stare, then said tartly, "I believe you could wait a little bit to talk about sex and Artemas Colebrook with Lily. Maybe just until the funeral flowers wilt on Richard's grave."

Maude shushed them both. The reporter began narrating. "Artemas Colebrook—a dynamic leader, a very private man, a man fiercely devoted to his family and its corporate *kingdom*. Now, he must confront the *awful* spotlight. Can he save his family from the Colebrook curse?" Taking a deep breath, the woman concluded, "Don't miss our exclusive report on the tragic roller-coaster ride to wealth and power of one of America's most elite families. Tomorrow, on *You Want to Know*."

"Kiss my big pink butt, woman," Maude said, and turned the television off. The three of them sat silently, brooding. Little Sis sighed. "How long ago was it that Artemas's wife died?" She tapped her forehead to dislodge the information.

"About five years ago, I think," Maude replied. "I remember, because Lily got the phone call about it during the middle of Stephen's first birthday party."

Big Sis cocked her head to one side, her eyes as bright as a crow's. "Who called her? Artemas?"

"No, no, that damned Tamberlaine called. He always kept her up on Artemas's doings, whether she wanted him to or not. I'd like to have strangled him, that day."

"What'd Lily do?"

"Well, what could she do? She cried and told Richard a friend's wife had died. Which was all she needed to tell him, as far as it went. Richard, bless his heart, never realized there'd been more than a childhood friendship between Lily and Artemas. It just never occurred to him. Lily never gave him any reason to wonder about it, you know. She told me there was no point worrying him over something that didn't matter anymore." Maude stared at Little Sis. "So why are you bringing it up now?"

Little Sis frowned. "When did Artemas hire Richard and Frank to design the Colebrook Building?"

Maude thought for a moment. "He hired them about two years after his wife died."

"Ah! See? Soon as enough time had passed for folks not to gossip, he put himself right back in Lily's life, even though she was married and had a son."

"Didn't do him any good," Big Sis interjected hotly. "Lily never encouraged him, did she?"

Little Sis slammed the remote control down on a coffee table. "Of course not!"

"Then what are you trying to say?"

"I'm saying that now, *nothing* stands between him and her. You know what's got to happen, don't you? *Fate's* got to happen, that's what."

Maude gaped at her, then said sarcastically, "Nothing stands between them?" She beat a hand on her knee. "A bunch of people are dead, including Richard, and Stephen, and Artemas's sister, and his brother's lying in a hospital with his leg torn up, and there are terrible questions about why that bridge collapsed and who's responsible for it—that's *nothing*?"

With a savvy nod to her less intuitive sisters, and in a tone as profound as a minister's, Little Sis said, "You'll see."

Cold February rain slid down the limousine's windows. The scenery beyond them was washed in gray hues—a low, hovering sky, drab, rolling hills blanketed in groves of wintry silver hardwoods and dull pines, where pockets of elite, upscale subdivisions could be glimpsed among the hills through gated entrances along the two-lane road. Occasionally a private drive curled off through the woods to some large house set on a hill by itself. Lily's house was one of those. Tamberlaine remembered, because he had come to see it not long after she and her husband finished it—she hadn't known he'd visited—so that Artemas could learn how she lived.

Tamberlaine knew the area would have been beautiful and peaceful, given any other time of year and circumstance. The communities in the foothills north of Atlanta's urban sprawl were being carved out of old farmland, and the aura of sequestered privilege mingled with tiny white farmhouses, old pastures, and here and there a dairy barn converted into a swank stable for expensive riding horses.

That was slim consolation for Lily's never getting her family's home back from Hopewell Estes—how often she had tried to persuade the man, Tamberlaine knew, and how diligently Artemas had tried for her. The situation had ended badly, and Estes would probably keep the land for the rest of his life, if only out of bitterness toward Artemas.

He sank back on the car's plush leather seat and tried to ease his mind with the deceptive serenity of its dark, whisper-soft interior. He glanced at Artemas across the way from him, staring with hollow lack of interest out the other window, probably not seeing the landscape at all.

The tailored black overcoat and exquisitely cut black suit, the gleaming black dress shoes and slender Cartier watch, marked a man of immense wealth and power. The set of the face was stamped with grim maturity; the body was heavier but still lean, thicker in the shoulders and chest than a young man's. The dark hair held featherings of gray at the temples, but those had appeared recently, almost overnight. The disgraced and powerless teenager Tamberlaine had met twenty years ago was only a pale memory.

Tamberlaine had been so close to the changes that he hadn't been aware of their accumulation. But all those years had merged in the past few weeks, since the tragedy at the new office complex. Since past and present had collided.

There was nothing youthful or spontaneous about this man he knew so well—as well as a son, Tamberlaine had often thought with affection. When had the change first become noticeable? Ah, that was easy to mark. After the trip to Georgia, twelve years ago. And each year since had added its own shade to the darkening patina.

Not a shedding of integrity or kindness—no, those qualities were still with him. But the ability to laugh, the flash of unfettered enthusiasm, a well of patience for his own failings and those of others—those attributes had dwindled. The marriage to Glenda, Lily's to Richard Porter, Glenda's death, now, what, five years past? And certain sorrows encountered by his brothers and sisters—each had left its mark.

Elizabeth was divorced. Michael's wife had died. Michael's asthma remained as virulent as it had been in childhood, and his grief was a deep, permanent wound. The family worried about him constantly.

Cassandra's obsession with her weight had resulted in a frightening bout with anorexia a few years ago, until Artemas and the others had strong-armed her into therapy. She had traded one obsession for another—a penchant for bedding, mistreating, and casting aside men. Artemas despised her irresponsible behavior but was powerless to prevent it.

Tamberlaine bowed his head, remembering Julia's stint of pure, lazy self-indulgence, and her steely determination to reclaim the family's respect. After graduating from college, she'd run with a pampered, useless crowd of Eurotrash and whining New York socialites, horrifying her siblings with visions of their parents' idle, depraved lives. But she'd redeemed herself with the Colebrook project. Dear God, how hard she had worked to prove herself to Artemas and the others.

He sighed. There were joys to count, also. He wished Artemas recalled them as easily as he could. The brothers and sisters had worked together with such pride and diligence, all proving themselves and earning respect in the family's expanding business interests.

Colebrook International had become what it was today because Artemas had understood the needs of an industrial world. Electronic and automotive components, surgical instruments, foundries for creating brick and tile—all were part of the empire. Crowning that empire was its smallest, but most beautiful, jewel: Colebrook China. Artemas had guaranteed its reputation and its future.

What they had built was rare in corporate America—a

network of expertly managed companies with well-treated employees. The withdrawal of Colebrook International from industrial ceramics involved in military uses had been a cause for celebration.

Though Elizabeth's marriage had failed, she had a pair of beautiful little boys, one now two years old, the other four, both a happy addition to the family. James and Alise had married and were devoted to each other, though James would never admit such maudlin pleasure. He had waited years before proposing to her, clinging to his independence until Alise's wounded patience had forced him to make the right decision.

Artemas and his siblings now shared a fortune. They maintained, either separately or together, a dozen magnificent homes, both here and in Europe. They collected art, endowed charities—Michael and Elizabeth supervised the family's philanthropic ventures—and were widely regarded as having reclaimed the respect their parents and uncle had squandered.

Yet Artemas was still driven by his work. He had few interests outside the family and its businesses. He did not play, or indulge himself. There had been a few women in his life since his wife. Each had been pleasant, intelligent, successful—but not one had been capable of holding his attention for long.

Now, as if some great, heavy doors had finally closed, not even a flicker of light showed through. It was lost—with Julia's death, with James's maimed leg, lost in the family's stark grief, lost in the horrible suspicions and unanswered questions emerging from the destruction at Colebrook's new offices—lost, most of all, in the knowledge that Lily MacKenzie Porter was permanently and irretrievably bound up in the disaster.

"When we arrive at her house," Artemas said slowly, not veering his deadened gaze from its place, "I want to talk to her alone. I brought you with me for appearances' sake, and because you've been the only link between us for so long. Seeing you might make her feel more comfortable. But primarily I want you to keep the others distracted."

Tamberlaine nodded slightly. "I believe I can charm—or at least distract—three aged ladies who, quite possibly, will be more upset about my presence than with the reason for your visit."

"Maude and her sisters are bizarre, perhaps, but not bigoted. You should know—you met them once."

"Not under amicable circumstances. I had the distinct impression they despised me."

"Only because you were there as my representative."

"Then what kind of welcome do you think either of us will receive today—regardless of the fact they're expecting us?"

"The same as I've gotten from the three of them over the past month. Alternately defensive and kind."

"And from Lily?" Tamberlaine asked the question gently. Nonetheless, he saw Artemas's eyes narrow with pain. Deep lines radiated from the corners.

"As usual, she'll answer when she's asked a question," Artemas said finally. "She'll look at me when she has to, and she'll be sure to say something kind about Julia and James. If she thinks I'm hurting too much to keep my control, she'll put her arms around me. Otherwise, she'll simply . . . she won't be there. She'll simply *exist*, with a look in her eyes as if she's holding on to her sanity with every ounce of strength and can barely wait until you and I and everyone else leave her alone."

Artemas steepled an arm atop the window's ledge and bent his head to his fingertips, rubbing the groove of tension between his brows. "The person I knew is . . . some part of her died with her son and husband. She'll never be the same."

Neither will you, Tamberlaine thought sadly. But both Artemas and Lily could heal, given time. Whether the healing might bring them together was another matter. Even their poignant, troubled friendship might not survive

the investigations and accusations looming ahead. The
worst, in some ways, was yet to come.

Tamberlaine cleared his throat. He had been their am-
bassador, intermediary, and counselor for so many years.
He prayed that the skill would not fail him now. "She came
to New York and stood in the background at Julia's funeral,
crying for you and your family," he reminded Artemas.
"Just as you came here, to Atlanta, to stand behind the
crowd at the funeral of her son and husband. The *friendship* you and she have always shared still exists."

Artemas dropped his hand to the window ledge and
resumed staring at the cold, bleak scenery moving them
closer each second to their destination. "Not after today,"
he said. "Not after she learns why I've come to see her."

"Lily? Sweetie, you have to get up. They'll be here any
minute. You don't want them to see you this way."

Get up. Keep moving. Pretend you have the strength. Lily
stirred, moved a hand vaguely, found the matted hair
hanging across her eyes, and pushed it aside. Her arm
brushed the plump pillow she'd drawn to her chest. She
opened her eyes and stared at the pastel ponies and cow-
boys on the pillowcase. She and Richard had planned to
buy Stephen a Shetland in March. Richard had already
marked off half of their ten acres to be fenced. He'd drawn
a blueprint for a small barn. She'd spent hours walking the
land, planning the riding trails.

Looking at the pillowcase became an exercise in fresh
horror. If she didn't force herself to move, she'd stare at it
until sleep blacked out the sight again. "I'm ready," she
lied, pushing herself upright on Stephen's small bed. She
braced her arms, squinted at Stephen's cheerful little bedroom, afraid of what else her grief would lock onto, and
waited for the dulling release to come. It did. She simply
couldn't imagine that any of this was happening, that
Stephen and Richard were gone. She became numb.

Aunt Maude and the sisters were gathered around her.
They looked so old, so worn. They had moved in without
a word—simply showed up with their suitcases a few

hours after the deaths. Even Little Sis, with her bright red sweater and tight jeans, her gray hair hanging in a jaunty braid, seemed to have aged. Big Sis leaned heavily on the lion's-head cane Lily had given her for her birthday a few years ago, frail as a shadow in an oversized blue jumper and print blouse. Aunt Maude's sturdy body had a slight hump at the shoulders, which she tried to conceal with the enormous shoulder pads of a double-breasted gray suit-dress.

But she still mastered her sisters—and now Lily—standing beside the bed with her gray pumps braced apart, holding out an outfit from Lily's closet. It was a dark wool jacket with gold buttons up the front and a slender matching skirt. "Get yourself out of those faded ol' jeans and that wrinkled flannel shirt," she ordered. "And let's get your hair brushed and pulled up."

"Where's Lupa?" Lily looked around frantically. "Where is she? She was right here next to the bed when I lay down."

"Oh, hell, I forgot about her," Little Sis said. "I put her outside to pee about an hour ago."

Lily bounded off the bed and ran downstairs. The gleaming hardwood floors covered in bright braided rugs made no sound under her bare feet. Richard had said a house that creaked was an embarrassment. He'd built their house to last. She darted through a foyer lined with a Shaker sideboard and soft watercolors of mountain landscapes on the walls, including a picture of her old farm, which she'd hired an artist to paint from photographs. Out on a wide front porch she looked around desperately. There was no big, funny-looking yellow dog parked near the heavy rocking chairs, no muddy paw prints on the welcome mat.

She darted back inside and ran through a large den, scraped one foot on the hearth's edge of the soaring field-stone fireplace there, and ran to the expanse of sliding glass doors that looked out on a large wooden deck surrounded by wintry gardens and lawn and huge old oaks, even now a pretty landscape. She'd designed it to please the eye at any time of year.

She shoved one of the glass doors open and bolted onto the deck. Icy rain pelted her. "Lupa!" The big, bedraggled dog crawled from under the deck, crept up the short flight of steps to the garden path, and wagged her bushy golden tail wistfully. Lily sat down on the steps and put her arms around the dog's wet neck. "Lupa, I'm sorry, I'm sorry. Why didn't you go around to the front porch?"

The mixed breed flattened her ears despondently and huddled inside Lily's embrace, burrowing her head under Lily's chin. No one could make Lily believe that Stephen's dog wasn't grieving. Lily rested her cheek on the dog's head and sheltered it from the rain. They sat there miserably, the rain soaking them.

"He's here," Aunt Maude called from the open door. "Lily, he's driving up *right now*. In a big black limousine. Please come inside."

Lily raised a hand in dismissal, then slid it back around Lupa's neck.

Eventually, through a haze, she heard sounds behind her—heavy, leaden footsteps advancing on the wood, then halting. Lupa dragged her head up and laid it across Lily's shoulder, woofing softly. Lily let go of her and twisted around, rain streaming into her eyes. She rubbed the back of one hand over them.

Artemas looked down at her. The one emotion that flashed through her mind was sympathy. His strong features were contorted in dismay and sorrow. A black overcoat hung open over his suit, and the rain was already slicking his hair. She had to go back inside, if only for his sake.

His expression stiffened. He held out a hand. She took it, and he pulled her up. His pain was hers; it radiated from the gentleness of his hand and the way he squeezed hers. She put her arms around him for a moment, and he shivered. His arms went around her tightly. They held each other without speaking, and she laid her head on his shoulder. His jaw was hard and warm against the back of her neck. For that brief moment, the comfort obliterated everything else.

"No need for us both to stand here in the rain," she said wearily, and stepped back. "Lupa, come on." The dog trailed them inside.

Tamberlaine stood in the room's center, frowning. Maude and Big Sis waited beside him. All three looked awkward and pitying. Little Sis burst into the den carrying two large towels. "Here." She draped a towel across Lily's hair and handed the other to Artemas. He dried his face and hands, then dropped the towel on the hearth. Little Sis held out her hands and nodded toward his damp overcoat. He shrugged it off and folded it in half before handing it to her, every movement precise and concentrated.

Lily was dimly aware of dabbing one end of the towel to her face as she went to Tamberlaine. He took her outstretched hand in both of his, and his face softened. Behind her, Artemas spoke brusquely, "I'll wait here while Lily changes into some dry clothes."

"I don't need to," Lily said. She dried her face and let the towel fall around her shoulders, then went to a fat blue sofa and sat down. Lupa stretched out on a rug beside her.

As if on cue, Tamberlaine turned to Maude and the sisters. "I would certainly appreciate a cup of hot tea."

"We can do better than that," Maude answered. She shot a wary look at Artemas. "We suspected we'd be extra baggage." Little Sis linked an arm through Tamberlaine's. "Come with us. We figured you for a cognac man."

"How astute. Thank you." He and the trio left the den. Artemas went after them and pulled its tall double doors closed. The only sound was rain pelting lightly on one of the wide skylights. The den, with its high, beamed ceilings and oversized couches, its heavy pottery lamps and bookcases, and the big-screened television in one corner, suddenly seemed too small for his presence.

Lily regarded him with dull lethargy. He stood with his back to her, his large hands still clasped on the doors' ornately carved wooden handles. "I always wondered what your house looked like," he said. "It's what I pictured—warm, filled with unique touches."

She found her voice. It was a raw scrape of sound. "Richard loved woodworking. He has . . . had . . . there's a wonderful workshop out back. He made those doors."

Artemas drew his hands off them. He turned and stood, motionless, his eyes troubled. His gaunt face belied the well-kept elegance of his clothes. Lily looked away from the sight. Dull pain stabbed at her throat. She looked like hell, but so did he.

"I wish I could put this conversation off," he told her. "I wish it never had to be. Certainly not this soon."

"What?" She felt distracted. Her mind wandered to Stephen's bedroom upstairs, to her and Richard's bedroom, the guest rooms, the downstairs with its den and large kitchen and dining room, and off the den, the large office she and Richard had shared. Her mind took in the whole house in the space of a few seconds. It was empty. She was empty, a mother with no child to hold. Artemas's sister was dead, his brother perhaps crippled for life. And there were questions about the Colebrook Building. She had known they'd come.

He looked defeated by her blank silence. "We have to talk about what happened, and why it happened." His voice was leaden, and his expression had become a mask of restraint.

"Some kind of accident. I don't know." Lily drew the towel into her lap, watching water drip from the curly strands of hair matted to her breasts. "I've asked myself questions. Every day, every night. I've screamed them at the walls in the shower, so Aunt Maude and the sisters can't hear. I don't know."

"Then you and I have been doing the same thing."

"The lawyers—Richard and Frank's lawyers—tried to ask me. They gave up. I have to call them when I can make sense. And there are investigators. The state's people. All of them. I have to talk with them."

"You have to talk to me first."

She raised her head, shocked by the command in his

voice. There was enough of her old self left to feel wary. And more coming to the surface. But he had been devastated too. She had to help him learn who'd done this godawful thing. If there was anyone to blame. "How is James?" she asked finally.

"There'll be another surgery on his leg tomorrow, to repair more of the muscle and nerve damage. He'll stay in the hospital for several more weeks. The house he and Alise have under construction isn't finished yet."

"And the rest of your family?"

"They're taking it one day at a time. Keeping each other—and James—from thinking too much. They have their homes here. They won't be going back to New York. We've taken two floors at a hotel as a headquarters, for now, until we can find an office building to lease. Most of our people have already moved here. We have to get them situated as quickly as possible."

"You're living at the hotel?"

"Yes."

"What about Blue Willow?"

"I still plan to restore it. Eventually."

She leaned back in the chair and let her head rest on the hard rim. "Everything you worked for, your dream—"

"My family is torn apart. That's my main concern." He paused, his face working silently, the large gray eyes searing her. "I'll never stop missing my sister, but Lily, your son—I can only try to imagine how it must feel to lose a child."

"I feel as if everything inside me has been cut out and burned." She heard her voice from a distance. It was dispassionate. An observer's calm tone. "And all that's left is this shell"—she gestured toward her body then laid her hands on the chair's arms—"this shell that walks around pretending to be alive. If I didn't need to find out what happened that night, I wouldn't have any reason to pretend. I'd put the muzzle of my father's old forty-five in my mouth and pull the trigger."

He exploded, making some furious, guttural sound and almost running across the room to her. He snatched her

out of the chair by her shoulders. Her bare feet strove for
a landing, sliding off the toes of his shoes. She gripped his
jacket and stared at him, barely keeping her balance. His
eyes glittered wildly. "Don't you *ever* think of doing that,"
he said between clenched teeth. "Goddammit, *swear* to me
that you won't. *Swear* it."

"I said *if* I didn't have a reason to go on. I *do*. I'm not
a coward—"

"I said *swear* it. Swear it on Stephen's soul." She
gasped. "Swear that you won't hurt yourself," he said
again, almost shaking her. "If I can survive, by God, you
can too."

"I swear. I promise. *Let me go.*"

Breathing heavily, he lowered her and released her
arms. "I'll give you plenty of reasons to want to live and
fight back," he said, the words low and fierce. He turned
and walked away, ramming his hands through his hair. He
took a deep, shuddering breath and dropped his hands to
his side. Lily looked at him in horror. What he was going
through equaled everything she felt. There were so many
old ties between them, so much that couldn't be described
or considered. Or denied. So much love.

She groaned and covered her face. *Richard, Richard, I
didn't mean to think that. I'll never think it again. It was over
before I met you. Forgive me.* Lily turned blindly and went
to the glass doors. Hugging herself hard, she forced herself
to concentrate on the future. She had to begin dealing with
her grief, subverting it, if only enough to do what had to
be done. Artemas's words suddenly snapped into focus. *I'll
give you plenty of reasons to live and fight back.* A chill
crawled up her spine. Fight back?

She pivoted to face Artemas. Her fingers dug into her
arms. She wanted to shield herself against the stark new
thoughts rising in her mind. "Did you come here to tell me
that my husband and his partner are accused of doing
something wrong?"

The look in Artemas's eyes froze her blood. "They were
the architects. They designed the building. They designed
the bridge. They worked closely with the contractor.

Everyone who had anything to do with the design and construction is being investigated."

Fury clawed at her throat. *Steady, now. Don't overreact. He's only stating the obvious. He has to do that.* "I'm not a fool," she said slowly. "I know the investigators have to study Richard and Frank's design of the bridge—that they wouldn't be doing their job if they didn't check every detail." She returned Artemas's relentless gaze. "But I also know that they won't find any mistakes."

His voice was low, anguished. "How can you be so sure of that, Lily?"

"Because there was only one thing Richard loved as much as he loved Stephen and me. His work. He lived for it. His pride in it was *everything*." Cold threads of panic were winding around her chest. How could Artemas suggest Richard's architectural firm might be at fault? "Do you think he would have allowed Stephen on that bridge if he thought it was dangerous? Do you think he would have let *anyone* go up there? That he would have gone up himself?"

"If he thought the risk were slight. If he and Frank Stockman miscalculated."

"No. *No.* You're saying they knew the bridge might not have been one hundred percent safe." Trembling with a sense of betrayal—she was stunned that Artemas could be pushing this angle—she realized her hands were pressed to her throat. The pulse there slammed against her fingertips. "Don't do this. Don't make ludicrous accusations. I understand your need to blame someone. Revenge, it's"—her hands formed into fists—"it's what I want too. But Richard isn't responsible. Never."

He shut his eyes. Without moving or speaking, he radiated deadly energy, a maelstrom of conflicting emotions. When he looked at her again, there was a kind of despondency in his eyes, but also that lethal drive. "I want experts of my own to look at every document. Every blueprint. Every materials specification. It may take months, but eventually we'll know what happened. But more important is *why*." He paused. Then, softly: "Richard was the structural engineer—he calculated the stress loads, designed the steel frame—"

"I know what my husband's work involved. And I know how meticulous he was about it."

"His professional seal is on every blueprint, every materials specification. Lily, if we discover that the failure came from Richard's calculations, I have to find out whether it was an honest mistake—or deliberate."

Her knees went weak. Nausea twisted her stomach. "You are talking about a man," she said between gritted teeth, "who had carpenters rebuild an entire wall of this house because it was one inch off vertical."

Artemas walked over to her—stood beside her, not looking at her, his hands clasped behind his back. The gray light filtering through the rain and the glass doors cast his face in ashen hues, like stone. "There is the possibility that Richard and his partner collaborated with the contractor to save money, or time."

"That makes no sense! The Colebrook project was a godsend to Richard. He and Frank staked their reputations on it! It meant everything—national respect, big clients, awards. They slaved over it for *the past three years*." She leaned toward him, grasping his shoulder fiercely. "He and Frank wouldn't have risked people's lives to save a few dollars on a hundred-million-dollar project."

"Unless they believed the bridge would be safe, regardless. If they gambled—and lost."

The pulse roared in Lily's ears. She felt the clammy, cold prickle of shock on her cheeks, and black shadows floated across her vision. But she would not show weakness before this man. She remembered all too well the cost of being vulnerable to him. She made her way to a couch as calmly as she could and sat down. There must be other answers to this horror. Ones she hadn't had the time or the presence of mind to consider. Only one thing mattered right now—Artemas was saying Richard might be responsible for a tragedy that had taken the lives of a dozen people, including their son's. A tragedy that marred the Colebrook name. All that had ever been paramount to

Artemas was rebuilding that name. All he cared about now was finding some way to protect that name and his family, even if it meant destroying everything she believed in.

"I want you to tell me if you knew or suspected that anything strange was going on," Artemas continued in the same, deadened tone. "Anything you can remember—comments Richard made, any odd behavior on his part, anything at all."

Her voice finally escaped from the knot of despair in her chest. "I won't help you make a scapegoat out of my husband. If you think I'll ever help you do that, you don't know me at all."

A muscle popped in his cheek. "My sister is dead. My brother will walk with a limp the rest of his life. Several executives from companies owned by Colebrook International were killed. For God's sake, Lily, so many lives were lost—and so many people will have to live with that grief. They deserve justice. My family and I deserve it. You're caught in the middle, and you have to think about what's fair, what's decent—no matter how hard it is to accept the truth. There's nothing I can do to protect you."

"I've never needed your protection. I've proved that."

"Lily, your landscaping business is tied to this. You worked on this project from the beginning."

"Are you forgetting why? That I didn't want any part of it—I didn't want Richard's firm to be part of it. That you coerced me."

"Coerced?" His face, lined with strain, became even more drawn. "I gave a struggling pair of young architects an opportunity no one else would have given them, and a talented landscape designer the chance to prove herself."

"You insinuated yourself into our lives, and I couldn't even tell Richard why. I couldn't hurt his pride. You knew that."

His shoulders slumped a little. "There's no point in arguing about my motives now."

"You're right," she said, her tone condemning. "Because I understood them a long time ago. You're capable of being ruthless to get what you want."

"I came here to ask you for access to Richard's personal files. I've been told he did most of his drafting at home. I want you to let my people go through Richard's files."

She stared at him. Her mind was hollow, except for one thought. *He wants to punish me for marrying Richard. He wants to shame me for having a child with Richard. He wants me to beg him for forgiveness.* "I chose my loyalties a long time ago," she said evenly, "and I won't desert them now."

"They'll ruin you. And if you don't cooperate with me, there won't be a damned thing I can do to stop it."

"So you're saying you have the power to save me?" She put her head in her hands. "If you had stayed out of my life, my son would be alive. My son is dead because of you."

It was as if all the room's light had been absorbed in his silence. When he finally spoke, his voice was a bare whisper, raw and stunned. "Your son is dead because of *Richard*. My sister is dead because of him. My brother is maimed. I'm going to prove that to you, even if you hate me for the rest of your life."

She watched him walk swiftly to the doors Richard had built with such loving care. The heavy wooden panels gave rough, protesting groans as they slammed into the walls adjacent to them. He left without a backward glance, his posture brutally erect. The doors closed behind him gingerly, as if bruised.

They gathered in the hall outside James's hospital room. The hall had the quiet, empty feel of evening, though bright, fluorescent lights played harshly on the white walls. Visitors' hours were coming to an end soon. Nurses worked silently at their station. The low murmur of a television came from the open door of a room across the way.

Michael pulled the door to James's room nearly closed. The hospital reminded him too much of the week he'd spent by his wife's side, watching her fade under the hideous spell of the aneurysm in her brain. He felt the same stark defensiveness as now. It wasn't possible that such a joyous, vigorous life could hinge on the workings of a tiny artery. It wasn't possible that his dynamic brother was trussed up by slings and bandages and humiliating tubes, in the bed beyond this door.

Cass leaned against a wall, her face bleak, her slender hands lying unfurled along the sides of her tan silk slacks. Several coffee stains dotted the white angora sweater she wore. Elizabeth wavered in place, her body so leaden with fatigue that the shoulders of her suit-dress seemed to be holding her up. She put an arm around Alise's shoulders, and Alise wearily tilted her head against her sister-in-law's. Alise held a clenched hand to her stomach. Michael noticed that blood had speckled the ivory blouse she wore. He touched her hand. She looked at it wistfully, then tucked a square of bloodstained gauze into a pocket of her long skirt. She had kept it when the nurses were changing one of the bandages on James's leg.

"I can't understand why Artemas isn't here yet," Elizabeth said. "If he doesn't get here soon, he won't get to talk to James again until after surgery tomorrow."

Cass stirred, brushed broken fingernails across lips chapped from being chewed constantly, and said hoarsely, "I remember Tamberlaine saying they might be late. I think they were going almost an hour's drive from here. Someplace in the suburbs north of the city."

Alise sighed. "Why did Artemas feel he had to see her *today*?"

"She's an old friend," Michael said. "He didn't want her to hear the news from one of her attorneys."

Cass's mouth curled in dismay. "An old friend," she echoed, acid in her tone. "Who probably knew that her husband and his cronies were screwing us over. Hell, she was even in charge of the landscaping. She had to know what they were up to."

"Not necessarily," Michael said. "Artemas doesn't think so."

"Does it matter?" Cass shot back. "Anyone connected to those bastards deserves to suffer. I say she's guilty by association. She was married to Porter. She knew what he was capable of."

"We don't know who did what yet," Elizabeth reminded her.

"Yes, but as soon as Oliver Grant caves in and talks, we will. If I hear his lawyers say 'Our client followed the architects' instructions' one more time, I'll strangle the S.O.B."

Alise pressed two fingers to the bridge of her nose. Her face was as pale as the walls. "I don't know who to hate."

"You will. We all will," Cass promised.

Michael searched the front pockets of his dark trousers, found the bronchial inhaler he always carried, and rolled it between his fingers like a worry stone. His chest felt tight, as if the soft cotton polo shirt were binding it. Dammit, he always had to deal with his asthma when he was upset, but he would deny it as long as he could. "Whether Grant talks or not, the facts will come out. If he and the architects were willing to undercut construction standards to save money, we'll know it, as soon as the investigators dig into all the invoices and work schedules."

"But *why* would they have been so desperate?" Elizabeth asked. "Couldn't they have just told Julia that the project would run over budget? There's no evidence that any money was embezzled. They weren't diverting the construction accounts. Perhaps they simply miscalculated the cost to complete the building. That happens all the time."

"Or they were sloppy and extravagant in managing the budget, then had to cover it," Cass answered.

"No, Julia was obsessed with tracking every expense. She'd have known if they were running over budget in some areas."

Michael felt grief pulling at the corners of his eyes. He tried to smile, but winced. "She always bragged about that. She could recite the per-unit cost of everything from the doorknobs to the filters in the air-conditioning system. And she knew labor costs to the penny. For each job title. One time she told me what the electricians were paid per hour, then whipped open that leather binder she always carried and pointed to her notes to prove it."

Elizabeth gave a painful little laugh. "She said she'd show us that she could bring even the Taj Mahal in on time and on budget."

Cass straightened ominously. "She was wonderful, and they killed her. And that bitch Artemas calls his *friend* is part of it."

Silence descended. Finally Michael said, "Our brother won't condemn an innocent person. But if she's not innocent, he won't hesitate to make her regret it."

"I know that," Cass told him, the fury fading from her eyes. Michael put one long arm around her and gave her a hug. Elizabeth and Alise moved into the circle. The four of them stood together, linked in faith.

An elevator door opened at the end of the hall. They gratefully watched Artemas stride toward them. He frowned at their huddle. "Has something happened with—"

"No, he's fine," Elizabeth said quickly. "We were just letting him rest a minute while we waited for you."

Artemas studied the weary, ragged-looking group protectively. Sometimes he had to remind himself that they were no longer children, nor he their surrogate parent. Michael and Elizabeth and Alise were thirty-one years old, Cass, thirty-three. He wanted to tell them that he felt broken inside, that today he'd lost more than they could imagine. But how could they understand? They only knew bits and pieces of the Mackenzie-Colebrook history, only that he had been planning to begin restoring the old estate at Blue Willow as part of the corporate move to Atlanta, only that Lily and he had been casual, distant friends over the years.

"How did your meeting with Lily Porter go?" Michael asked.

Artemas shook his head. "Badly." Later he would have to relay the important points to them. God help him, there might be no way to prevent them from hating

Lily and wanting to punish her. His eyes felt hollow and grainy. His throat was raw. But he had a role to play here, and he would not let them down. He never had. He cleared his throat and said brusquely, "Let's go see James."

Sixteen

The office she and Richard had shared was a large, handsome, comfortably folksy room of oak walls and muted colors. Big windows fronted the azalea groves outside. Soft print drapes were drawn over them now, keeping out the cold black night. The room was cast in shadows from the lamps.

It felt like a prison.

Lily sat on the floor, with file folders stacked around her and notepads spilling onto the thick beige carpet. Perspiration trickled between her breasts and down her armpits. The ink pen couched in a fold of her sweatshirt was leaking a dark blue blot onto the gray material. As she scanned yet another page from the files, she brushed the pen aside heedlessly. It began staining the carpet.

Her energy was devoted to searching for any clue, any salvation.

Two of the architectural interns who had worked for Richard and Frank had crammed an extra chair in front of the computer on Richard's desk. Side by side, their eyes bloodshot and faces strained, their shirtsleeves rolled up, they peered in tandem at the screen, scanning section after section of blueprints on the CAD system. The firm's comptroller, a prim-mouthed, middle-aged woman who looked

stern even in a blue jogging suit, sat at a table with folders
from Richard's file cabinets spread before her. She bent low
over them, pursing her small mouth and occasionally
pushing a pair of black reading glasses up the narrow
bridge of her nose. The firm's chief attorney was sprawled
on a couch in one corner, reading copies of correspondence Richard had kept at home.

"I'll bring another pot of coffee," Little Sis said from the
doorway. She didn't mind everyone seeing her in her plaid
nightshirt and fuzzy slippers.

Lily shook her head dully. "No, go on to bed. Please.
Maude and Big Sis already have."

"You all need some sleep too. 'Specially *you.*" She
frowned at Lily.

The thought of confronting the bedroom filled with
Richard's clothes and other personal items, and the king-
sized bed they had shared, or of having to walk past
Stephen's room to get to it, made a dry cavern behind Lily's
eyes. "I can't. I'm sending everybody else home soon, but
I can't sleep."

Little Sis grumbled and disappeared back into the den,
her fuzzies scuffing aggressively on the wooden floor.

"There's nothing new here," one of the interns said,
rubbing his eyes. The other young man pushed a key, and
the computer monitor went dark. "No changes in specifications, no amended drawings for the bridge. Just the original blueprints."

Lily looked at the pair with weary bewilderment.
"Richard kept copies of everything. Drawings, notes, letters. So he wouldn't be inconvenienced when he worked at
home."

The attorney, a large gray-haired man whose reputation
for brutal honesty had always impressed her, steepled his
fingertips under his chin and leaned forward, lost in
thought. "So it's possible that the design work on the
bridge—and any changes made to the design later—was
done at the firm's offices and not here."

She said quickly and firmly, "Marcus, he did *not* alter
the design, and he wouldn't have let Frank do it, either,

not to cut construction costs. Never. Don't even suggest that he might have."

Marcus sighed. "Let's look at what we know for certain. Frank and Richard had a half-dozen other clients—other projects underway—besides the Colebrook Building. Frank concentrated on the aesthetics. Richard was primarily involved in structural analysis."

She nodded. "Frank was the artist."

One of the interns added, "I've seen him spend hours debating the shape of the bricks to be used in a facade. And when he talked about the bridge in the atrium of the Colebrook Building, he said he wanted a masterpiece. Something so graceful it seemed to defy gravity."

"It *was* a masterpiece," the other intern said. "And there was no sacrifice of structural integrity in the design. Richard reinforced every crucial stress point by fifty percent over maximum load. We sat in on the discussions he had with Frank about it. There were a lot of them."

"But those specs must have been changed at some point," Marcus noted. "When? And why weren't any of the interns aware of it?"

"We were assigned to other projects. There was a lot going on. The recognition the firm got from the Colebrook Building kept bringing in new clients."

Lily bit her lip until it throbbed. All the hopes, all the plans for expansion—destroyed, along with her husband, her son, and all those other lives. Last fall the firm had moved from a suite of rented offices into its own building, a beautiful two-story complex Frank and Richard had designed, with space for the additional staff they had hired.

"I'm certain Richard didn't change the bridge specifications," she said abruptly. "If he had, the revised blueprints would be here on his CAD system."

Marcus stared at her intently. "But that suggests Frank could have changed them without Richard's knowledge." He glanced at the interns. "Would that have been possible?"

They traded speculative looks. "Yeah," one said. "But there was no good reason for it."

Lily felt as if the blood were draining from her head. Dizzy, she took a shallow breath and rubbed her temples. Could Frank have done something behind Richard's back?

"We may never know exactly what happened," Marcus reminded them. "Unfortunately, that means we may never be able to conclusively clear the firm from liability."

Lily stifled a moan of despair. They had reached a dead end.

The comptroller, Mrs. Lacey, closed a file and removed her glasses. Lily had never liked the woman, though she was very good at her job. There was something self-righteous about her. Frank and Richard had hired her from the established firm they'd worked for after graduating from college, and the first time she and Lily met, Mrs. Lacey told her it was God's will that they hire her to work for them when they started their own firm. Nothing to do with pay raises.

"We must face the possibility of scandal and have the courage to place the blame where it belongs," Mrs. Lacey said now. "Pride goeth before a fall, and as much as I respected Frank and Richard, they were sinfully proud men."

Lily got up slowly, went to the table where Mrs. Lacey sat, retrieved the woman's stern little purse from the floor, and set it in front of her. Bending down so that she was on the same level as Mrs. Lacey's startled, rebuking eyes, she said, "Get out of my house and don't come back."

Mrs. Lacey gasped. "Mrs. Porter, you're not being rational. *Really*—"

"*Out*," Lily commanded, and slung the purse. It thudded against the doorframe.

"Easy now," Marcus said quickly, leaping up and coming to Lily. He clamped a hand on her shoulder.

Lily leaned closer to Mrs. Lacey. The woman's eyes flickered with fear. "Richard was good to you. He was good to everyone. And the least you can do is believe in his innocence—and Frank's." Lily's voice shook with violence. She raised her head and stared at Marcus. "And you too." Then the interns. "All of you."

When she was disconnected from her pain, she reacted

with plodding determination—hypnotized by any chore that crossed her path. But when something provoked a fresh wave of agony, she lashed out recklessly. Suddenly she wanted to grab Mrs. Lacey by her short brown hair and drag her out of the chair. "Don't preach *sin* to me," Lily told her. "You're just worried that somebody'll accuse *you* of something."

"Lily, calm down," Marcus interjected. "No one's trying to accuse Richard. We're trying to get the facts."

Mrs. Lacey sniffed. "But *I* won't allow myself to be coerced into ignoring my suspicions."

Lily slammed a fist on the table. Mrs. Lacey bolted, barely pausing to snatch her coat from the back of the chair and her purse from the floor. She whirled around, backing from the office, her pallid face contorted with fear and disdain. "I have my own reputation to think of!"

Lily started around the table. Marcus grabbed her by one arm. "*Leave,*" he told Mrs. Lacey. She spun on her heels and hurried off. Lily struggled to get free of the attorney's grip. "Lily, she's the least of our worries," he said. His voice penetrated her fury. Lily sank down in her vacant chair and stared grimly at the file folders there, listening until she heard the front door slam. Awkward silence filled the room.

There was a rattle and crash. Her head jerked toward it. One of the interns scrambled out of his chair. The office's answering machine lay upside down on the floor. "Lily, I'm sorry," he mumbled. "I was thinking of ways to strangle her, and my hand slipped."

"What happened?" Little Sis asked. She had returned at a run, and stood in the doorway, again.

"Chuck just knocked the answering machine off." Lily leaned back in the chair and shut her eyes. The intern replaced the machine next to the phone on Richard's desk. "Don't worry about it. It was broken anyway."

Little Sis shuffled in. "No, it's not." She checked the connections and punched a button. The answering machine whirred smoothly. "It just didn't have a tape in it.

And it had been unplugged. I noticed one day. Got a new tape for it. It works fine."

Lily straightened quickly and opened her eyes. Her mouth went dry with bewilderment and dread. *Richard had said it was broken. When? How long ago?* Her thoughts whirled. She pressed her fingertips to her forehead, dug her nails into the skin. *About a week before he died.*

Why would he lie about it? Had he simply made a mistake? Or had there been recordings of conversations he didn't want her to hear?

"Lily?" Marcus spoke her name worriedly. He was rubbing her shoulders. She felt dazed.

"She needs some rest," Little Sis snapped. "She hasn't slept more than an hour or two a night since Artemas Colebrook came to see her, and that was a week ago."

Lily dragged herself out of the chair and looked at the group. She would hold herself together by sheer willpower until she was alone. "Y'all go on home. And thank you for coming." She turned to Marcus and clasped his hand. "I'm sorry I'm not able to look at this objectively. I'll pack all these files up and send them to you. I know you have to have them."

"Yes," he said gently. "Don't turn anything over to Colebrook. He had no right to ask you to help him."

"He has a right," she said. "But I can't let him turn that into a crusade against Richard."

After Little Sis herded the men outside, Lily shut the office door. She walked numbly to the answering machine and ran her fingers over it. She was seeing Richard, remembering small details the fog of grief had shut away from her until this moment.

How strained and jumpy he'd been at the office ceremonies. How he'd been that way for days—at least a week—beforehand. She shut her eyes and recalled waking up just after dawn once to find him down here, with the door shut, talking on the phone. He'd looked upset when she'd opened the door, and he'd ended the conversation quickly. When she'd asked him what in the world he was doing at that time of morning, he said he'd called Frank to go over last-minute details again. Julia Colebrook was hounding them about some minor problems, as usual.

She remembered him yelling at Stephen the next night for leaving toys scattered on the couch in the den. Richard had never raised his voice to his son before. And when Stephen burst into tears at the shock of it, Richard had hugged him desperately, looking very close to tears himself.

She remembered reaching for Richard in bed, thinking she could break through his bewildering moods that way. He'd shoved her hands aside, then apologized profusely, then gotten out of bed and gone downstairs to the office. She had followed and found him staring at the computer. At the Colebrook blueprints.

All of it could have been ordinary nervousness over the project. But none of it was remotely like the man she had known since college.

Lily paced the office, her hands latched behind her neck. Her legs felt like rubber. Without knowing why, she went to her drafting table near the windows. Bookcases on the wall beside it overflowed with volumes on landscape design and horticulture, with framed photographs of Stephen and Richard. She clutched the edge of a shelf and bent her head to it. From the corner of one eye she glimpsed books jumbled in front of something that was barely visible behind them. Blue and white.

She shoved the books aside and cupped her hands around the Colebrook teapot. It had resided there for years. Richard, who'd known that her family and the Colebrooks had been neighbors, had assumed it was a gift the family had received long before her birth. She had let him believe that small fable, because she never discussed Artemas with anyone, not even Richard.

Shivering, Lily jerked her hands away. She should never have let Artemas return it to her. Touching it filled her with guilt, as if she'd betrayed Richard. She sank down on the couch. She'd married the best man for her, a man who hadn't measured his love for her against his ambitions and loyalty to his family. A man who kept no secrets from her. Had she been wrong? *No.* Her life had unfolded as it should. Shutting her eyes, she remembered.

She was bent over a dresser in the tiny attic bedroom of Aunt Maude's house. In the fall she'd move to a dormitory at college, down in Atlanta. A window fan pushed the sticky afternoon air across her flushed face. Boxes and paper bags were strewn around the room. It seemed impossible that she could fit her things into the cramped dresser and closet. Impossible that she could never go back to her own home. Impossible that she'd lost Artemas.

"Someone's here to see you." Lily pivoted quickly at the sound of Aunt Maude's voice. "From New York."

Her hands closed tightly around a stack of folded white socks. *Artemas. He's come back to get me,* was her first thought, but it died when Aunt Maude shook her head. "Not *him,*" Aunt Maude said, her tone gentle but stern. "He sent someone else. A Mr. Tamberlaine."

Lily bolted past Aunt Maude and went down the short, narrow stairs to the second floor. Squaring her shoulders, she made herself walk slowly down the long stairs to the first floor. Her heart pounded.

Mr. Tamberlaine was as well dressed and courtly looking as she remembered from her trip to New York in March. He didn't see her immediately because he stood with his back to the parlor's arching entranceway. Little Sis was planted in front of him. One of his large, dark hands lay stiffly in her pale ones. She prowled over his palm with a fingertip. Big Sis sat in a chair by the window, chewing tobacco and peering at him avidly.

Lily stopped in the doorway and said nothing, her voice trapped in her throat. She glanced down the front hall. Through the screened door she saw a sedan with an Atlanta taxicab company logo waiting by the curb. Mr. Tamberlaine wasn't going to be here for long then. And she doubted Artemas had sent him here to get her. The last shred of hope melted.

"We never had a colored man dressed in a nice suit as

a guest in this house before," Big Sis announced. "It'd be exciting, except you're here for no good."

"I assure you, that's not the case," Mr. Tamberlaine said. He sounded awkward. Leave it to the sisters to derail his dignity.

"The pain is clear," Little Sis concluded, pointing at his hand and tilting her head back to stare at him with narrowed eyes. "The pain of the African enslavement."

"I come from many generations of New Yorkers," Mr. Tamberlaine answered, his deep voice exasperated. "There hasn't been an African or a slave in the lot since 1798. My grandfather ran one of the largest banks in Harlem."

"You know what I mean. You've suffered the pain of racism. And you've been an outcast as much as a hero to your people, because you've succeeded in the white world."

"Undoubtedly."

"But there's pain in your love life too. Losses. Terrible disappointments. They're all here—you haven't resolved them."

He didn't say anything. Lily watched the rigid line of his back become a little straighter. "I'm divorced," he allowed. "I have a mentally retarded daughter who's been institutionalized since birth."

"Hah! I knew it!"

Lily entered the room. She almost felt sorry for him. He turned when he heard her footsteps. "Miss MacKenzie," he said gravely, and gave a little nod.

"Don't talk to him," Big Sis said, and hawked tobacco juice into a coffee can balanced on her lap. "He's odd. What's his job—chief messenger?"

"I am chief financial officer for Colebrook International," Mr. Tamberlaine intoned grimly.

Lily scrubbed her hair back and exhaled. This was going nowhere, fast. "Would y'all mind if Mr. Tamberlaine and me had some privacy?"

"Yes," Aunt Maude said. She had come downstairs and now commanded the parlor doorway, watching them angrily. She shook her finger at Mr. Tamberlaine. "What do you want, you henchman? What other heartache is Artemas Colebrook sending into Lily's life?"

"Aunt Maude!" Lily flung out her hands and looked from her to the sisters. "Please."

"Shut up, Maudy," Big Sis said. "Leave 'em be. He'll be gone soon enough."

Aunt Maude grunted and stomped down the hall toward the back porch. Little Sis took Big Sis by one arm. As they left the room, Little Sis peered back over one shoulder at Mr. Tamberlaine. "You have kind brown eyes. Better live up to them."

When they were finally alone, Tamberlaine went to a table draped in a crocheted doily and opened a bulky leather tote sitting there. Lily watched in speechless silence as he removed the Colebrook teapot and set it on the table. "He asks that you keep this. It has always been yours, he said."

Her eyes burned. She swallowed hard and said, "Is that the only reason he sent you? To bring that teapot back here?"

"No." Tamberlaine faced her. He was old enough to be her father, and she couldn't help feeling respectful in his presence. The sadness in his face touched a chord. "I wanted to apologize to you. My idea, not his. No matter how good my intentions, I contributed to the loss of your home."

She exhaled wearily and sat down on a delicate little settee, knotting her hands over the bare knees that protruded from baggy cutoff jeans. "He shut himself away, so even a friend couldn't get to him. I don't understand all the reasons why, but it was his doing, not yours."

"You are very gracious. Thank you."

She shrugged, a miserable attempt at nonchalance. "Tell him I'll keep the teapot."

Tamberlaine nodded. "He realizes you may not want to contact him again. I'd be honored if you'd contact me, should you need assistance in any way. Indeed, I'd like to keep abreast of your progress at school and anything else of importance in your life."

"So he can know without having to ask me himself?"

"Yes."

Tamberlaine sat down in a chair near her and said, "He cares deeply about your friendship."

She leveled her intense, searching gaze on his. "Will you tell me about the woman he's . . . involved with?"

"What would you like to know?"

"Her name. How old she is. Things like that."

He told her briefly, only the basics, and each bit of information carved a deep niche. "Is she somebody important?" Lily asked.

"I'm not quite sure how you mean that."

"A society type. Well-to-do."

After Tamberlaine told her Glenda DeWitt's father was a United States senator, Lily didn't need to know anything else. She realized Tamberlaine was watching her carefully. "There's only one thing I want you to do for me," she said. "I want you to promise to call and let me know if he marries her."

"Young lady, if that is your dearest wish, you have my promise."

"It's not my dearest wish." She looked at him. "Not even close."

He bowed his head slightly, an acknowledgment. "Unfortunately, it's the only one I can grant you."

She took the teapot into the backyard and set it on the stone walkway to the old shed that served as a garage. Aunt Maude and her sisters gathered around. They were solemn and fidgety but seemed reluctant to encourage her one way or the other. Lily pulled a loose brick from an edging on a flower bed, knelt in front of the fragile little vessel, and raised the brick over it.

The brick crashed down. Flecks from its red surface scattered on the stone. The teapot was unharmed. She hadn't meant to miss.

Lily dropped the brick and sat back on her heels. She was shaking. Finally she took the teapot and hurled it across the yard. It bounced on the lawn, and the lid flew off. But it didn't break.

"I could get a hammer," Aunt Maude said.

Big Sis hissed at Maude. Little Sis came to Lily and patted her shoulders. "This is a sign, honey. It can't be broken. It's part of your life. Put your memories in it and keep 'em safe."

Lily stumbled to her feet and retrieved the pot and its lid. For the first time tears slipped down her face. She set the lid back in place and started into the house. She would pack the teapot away, use it as a challenge. When she could take it out and look at it again without hating and loving Artemas at the same time, without hurting the way she did now, she'd know she was done with him.

She was sitting at her desk, studying for spring exams, in the small dorm room she shared with a cheerful little music major named Hai, whose family had immigrated from Vietnam during the seventies. When the phone rang, Hai answered it, laid her cello and bow aside, and handed the phone to Lily.

"Tamberlaine calling," the deep voice said, as always. He'd contacted her a half-dozen times over the months, just to chat, he said. As if Mr. Tamberlaine were a chatterer. Her heart stopped every time. As always, she asked immediately, "Got any interesting news?" Both he and she always knew what she meant. "None," he always said, and then she could start breathing again.

But this time he said instead, very kindly, "I made you a promise last spring, Lily."

She clung to the phone, not wanting to hear or believe, feeling the sick, icy slug of panic and the fire of defeat. Until that moment she hadn't realized how much she'd hoped for a miracle. How naive she'd been. "He married her," she said numbly.

"Two days ago." Mr. Tamberlaine paused. Then, even more gently: "May I continue to call you, from time to time?"

"Is that what he wants?" she asked, her voice hollow.

"May I continue to call you?"

In evading her question, he answered it. Artemas was

married now. He would not betray that loyalty, not even in some harmless way, and Mr. Tamberlaine wanted her to know it. She bowed her head. No more false hopes, not anymore. "I'll be here, if you want to call."

He asked if there was anything he could tell her; anything she'd like to know. No, what did the details matter? She said good-bye and put the phone down. Her hands clenched it tightly, then surrendered.

She was done with the past. Done with it.

Hai's head came only to Lily's shoulder, and when Hai pushed her, it was like being bulldozed by a toy truck. "We'll have fun. Go inside," Hai commanded. "They're normal. You'll see. Not like you think fraternity men are."

Lily stood resolutely on the sidewalk beside her Jeep, feeling the pinch of new high heels and a sense of muggy dread. It clung to her like the warm spring night, seeping in through the soft fabric of her white trousers and thin white blouse. The gold belt around her waist felt too tight.

"This place looks like somebody forgot to condemn it," she said, gazing at the shabby brick-and-wood house fronted by a half-naked lawn and old, drooping oaks. Young men in haphazard suits—some wearing jeans with their jackets and ties, some wearing shorts with jackets and no ties, one wearing a Grateful Dead T-shirt and dress slacks—were huddled around a keg of beer set on saw-horses. The women mingling with them wore everything from cocktail dresses to cutoff overalls.

It was, Lily admitted, an appealingly bizarre group. "Move," Hai prompted, poking her in the lower back. "What's wrong?"

"I'm just not psyched up for this. I don't know what to say to all those guys." *I don't care about meeting them,* she added silently.

"You say, 'Give me some beer and show me where the food is.' Come on, Lily, it's time you developed some extra-curricular activities."

"Give me a minute. I just want to stand here and look around." Dingy urban streets bordered the house on two sides. Downtown Atlanta had surrounded the campus of Georgia Tech decades earlier. Now, the fringes of the campus had the seedy feel of old neighborhoods on the verge of urban decay.

A better-kept but equally old bungalow next door seemed to be trying to hide behind huge shrubs and a tall fence. The other houses crowding up to the sidewalks and each other couldn't be younger than World War II. Across the intersection was a flat brick house of later vintage, maybe the sixties, judging by its uninspired modernism. Old sports cars and battered sedans lined every available foot of curb space.

"I thought fraternity houses were supposed to look like mansions," Lily commented. "I thought that *Animal House* stuff was a joke."

"This is Georgia Tech," Hai said impatiently, as if that explained everything. She tossed back shoulder-length hair as black as a crow's wing. "Engineers and such. They are, hmmm, *inventive*." She and Lily started up a cracked flagstone walkway to the house with the scruffy lawn.

Elvis's "Love Me Tender" suddenly blasted from enormous speakers on the house's low concrete veranda. "They are *loud*," Lily said, squinting.

"They love to invite women from Agnes Scott to their parties," Hai called over the music. "Because there still aren't very many women students at Tech."

"You mean these guys are desperate for women. That's what you mean!"

They covered their ears and made their way onto the porch. Someone stuck a plastic cup of foamy beer into Lily's hand. A fat, shaggy dog trotted out through a front door blocked open with a car battery. "That's Mandy!" Hai shouted. "She's their mascot!"

Lily stopped to scratch Mandy's head. The dog reared up and lapped her tongue in Lily's beer. "I like Mandy," Lily shouted. She carried the cup to a corner and put it down, leaving Mandy in tail-wagging happiness.

With Hai tugging at her arm, she ventured inside. The living room was filled with people. It smelled of beer and pine cleanser, and the furniture, like the woodwork, had seen a lot of abuse. A mantel filled with intramural sports trophies decked a fireplace littered with empty beer cups. Beyond the living room was a narrow hallway lined in bulletin boards. "The women's toilet is down that way!" Hai shouted helpfully, pointing. She led Lily in the opposite direction, through a wide doorway into some kind of communal meeting room, judging by its size, the old Ping-Pong table covered in food, and a ratty couch in front of a television set in one corner.

There were more kegs of beer, more people, and big doors leading to an open deck above a small parking lot. Lily stepped onto the deck, grateful because Elvis's volume was only a dull roar there. She looked down at some kind of monstrous, hulking piece of automotive machinery that squatted in the lot's corner. She moved farther along the balcony, away from the open doors, and leaned both elbows on the wooden railing. After all she'd been through in the past year and a half—her parents' deaths, all the changes, Artemas—she felt so lost and empty inside. The hollowness couldn't be filled by crowds or noise. Hai wandered out and joined her, looking exasperated. "You have to make an effort!"

"I will. Eventually."

Hai waved her beer at the strange piece of junk in the parking lot. "That was their entry in the Rambling Wreck Parade, at Homecoming. I don't think it runs anymore. I don't think it ran very well to begin with."

"It sets performance art back a few thousand years, but I sort of like it."

"This is a great place! You'll see!" Hai pivoted, the full pink skirt of her dress whirling. "Frank! Hello! Come meet my roommate!"

A lanky young man stepped outside and caught Hai in his arms. He wore a beautiful pinstriped suit with a gold tie bar. His dapper appearance was such a contrast to the others' that Lily studied him with surprise.

Winding one arm around Hai's delicate shoulders, he gave Lily a jaunty once-over. "Hai, darlin', I thought you just pretended to have a roommate so I couldn't spend the night with you," he teased. "But she actually exists." His voice was one of those rare molasses-and-champagne drawls that must have been bred in some rich little southern town far from Atlanta. This fellow was the kind who drove a little sports coupe his daddy and mama had given him, with a country-club I.D. decal on the windshield and a FORGET, HELL! bumper sticker. He probably had more than a few ancestors named Beauregard.

"I'm for real," Lily said. "Are you?"

He laughed. "Allow me to introduce myself. I'm Frank Stockman, the most charming and talented brother you're likely to meet here tonight."

"Lily. Lily MacKenzie." She stuck out a hand. He lifted it to his lips and kissed her knuckles. Lily scowled benignly and withdrew it. Hai shook her head and chuckled. "Lily, Frank's a senior in architecture. He's about to graduate. He's been here so long they call him the Old Man. They let him and the other Old Man move into the attic. The two of them turned it into an incredible two-room suite. They put in skylights and a wine rack!"

"Au contraire," Frank drawled. "I have a wine rack. My partner in the penthouse suite prefers chocolate milk."

"Richard doesn't drink?" Hai looked amazed. As an aside to Lily, she explained, "Richard's a senior in architecture too. But he's the opposite of Frank. Believe it or not, they're best friends."

"Odd, isn't it?" Frank said blithely. "If he weren't such a likable bore, I'd have gotten rid of him years ago." Frank swiveled his attention to Lily. "Speaking of Richard, I came out here on a mission. I doubt you noticed, but when you walked through what passes for our community room—" he gestured drolly toward the doors—"you were being stared at. My friend took one look at you and jabbed himself in the mouth with a barbecued chicken wing. Would you care to meet him?"

Lily stifled her lack of enthusiasm. "I guess so, if he's wounded or something on my account."

Frank gestured gallantly toward the door. "Follow me,

darlin'." As Lily walked past, he added, "Oh, and don't mention that I set up this little introduction. He hates it when I'm devious for his own good."

They angled through the crowd. Lily immediately sensed their destination. The giant, ruddy-faced young man towered over everyone else, and he was staring at her from a place near the windows to the balcony. She wondered if he'd been watching her since she'd walked outside.

His sport coat fit him badly, and the slacks he wore with it were a nondescript shade of brown. His tie was askew, and his dark hair had a cowlick. She glanced down at his shoes. Thick-soled suedes, a little scuffed. Still, his broad, handsome face had an appeal that drew her attention, and her first impression was comfortable. He reminded her of a big, friendly couch.

Frank waved a hand. "Lily, this is the very honorable Richard Porter. Richard, this is Lily MacKenzie. She's from Scott. Hai's roommate."

Richard Porter's face turned three shades of red, but he put out a huge hand. She shook it. It was a good hand, hard and callused, and he was so formal, so awkward and gentlemanly, that she wanted to pat the side of his face and tell him to relax. He reminded her of all the rugged, tongue-tied men at home, like her father, in that way.

"You're the tallest woman I've ever seen," he said. He was gazing at her like a stunned bull, she thought. His voice was thick with an accent close to her own, and as deep as a mountain hollow. She recognized a kindred spirit. It was like a warm homecoming, something she needed desperately.

"Where are you from, boy?" she asked.

He looked pleased by the twang in her own voice. "North Carolina. Up around Asheville. How about you?"

"Ever hear of MacKenzie, Georgia?"

"Uh, no. But I'd like to hear all about it."

"It's not far from Victoria. In the mountains."

"I've heard of Victoria." He was bending close to her, trying to listen over the music. She smelled an overdose of Old Spice. She'd never known anyone under sixty who used Old Spice. It was familiar and reassuring. Dependable.

Some jolly idiot was dancing too close, bumping her, a beer sloshing over his hand. Richard stepped between her and the bleary-eyed partyer, as effective as a wall and twice as protective. The younger, smaller frat brother bounced off Richard's arm. Richard scowled at him. The brother looked abashed and respectful, as if he'd slammed into a monument.

Lily pointed toward the balcony. "Want to go outside, where we can talk like normal people?"

Richard looked relieved, and nodded.

They sat on top of the wreck. It had a full-length car seat bolted to steel shanks. Climbing up had been her idea, and he seemed enormously impressed. Dusk deepened around them, and the lights and noise of the fraternity house seemed distant.

He opened up under her casual questions, telling her he came from a family of construction workers, that his mother was dead and his father was tied to a new wife and her small children. Richard had no brothers or sisters of his own. He was the first one in his family to attend college. He and Frank Stockman already had internships lined up with a big architectural firm here in Atlanta.

When Lily told him she was working weekends for a landscaping contractor and wanted to get into that business after she graduated, he said, solemnly and without the least bit of flattery, "You're perfect."

"Well, nobody's ever said *that* to me, before," she answered. "Boy, have I got you fooled." She looked away, pensive and yet glad he'd said it. She was greedy for someone to talk to, to care about, for somebody to care about her.

"What are you so sad about, Lily MacKenzie?"

"Nothing." His voice was so somber and kind. She turned toward him, studied the sincerity in his face, and watched a lightning bug blink its fairylike yellow glow on his shirt collar. "Hold still," she said. She scooped her finger under the bug, blew gently on it, and it fluttered away. "When I was little, I'd catch these and keep 'em in a mason jar until I went to bed. Sometimes I'd turn 'em loose in my room and watch the show."

"I did that too," he said. "I had pet squirrels, and lizards, and a raccoon once."

"Me too."

They were silent. It was an easy silence, even if she felt the intense interest coming off him in waves. Strange, how she could crave his company so quickly, but in such a different way than she'd wanted Artemas's. Maybe life was safer this way.

He didn't seem to know what to do with his handsome, oversized hands. He kept laying them on his knees, then knotting them together. Now, he was fumbling with his tie.

Lily snagged one of them. "You're making me jumpy, boy," she drawled. "Are you always this fidgety?"

His shoulders slumped. "Never." He looked at her strong hand cupping his. His long, blunt fingers curled carefully through hers. She leaned back on the car seat and looked at the stars that were beginning to appear straight overhead. He settled beside her. Peaceful, that's what this was. The first peaceful moment she'd had in so long. She wanted to preserve it, build on it, see if there could be more to life than disappointment.

"I could get used to this," he said. "I'd love to get used to this."

Lily felt the careful, warm grip of his hand tightening on hers. She shut her eyes, concentrating on it. "Me too," she whispered.

Lily woke to the touch of Little Sis's hand smoothing the hair back from her forehead. She was still on the couch in her and Richard's office. Her face was damp. "You were crying," Little Sis said. She was kneeling beside the couch. "Come on, now, let's go upstairs. I'll lie down with you until you get back to sleep."

Lily took her hand and held it tightly. The pain came roaring back, tearing at her chest. She drew her knees up and bent her head to them, sobbing brokenly. "I want Stephen," she moaned. "I want Richard."

"Oh, honey," Little Sis crooned, putting an arm around her. "It won't always hurt like this. Just give it time. You'll always miss them, but eventually that'll only be one part of who you are, instead of the whole shebang."

"I have to know what caused it," Lily said, panting for air. She laid her cheek on one knee and looked at Little Sis. "What if Richard, oh, God, what if—"

"That's a question you can't answer tonight. And if you don't take care of yourself, you'll be too crazy and sick to ever find the answer." Little Sis huddled next to her, rocking her a little.

"I have to do *something*. I have to make Artemas see— make his family see—that it couldn't have happened because of Richard."

"There's nothing you can do except hunt down the facts and hope for the best. I don't think the Colebrooks can hate you for having faith in your husband. I know Artemas can't."

"Yes, he can. He does."

"He's so full of grief and confusion, he doesn't know which way to turn himself, right now."

Lily said no more. Retreating inside herself, she gave into the slow, soothing rhythm of Little Sis's rocking, and finally she knew what she wanted to do next. *I have to talk to them. I have to make them understand.* Something Artemas had said the other day came back to her, but she told herself it didn't matter. *If you won't cooperate, I can't protect you.*

Seventeen

The scotch was a good companion tonight. It asked no questions, made no demands, and muffled the sharp edge of frustration and despair. Artemas tilted the half-empty bottle over a glass where only slivers of melting ice remained. Where was the peaceful lethargy he wanted? Setting the bottle back on the small table beside his chair, he cursed the steadiness of his hand.

With the tumbler dangling from his fingertips, he leaned his head back on the chair's thick upholstery and stared at the suite's chandelier. A flash of self-awareness caused him to grimace. He saw himself at the moment as a stranger would—slumped in the big armchair in the center of the main room of a large, magnificent hotel suite, lit only by the crystal lamp on the table beside his chair and the faint glow of the lights from the tall buildings beyond the open draperies of the hotel's enormous windows.

A stranger would note that he had carelessly dropped the coat of his fine dark suit on the floor, with his tie atop it, that his linen shirt was wrinkled and half-open, that there were smudges of cigarette ash on his trousers. Despite the air of exhausted unconcern, he had not gotten around to removing his shoes.

The melodrama of his self-image did not appeal to him.

He shifted wearily, stretching one leg to its full length, the other remaining bent, balancing a bulging leather portfolio on the thigh. Flipping it open, he lifted a sheet of neatly formatted notes that Tamberlaine and LaMieux had prepared.

Here, waiting for the scrutiny of his vengeful family and the team of aggressive and highly skilled attorneys Colebrook International retained, were dossiers on everyone who had been significantly involved in the Colebrook office project. There were dozens—subcontractors, real-estate brokers, bank executives, local and state government officials.

Colebrook International had taken out huge construction loans, but had still funded at least half the cost of construction directly. Regardless, the liabilities had been small. Atlanta was eager to lure new jewels into its Olympic-caliber crown. There had been generous tax incentives. Artemas remembered how easy it had been to pitch the move from New York to his brothers and sisters. Without dwelling sentimentally on the estate at Blue Willow, which he planned to restore, or the family's southern heritage—and without mentioning his even more personal interest in relocating—he had convinced them that a lucrative and more gracious new world waited for them here.

He had convinced them, and now Julia was dead. Artemas drained the glass in one swallow, shoved it onto the table, and picked up the portfolio. Most of the people who were profiled in the report had been relegated to a paragraph or two of basic facts. Those could wait. Rifling the stack of dossiers, he found the pages he wanted, dropped the rest of the portfolio on the floor, and began to read. He knew it all already—from Tamberlaine's reports over the years, from his own contact with her—but seeing all those years reduced to lines of facts and dates tortured him.

Lily Amanda MacKenzie Porter. Named after a flower and her grandmother MacKenzie. Thirty years old.

Bachelor's degree in botony, with honors. Married for seven years. Award-winning landscape designer. Two terms as an officer of a state horticulture society, one as secretary, the other as vice president.

No criminal record. Her only brush with notoriety had been the brief loss of her driver's license several years ago, for an accumulation of minor speeding tickets. She'd paid a small fine, attended the state's three-day school for violators, gotten her license back. She had remarked to Tamberlaine that she enjoyed getting to know her fellow miscreants, especially the bikers.

No church membership, though she and Richard had attended a moderate Baptist church occasionally. They had a small circle of devoted friends, ranging from construction workers to her old college roommate, Hai, a cellist with the Atlanta Symphony. What few parties they gave were casual, usually barbecues. She remained close to her aunt Maude and the sisters, and had been very generous to the trio, giving them vacations in Hawaii and paying for a new roof on Maude's aging Victorian house.

She had met Porter when she was a freshmen at Agnes Scott and he a senior at Georgia Tech. She had dated no one else, had lived with him eventually, and had married him the summer after her own graduation. The wedding had been held in the backyard garden at Maude's.

By then Porter and Stockman were junior partners in one of the city's largest architectural firms, and Lily was manager of landscaping design and maintenance operations for a nursery wholesaler. Stephen was born just over one year later.

That was the same year Richard and Frank started their own firm. She quit her job to spend time with the baby and work as a freelance designer. Her clients recalled her striding vigorously around construction sites in brogans and overalls, a notepad in her hands and Stephen snuggled against her back in a cloth knapsack she'd converted into a baby carrier.

Now, she was one of the most respected landscape

designers in Atlanta. She and Richard had lavished attention on their sprawling, six-bedroom house set on prime
land outside the city. She still drove a Jeep—but a new
model every other year—and she was just as likely to be
seen behind the wheel of their big Lincoln, or one of her
and Richard's two oversized pickup trucks, or the restored
Corvette that had been Richard's pride and joy. They
owned a thirty-foot sailboat berthed at a coastal resort in
South Carolina, and they had traveled frequently, always
with Stephen happily in tow, taking vacations all over the
States, going to England and Scotland for several weeks
last summer.

Artemas poured himself another drink. He rubbed the
glass to his forehead and shut his eyes.

There was so much about the past twelve years that
couldn't be included in a few pages of typed notes. She
had married Porter reluctantly—at least, that was the way
Artemas saw it. She had been content with their live-in arrangement and saw no reason to change. Porter finally became so desperate, he'd threatened to walk unless she
made a commitment.

Richard had confided to Frank Stockman that he was
bewildered and hurt by Lily's unfathomable behavior. After
all, they wanted the same things—a beautiful home, kids,
success. He was crazy about her—had been from the first
moment he saw her—and she seemed to love him too. She
had never so much as looked at anyone else.

You poor, dumb bastard. She must have still loved me
then. She hadn't given up yet, Artemas thought, clutching
the glass. He would always believe that.

Artemas knew all these details about Richard and Lily's
early relationship because Stockman had told Tamberlaine
during preliminary discussions about the Colebrook Building, when Tamberlaine was cultivating Stockman's love of
martinis and gossip.

When Lily had married, Artemas sent her a complete
set of Colebrook's finest bone china—the white Avalon—as
a wedding present. She responded with a crisp, polite

thank-you note. Tamberlaine deduced that she immediately donated the china to a charity auction for the Humane Society.

A swallow of scotch chased that memory. He scowled at the pages lying on his knee. Perhaps to provoke her, but also because he wanted to reclaim a glimmer of their old affection, he'd sent an enormous toy bear when Stephen was born, and a smaller one every year after that, on Stephen's birthday. Tamberlaine assured him that she'd kept them all, and that she still had the Colebrook teapot.

When Glenda died of kidney failure related to her diabetes, Lily wrote to him—a brief, kind letter of sympathy. He had wanted to call her in gratitude, but stopped himself. Lily was happily married; she had a child. He couldn't say to her what he loathed admitting even to himself—that he grieved for his wife and had cared about her deeply, but felt cleansed of the lie he had lived for years. Now, he was free to pursue his own happiness again.

But how? Lily would never leave her husband, the father of her child. Fidelity was as much a part of her as her blue eyes and fiery MacKenzie hair. And so he had done what he could to be part of her life, even a distant part.

Richard and Frank were struggling to make a name for themselves. They were too young and unknown to compete for prestige projects against the large, established firms. Artemas had changed all that. The Colebrook project had given them fantastic opportunities. But to Lily, it had been a threat from the beginning.

The day she'd come to New York to confront him— this time secure in the knowledge that Tamberlaine had arranged an appointment—was vivid in his mind. So many years had passed since that time at the farm. So many years since they'd stood face-to-face. The tension simmering between them pulsed with rediscovery and the unspoken memories of the brief period they'd spent together, the night they had shared. Though she would never admit that current still existed, he doubted she could deny it either. Her attitude was accusing, defensive, almost fearful.

"Why are you doing this?"

"Because I was never able to get the farm back for you."

"Richard doesn't know about any of that. He thinks you're just an old childhood friend of mine."

"Isn't that all I am?"

"You know what I mean. I never told him the rest."

"He never asked if he was your first?"

"He asked. I told him there had been someone at home, who didn't matter anymore. That's all he wanted to know. He's one of the most trusting people I've ever met."

"Or one of the least inquisitive."

"Maybe I wanted to keep a few good memories, and I couldn't justify that if he knew everything. It would have worried him when there was nothing to worry about."

"Then why suspect my motives now?"

"Don't you realize what it would do to his pride if he thought he and Frank hadn't earned the Colebrook project on their own merits?"

"Do you think I'd have chosen them if they weren't deserving?"

"No, I learned a long time ago that you do what's best for the Colebrook name, regardless."

"Then there's no need for you to tell him about our history."

"He's my husband, and I love him. I don't like to keep secrets from him."

"Then tell him."

"You know I won't. You *know* it, and you don't care if that makes me feel like a traitor."

"Consider me a friend who has his best interests at heart, as well as yours. That should soothe your over-worked conscience. I'm trying to help you and your husband, Lily. All I want in return is to hear you say the past is forgotten."

That had forced her into a corner. He was certain she couldn't honestly say it. The look in her eyes told him so. Finally she answered, "It may not be forgotten, but I stopped letting it control my life a long time ago."

"Then we've reached a truce. Good."

"You mean you've settled some kind of debt you think you had."

"However you want to interpret it. May I ask one favor of you to cement our new understanding?"

"You can ask, and I'll let you know what I think."

"Will you design gardens for the Colebrook Building? Exterior and interior. With a blue willow as the centerpiece."

Her speechless, almost painful regard had made him fear she'd say no. He wanted her touch on the building. He wanted to be surrounded by it. Eventually, looking defeated, she had agreed. "I'll have to ask Joe Estes if I can buy a willow from the grove at the farm," she said wearily. "I haven't been back since . . . Aunt Maude says he's let the place get run-down. I didn't want to see it." Then she'd squared her shoulders and studied him proudly. "But you'll get your blue willow."

He nodded, afraid if he tried to say anything else, it would sound too relieved. She gave him one last look as she walked to the door of his office. "After all, it's only a damned tree."

Only a tree. And they were only friends. The past had no power. He could live with those lies if she could.

Artemas stirred, breaking the memory's spell. He dropped the pages about her to the floor. No one but he cared about the absent details, the heart and soul behind the facts. The irony of it was that those details would only complicate matters now. To his siblings and business associates they would set off alarms, make them wonder if he could be objective about her and take whatever action the situation demanded. He could.

The dossier did not reveal how many times he'd contacted Hopewell Estes over the years, trying to buy the farm back for her, and how diligently she'd tried, also, according to what Tamberlaine had heard from her. Hopewell had never budged. His wife was dead, his son was all he had left. *Joe loves that place,* he always said.

Two years ago Artemas had sent people to do routine maintenance on the mansion at Blue Willow—with instructions to discreetly check on the farm's upkeep. He'd been furious when they found the farm overgrown, the house empty, and well-tended plots of marijuana hidden in the mountain hollows—not only on the old MacKenzie land, but on the estate as well. Joe Estes had moved to a quarter-million-dollar condo in Atlanta and drove a Ferrari.

Small wonder that he'd wanted access to so much empty, privately owned forest. Small wonder that his despondent, defensive father could not risk selling the MacKenzie place.

Ending Joe Estes's career had been a simple, discreet matter of placing a few calls to the right people. Drug agents had descended on him. He had gone to prison. Somehow, the rumor of Artemas's involvement in his downfall had gotten out. Hopewell had sworn to keep the farm, out of spite. A dead end, after so many years. Lily knew what had happened. Artemas had explained. If anything, she'd seemed relieved. It was finally over, she'd said.

But it was not over. It was just beginning.

Artemas got up and paced, his chest tight with helpless rage.

Everything she owned was mortgaged to the hilt. The house she and Richard had built so lovingly, the acreage around it, the sailboat, the cars and trucks. Richard and Frank, apparently flush with visions of the grand future that had come their way since taking on the Colebrook project, had built themselves a $2 million office last year, using their personal assets to acquire the loans. Porter and Stockman had risked everything, and for that their possessions would belong to the banks, the courts, the victims. A complete and brutal taking, in which Colebrook International would be the chief litigant.

Artemas threw the glass against a wall. The force sprayed shattered pieces. The sharp sting on his cheekbone and the dampness of blood were distant concerns. His head bent, his hands hanging limply by his sides, he thought, *She lost her husband and son because of me. Now she'll lose her home too. Because of me.*

• • •

Artemas pushed the door open and got out before his driver could reach him. "Wait here, George," he told the steely older man who snatched at the limousine's door and held it dutifully, as rigid as a soldier at attention. "I won't be long."

George shifted anxiously and touched a hand to the brim of his black cap. "I've worked for you a long time, Mr. Colebrook. I hope you don't mind me saying that you've got the balls of an elephant, but I've never seen you do anything, well, *reckless*. I've figured out who you're here to see, and, well, sir, it has me worried."

"I'm not going to kill him, George." The tone of voice was lethally soft, not reassuring. "I'm just going to make him wish he'd never been born." Artemas's attention was riveted to the building in front of him. The bustle of Atlanta's busy streets and the office workers passing on the sidewalk might have been a thousand miles away. Cold air curled inside his open coat and sank into the dark wool of his suit. He welcomed the sensation against the heated tension in his skin. His bare hands felt hot against the sides of his trousers. Bright sunlight glinted off the tower of glass and steel awaiting him but did not penetrate his narrowed eyes. Violent justice was what he wanted, but no, he wouldn't lay a hand on Oliver Grant. That would have ended his revenge too quickly. He wanted Grant to suffer.

The lobby was bland and cramped and utilitarian, a stark contrast to the soaring beauty that had been the Colebrook Building. He had come here several times over the years, with Julia, to discuss the project in its planning stage. His skeptical sister had wondered at the artistic skill of a contractor who chose to work in such an uninspiring place.

His business is construction, Artemas had counseled. *Leave the creative genius to the architects.*

That memory was sour in his throat. He had chosen the architects. Stockman and Porter. They had recommended Grant as the contractor.

My sister would be alive if I hadn't insisted on Stockman

*and Porter. If I hadn't wanted to move Colebrook International
to Atlanta. If I hadn't wanted to be close to Lily, and prove
something to her. If I'd stayed out of her life, her son and husband would be alive too.*

His inner conflict brought fury and frustration. His
shoes clicked an efficient, swift tattoo on the lobby's granite floor. Decisions. Guilt. Sorrow. Revenge. His dream had
been noble. Selfish? Yes, that too. *Lily, Lily, I never meant to
hurt you. I meant to win you back. God help me.*

His jaws ached from clenching his teeth. On a direct-
ory positioned on the wall beside a dull-witted abstract
tapestry he found the contractor's suite number. During
the brief elevator ride up he stood in the center of the
compartment, staring at the doors.

When he stepped off the elevator at the floor occupied
by the building firm, his skin crawled with disgust. A receptionist at the lobby's desk stood quickly, recognition
and alarm flooding her expression. He walked past her
without speaking, ignoring her startled "Do you have an
appointment, Mr. Colebrook? *Mr. Colebrook?*"

He strode past secretaries in an open area, bathed in
their stares and whispers. His destination was one of the
doors in the office suites beyond them. The small brass
plaque there bore Grant's name.

He slammed a hand against it. The door groaned; its
latch popped. It burst inward.

Oliver Grant, standing near a window with a portable
phone against one ear, whirled in shock. When he saw
who the invader was, the phone dropped to the carpeted
floor. Grant leaped toward a desk littered with paperwork
and punched a button on a phone console there. "Call the
police," he ordered, his voice frayed.

Artemas slung the office door shut and advanced on
him with long strides, reaching out as he did. He shoved
the phone console onto the floor. Grant backed away,
holding up both hands, palms outward. "The media will
climb all over both of us. We don't need any more negative
publicity."

Artemas gave him a killing smile. "The truth won't be

negative to me. It'll be a goddamned pleasure to see the truth made public."

Grant had the short-legged, lantern-jawed demeanor of a bulldog, but a muscle twitched near the corner of his mouth. His flat face had a haggard pallor from weeks of intense stress, and his thinning brown hair stood out in wisps from the sides of his head. His thickly sinewed forearms, showing beneath the rolled-up sleeves of a dress shirt, gave evidence of a career that had been bred in the dirt and sweat of a laborer's dreams. But framed photographs of Grant with the city's social elite lined the walls, and a Mercedes key ring peeked from amid jumbled papers on the desk.

"Your ambition should have been tempered by honesty," Artemas said, scooping the key ring into his hand then dropping it in a trash can by the desk. "Because now you're going to lose everything. How will you like prison life? Think about it."

"Talk to my lawyers. I have nothing to say to you."

"Then just listen. *Listen,* you sleazy son of a bitch." Artemas pulled a sheaf of folded papers from inside his jacket and threw them on the desk. "That's the transcript of a statement Avery Rutgers gave my people this morning. His conscience got the best of him, not to mention the fact that he's scared shitless." Artemas leaned forward. The words slid softly, coldly, from his lips. "Your own quality-control inspector says the concrete used in the bridge's supporting walls wasn't allowed to cure properly."

Grant wavered as if caught by a gust of wind. His hands dropped to his sides, then fumbled vaguely. "That's a lie. Get out. My attorneys—"

"He says he told you as soon as he discovered it. And that you told him to keep his mouth shut or he'd lose his job. When he brought the subject up again, you said the architects had checked the problem out and agreed that it was insignificant. That's ludicrous."

Grant collapsed slowly, catching the back of a plush leather chair behind the desk. It swiveled toward him, and he sank into it. His mouth hung open. His eyes glazed over. "There's no proof."

Artemas dropped another folded document on the desk. "Core samples of the concrete have been analyzed. Rutgers was right about it. Look at the report."

"Oh, God." Grant moaned and put his head in his hands.

Artemas was dimly aware of straining forward over the desk, of violence rising up blindly in him. He wanted the man's throat between his hands—he could already feel his fingers crushing flesh and cartilage. He wanted to see all the death and betrayal, all his grief, mirrored in Grant's dying gaze.

You can't. He still has answers to give.

His fingers bit into stacks of papers, crushing them in substitution. Contempt and rage were overwhelming him. Restraint made him tremble. "I want to hear you admit that Stockman and Porter never knew you'd screwed the structural safety of their design."

Grant lifted bleak, groggy eyes to his. Two of the building's security guards burst into the office. They dragged at Artemas, binding their arms across his chest, cursing. His gaze never left the contractor's. Grant's sagging face contorted. The viciousness of a trapped animal replaced defeat. "They *knew*," he said, spitting it as if in triumph. "They let it pass. They approved it."

His words landed like fists. Artemas recoiled, stiffened. The guards gripped him tighter, as if their threat was responsible for holding him motionless. A prayer rose in his mind. *Let him be lying. Don't let Richard Porter be part of this.*

Through the pulse roaring in his ears, he heard Michael's deep, anxious voice speaking his name. He felt a hand on his shoulder, sensed Michael beside him and the guards. "George called from the car phone when you left the hotel," Michael was saying. "I followed you." He jerked furiously at the guards' arms. "Goddammit, let him *go*." Michael began to cough but continued fighting. One of the guards twisted and rammed an elbow into Michael's chest.

Artemas jerked away from them, caught one in the face with his fist, and shoved the other one aside. Michael was bent over, gasping, one hand unzipping the leather aviator jacket he wore with jeans, fumbling inside past a white sweater, searching the inner pockets. "I'm all right," he said, as Artemas grasped him by one arm. He found his inhaler and straightened, shaking his head. His dignity and self-rebuke were fierce. He jerked his arm away from Artemas. "All right." Artemas's chest heaved as deeply as Michael's. He pivoted toward Grant. "I don't believe you."

Grant rose like a drunken boxer, gripping the edges of his desk and swaying, his vindictive gaze boring into Artemas. "You will. I'm not going to hell alone. Ask Lily Porter to tell you what *she* knows. Ask her why Stockman and her husband and I were all so goddamned crazy by the end. Then live with *that* truth!"

Two police officers ran into the room, then halted. "I want these bastards out of here," Grant yelled, pointing at Artemas and Michael. Artemas raised a hand in warning as the officers stepped toward him. The terrible dread inside him became fierce efficiency, a litany of commands. *Turn away. Take Michael to the hotel. Make certain he's recovered. Go to Lily. Make her talk.*

Eighteen

The click of her flat blue shoes was the loudest sound Lily had ever heard, and every step closer to the door of James Colebrook's hospital room made a sharp throb in her pulse. She had come once before. The memory was fuzzy; maybe it had been the week after the funerals. Almost six weeks ago. Eternity. Yesterday. Aunt Maude had insisted on driving her here that time, thank God.

Lily remembered standing at the foot of his bed, staring at him speechlessly, lost in the horror, seeing the tiny clear tube running from under the sheet to a yellowish bag attached to the bed's lower railings, and his leg, swaddled in white from hip to foot and hanging in slings. His face had haunted her—eyes closed, asleep, deathly white, a limp shock of hair the color of Artemas's feathering his high forehead. He resembled Artemas so much—with the same sharp cheekbones, the same harshly sculpted mouth, but his features were leaner, more elegant.

His wife had been the only other person in the room. She had risen from a chair and come to Lily silently. Lily recalled looking down into a stunned, pretty face framed by straight, mink-colored hair. She recalled holding out a hand to Alise Colebrook, and that Alise had taken it.

Whatever they had said to each other had been compassionate, and there had been quiet tears. Lily wasn't certain how long she'd stood, watching James sleep, holding his wife's hand.

She stopped outside the open door, her heart hammering in her throat. Her body reacted to emotions she didn't know she felt; everything was buried too deep. She knew she was nervous because she felt the physical sensations, but her mind was calm, almost sluggish. She heard voices inside the room. Several different ones, but all female. Then a low murmur. Masculine.

She had to make these people understand that there was no reason for them to suspect Richard.

She brushed a hand over her clothes and glanced down, stalling for time. Straight dark skirt, white blouse, camel-colored cloth coat. Black hose, blue shoes. Blue purse dangling from the other hand. Wide gold wedding band and large diamond engagement ring. Nails bitten to the quick. Long dull braid of hair fastened with a black band, lying on her right breast. She plucked a dozen stray wavy strands from her coat's lapel. Her hair was falling out all over the place—streaking the throw pillows on the den's couches, clogging the shower drain, filling her brushes. Nerves, Big Sis had said.

The respectable inventory reassured her that she was thinking rationally. She hadn't noticed much about the selections while she was getting dressed.

She started to knock on the door, then lowered her hand. Knocking seemed too polite, as if she were about to breeze in carrying flowers and a fruit basket. Lily lifted her chin and walked slowly into the room.

When they saw her, there was shocked silence. She halted just beyond the corner of the bathroom wall, where the room opened up. Their faces flashed across her mind like slides changing too fast. Cassandra. Dark accents. Whip-thin. Standing. Elizabeth. Blond. *Zaftig*. Standing. Alise. Delicate. Sitting on the edge of a chair.

Lily's breath rattled in her chest. *James*, finally. No sling. No catheter. A pillar of white extending from his left hip, lying parallel to the ridge his right leg made under the sheet. He was sitting up with bright white pillows stuffed behind him. A silky black pajama top hung loosely on his powerful shoulders and chest.

His face was pale and furious. "I suppose," he said in a low voice, "you didn't have the guts to face the cripple until now."

The words felt like a hand shoving her chest to her backbone. Lily looked at him with dull agony, struggling to breathe.

Alise leaped up. "James, she came here before. I told you." But the look Lily received from her contained icy dignity. There was no compassion in it. "You shouldn't have come back."

James appeared not to notice either his wife's fiercely soft words or her loyal, protective movement to his side. "If you're looking for my brother, he's not here. He might be interested in hearing whatever you came to say, but I'm not." His gray eyes were hard on Lily's. His mouth took a crueler slant. "And when this family is finished with you, you'll know better than to expect any welcome from *him*, either. In fact, he's trying to find you, as we speak. I'd say your illusions of friendship won't survive much longer."

Lily dragged her voice from the clenched fist inside her throat. "I'd trade places with you if it would change what happened—if it brought back my husband and son, or your sister, or any of the others who died."

"What a nice sentiment. What a useless sentiment."

"Have you all made up your minds?" she asked, looking from him to his wife and sisters. "Without any evidence?"

Alise's eyes were shuttered. She said nothing. Cassandra's expression was as vividly contemptuous as James's. "The evidence is accumulating at a dazzling pace."

Lily shook her head. Were they blind? "What evidence? There's *nothing*."

"God fucking damn," Cassandra said.

Elizabeth Colebrook stepped forward, scrutinizing Lily as if she were an unfinished china pattern. Her expression was akin to Alise's—restrained, disgusted, but not blatantly cruel. "You obviously haven't heard from your attorneys yet."

"Heard *what*?"

James leaned forward quickly. The careless movement made him grimace, and he panted. The ruddy splotches of color on his cheeks gave him a feverish look. Alise uttered a small cry of dismay and knelt on one knee by his hips. She clasped his shoulders. "Please, don't. You have to rest."

Again James ignored her. The hatred in his eyes twisted Lily's stomach. "Avery Rutgers," he said.

"I don't know him."

"Oh? He worked for Oliver Grant."

"Dozens of people did. Either directly, or through sub-contractors."

"Rutgers was Grant's quality-control expert. He couldn't quite reconcile that with the deaths of more than a dozen people. He called our attorneys this morning."

When Lily only frowned in desperate bewilderment, Cassandra interjected, "He said the concrete used in the bridge was shit. That Grant knew and didn't replace it. And when Artemas confronted dear, doomed Mr. Grant, he confessed that your husband and his partner knew as well. They knew the bridge might not be safe, but they didn't do anything."

Lights burst in Lily's vision. Her face felt cold, her legs like rubber. All these weeks, she'd never come so close to fainting. She took two wavering steps toward a wall and leaned, facing it, her forehead bowed to the hard, cool surface. Oliver was responsible. Not Richard. Not Frank. She'd never believe they'd collaborated with Oliver. She wanted to kill him. She wanted to drag him to Richard's and Stephen's graves and kill him with her bare hands.

Her one goal was to get out of here and find him. Through a haze of black hatred she heard James's voice, speaking to someone else. ". . . immediately. I won't have her pass out in my room. I'll let her lie on the floor like a goddamned piece of trash, if she does."

"We'll send someone as soon as we can, Mr. Colebrook," came the grainy, disembodied answer over the nurses' intercom.

Lily pivoted unsteadily, fury surging into her muscles. "It's not true. I don't care what you've been told. Whatever Oliver did, he did alone."

His face convulsed in rage. "The only question is, how much did *you* know?" James was shouting. "And if you don't know what your husband was capable of, what does that say about your judgment?" Sweat glistened on his face and stained the front of his shirt. The others were agitated, closing in around him, trying to push him back on the pillows. "Anyone who fucked—anyone who even *smiled* at—the bastard or his partner is responsible for doing this to me!"

Lily snapped. She lunged to the end of the bed and clung ferociously to the foot railing. "Does that include *Julia*? Do you condemn your own sister for falling in love with Frank Stockman? Do you think she believed she couldn't trust him? What blame should that place on *her*?"

The hideous accusation registered in their gasps. She noted their horrified expressions, and her blood froze. *They hadn't known about Julia and Frank.*

"Close the door," Artemas said.

Lily straightened slowly and turned to face him. He was formidable—his eyes half-shut, head up, the dark brows pulled together in fierce concentration, his mouth harsh. The somber, beautiful suit he wore and the long black overcoat seemed too civilized for the look on his face, and the way he stood there—like some towering magistrate, weighing her fate—would have frightened her if she hadn't been soaked in rage.

Tamberlaine stood just behind him, looking troubled and alarmed. Michael Colebrook shut the room's door and positioned himself beside Artemas, staring down at her with openmouthed dismay. "What did you just say?" Artemas asked. His voice was low but commanding.

Lily returned his merciless gaze. The truth his siblings had just given her rejuvenated the dignity that had escaped her so often during the past weeks. She remembered the

kind of person she'd been before. She wouldn't be anybody's victim—especially not his. "Julia loved Frank. It was
something that developed a year or so into the planning
for the Colebrook project," The calm, sturdy sound of her
own voice reassured her. She was as dispassionate as a
hired assassin. When she finished here, she would track
Oliver down. The consequences didn't matter.

"Go on," Artemas ordered, staring at her. His eyes were
narrowed with a different kind of consideration. Concern?
Did he sense her cool madness?

Lily exhaled and tried to concentrate on the conversation at hand. "Once the building was under construction,
she spent most of her time in Atlanta. She and Frank were
staying together every night—at her hotel or his house. It
ended about a year ago."

"I don't believe it," Cassandra said. "How do you
know?"

Lily turned her head slightly and said over her shoulder, "Because Frank didn't make any secret of it to Richard
or me. Because Julia talked to me about it. To be specific,
because I accidentally walked in on them once, in a
construction trailer. They weren't using the desk to study
blueprints."

She met Artemas's eyes again. There was a shadow of
pained belief in the mask. She hurt for him, but couldn't
relent. "Frank had a live-in housekeeper. Ask her. She can
tell you how often Julia stayed with him when she was in
Atlanta. Ask Oliver Grant. He knows. Some of his men
used to complain that there ought to be a Do Not Disturb
sign on the construction trailer's door when Julia was in
town."

Artemas said slowly, "There was no reason for my sister
to keep a secret like that."

"She worried that y'all would think she'd compromised
her supervision of the building. But I assumed she'd confided in at least one of you. Or that you suspected."

It was obvious, from the looks that passed among the
group, that no one had been informed. She glanced at
James. His strained expression was infused with a quieter,

more poignant rage. "What you've described wasn't *love*. It doesn't mean a damned thing." His large, pale hands knotted in the sheets.

Artemas's voice cut through her. "Have your attorneys discussed the accusations that came out today about Richárd and Frank?"

"I learned about them the hard way, a minute ago, from people who think they're true."

If there had been even a flicker of sympathy in his eyes, it was gone. "Don't blindly defend Richard. This family deserves better than that."

"My husband deserves better than to be judged by the claims of a building contractor who's looking to save his own ass."

"Richard and Frank were desperate to have the Colebrook Building turn out perfectly. They needed the big-money clients it brought them. You can't deny that. Richard knew he stood to lose everything you and he owned if they failed. He used your personal property to acquire loans he and Stockman needed to build their new offices."

"I know. I agreed to it." She'd been trying not to think about those loans, or how they would be handled now.

"Do you realize how many lawsuits there are going to be? That the firm will end up in bankruptcy—and every asset connected to it will go to pay the debts? Will you still forgive Richard when you lose your house and everything else?"

"I've already lost what I loved most," she said, her voice hoarse. "There's nothing to forgive Richard for. No reason to believe Oliver isn't lying."

"If there's proof to back him up, I'll get it." He took a step toward her. Unspoken threat seethed in him. She absorbed it without flinching. "What else should you tell me about Julia?" he asked. "Grant said, 'Ask Lily Porter. She knows why we were all so crazy toward the end. Ask her about Julia.'"

"Frank broke off their relationship when she started talking about marriage. I won't defend him—he was stupid about it, and tactless, and I understood why Julia enjoyed making him miserable after that. But she took revenge on Richard, too, and Oliver, and me—everyone connected to the project. She'd always been hard to please. They'd never been able to make her understand that nothing runs smoothly about a project as large as the Colebrook Building. There are delays, mistakes, changes in plans, unexpected costs. Budgets that were approved before construction began have to be altered.

"But she wouldn't listen. And after she and Frank broke up, nothing was good enough for her. She threatened to sue if the project came in one penny over budget or one day late. She *knew* Richard and Frank couldn't afford a lawsuit, not with all their money tied up in their new offices. She knew the economy had hurt Oliver's business, and he was struggling to stay out of debt. She made everyone frantic by the end." Lily's hands rose in fists. "I watched Richard exhaust himself worrying about it. He had chest pains. He couldn't sleep. I'll never forgive her for what she did to him."

James interjected in a deadly tone, "Are you saying our sister pressured those gutless wonders so much that they'd do anything to survive, even if it amounted to criminal negligence?" His voice rose. "Goddammit, are you blaming her for what happened?"

Elizabeth Colebrook moaned and put her hands to her throat. Alise sat limply beside James, shaking her head. There was revulsion in Cassandra's face, denial in Michael's, warning in Artemas's—the silent assault made Lily's skin crawl. Until that moment she hadn't realized where the story about Julia was leading. It sank into her like a knife.

"Are you accusing our sister?" Elizabeth echoed.

Lily shivered. Artemas snapped a hand forward and gripped her shoulder. His eyes bored into hers. "Lily?" he said evenly.

She tasted the coppery tang of blood where she'd chewed the inside of her mouth. "Nothing excuses what

Oliver—and Oliver alone—chose to do. He was a coward, and innocent people are dead because of him, and—"

"Stop it." Artemas pulled her off-balance, his hand like a wedge under her arm. "Have the courage to admit that Richard might have been involved too. For God's sake, if you ever loved—" He paused, the muscles working in his jaw, drawing her distorted attention to the mysterious pink cut on one cheekbone. "Do you love him so much," he continued, "so much that you can't believe he could be at least partially responsible for your son's death?"

"He's the one man I've never doubted. I won't start now."

There was a flash of anguish in his eyes, so private and brief, only she was close enough to see it.

He lowered his hand. The cold facade dropped over his expression again. "Then perhaps you can understand the kind of faith this family has in Julia."

Blind faith, she thought. Lily regained her balance and wrenched his hand off her shoulder. "Your sister set the rules. She made them impossible to follow. She asked for trouble, and she got it. I'm telling you she's got to share the blame."

James made a guttural sound of fury, matched by Cassandra's keening one. She sprang forward. Her balled hand caught Lily in the mouth. There was chaos then—Artemas pushing between the two of them and uttering his sister's name like a curse, Elizabeth and Alise catching Cassandra by the arms, Michael vaulting to James's side and snagging him by the shirt as James struggled to push himself out of the hospital bed.

Lily staggered back, raising a hand to the blood at one corner of her lips. Despair and horror at the ruin that had come to Artemas's family and her own welled up inside her. Mr. Tamberlaine was suddenly beside her, a steadfast force who supported her with an arm under her shoulders. She couldn't see Artemas's face—he was turned away from her. But something in his expression made the others freeze. Even James stared up at him with fading violence. A chill crept up Lily's spine. They were looking at Artemas the way people looked at a terrible accident on the highway—wincing, as if afraid they'd already seen too much to let them sleep peacefully at night.

He turned toward her. She knew she'd see that haggard, tormented face in troubled dreams. She wanted to take him in her arms, pull his head to her shoulder, croon one of the wordless, soothing melodies she had used when Stephen was hurt or frightened. He lifted a hand toward her. Moving as if ancient and weary beyond imagining, he touched a fingertip to the bloody corner of her mouth. The feathery caress was gone immediately, his hand returning to his side. It nearly destroyed her. He was defeated.

"I'm sorry," he said in a voice hollow with despair.

Lily bowed her head, returning the apology. Tamberlaine said gently, "May I walk you down to your car, Lily?" She nodded. As she went toward the door, she hesitated and looked back at the shaken, white-faced group around Artemas. "I've known you all my life, even though we never met. I read so much about you in Artemas's letters. I thought of you as my other family. I don't want to hurt any of you."

"We're not your family," James said. "And we never will be."

She couldn't look at Artemas again. She turned and walked out.

The cold night wind tugged at loose strands of her hair and whipped her open coat around her legs. She walked from the Jeep to a low wall in the park across the street from Oliver's house. The two-story Mediterranean was surrounded by an eight-foot wall of white stucco, with a courtyard and fountain beyond the ornate black gate, which stood open.

Every light, inside and out, was blazing. The blue strobes of several police cars flashed across her face, a surreal addition to her shock.

In the shadows just outside a street lamp, she sank down weakly on the wall, her fists shoved in the coat's large pockets, staring at the unexplained scene at Oliver's house. A hand closed on her shoulder. She jumped. Artemas stood over her. Her gaze darted up the street. A large, inconspicuous sedan was parked behind the Jeep. "You were following me," she said.

"I had one of my private security agents follow you," he corrected. "He called when you left your house and started back to Atlanta."

He sat down beside her. One hand moved swiftly to her coat pocket, clamping her wrist. The other slid inside. It happened so fast, she didn't have time to protest or pull back.

He withdrew the heavy revolver and cupped it in his palm. Lily slumped a little and said nothing. Her mood was lethargic, as if she'd walked out of a nightclub in the wee hours of the morning, tired and a little drunk, to find the world deceptively peaceful and quiet. All she could think was, He knew I'd try something like this. He knows me that well.

He sighed and looked at the gun, his shoulders sagging. "My people have been watching Grant too," he said finally. "They managed to get some information after the police and paramedics arrived." He opened the revolver's chamber and dumped the bullets into his hand. "Grant lay down in a bathtub and slit his wrists. His wife found him."

Lily thought about that for a moment. She had been robbed of her revenge then. Nothing seemed real; not sitting here with Artemas after all that had happened earlier tonight, not the fact that she'd come here to threaten Grant, perhaps even kill him. Because this was too strange to be happening. "Is he dead?" she asked.

"Yes. I was told over my car phone that the paramedics left about fifteen minutes ago, with his body."

Lily shut her eyes and exhaled raggedly. He handed the empty revolver to her. "For once in our lives, fate worked on our behalf." He rose, stepped around to her other side, and gestured toward that pocket. She put a hand over it and shook her head. Bending over, he calmly pried her hand away and reached inside. He went very still when he extracted a small stuffed bear. Lily took it from him and slid it back into her coat.

He didn't ask if it was one of those he'd sent every year on Stephen's birthday. He didn't have to. He knows that too, she thought.

His face was infinitely sad. "I wish—"

"Don't. It won't change what you have to do, or what I have to do."

The poignant thread between them faded into stark silence. He straightened. "You're right."

She got to her feet and stepped past him, dropping the revolver in her other pocket. "I wanted to hear Grant say what he said to you. I wanted to make him admit he was lying. If he wrote any kind of confession before he . . . I want to see it."

"If he left information, we'll get it. And I promise you'll know."

Their voices were low and weary, like those of couples who had lived together so many years there was no pretense of pleasure left. They walked to their vehicles. He halted on the curb, and she felt him watching her as she went to the Jeep. She stood there in a daze, her hand on the door. Ticking like a bomb inside her was the agonizing fear that what Grant had said might be true, that Richard and Frank had gambled on the bridge's safety because they were desperate to save time and money. And that neither Artemas nor his family would ever concede that Julia's unreasonable demands had been the catalyst.

She stiffened and looked at him. "From now on it'd be better if you and I talk only through our attorneys. I couldn't stand another scene like the one at the hospital tonight. It doesn't do your family, or you, or me, any good."

Artemas stared at her without speaking. The bitterness and fatigue in his face made him appear cruel and older than his years. Inclining his head slightly, he nodded his agreement.

•   •   •

A courier's envelope from Oliver Grant was waiting for him at the hotel. His chest constricted with dread. He opened it under the small, private light of a desk lamp in his suite.

When he read the scrawled letter inside and realized that what Grant had told him could undoubtedly be proved, he sat back in his chair, letting the letter fall, unheeded, to the floor, out of his reach, beyond his control, as he stared into the blackness outside the windows.

Gulping for air, James pulled himself across the floor to the bath's oversized white tub and leaned against the side. The floor was brutally hard under his bare hips. His injured leg throbbed inside its bandages, and every movement bumped the thigh-to-ankle steel brace, sending shards of agony through his body. He wanted to cry, but rage and steely willpower held the tears back. No one, not even Alise, realized the depth of his humiliation or the terror he had of being helpless and pitiful.

Sweat poured down his face. He tilted his head back and studied the handles and shower head high above him on the white tile wall. Goddammit, he was going to wash himself without help this morning. He'd been reduced to goals that small.

Ripping at the buttons, he removed his damp pajama top and slung it aside; then, grimacing with revulsion, he stared at his naked body, hating the loss of muscle definition in his belly and the way his penis lay like a limp victim. After the doctor had reduced his pain medication and he began waking up with erections, he'd made a few halfhearted attempts to stroke himself. Alise had insisted on trying as well. Her gentle attention had only made him feel pathetic.

He didn't want Alise to touch him that way. He wasn't a man anymore. His love for her and his desperate need for the tenderness they'd always shared were buried under layers of frustration.

James gritted his teeth and pulled himself upward, using the sink. His good leg felt weak, and his bad one dragged like a dead weight. Finally he collapsed on the side of the tub and rested his forehead on the sink's cool white lip.

"James. Oh, God, honey, what are you doing?" Alise stood in the bathroom doorway, a garment bag sagging across her arms. She dropped it and bounded to him, her hands out.

He straightened furiously. "No. Leave me alone." She halted, hovering over him and looking distraught. The desirable sight of her in a trim gray suit and softly draped blouse, with her slender, shapely legs straddling his grotesquely outfitted one only made his frustration hotter.

"Get out," he ordered. "I don't want your help. I keep telling you that. Believe me, for once."

"James, *please*. You can't go on this way. There's no sense in you being defensive and embarrassed around me."

The tendons strained in his neck. He wanted to hurt someone, anyone. Even the person he loved most. "You like mothering me," he accused, his tone low and ugly. "It makes you feel important. I'm sick of it."

She recoiled as if he'd slapped her. Her hand covering her mouth, her eyes squinted shut, she sank onto the closed toilet seat and hunched over, crying silently. James strangled on regret. His hand wavered toward her, then clenched. Jerking it down, he said in a softer, more controlled voice, "I won't be treated like an invalid. Especially by you. I may be useless, but I'm not pitiful."

"You stupid bastard." Propping her elbows on her knees, she jammed the heels of her hands against her forehead and rocked slowly, her eyes still shut. "We still have a life. *You* still have a life. There's so much work for you to do. Your family needs you. The company will be moving into temporary offices as soon as some are leased, and the other building has to be sold, and you and I have a huge house waiting to be finished. And next year, we'll try to get pregnant—"

"No."

Her head jerked up. Her eyes were incredulous, pleading. "We agreed. We've been married for five years."

James felt as if he were being torn apart. "I see my

brothers teaching my children to play baseball, because I can't run. I see my children telling their friends that their father is handicapped. I see a hundred other scenarios such as those."

Alise moaned. "You've lost your mind."

"No, that's the one part of me that still works perfectly." He flung a hand toward the garment bag. "Hang that on the door. Wait outside."

She stood, wavered unsteadily, and looked down at him with a shattered expression. "I love you too much to believe you're always going to act this way. That faith can keep me going for a long time. Please don't shut me out forever. I couldn't stand it."

After she left and closed the door, he leaned his head on the sink, turned the water on full blast, and cried.

The meeting was called in the offices of the law firm that represented Porter and Stockman. Holding it there was a small favor Artemas could do for Lily, letting her meet with them on turf friendly to her. He would not have asked his siblings to attend, but she insisted. Her courage broke his heart. She and the architectural firm's attorneys already knew what Oliver Grant had written before he died.

"They're late," Elizabeth said, leaning her elbows on the long conference table and smoothing her fingertips over her temples. "I want to get this over with."

"I doubt she's anxious to see us again, after the other night," added Michael. He leaned back in the chair next to Elizabeth's and shook his head. "I can't blame her."

Artemas stood by a window in the large, handsomely appointed conference room, his hands clasped behind his back. He pivoted and studied the assembled group. Elizabeth, Michael, and Cass. Several Colebrook attorneys. James near the end of the table, pale and stiff in a special wheelchair, with his leg extended on its raised footrest. It was good to see him in a suit again, even if the weight he'd lost over the past six weeks made the sharply fitted black coat hang badly. Alise had asked his tailors to alter the left leg of his trousers. They had shortened it to the thigh and

widened it, to accommodate the cocoon of bandages and
steel.

Alise had pulled a chair up behind his—to leave room
at the crowded table, she said, but her eyes were swollen
as if she'd been crying before Michael arrived at the hospi
tal to help her bring James here. Since James couldn't see
her from her position, he didn't know that her gaze rarely
left him, or that her expression alternated between anger
and sorrow.

A heavily paneled door opened across the room.
Marcus DeLan, the law firm's senior partner, ushered a
small, wiry, reluctant-looking man in a cheap blue suit to
a place at the far end of the long table. "Sit here, Mr. Spencer," DeLan told him. Spencer dropped quickly into the
chair and fixed his gaze on the gleaming mahogany tabletop. His thin, heavily oiled brown hair was as shiny as the
table.

"I expect Lily at any minute," DeLan said, and left
the room.

Artemas went to Spencer and shook his gnarled hand.
A lifetime of heavy labor and skilled carpentry work was
stamped on them. "Thank you for coming to yet another
meeting filled with attorneys, Mr. Spencer. You won't be
asked to give another formal statement. Just tell Mrs.
Porter what you've told the state investigators and my
attorneys."

"Yeah, this un's for Mrs. Porter." There was a defensive,
anguished note in Spencer's voice. "If it wadn't a courtesy
I owe her, I'd just as soon have all my fingers broke in a
vise. She don't deserve none of this. And I ain't sure Mr.
Porter does, neither. Him and her was awful nice to me
over the years. They never acted like they was better than
the workingmen."

"I understand why this isn't easy for you." *Better than
anyone else in the world,* Artemas added silently. He introduced his brothers and sisters.

The door opened again. Artemas's chest constricted.
DeLan entered and stood aside. Lily walked in. She was
tall and stately in a dark suit, with her mass of red hair

pulled up. Large sunglasses covered her eyes. Her cheeks were gaunt. Michael stood, ignoring Cass's snort of dismay at his etiquette. Spencer popped up and hurried to her. "I would never have said nothing to you or anybody else if Mr. Grant hadn't put my name in that letter of his," he told her poignantly, and when she took both of his hands in hers, his leathery face contorted with emotion. "I guess he heard I'd talked to Mr. Porter. I was scared to tell, scared I'd get in trouble somehow."

"I know, Spence." Her voice was a raw whisper. Her shoulders had a defeated slump to them. Artemas stood motionless, hating what this day was doing to her.

"But it weren't just bein' scared," Spencer continued. "I didn't want to lay nothing on Mr. Porter. He was always straight with me, and when he told me he'd do something about that bridge, I believed him. I reckon I still do."

Delicate muscles flexed in her jaw. When she spoke again, she sounded stronger. "I wish we could know everything he was thinking, but we can always believe he did what he thought was right."

"Yes'm. Yes'm."

James made a low sound of anger. Artemas shot him a warning look, but James was staring vindictively at Lily. So was Cass. Michael sat down slowly. He and Elizabeth watched her with thoughtful frowns.

Marcus DeLan took over then, shutting the door then gracefully showing Lily to a chair and taking the one next to hers. Spencer returned to his chair and slumped. Artemas walked back to the window and stood where he could study her without being noticed by the others.

Lily removed her glasses and folded them carefully on the table. Her blue eyes were hollow as they rose to him, devoid of emotion. She turned slowly and looked at Spencer. "Tell me everything you know, please."

The little man clenched his hands on the table's edge. "I was building forms for the concrete crew, while they was pourin' the support walls and bridge. I heard 'em talking— sayin' Mr. Rutgers was ridin' 'em too hard. They don't like those quality-control snoops—the boys think nobody knows their business better than them. Anyhow, I hear that kind of complainin' all the time, so I didn't pay much attention to it."

"When did you hear all of this?" Lily asked.

"A couple of months before we turned the building over to the painters and all."

"What do you mean, 'painters and all'?" Cass asked sharply.

"The interior-decorating crews," Artemas explained. "Carpet, tile, wallpaper, that phase of the building."

Lily's eyes had never left Spencer. "You didn't say anything to Richard then?"

"No. Maybe Mr. Grant thought I'd heard something I shouldn't, 'cause he sent me to work on a building across town. But maybe a couple of weeks before the Colebrook Building was all done, I come back to do some work on the molding in the big offices upstairs."

"Why?"

Spencer ducked his head and glanced warily at Artemas and the others, then told her, "Miz Colebrook said she could see some of the nailheads. She wanted all the molding ripped up and new molding put down. I coulda fixed them nailheads so nobody'd notice, but Mr. Grant said she'd notice, so it had to be done all over."

"Get to the point," James interjected.

Lily swiveled slightly. Her fathomless gaze held James's. The room seethed with silent confrontation. Artemas stepped forward. "Please continue, Mr. Spencer."

Lily turned toward the carpenter and waited. Spencer sighed. "When I was doing that molding work, I seen Mr. Porter again. He stopped by to shoot the breeze with me, the way he always done. And I said, just talking about nothing, you know, I said, 'When we was working on the bridge, I thought the concrete boys was goin' to lay into Mr. Rutgers. He's lucky he didn't find no batch of wet mix in the front seat of his car.' "

Lily exhaled raggedly. "This was only a week or two before the building opened?"

"Yes'm. Mr. Porter asked me what exactly I meant, and

I told him Rutgers had given the boys all sorts of grief about the concrete not being let to cure long enough, and Mr. Porter got this look on his face like, like he was going to have a heart attack. He was *mad*. And *scared*. I ain't never seen him look that way before."

Lily steepled her hands against her mouth. Her eyes were half-shut, a tortured expression in them. "What did he say?"

"He asked me if I'd told anybody else. I hadn't. I said, 'Mr. Porter, do you think Mr. Rutgers and Mr. Grant let something bad slip by?' And he said—I remember exactly, because I was staring at him hard, and worried—he said, *'If they did, this building isn't going to open until it's fixed.'* That was all. We didn't talk about it again. I didn't see him no more, after that day."

Lily's eyes closed. She sat there, her hands almost in an attitude of prayer against her lips, misery seeping from every inch of her expression. Marcus DeLan touched her arm. She settled back in her chair and slowly lowered her hands into her lap. Exhaling, she opened her eyes and gazed at the tabletop, as if seeing nothing. Spencer bowed his head and mumbled, "He wanted to make things right. Maybe he just couldn't, for some reason."

One of the Colebrook attorneys said, "I'm afraid that what Mr. Porter and his partner did or didn't do next is beside the point. It's clear they knew there were questions concerning the bridge's safety, and they either took no steps or inadequate steps to remedy it. They and Oliver Grant are responsible. That will have to be Colebrook International's official conclusion on the matter."

"Case closed," James said, his voice curt. "I have some sympathy for you, Lily, I really do. I'm willing to believe you knew nothing about your husband's lack of ethics. But you'll have to live with what he did for the rest of your life."

Artemas strode to the end of the table, planted both hands on it, and leaned toward his family, his fierce attention focused on James. "We're not here to punish Lily. If anybody here doubts that she's suffered as much as we have, then leave the room. I don't want to hear it."

Cass pressed forward. "We may have some sympathy for Lily but I, for one, want to hear her apologize for implying that our sister had anything to do with what happened."

Lily lifted her chin. Her eyes glittered. "That fear is something all of *you* are going to have to live with. And you're going to have to wonder if she knew about the bridge too and did nothing."

Artemas heard the rattle of his own breath, the sickening implosion of the fear that had crossed his mind more than once, the fear he could never bring himself to voice. Cass was rising from her chair, furious. James clutched the arms of his wheelchair. Michael and Elizabeth looked stunned. Artemas met Lily's gaze and said the only thing he could. "That's not true. It could never be true. I don't ever want to hear that from you again."

She pushed herself up from the table, unsteady but stiffly erect, and shook her head. "God help you, you'll never know for certain, and you'll never have any more peace of mind than I will."

Artemas watched in speechless despair as she left the room. She was right.

A few months later, as the home she and Richard had created so lovingly became a showplace of flowers and blossoming trees, Lily packed to leave. She would live with Aunt Maude for now, while she decided what to do next.

Almost everything she owned had been sold to settle legal fees and the debts tied to Richard and Frank's architectural firm. Colebrook International had filed suit, as she'd expected. That was what Artemas had to do, a corporate decision he could not escape. She understood, but her bitterness was too deep to forgive it.

Artemas came to see her the day before she left. It was a terrible, grim visit, with Aunt Maude and her sisters refusing to budge from their presence, watching him warily. He asked if she'd accept help from him. He wanted to loan her—hell, give her—the money to start over, somewhere else. Whether the offer was sympathetic or merely an attempt to keep her from moving back to MacKenzie—or both—she hadn't cared. He had looked angry but not surprised when she turned him down.

She moved through the empty rooms, touching the woodwork, stooping to pick a bit of lint from the carpet or wipe distractedly at smudges on the walls. *If you can't bend, you'll break*, Mama would have said. She felt very close to breaking.

Part Three

Some parts of your small hill I will resign,
For it is yours, but where your hill is done
I'd love to add new worlds for us to roam,
For all my worlds have ended at your
    home.

Georgia poet

Nineteen

January second. The new year was one day old, and the specter of next week's anniversary darkened it.

Artemas threw a file of notes on his desk and swiveled toward his office window. The uninteresting parking lot and muddle of generic, glass-and-steel office buildings nearby only reminded him that this building they'd leased was a poor substitute for the neo-Gothic grace of the Colebrook Building, with its wooded, parklike surroundings and gardens.

He'd authorized his attorneys to sell the Colebrook Building to a group of real estate investors. They would renovate the lobby. There would be no bridge, no magnificent garden centered around a blue willow.

Artemas got up and paced. He could have kept the building and occupied it as planned. Maybe that would have been perceived as a courageous gesture. Not to him. It would only sicken his family and the families of the Colebrook executives who'd been killed. He knew he would have relived that night every time he walked through the lobby.

He halted to watch, with dull relief, as workmen took down a huge Christmas tree atop an office building across the street. Christmas had been an exercise in pretense.

They'd gathered at James and Alise's new home, a brooding stone mansion set on the Chattahoochee River. The place had the medieval atmosphere James had always loved. Considering everyone's mood, the holidays had been as pleasant as being held prisoner in a dark, sumptuous dungeon.

He wanted to know how Lily had spent her Christmas. He wanted to know her plans, and everything she'd done during the months since he'd last seen her. He had forced himself to give her the time and privacy to recover, as he was recovering. Tamberlaine called her regularly, but learned very little.

"Artemas? I need to speak with you. It's urgent."

Artemas turned and saw Tamberlaine standing in the doorway. The coincidence of thinking about him and then having him appear seemed uncanny to Artemas. "Come in. I was distracted. Sorry."

"You were a thousand miles away."

"Much closer than that." *Fifty, perhaps. It's fifty miles to Blue Willow.* He would be moving there in a few months. The fact that Lily was living nearby with her aunt meant they would have to deal with each other, and it must be done delicately. No confrontations, no aggression, no manipulation. Trust could only be rebuilt by slow, careful degrees.

"What is it?" he said, studying Tamberlaine's grim expression.

Tamberlaine shut the door. "There is talk among the workmen at the estate." Tamberlaine hesitated, then added, "They say someone has been cleaning up the MacKenzie place. As if planning to live there. I suspect it's Lily."

Hopewell's angry pounding made the Christmas wreath swing back and forth on Maude's front door, and red berries flew off sprigs of nandina tucked among the cedar boughs. A lithe form hurried up the hall, making a red-and-gray blur behind the panes of frosted glass. Little Sis slung the door open and stared up at him.

"Why, Happy New Year, Hopewell." Her eyes were

bright and exasperated, but a little flirtatious, too. Hopewell stared back awkwardly, his mouth working but not saying anything.

Damned woman. She had grandchildren. Ought not to look at him that way. She always looked at him that way.

A clump of plastic holly and red ribbon was tucked rakishly in the knot of gray hair pinned on top of her head. She gave her glittery red sweater a jerk, crossed one blue-jeaned leg over the other, and leaned against the doorjamb. Little pink-quartz crystals jiggled below her pierced earlobes as she shook her head.

"Don't you beat on our door," she added. "If you'd let me know you were coming, I'd have gotten out some wine and gingerbread cookies."

He shoved his fists into the pockets of his ancient coat so hard that the already torn seams gave a little more. "Lily's not here, is she? I bet you all know where she is. Do y'all take me for a fool? Did you think I'd never hear what she's been doing all these months? Did you think she could do it right under my nose?"

Little Sis eyed him with fading cordiality. "If you weren't a grubby old hermit who stays at home watching TV all the time, you'd have figured it out before now."

"What I do with my life is none of your concern, you prissy old bat!"

"Somebody ought to be concerned about you! For years you've let your store go to hell, your house go to hell, and now you look like a seedy bum! Your life didn't end when your wife died and Joe went to prison for growing dope!"

"I want to talk about Lily!" He stomped a scuffed cowboy boot on the porch floor. Another nandina berry fell off the wreath. Thrusting his grizzled jaw out, he leaned toward Little Sis menacingly. "She's been hanging out at the farm since she moved up here last May, huh? Herbert Beatty at the garden center in Victoria told me she came in back in the spring to buy seeds and fertilizer. I knew she hadn't planted nothing *here*—"

"She's not hurting anything."

Little Sis poked him in the chest with a fingertip. "She went out to see her old homeplace one day, and she came back with some of the spunk in her eyes, and she told us the only thing that made her feel better was working there. She knew you wouldn't approve. So we kept it quiet. Goodness, all she does is drive over there every day with a few of our yard tools and get some exercise."

"What does she want? I'm not gonna sell the place back to her!"

"She couldn't buy the place back even if you offered. The bank didn't leave her with much more than a pickup truck and that ugly dog of hers."

"Colebrook wants her to have it! I'll never give that bastard the satisfaction! Not after he had his people sic the law on Joe!"

Little Sis eyed him warily. "If you tell her she can't dabble around the farm anymore, I swear I'll send so many bad vibrations your way, you'll feel like an out-of-tune piano."

"Don't talk that nonsense to me. I, uh, maybe I *don't* care if she hangs around at her old place. 'Long as she doesn't expect to own it again."

She brightened. "Why, Hopewell, if you leave her alone, I might just send *good* vibrations at you." Looking at him wistfully, she added, "I'd like to, you know. You and I aren't too old to—"

"I've got no use for a woman who wears pieces of quartz rocks like they were some kind of magic totems and talks like a hippie and runs a store full of books by that Shirley MacLaine. *Are you gonna tell me where to find Lily today?*"

Little Sis straightened like a rocket. "You closed-minded old goat. Go on. She left here a few minutes before you showed up. She was heading out to the farm."

"Thank you, ma'am," he said tersely. Turning on his run-down bootheels, he stomped down the porch steps and strode toward a shabby truck. He heard Little Sis slam the door behind him. He didn't need her meddling sympathy or her outrageous, girlish hints. He did need revenge on Artemas Colebrook. Maybe, just maybe, Lily was a means to getting it.

Lily had just finished putting her Christmas ornaments on the small cedar tree that had taken root at the edge of the yard when Mr. Estes drove up the old driveway, now rutted and lined with groves of young pines that had crept into the front pastures.

She tossed a cardboard box into the back of her truck, sat down on the tailgate, and wearily draped an arm around Lupa's golden neck. A cool breeze crept down from into the hollow as if funneled gently through the hills around it. The cedar tree swayed. A blob of papier-mâché that vaguely resembled an angel—Stephen had made it in kindergarten—bumped against a crystal ornament etched with her and Richard's wedding date. Starched, crocheted stars made decades ago by Grandma MacKenzie floated like tethered snowflakes. The tree's stiff needles clung to tiny, brightly painted wooden sleighs and nutcracker men Richard had created in his workshop.

Staring at the tree, she had never felt so lonely in her life. Needing to huddle inside her own skin, she pulled up the collar on her quilted jacket, then wiped a sweaty palm on the thigh of her jeans and watched Mr. Estes park in front of the old farmhouse with its vacant, staring windows and peeling paint. He stalked over to her with a grim expression on his face.

He gaped at the decorated tree. Feeling exposed and foolish, Lily said grimly, "I put the ornaments on it when I'm here, and I take 'em off when I leave. I know Christmas is over, but I just wanted to see 'em one more time before I pack them away."

She struggled against bitterness. "The least you could have done was block off the road so people wouldn't dump garbage out here." She jerked her head toward the overgrown field beyond the creek and the willows, and the village of gravestones at the base of the hills. "You know what I found in my family's cemetery plot last spring? *Beer cans and a dildo.* If you don't know what a dildo is, sir, I'll explain."

Mr. Estes shifted from one foot to another. His furious teetering reminded her of an upset R2D2. "You watch your mouth. I'm not here to win no popularity contest."

She jumped off the tailgate and advanced on him, hands clenched by her sides. Lupa bounded down and circled them, growling softly. "You've never had any sympathy for anybody but yourself. I had a son, too, Mr. Estes. I wanted the best for him, just like you want for Joe. He's gone, and I'll never get him back. Joe'll get out of prison someday. You've got everything to look forward to. Can't you leave me alone? Even if I never get this place back, I need to put my hands on it, clean it up, sit under the willows, listen to the creek." Halting, she shook her fists at him. "Working here has given me a small sense of satisfaction and purpose."

"Good. *Good!*" Mr. Estes shouted. "Then you stay here and make Colebrook mad as hell."

She stared at him. The swift, thready racing of her heart made her dizzy with hope. His offer was so unexpected, she blurted, "Are you having a stroke?"

"Don't argue with me!" He ducked his head and muttered, "If you want to stay, *stay.* All I'm sayin' is, I'd, uh, rent the place to you."

She stepped forward eagerly. "I haven't got enough money to pay rent. But I could work for you. Pay you that way." He took a step back and looked at her in astonishment. The vague, fragmented ideas she'd been mulling over for so long suddenly crystallized. Lily found herself telling him about them at breakneck speed. A greenhouse. A nursery. For perennials—sweet william and yarrow and columbine and dozens of others—old-fashioned plants that people were starting to favor again.

Mr. Estes began waving his hands. "I don't have no interest in—"

"You need something to work for, Mr. Estes. So do I. You make an investment, and I'll manage the place. We can build something out of this mess. Prove to people around here that neither one of us is ready to lay down and die."

"I don't care what nobody thinks. You sayin' I'm *ashamed* on account of Joe?"

"Yes, sir, and I think you're eating yourself up with it."

His head arched like an angry rooster's. "You don't want a job, you want to order me around. Pffft. I ain't got the time or the patience. You're one of them that's got all the answers when nobody's asked you a question. Just like Little Sis."

"We could call it Blue Willow Nursery."

His mouth halted in midprotest. His eyes narrowed. He pulled his hat off and ran a leathery hand through a thick shock of white hair that looked as if it had been cut with a pocketknife. "Colebrook'd hate that, wouldn't he? His whole family would have a fit."

"The Colebrooks have no legal claim on the name. It came from my family, from the willow my great-grandfather gave the Colebrooks when they built their estate. It's mine more than theirs."

"You really want to make a point, don't you?"

"I want respect and fair treatment." She shuddered, then walked back to the truck, her hands on her hips. "I won't run from them. I won't forget about them. I won't let what they said about my husband make me hide from the people in my own hometown. If I did that, it'd be as good as saying I'm ashamed of Richard. No. I'm here to stay."

Lily slumped on the tailgate and rubbed her forehead. Mr. Estes began pacing, twisting his hat, slamming it on top of his head, then taking it off again.

"Just who's gonna buy these old-fashioned plants you want to sell?"

She smiled thinly. "Nostalgia is big business, Mr. Estes. People'll come here from Atlanta for the same reason they come to the mountains. Don't worry. I can make this place a success."

Mr. Estes stopped pacing and faced her. "All right, it's a deal. You live here and run things. Work up a plan. I'll let you know how much money I can put into it. Maybe ten thousand dollars. That's all."

"I warn you, you won't make your money back right away. It'll take upward of a year to get set up, and a lot longer than that to build recognition."

He nodded toward the old house. "I'll get the electricity turned back on, but I'm not investin' any money in fixin' it up."

"I've got a little savings. And I've got something I can sell to get a little more. I'll get by." She thought of the Colebrook teapot, then lifted her head and looked around, her throat aching with hope. "I've got what I need. Thank you."

A shiny new metal gate hung between two sturdy railroad ties at the end of the driveway. Artemas touched the padlock and took in his surroundings with dismay. The forest seemed to press around him, whispering and brittle with winter. As he'd driven the long, winding dirt lane from the paved road, he'd felt as if he were going back in time.

But time had not paused here.

Fallen hog-wire fences were all that marked the old pasture boundaries, as if struggling valiantly to contain thick groves of waist-high pines. The house and barn sat in the distance, looking abandoned and forlorn. The willows, bare of leaves, stood out against a cold blue sky. Lily's large red truck was parked in the yard.

He stepped over the crumpled fence and walked swiftly up the drive, a black windbreaker curling back from his sweater and corduroys. He saw the jumble of trash piled in the side yard where Mrs. MacKenzie's flower beds had flourished. Rusting appliances and tires were piled nearby. White paint was peeling off the house. The barn was a hollow shell, with pieces of tin missing from the roof and gaping holes in the sides. God, how awful she must have felt when she saw the place like this.

Only the willow grove remained beautiful and dignified. Beyond the creek she'd cut a small clearing in the pines. It was scarred with small stumps, charred piles of debris she'd burned, and mounds of pines waiting to be burned.

He went to the house, pulled the warped front door open, and grimaced at the musty scent of dark, empty rooms. Even in the dim light he saw how Joe Estes had ruined the interior. Cheap paneling covered the walls of the main room. The handsome pine floor was hidden under matted shag carpet. He yelled Lily's name, his voice ringing with anger—anger at this scene, at the gut-wrenching sympathy he couldn't indulge, at her for making him so hopelessly eager. The name echoed unpleasantly. He slammed the door and walked across the yard, searching.

She must be in the woods somewhere, walking, exploring, doing what had always meant so much to her. Or hiding? Hiding from him, watching him from some vantage point, the way she'd done the day he'd left here so many years ago. If he tilted his head back and yelled that he loved her, it would change nothing, just as it had changed nothing then.

By God, this time he'd find her. He strode to the creek, crossed its shallows on a path of flat rocks laid down by some long-dead MacKenzie, and skirted the clearing, scowling at the piles of burned timber and the rising hills beyond. The view from the farm's valley was magnificent, as he lifted his eyes to gaze up to Mount Victory, which poked its bald granite dome into the sky. He angled around a jumble of broken limbs and came to a shocked halt.

Lily sat there, facing the mountain view, her long legs crossed, her mane of red hair flowing around her shoulders, every stitch of her clothes piled beside her.

Indelible images slammed into him. Large, high breasts with wide, dusky red tips. A long, slender back flaring into luscious hips. A flash of red between her thighs. But even more, he reacted to the deep emotional tug of the loneliness and grief in her face. He had not seen her since spring, the day she was preparing to move from her and

Richard's home. That she had been suffering so harshly since then, and was still in such despair, tormented him.

His hiking shoe snapped a twig. She exploded into action, scrambling to her knees and facing him, her tear-streaked face contorting, one arm rising quickly to shield her breasts, the other snaking across her thighs. She slipped sideways onto one hip. Her eyes were strangely unfocused yet angry. "Mine. It's mine. You can't ruin it. You're spying on me. Go 'way."

His attention went to the half-empty bottle of bourbon tilted against a hummock of dead grass, and he made an animal-like sound of helpless pain. Sorrow and frustration left little room for kindness. He vaulted to her, sank to his knees, snatched a flannel shirt from her jumbled clothing, and threw it at her. "It's not even fifty degrees out here. And anyone could have walked up on you like this."

She shoved the shirt aside. "Only you." She hunched down, her arms sagging then clenching tight over her nakedness, and gave him an agonized look that radiated fury and ruined privacy. "Leave. *Leave.*"

"If you can't stand me, then why the hell are you here?"

"My home. *Home.* You thought I'd run? You thought I'd let you make me feel like dirt and not fight back?" She jammed a hand into the ground. "It's clean here. I'm clean." She threw a clod of damp earth. It grazed his cheek. Something snapped in his control. He lunged at her, jerked her arms aside, then whipped the shirt around her shoulders. "Get dressed."

She hissed and drew a hand back, but fell off-balance. He pushed her over and straddled her, his knees clenching the sides of her hips. Her loose-limbed struggling accomplished nothing but the lurid writhing of her belly and breasts. He shoved one of her hands into a shirtsleeve. She caught him in the jaw with her free hand. He clamped her arm down.

Bending over her, he stared into her eyes. Something in his expression frightened her enough to temper the fury. Before the fear could fade, he rammed her hand into the other sleeve and closed the shirt over her breasts. "Hello,

neighbor," he said with ugly sarcasm, and sat down beside
her. The shirttail was draped halfway up her stomach. Her
long legs were half-bent, her feet and ankles rust red with
dried mud. Artemas flicked the shirt over her thighs and
cursed.

She gulped short, shallow breaths. Finally one hand
rose to her shirt. Holding it together, she pushed herself upright. "I guess Tamberlaine tol' you what Mr. Estes
and me—"

"Hell yes, he told me."

"Nothing you can do about it." She reached for the
bottle. Artemas beat her to it and flipped it upside down,
then jabbed the tip into soft earth covered in brown pine
needles.

"There's nothing worse than a mean drunk. We can't
talk unless you're sober." He leaped to his feet, pulled her
up after him, and started toward the creek. She dug her
bare heels in and stumbled when he plowed ahead despite
her resistance.

He dragged her into the shallow creek, turned, and
scooped her legs out from under her. She sat down hard
on the sandy bottom. Immediately he was on his knees beside her in the icy, foot-deep water.

Lily gasped. The cold penetrated her bones. She
couldn't believe he was doing this. Hugging herself, she
tried to wrench away from him. One of his hands sank
into the back of her hair. He held her still and cupped water to her face, scrubbing it vigorously.

"Stop," she ordered, her voice small and weary. Twisting her head away and shutting her eyes, she hunched
over miserably. The water flowed around them with peaceful gurgles, chuckling at their torment without compassion. She heard the ragged sound of his breathing. "God
damn you, Lily," he said, his voice soft and hoarse. "This
is killing me."

She cried—helpless, humiliating, drunken sobs. "I
know. I wish you never had to see me again. But I can't
leave here."

"Oh, God." It was a groan of despair. "I don't want you

to go away, but I can't do anything to help you." He
latched both arms around her waist and, half carrying her,
pulled her to the bank. They leaned against each other, her
head bowed by his shoulder, both of them shivering.

"Tomorrow, it's been a year," she said, struggling to get
the words out of her throat. "It seems like forever. It seems
like yesterday. I miss them so much. The loneliness—God,
the loneliness. It makes me feel crazy things. Friends came
up from Atlanta last week. Hai and some others. I wanted
them to stay with me—anyone, to stay with me. Richard's
cousins from South Carolina came to visit at Christmas. I
could hardly stand to let them leave. They felt so sorry for
me—one even asked me to move up there and live near
them." She beat her fist on one knee. She knew she was
babbling, but she couldn't stop. "Richard would want me
to go live with them. But I can't. This is my home. This is
where I have to stay—and fight for our honor."

Artemas leaned his head against her hair. "*Your* honor
has never been in question."

"Oh, yes. He belonged to me. And our son . . . our boy
deserves a better memorial than this gossip and accusation
about his father."

Artemas kept one arm around her back, tight as a vise,
holding her to him. "There must be something to look forward to. There has to be."

"Work. Making something out of nothing. And forgetting. I feel them going away, a little. It hurts. It hurts to
feel them fading. I don't want them to go."

"We have to let them go."

"I can't. Not with all the doubts, everything we'll never
know. Don't you think about that? Not knowing exactly
what happened?"

"Every day. And I think about not knowing what will
happen to you. Then, finding you alone and hurting like
this . . ." His voice trailed off. He put both arms around
her and kissed her forehead roughly. He was the only
warmth in the world, and she couldn't bear to move away.

She moaned and tilted her face up, blindly yearning to
give back his comfort, to make some small sacrifice of bit-

terness. He kissed her eyes, a fervent and quick caress, and she sagged against him. His face was wet and cold, his mouth like a smooth fire in comparison.

Connect. Survive. Forgive. Crying again, she pressed her lips to his, and he responded. For the briefest of eternities there was no need to think of anything except him. Then remorse flooded her. She faced forward, her eyes squinted shut. Gritting her teeth, she groaned Richard's name.

Artemas caught his breath, then exhaled in one long, exhausted sigh. "I'll drive you to your aunt's house." His voice was flat, dead.

"No." Dragging a hand over her ravaged face, she stared straight ahead, trying to repress the thought that she'd betrayed Richard and Stephen. And herself. "Don't come here again. Mr. Estes doesn't want you to set foot on the place. And neither do I."

Artemas took her firmly by the shoulders and twisted her to face him. "That's guilt talking."

He got up and walked away in grim silence, crossed the creek, and stood, his back to her, his broad shoulders hunched. Several long minutes passed before he heard splashing sounds from the creek. He turned and watched as she knelt on the bank near him, dressed in jeans and a quilted blue jacket over the wet shirt that was plastered to her breasts and stomach. She tied the laces on her thick-soled work shoes, scooped the ragged hair back from her face, and stood, unsteady but in control again.

"This place can't be what it was," he said slowly. "Under the circumstances, nothing can be wonderful again. All we can do is accept that."

"Including Blue Willow?"

"I'll settle for believing that there are places and memories worth preserving, and something meaningful in saving them."

"Heady philosophy for a man who remade the family fortune by marrying a senator's daughter and selling ceramic technology to the military."

"It beats the hell out of being a victim."

She shot him a hard glance. "Like me?"

"You're a victim if you equate blind faith and suffering with nobility."

"You mean, sitting naked in the cold won't get me into the Gandhi Hall of Fame? *Damn.*"

He frowned at her sarcasm. "All it might do is get you raped by some wandering hunter who thinks you're fair game."

"Well, if that ever happens, I'm sure your family will have a celebration."

"That's a vicious and unwarranted thing to say."

"Is it? They probably think I moved back here to get in your good graces again—and maybe into your bed too."

"Did that unscrupulous bastard you were married to teach you this gutter-level cynicism?"

"My husband—" She tried to say it calmly, but her mouth trembled and her composure shattered. "My *husband* was the least cynical person I've ever met. And he died holding our child in his arms and trying to protect him."

Artemas winced, as she put her hands over her face and turned away. "Lily," he said desperately, reaching toward her. "*Lily.* Let me make things easier for you. I can give you the money to buy this place back. I can—"

"Oh, my God." Her shoulders shook. She twisted from the brush of his fingertips and stared at him. "Do you think I'll ever take any help from you? Do you still believe you can run my life and get whatever you want?"

Artemas dropped his hands to his side. "Yes."

She inhaled sharply. "Goddamn you."

He turned and walked back up the long driveway. Their futures were no less bound together now than they had been the day she was born.

"She's poison," James said. "And Artemas doesn't seem willing to acknowledge that."

Tamberlaine leaned back in the plush chair of his office, one hand bent to his chin, studying James and the others with deceptive calm. He feared their undercurrent of agitation and bewilderment. It was divisive—something the family had never had to deal with before. "What would you have him do?" Tamberlaine asked. "Abandon an estate that has great significance for this family simply because Mrs. Porter has chosen to live at a home that has equal significance to her?"

"He could pressure her to leave," Cass interjected. "Instead of telling us he's accepted the situation."

Tamberlaine shrugged elegantly. "That doesn't imply he intends to hand out a welcome mat for her."

Elizabeth frowned. "Tammy, this friendship they've always had—is there any reason to think it was ever more than that?"

"No. As I've said before, he spent time with her family, as a child. He and she corresponded with each other over the years. It was quite innocent and sentimental." Tamberlaine carefully hid his remorse at lying. Artemas had confided the truth to him years ago. It was a confidence he would never break.

Elizabeth sighed. "Do you think she's deliberately trying to harm us in some way now?"

"No. I believe Mrs. Porter is a very honorable person, who feels she has as much right to her heritage as Artemas does to his."

Michael leaned forward. "But she must realize that she's exacerbating a painful situation."

Tamberlaine scowled. "It has been widely publicized that the architects as well as the contractor bear the responsibility for the bridge collapse, and that your brother has pursued their liability to the hilt. No one can claim that he let his friendship with Mrs. Porter hinder his duties to Colebrook International—or to this family."

James cursed. "We'll never have any peace as long as she's living near the estate. And that's exactly *why* she's there—to show us she can do as she damned well pleases."

Tamberlaine's patience for James's bitterness had faded months ago. James seemed intent on destroying the future, not rebuilding. He scanned the assembled group with deep sorrow.

James, dressed in tailored black pinstripes, stood by a

black marble fireplace as if drawing from its coldness, rigid and alert, one hand white-knuckled on the handle of a metal cane—one of the generic, tripod-footed devices furnished by his physical therapists. Alise sat near him in an armchair, her slim, fashionable black dress making her look even more subdued than usual.

Cassandra looked ready to dine on Lily's pride as she prowled the room in snug red silk, a brilliant scarf fluttering over one shoulder. Elizabeth sat in a prim little armchair with her knees pressed tightly together under a demure gray suit dress, her blond hair curling sweetly around her face, her toddler drooling on her jacket sleeve. She was tall and imposing, but her face had a perpetually timid look, as if she suspected someone might creep out of a corner and shout "Boo" into her ear at any moment.

Michael, kind, gentle Michael, sat in a chair nearby, his long denimed legs extended and crossed above suede loafers, a houndstooth jacket hanging over a rumpled sports shirt, sandy brown hair shagging over his pale forehead and large hazel eyes.

They were deeply decent and loving human beings, all of them, and seeing them descend into vindictiveness and suspicion made Tamberlaine sick. He shook his head slowly. "James, you seem to forget—all of you are forgetting, I think—that Mrs. Porter has done nothing more heinous than love and trust her husband."

"She said that Julia knew the bridge was faulty, and ignored it," James retorted. "She said that Julia bullied her husband into compromising standards. There's no excuse for accusations like that, and there never will be."

Alise moved a hand wearily. "I think we should try to understand Lily's point of view, even if we don't agree with it. She's lost so much. Her bitterness may be misguided, but it's not surprising." Alise looked at James. His fierce gaze made her clench her hand in her lap. "We have to get on with our lives."

He gestured sharply toward his bad leg. "Yes, I know how much you're looking forward to cheering for me when I try out for the Olympic track team this spring."

Alise flinched and turned away. There was awkward silence. Cassandra halted her pacing and scowled at her brother. Elizabeth and Michael seemed equally dismayed.

Tamberlaine rose to his feet. *"James."* His voice was like soft thunder. "Alise has a great deal more respect for you at the moment than I do." He left the large office, slamming the door behind him.

The brooding silence became oppressive. James limped to Alise, hesitated, then dropped a hand to her shoulder. She put hers over it, but her expression remained drawn. Finally Cassandra bluntly summed up their mood: "We have to keep a close watch on Lily. That means spending time at the estate. Artemas has said he considers it the family's home. Given that excuse, we can make certain—discreetly—that she doesn't worm her way into his life."

There were general nods of agreement. James's face was as closed as a vise. He turned from them, frowning. He would keep his own counsel, and make his own plans.

Michael wandered miserably through the rooms of the large apartment he and Kathy had shared. It was crammed with books and paintings, sculpture, and ordinary, pleasant, comfortable furniture. Even if he spent most of his time at a town house in Atlanta now, he would never sell this place. He touched Kathy's clothes, still hanging in the walk-in closets of the bedroom, spread her perfume on his hands, and stood for a long time studying photographs of her that covered one of the bedroom walls.

He fought the urges as long as he could, and anxiety made his chest constrict. A deep drag on one of his asthma inhalers eased the attack, but he knew nothing but action could solve the other problem. He phoned downstairs to have the doorman call a cab. By the time it arrived, he had changed clothes and was waiting impatiently on the curb in the muggy air, his jogging shoes soaking up a puddle from a recent rain.

He had the cabdriver drop him off a block from his destination, preferring not to cause idle gossip. Dark, silent brownstones and small shops gave no clue that, a century earlier, this had been a tree-lined boulevard fronting the in-town mansions of the very wealthy. But the imposing stone wall at the end of the block hinted at remaining grandeur. It enclosed an acre, a fortune in land at New York prices.

Michael retrieved a key from his jeans' pocket and unlocked a tall, narrow gate of black iron. Stepping inside, he locked it behind him and stood still, absorbing the place's leaden reality. Scattered among old trees like morbid playhouses were the Colebrook mausoleums.

A half-moon had come out from behind high, scudding clouds. He didn't need the moon; he had found her crypt in pitch-darkness many times. He picked his way up a path to the newest mausoleum, a broad, stately monument in white marble, with a door made of steel grate in an ornamental pattern of overlapping *C*'s.

Another key unlocked that door, and then Michael was inside, sitting cross-legged on the cold floor next to her, tracing her carved name on the wall with trembling fingertips. The past two years disappeared; she was alive again. Michael laid his cheek against her name.

He tried never to think of Kathy inside the coffin, just as he struggled every day not to think of her cradled, warm and loving, in his arms, whispering his name.

"Hello," he whispered. "I know you don't want me to come here like this. But I have to." He huddled as close as he could and shut his eyes. He and she had been soulmates since their freshman year at college, both of them psychology majors, she Jewish, from a family of academics, he benignly cynical about religion in general, and from a family whose name meant wealth and decadence. They had never spent a night apart until she died. There would never be anyone else for him.

He acknowledged James's reasons for hating and distrusting Lily Porter. James sought someone to blame for every limping, painful step he would take for the rest of his life. Michael doubted James or anyone else in the family—even Elizabeth, with whom Michael had the close, intuitive bond of a fraternal twin—would approve if they knew he had always admired and sympathized with Lily.

He could never punish her for loving her husband so much that nothing else mattered. He understood that pain too well. Touching Kathy's name again, he cried against the cold stone.

Twenty

Edward Tamberlaine bent to pet Lupa. If he ever wore anything less formal than a handsome double-breasted suit, Lily had never seen it. His skin was the color of rich chocolate, his hair short, trained into graceful waves, and salted with gray. Inky-black freckles were sprinkled over the bridge of his flaring, elegant nose. He smiled somberly as he came toward her, leaving his car parked in the yard.

Lily watched from her place in what had been the front pasture—now a muddy, flat expanse cleared by the bulldozer Mr. Estes had sent. She set a bucket of grass seed down and walked swiftly to meet Tamberlaine. The breeze made jonquils sway along the shallow ditches that bordered the drive, where they had bloomed every March as long as Lily could remember. Deep orange daylillies would take their place later in the spring. No amount of desertion or neglect mattered to them. When she had the time and a little precious money to allocate, she would reward them with mulch and fertilizer.

Her hands were chapped and scratched, her nails chewed to the quick. Aching muscles and bruises had become everyday companions over the past two months. She made long lists of tasks and began work before dawn most days, fighting the weight of grief and depression that always hovered like a shadow just beyond conscious thought. If she stopped moving, she started thinking and sank into bleak moods.

"How are you, Lily?" Tamberlaine asked.

"Fine," she lied. Feeling a little awkward, she tucked a jonquil into a buttonhole on his lapel, then stepped back. "Now you look ready for spring."

"I came up to the estate to see the progress. I couldn't help stopping by here. I hope you don't mind."

"No, of course not." He was here on Artemas's behalf, to see what she'd accomplished so far. She was certain of it.

She followed his curious gaze. The mountain of garbage was gone, though a pile of discarded shag carpet and torn paneling lay in the front yard, waiting to be hauled away. She wanted every hint of Joe Estes out of the house. Mr. Estes had looked dour but said nothing when he'd noticed her intentions.

A long concrete foundation had been poured toward the front of the cleared pasture, with a smaller pad nearby. She pointed toward them. "The little one is for an office and shop, eventually. The other one is for a greenhouse. The rest of the clearing will be used for nursery beds."

Tamberlaine nodded. "And you've had the lane from the paved road widened a bit and graveled, judging from the looks of it as I drove in."

"The road was washing away a little more every time it rained. And little trees were trying to take over."

"It's a fine road now."

His solemn praise made her slide her hands in the back pockets of her khaki trousers and try to appear nonchalant. "So what's the news, Mr. Tamberlaine? Has he moved in yet?"

"Yes. The house is functional, but hardly comfortable. He moved into a suite of rooms his grandparents had occupied. It's rather spartan."

"I'll tell you the truth. I slip through the woods sometimes and stand just out of sight, by the lake, to watch the work. There must be a hundred people around the place.

He'll need to hire a top landscaper to restore the gardens. I could give you a list of names, if you won't tell him where you got 'em."

"He doesn't plan to renovate the gardens anytime soon."

She frowned. "But he's had everything cleared around the mansion. And on the hill above the lake."

Tamberlaine said softly, "I expect the gardens are more personal to him than the house. Perhaps he doesn't like the idea of having some stranger design them."

An invisible hand pressed on her chest. She looked at Tamberlaine. She'd almost forgotten that he rarely contacted her without dropping some bit of information—and usually for a reason.

"I'm gonna start calling you Machiavelli, if you keep scheming like this."

A pensive smile crooked the corner of Mr. Tamberlaine's mouth. "I'm afraid I've grown too fond of my role over the years. I would like to see this heartache resolved between you and him. And the others."

"I don't think that's possible." She linked an arm through his. They walked down to the creek. "They're like family to you, aren't they?" she asked gently.

"Yes. But then, so are you." They stopped under an enormous willow. He sighed and caught one of the draping tendrils in his free hand, studying the tiny new leaves. "Dusky blue-green, even in infancy," he mused. "What a marvel."

"I could dig up one of the saplings for you." She nodded to the small trees spreading out around the grove's edges. "These willows are hardier than most kinds. And they breed like mice."

He cleared his throat and said gruffly, "I'd love to have a blue willow at my house."

"I'll send you one."

"Would you believe that I bought a twenty-room Italianate villa near the governor's mansion? I believe I'm the first black man my neighbors have seen who isn't wearing a butler's uniform."

"Aw, it's not like that anymore." She tugged at his coat sleeve. "Get yourself a white butler named Billy Bob."

He laughed. "Perhaps I will." Tamberlaine studied her with somber amusement from under bushy brows. As he continued to look at her, a pensive look replaced his smile. "He has never directed me to explain his behavior to anyone, on his behalf. His actions often speak for themselves. Forgive me if, in this case, I step over the boundaries of my duties and speak on a personal level."

"I'd appreciate that. Go ahead."

"He may appear aggressive and even self-serving to you, but he is *not* someone you should consider an enemy."

Her hands shook. She wound them into her pockets and stared at the creek, seeking answers in the ever-moving water. "I know that. But he's trying to fix my problems for me, and he considers my loyalty to Richard something that needs *fixing* along with the rest."

"The desperate state of his family never allowed him to choose between *taking care* and *taking over*. There was simply no gray area for him. There still isn't."

"He's going to know where the gray areas are with me." She gestured at her land, including herself in it. "Maybe that's one of the reasons I came back here. To prove that he can't take care, take over, or ignore me."

"And perhaps to prove to yourself that you don't want him to succeed?"

She was silent, shaken by his insight. "Yes," she admitted finally.

After he left, she returned to spreading grass seed on the stripped earth of the old pasture, but a new, indefinable darkness hovered over her. She found herself studying the dense woods across the road that fronted the pasture. Artemas had come back, as steadfast as the jonquils and daylillies along the driveway. So had she. Both of them had kept some part of an old promise. The rest was hopeless. Her hand wavered, halted. She shut her eyes against sorrow and dread.

On the other side of those woods, so close that when

the wind was right she could hear the sounds of heavy
trucks and bulldozers, saws and jackhammers, Artemas
woke, slept, and dreamed his own memories at Blue
Willow.

Artemas set the Blue Willow teapot on a crude table made
of sawhorses and plywood in the center of the upstairs gallery, stood back, lit a cigarette, and studied the small, delicate vessel grimly. It looked as if it were waiting for
interrogation under the harsh light of a construction light
clamped to the top of a stepladder by the table.

   Last week Lily had sold it to Svenson's Fine China and
Crystal Shop, an elite Atlanta dealer, for five thousand dollars. Artemas had suspected she'd go to Svenson's if she
ever disposed of the teapot. His discreet inquiries into her
life over the years had revealed that she'd bought all her
china and crystal from the dealer. Not Colebrook china,
no. She had never bought any Colebrook china.

   So he'd had Mr. LaMieux, who handled all such secre-
tarial chores for him, leave word at the dealer's that he'd
pay top value should anyone ever bring in a piece of old
Colebrook Blue Willow.

   He'd bought the teapot back.

   Artemas understood how much she needed the money.
What hurt was knowing that she'd rather sell something of
such sentimental value to strangers than ask him for help.
Despite some of the things he'd said to her, he wanted to
be part of her life. That need was a constant torment.

   Restless, he left the large, empty gallery with its high
ceilings and mahogany bookcases waiting to be restored
and opened one of the towering glass doors to a balcony.
Pulling a heavy terry-cloth robe closer around his bare
chest, he stepped onto smooth stone tiles. They were cold
and damp with dew under his bare feet. The sky was
salted with brilliant stars. He mashed the cigarette out on
a wide stone balustrade, then carefully brushed the ashes
off the edge and dropped the butt into a pocket of his
robe. Abruptly he realized how ridiculous his concern was,
considering the rough state of most of the mansion's inte-

rior, the clutter of drop cloths, dust, debris, and materials scattered throughout three stories of rooms and hallways.

He leaned against the balustrade and looked at the newly cleared terraces far below. Gardens had once stair-stepped down the hill toward the distant, starlit mirror of the lake. He remembered Lily writing to him once, as a teenager, that there had been trellises filled with roses. She had said that even after the trellises rotted and fell down, years passed before the roses were choked out completely by briers and pines. The last few clusters of pink and red blooming in the thickets had made her think of elegantly gowned ladies displayed in a prison. She had wanted to rescue them.

Now, the terraces waited for her attention. He knew it could never happen, and that he shouldn't put off hiring a landscaper. With every day that passed, he would look at the cleared spaces around the house and only think of the impossible. It was reckless, like buying the teapot. For once in his life, he verged on losing control over selfish obsessions, a dangerous indulgence.

He lit another cigarette. The pinpoint of red flared then disappeared, its invisible heat merging with the darkness.

The man was a stranger. Strangers usually came to Hope-well's door to sell, beg, or preach, all of which he despised. Well-dressed strangers stepping out of late-model foreign cars with leather briefcases were twice as suspicious.

Hopewell moved quickly out of a rump-sprung arm-chair in front of the television. Anger was the only thing that made him move this fast anymore. He slapped at his creaking knees and stomped through a living room strewn with dirty clothes and the remnants of frozen dinners. He had the front door open before the stranger reached the porch.

Hopewell didn't bother opening the outside screened door. He waited behind it, glaring through fist-sized holes in the mesh. Beyond the stranger, a weedy meadow large enough for a baseball field stretched between Hopewell's big clapboard house and the road to town. He liked his privacy and didn't care for appearances, dammit. Couldn't the stranger tell from this ailing, secluded house and the scowl on his face?

"Mr. Estes?" the man asked. He had smooth, polished hair and nails.

"I don't want no insurance," Hopewell retorted, and started to slam the inner door.

"I'm not selling. I'm buying." The man stepped closer, smiling without showing any teeth. "I'm buying your co-operation. In return, I can guarantee your son's future."

Hopewell held on to the door. He couldn't make him-self shut it. "Who are you?"

"I represent someone who has your son's best interests in mind. Someone who wants to make certain he passes his parole hearing next year. Someone who'll take care of him once he's paroled, so he'll have every chance to start a successful new life and make you very proud."

The door was opening wider. Hopewell couldn't help himself. "What do you mean, exactly? Whose mouthpiece are you?"

"That's not important, Mr. Estes." The man pulled a creamy, embossed business card from inside his coat and held it to a hole in the screen. Hopewell read a law firm's name that meant nothing to him. "Who for?" he repeated.

"May I come in? This will only take a minute. And I assure you, you'll want to hear my proposal, for your son's sake."

Hopewell clutched the door. For Joe's sake. That was the whole measure of his life, and of his poor Ducie's dying wishes. "Come in."

The lawyer sat on the edge of a couch that smelled of stale cigar smoke and sweat. Hopewell loomed over him, waiting. Opening his briefcase, the man removed a slender stack of pages divided by stapled corners into three sets. He shut his briefcase and laid them on it, then looked up at Hopewell. "The client I represent will do everything possible to ensure Joe's release next year. Assuming that's accomplished—and I believe it will be, since Joe has been a model prisoner—my client will arrange money, a job, a fine house, and a powerful amount of discreet intervention should Joe ever have any more, hmmm, shall we say, *difficulties*."

"Joe wants to race cars. That's what he was spending that damned drug money on. Mario Andretti—that's who he wanted to be."

"Then my client will spend whatever is necessary to sponsor him and help him achieve that goal."

His mouth open, Hopewell slumped in an armchair padded with dusty newspapers. "Why? What's the catch? What does your 'client' get out of this?"

The lawyer spread his hands on the paperwork, like a TV evangelist getting ready to perform a healing. "All my client asks in return is that you evict Lily Porter from the property you own."

Hopewell strangled on the dilemma. It was as if those pale, healing hands had gone around his neck, and they were squeezing so hard that self-respect and disgust kept trying to get past them but got pushed down. "I . . . I can't," he said.

"You and she have signed a formal contract?"

"Yeah. She drew one up. A year's lease. February to February. I'm not gonna break it. I'm just not. Don't ask me to." *There. A good show of honor.*

"Hmmm." The lawyer frowned mildly. "Then the term of the lease will end at about the time of your son's parole. I suppose that will have to be acceptable. You'll agree not to renew Mrs. Porter's lease, and prohibit her from remaining on the property in any capacity."

Hopewell leaned forward. His ears buzzed. He felt in a shirt pocket for the blood-pressure medication he took whenever it damn well suited him to care, and popped a tablet into his mouth. The lawyer watched him with a patient stare. "It's him, isn't it?" Hopewell said, his voice tinny. "It's Artemas Colebrook. He's behind this."

"I can't reveal my client's name. But your guess is mistaken."

"Liar." Hopewell put his face in his hands. Joe's future or revenge. Joe's future or self-respect. Joe's future. Joe was weak-willed. Hopewell had suffered agonies thinking about the new trouble he'd probably get into once he left prison. Here was a way, maybe the only way, to give Joe a chance to do right. Maybe it was revenge enough to make Artemas Colebrook spend money on Joe.

As for Lily, well, she'd brought Colebrook's meanness on herself, hadn't she, by coming back to the old place when she knew it would only cause trouble, and by being married to a criminal?

No, this is wrong, this is shameful, what you're thinking of doing to her.

This was for Joe. Joe was his blood. Lily wasn't.

The lawyer had a gold pen out. He was adding precise little lines of script to his papers. Waiting for the inevitable.

Hopewell rose to his feet unsteadily. "You get your ass out of my house, and don't come back."

The lawyer laid two more of his business cards on a coffee table littered with crumbs and empty soft-drink cans. "You'll have almost a year to decide. My offer will remain open." The man stood and smiled. Again, no teeth showed. "Have a good day, sir."

Hopewell swayed in place, trapped by desperation, as the visitor walked out. Staggering to the front door, he shut it hard, then stood for a long time, paralyzed, looking at the cards without touching them. Finally, he picked them up by the edges and moved leadenly to a battered old desk in one corner of the living room. He wavered over the trash can beside it. Slowly, as if carried by the pointer on a Ouija board, his hand moved to a half-open desk drawer, and dropped the cards inside.

"James?" Alise moved through the darkened rooms of their private wing, searching for him, a robe wrapped around her nightgown, shivering. It was like this almost every night—she woke to find him gone. She followed him each time and discovered him sitting in the dark somewhere, either inside or out on the lawns that fronted the Chattahoochee's vast, gleaming ribbon of water.

She saw a light coming from the study down a hall and felt her way along by a wall covered in a tapestry depicting some violent scene from medieval England—sharp-faced warriors on prancing horses, lances extended. His affection for the pageantry of ancient wars mingled uncomfortably with her insistence on soft pastels and abstracts, giving the mansion a peculiar division of personalities. When they'd designed it, she'd thought the contrast exciting; now, it contributed to her anxiety, and to the sense of separation she felt even when he touched her.

He was lost in thought at a heavy dark desk under the light of a small lamp, one fist curled under his chin, his face, in profile, as sharp and fierce as those of the knights on the hall tapestry. A burgundy robe was loosely tied at his waist, revealing the lush mat of dark hair and heavy muscles of his chest. Along with daily therapy sessions for his leg, he had returned to his former routine of working out with weights an hour each day. Watching his weak, determined struggles in the early months had agonized her. Telling him that he was pushing too hard, too soon, had infuriated him. He didn't want her advice or her sympathy.

One end of the robe had fallen away from his leg, propped on a cushioned footstool. Scars scooped out long dents in the muscles of his thigh, and the most recent skin grafts made crazy-quilt patches. His knee and ankle were misshapen bulges.

She padded into the study's towering, richly carved shadows and halted, despair clawing at her throat. Nothing she said ever made any difference. James looked at her with his eyes half-shut, then leaned back in the tall-backed, upholstered chair as if it were a throne. He flipped the robe over his leg as he did. She wanted to scream at him that she was no prying, morbidly fascinated stranger.

Alise went to him and climbed into the chair, her knees sinking into the thick cushion on either side of his thighs. She held his brooding gaze as she lifted her robe and gown, daring him to reject her and what passed for intimacy between them these days. He didn't. Wordless hunger flashed in his eyes. He grasped her hips and guided her into place as she put a hand between their bodies. Together they accomplished the blunt joining.

Rocking against him, her arms around his neck and her face pressed to his hair, she mourned for their serenity and tenderness. When he finally, convulsively, embraced her and groaned against her shoulder, she clung to him, tears sliding from under her closed lids. They sat there in dreary silence, his arms squeezing her, one hand rising to cup the back of her head. She muffled her anguish against his dark hair.

He wouldn't be happy until he punished someone for what had happened to his family and himself. But there was no one left to punish except Lily Porter, who didn't deserve it. And James wouldn't stoop to ruining an innocent person's life. Alise would never think him capable of that.

Twenty-one

Lily found a retired farmer over in Victoria, which had turned into a tourist town full of bed-and-breakfasts and antique shops, and bought his tractor. It was forty years old, made to last a thousand more, but a bargain because the transmission was stuck in second gear. Unless a miracle occurred, it would spend the rest of its days chugging along at five miles per hour, popping wheelies whenever it wasn't weighed down with a harrow or plow, permanently denied the pleasure of first, third, or reverse.

It came complete with its own toolkit, contained in a green army-issue ammunition box bolted to one rusty fender, and a specially cut length of two-by-four, to wedge on the clutch pedal whenever she wanted to hop off and push the tractor backward. Probably because he felt sorry for anyone desperate enough to buy his tractor, the owner offered to customize it. He bolted a square of plywood onto the frame, just behind the hard, springy metal seat, so Lupa could travel with her.

When she, Lupa, and the tractor chugged up the paved road beyond the farm's driveway, they met one of the estate's guards in his Land Rover. The man stopped to watch and almost laughed himself silly. Lily gave him a curt nod and drove past, halted in the weeds on the far shoulder, hopped off, dug with her long-handled posthole diggers for a few minutes, then set a pine post into the ground, onto which she'd already bolted a large black mailbox with BLUE WILLOW GREENHOUSE AND NURSERY in gold stick-on letters across both sides. She poured a bag of concrete into the hole, then chased it with a bucket of water. The mailbox could take a hit from a tractor-trailer without budging.

It was plain. It was utilitarian. It was out of place. It was a statement. She climbed back on the ancient tractor, slipped the clutch off, and held Lupa by the ruff as the tractor gave a little leap. They went rumbling back down the graveled road into the woods, with the guard staring after them.

This would be reported immediately, she suspected.

It was. The next day there was a faxed memo from Artemas, in her new box.

Still throwing those rotten apples, aren't you?

"What happened to my lawn jockey?" Hopewell demanded, pointing to the vacant spot where it had been when he'd left it, then glaring at Little Sis, who strolled out of the new greenhouse with her hands latched behind her back. He hadn't expected to get out of his truck and find *her* here. She halted in the middle of the graveled area that had just been finished. Lily wanted to keep the entrance to the greenhouse and nursery separate from the driveway to the house. Hopewell was trying to give Lily everything she asked for. Guilt gnawed at him. And looking at Little Sis only made him feel worse.

"Your little grinning black lawn jockey?" she echoed, tilting her head to one side. "It had an accident."

"*What?*"

She sighed. "I shouldn't have bought that new Cougar. Too much car for me. I stepped on the gas, and *wham.* Before I knew it. I'm sorry."

Hopewell threw his hat on the ground. The June sun was no hotter than his temper. "That jockey wasn't hurting nothing!"

"It was a redneck ornament. I hated it. What's more,

Lily hated it. You carried on about it so much that she quit arguing, just to make peace. She was going to paint it white. I took matters into my own hands." She smiled sweetly and ambled up to him. "You're no redneck. You're just a moody old bear who needs a hug."

She looked as if she might give him one. He cleared his throat and said, "Lily hated my lawn jockey?" His voice squeaked.

"Yes. She tried not to hurt your feelings about it, but you're denser than a rock. I'll just keep chipping away at you until I find a crack." Little Sis stepped closer. She lifted one hand and toyed with the collar of his thin cotton shirt. "And then I'll slip inside."

She smelled of cinnamon. Or maybe it was just the residue of that damned incense she sold at her store. Either way, she smelled good. She liked him. Why, he didn't know. But he knew she wasn't going to like him next winter, when he told Lily to leave here. "Yes," she purred, stroking his collar, "I'll just slip right inside you, you big old rock."

"Like a damned kudzu vine," he retorted, but he was frozen in place, feeling like a heartsick boy. She put her fingertips to her lips—God, the woman was too old to wear such bright red lipstick—kissed them, then touched a red tip to his cheek. "You hush about that lawn jockey," she whispered.

He finally found his voice. "If Lily hates it, I won't say nothing more. But I have some ceramic deer in my basement—"

"I think I might accidentally run them over too."

Hopewell backed away, swept his hat from the ground, and waved it at her as if she were a pestering yellow jacket. "Is there *anything* of mine you won't try to run over?"

She buzzed forward, slipped an arm through his, and looked at him from under long gray eyelashes coated in black mascara. "Lily's like a daughter to me. I want to help her." She paused, and her coyness faded. "But I'd like to be friends with you, Hopewell."

He could have resisted anything but the serious, yearning expression on her face. Friends. Maybe, *maybe*, if he tried to be sweeter to her, she'd forgive him when the time came to sacrifice Lily's trust for Joe's sake. He stared at her wispy, liver-spotted hand curled around the crook of his bare arm. Her long red nails were the sexiest damned things. "I guess we're friends, whether I want to be or not." Tugging her hand off his, he clasped it gently for a second. Her face lit up. Hopewell let go quickly and walked back to his truck. His eyes burned. Suddenly he knew that losing Little Sis's crazy affection was going to hurt more than he'd ever thought.

Timor Parks was a leather-faced, middle-aged little man who'd gone to high school with Lily's daddy. Even though he was old enough to be her father, he was too shy to say more than a few words to her. His sons were her age and older, and they didn't speak either. As she recalled, the one who'd been in her class in high school hadn't had much to say then. Since she didn't want companionship or conversation, she and the silent Parks men got along comfortably. He and his sons said hello, good-bye, and not much in-between.

They helped her clear the other pastures, sawed the trees into logs, then placed them in neat stacks for use as firewood. She spent a week from sunup to sundown dragging brush and branches to several huge burn piles. Timor and his burly sons refitted the house's well with a new pump and concrete cover, and repaired the septic tank.

When she wasn't working alongside the sweating, non-speaking Parks clan, she tilled and plowed her newly cleared land, wrestling the lurching old tractor until the steering wheel rubbed enormous blisters on her palms. She slapped bandages over them and wore two pairs of gloves, but kept working.

Lupa stayed close by each day, stretched out happily in the fresh spring sunshine and cool dirt. She had settled into her job of chasing off the deer and rabbits that tiptoed around the clearing at night.

Lily grew leaner, living off cheap sandwiches and clear, sweet water from the new well. She was at work when Timor and his boys arrived in the morning, and still going when they left at dusk. An enormous garden plot took form, with trellises for beans and neatly lined-off rows for the seeds she planted. She didn't have much money, but she'd eat well. The Parks boys repaired the house's neglected wiring and installed the sturdy secondhand stove and refrigerator she bought. After Joe had achieved his illegal prosperity and moved away, thieves had taken the old appliances.

She fertilized the grove of apple trees beyond the backyard and hoped they'd produce a few apples by fall. She despaired of reclaiming the old barn, which Joe had ignored. Sheets of rusty tin had fallen from the roof, and there were holes in the sides where rotten boards had dropped away.

Timor came over to her in the garden when he arrived one morning. She was down on her knees planting a hill of squash. "You work harder than any woman I've ever seen," he said.

Timor had spoken. Amazed, she looked up in awe. Sweat dripped from under a tractor cap she'd bought at a seed store in town. Her overalls were covered in dirt and chalky fertilizer.

"Mr. Parks, you never saw my mama work."

He was carrying a large cardboard box. His sons hung around behind him, near their old truck, watching silently. He shifted from foot to foot, cleared his throat, and finally said, "Seein' as how I'm thankful for the job you sent my way, and how I admire what you're doin', I brought you a gift. You want some Rhode Island Reds?"

"Yes, sir!" She jumped up and looked into the box. Two dozen fluffy chicks were huddled in the bottom. Some were pink, others were purple, and a few forlorn ones were green. "Easter leftovers from my cousin's pet store down in Atlanta," Timor explained, looking disgusted. "But they'll grow out of it."

"They're wonderful. Thank you."

She lay in bed that night, listening to their soft, sweet peeps under the light she'd strung over their box to warm them. Through the screened windows and door she heard the night sounds—owls with their giggling whistles, a fox barking, insects beginning to hum with the new season. Beside her on the sleeping bag, Lupa snored. The world was quiet and achingly innocent. She thought of Stephen and Richard, and with a disturbing sense of loneliness, Artemas.

Rising in anguish, her hands wringing the tail of her floppy T-shirt, she went, barefoot, outdoors, and planted zinnias in the moonlight.

Mr. Parks and two dozen other people from the community, including Aunt Maude and the sisters, arrived unannounced one morning, trailed by an old logging truck stacked with faint green translucent fiberglass siding. They knew she needed the barn as a second greenhouse. They had come to repair it. Aunt Maude and the sisters had paid for the materials. "An early birthday present," Aunt Maude said.

Mr. Parks stepped forward uneasily, gulped on his shyness, then added, "We know Hopewell Estes ain't giving you much to work with, and we know the Colebrooks ain't happy to have you here. But we're glad to have you."

When Lily sat down on the edge of the porch with one hand pressed to her mouth, Big Sis tottered brusquely among the awkward group, waving her cane and telling them to get busy. Little Sis, decked out in overalls decorated with rhinestones and embroidered flowers, wandered over and sat down beside Lily. "You've got family, friends, a home—even if it's only yours on lease—and work to do," Little Sis told her. "Don't sit here looking like you're about to bawl."

Lily put an arm around her. "I'll hang on to all this good stuff like a miser."

"There's got to be more to your life than wanting some kind of vindication from the Colebrooks."

Lily held out one hand, palm up, as if trying to weigh

unseen fears. "I want justice for Richard. I want acceptance for who I am, for the quality of my word—my honesty. I want to feel satisfied that I've stood up for what I believe, and I want"—she lowered her hand and looked at Little Sis—"I want to feel there's some rhyme and reason for why my son is dead." She shook her head. "That's asking for the impossible, I know." The next words came hard. "Maybe Artemas and I are the guilty ones."

Little Sis gasped. "What? How?"

"If we'd never cared about each other, if I hadn't made him feel responsible for me having to sell the farm, if he hadn't tried to make that up to me years later, by hiring Richard's firm—"

"Listen to me, Lily Amanda." Little Sis snagged her hand and gripped it fiercely. "Loving somebody doesn't make you responsible for their weaknesses, even if you put 'em in the position that brought those flaws to the surface. Richard, and Julia Colebrook, and the others—they made their own mistakes. You and Artemas have to live with the consequences, but don't ever think you caused them."

Lily rubbed her forehead and tried to believe that. "The consequences are that he and I can't overcome *anyone's* mistakes—including our own." Looking at the people who were bustling around, trying to help her while all she could do was mourn unchangeable sorrows, she rose to her feet. "But no, I'm not going to sit here brooding over what can't be changed."

"Wait!" Little Sis stood. Turning Lily's hand upward, she pointed to the palm. "There's still hope. You and he have come back together, just like I predicted."

Lily flinched. The truth of Little Sis's old soothsaying made chills on her skin. "You never said it'd be happy. Or that it would have anything to do with love."

There was a portentous silence. Little Sis appeared to be sorry she'd brought this subject up. Pursing her lips as if considering whether to lie, she hesitated, exhaled, and said, "I think you do love him. I think you always have."

"Don't." Lily moved away, shaking her head. "Don't—"

"And he still loves you. That explains a lot."

"No. You're wrong." Pulling a pair of work gloves from her jeans pocket, she hurried to help unload siding from the truck, as if action could erase thought. Little Sis dogged her steps and clamped a hand on her shoulder. Lily halted, pretending to study a sheet of siding, paralyzed. "I don't know if loving each other is meant to make you happy," Little Sis told her. "I just know that you do love him."

Lily sat down in Mr. Svenson's cramped little office. Beyond a glass door a world of china and crystal glittered under soft lights. Her eyes felt grainy. She had slept worse than usual last night. She'd had another nightmare. The terrible dreams had started soon after Richard and Stephen's deaths, and still continued.

Sometimes she saw them climbing from the debris of the bridge, mangled, grotesque, begging her to believe they weren't dead. Sometimes she saw them beautifully perfect and serene, but trapped behind an invisible wall. Sometimes she heard them calling to her from some dark, unfathomable place her eyes couldn't penetrate. Last night she'd heard Stephen's voice in such vivid detail that she woke up crying for him.

Finally, around dawn, sitting at the old kitchen table she'd bought last week at a flea market, she'd dozed with her head on her arms. And dreamed about Artemas. His presence had been all around her, wordless and powerful, and she dreamed of shutting doors as Richard and Stephen tried to walk toward her, of turning away, toward him.

She'd spent most of the day trying to forget that dream. Finally she'd driven down to Atlanta, convinced that settling one uncertainty would help settle the rest. For her own peace of mind, she wanted to know that the teapot was gone.

Mr. Svenson's assistant stepped into the office and shut the door. "Mrs. Porter," he said happily, his gaze as delicate as the wares in the showroom, but no less exclusive. She knew how out of place she looked now, in her jeans, leather work shoes, and old T-shirt, with her hair knotted up in a bandanna. She looked like the kind of person who couldn't browse in the shop without being scrutinized by wary salesclerks. "What can I do for you?" the assistant asked, sitting down at the desk. "I'm afraid Mr. Svenson is out of the shop today."

"I sold a Colebrook Blue Willow teapot to him a while back. I just wondered who bought it."

"Oh, yes, I remember. Such a rare piece. Colebrook stopped making the Blue Willow pattern just after 1900. And we dated your teapot between 1850 and 1870. Mr. Svenson was delighted."

"Could you check your records and tell me if someone bought the teapot?" She tried to sound casual, and gave him a sheepish look. "I know it sounds silly, but I'd just like to know if it got a good home."

"Oh, certainly, I understand. One moment." He turned to a computer terminal on the desk and began typing. Lily cradled the big cloth tote she carried as a purse and reminded herself not to wad it between her nervous hands. As usual, it contained sandwich bags with plant rootings she'd gathered from the roadsides. She never tampered with endangered species, just the ordinary wildflowers—yarrow and crown vetch, daisies and coneflowers.

Of course, she would have to buy plugs—rootings—of most other flowers from commercial growers, to build parent stock from which she'd propagate next year's plants, but she loved knowing that some of her inventory had come to her as freely as a gift from the land.

The rootings nestled in her bag would join the seedlings arranged in neat trays in the greenhouse. She nurtured her flock with obsessive attention, and only during the bleakest times, such as last night, admitted that her life had become a constant drive to salvage and rescue—and love—things that would never fill the void.

"Here it is," the assistant said, squinting at the computer screen. "Good Lord. We didn't keep it long, did we? A Mr. LaMieux purchased the teapot from us the same day you sold it." He sighed and sat back, unaware that she was stunned. "I'm afraid all I can tell you is that he paid with a personal check and has what appears to be a post-office-box address, here in Atlanta."

There couldn't be a different LaMieux from the one she knew, who'd waltz into this shop and buy a Colebrook teapot as soon as she'd sold it. Mr. LaMieux had been sent here by Artemas. Artemas had been watching her. She thanked Mr. Svenson's assistant and walked out, then broke into a run toward the truck as soon as the shop's security guard politely closed the door behind her.

Twenty-two

The landscape outside the truck's window was a blur. She passed cattle pastures, chicken houses, apple orchards, and wide, empty fields ripe for planting. Every house had a garden patch beside it; most had satellite dishes.

Her heart began to race when she reached the turnoff for MacKenzie. She took a narrow paved road and then another. She'd go straight to the estate. If he was there, she'd say—what? She wasn't certain. Only that she had to know why he wanted to control her life.

Finally, her throat dry, she crossed the bridge over the shadowy Toqua River and entered a different world. Not her land. Nearly hers, though, in spirit, and an integral part of her image of home. A narrow two-lane highway veered off to the right, seeming to disappear into a tunnel of forest.

Blue Willow Road. The farm's driveway was three miles down, past the estate's entrance. The estate's clocktower sat in a grassy clearing in the corner of the junction between Blue Willow Road and the highway.

The sight of the Gothic stone tower, its steep blue-tiled roof looming high overhead, made her stop her car and gaze upward with tears on her face.

Blue Willow. She had roamed its deserted forests,

fished in its lake with her father, daydreamed in the beautiful, forgotten gazebos, played princess on the mansion's awesome, windswept loggia, peeked through cracks in the boarded-up windows, picked flowers in the overgrown gardens. She wondered if Artemas thought about that as often as she did. With startling ferocity she hoped he never hired an outsider to re-create the gardens. *Her* gardens.

The estate began where the river formed its eastern boundary. Darkly forested land rose sharply on her left, but on the estate's side it sloped gently upward from the road. Blue Willow Road cut through the estate's southern edge until it finally met with the road to Victoria, seven miles away.

The Colebrooks had built it, then donated it to the county so people could take the shortcut to the neighboring town. In 1900, that shortcut had meant a lot to the locals, Lily recalled her grandfather saying. The Colebrooks were generous to their neighbors back then.

Lily sat there anticipating the last three miles to the farm's driveway, suddenly afraid that she was going to say all the wrong things, accuse him, hurt him, let him hurt her again.

Deep, melodic chimes sounded from the clocktower. Even the clock was serving him faithfully, again. Keeping *his* time.

Stomping the accelerator, she sent the truck rumbling down Blue Willow Road. The unkempt laurel lining the roadside had been trimmed back, and the old, gnarled dogwoods were carefully pruned. The ground was freshly tilled and sprayed with green material she recognized immediately as a seed-and-mulch mixture.

She reached a widening apron of pavement that curled off in a spur to the estate's gate. The gatehouse, once an empty shell with the leaded-glass windows broken out and kudzu covering the walls, had been fully restored. Dark blue shutters ornamented the new windows. The stonework had been cleaned of graffiti. The kudzu was gone.

The majestic old iron gate, with its matching patterns of willows, had been repaired and painted. It stood open.

A stocky gray-haired man in a security-guard uniform exited the cottage's side door quickly and planted himself in front of the open gate, watching as if he expected her to roar through like a lunatic, which, she realized, she'd given him some reason to expect. He even rested one hand on the heavy pistol holster on his belt.

Lily lifted a hand in greeting, but drove past. She wasn't going to *ask* to be announced, like some god-damned stranger.

The old hardwood forest closed around her. She crossed MacKenzie Creek at the stone bridge, which had been cleaned and freshly mortared, the banks around it cleared and planted with ivy.

When she reached her mailbox and driveway, she pulled onto the secluded road and parked, then got out and started through the woods. She could find her way to the estate's main road blindfolded.

The land had not emerged yet from decades of neglect. The walk took her along an eerie pathway of fallen trees and tangled undergrowth. A mile inward the one-lane road split and formed a circle. She looked at the majestic, gnarled willow at the center of the circle, standing alone in what had once been a small park. Lily averted her gaze from it, remembering how she'd considered it her own, how she'd claimed it that day as a child, the pockets of her overalls bulging with soft brown apples, and how Artemas had stepped underneath, an unsuspecting victim who had terrified and then enchanted her.

The undergrowth and the ground around the thick, sinewy roots had been cleared. The commemorative plaque that had been there when she was a child was gone.

She walked faster. The land rolled and dropped, and the road followed its contours, taking her deeper into the Colebrook world with every second. Newly graveled service roads curved out of the woods to meet the main drive. She knew them by heart. They led to the lake, the guest houses, and across the river to the estate's dairy barns, fields, and stables. A small fiefdom had existed here, self-absorbed and self-sufficient.

Her palms were clammy and her chest tight with emotion. The strain of the past months had taken its toll. She knew that, and struggled to keep calm.

The road rose and curved up the side of the big ridge that ran through the heart of the estate. She came to a pair of granite boulders fifty feet tall guarding either side of the road, with willows carved into their rugged contours. The craftsmanship was so expert that the carvings seemed natural. Decades of wind and weather had softened them. They might have been drawn by rivulets of rain rather than human hands.

A hundred yards beyond them the road uncurled suddenly at the top of the ridge, emerging from the woodlands with an abruptness that made her heart rise in her throat. Sunlight burst onto raw red earth—the old meadows, fanning out from either side of the road. They had grown up in pine forest when she was a child, but were now cleared again, and waiting to be replanted.

She looked into the distance, and her breath caught. Rising from the far side of the ridge, the estate house lifted steep, gabled roofs of weathered blue slate against a dark blue sky with curls of pink clouds above it, shot through with beams from the descending sun. Long shadows were creeping over the land.

Keeping to the road, she strode past the cleared foundations where collapsed greenhouses had been, cracked foundations, and piles of construction debris. The house was surrounded by scaffolds. Any workers who had been there were gone for the day. Toward the south end, the curving glass roof of the palm court, once dotted with gaping holes, was covered in black plastic.

Utility poles had been jabbed into the lawn. Heavy electrical cables stretched from them to open windows on the main floor. With all the lines and equipment around it, the mansion resembled a surgery patient receiving intensive care.

She halted in the wide cobbled courtyard in front of

the main entrance and considered the enormous front doors. Their stately glass and wood, covered in intricate patterns of black wrought iron, belied the mansion's disarray. Was there a butler still to command those doors? She ran up the steps and pressed a buzzer set in the stone wall on one side. If it worked, the chimes were too muffled to hear. Tapping a heavy brass knocker, she felt insignificant and angry.

The doors were locked. She beat on them with both fists and yelled for Artemas to let her in. She wanted to scream that he couldn't buy back the past.

Deep inside the house came the quick, soft thud of feet on stone. The doors cracked, shuddered. One swung inward abruptly. Artemas stood with his feet braced apart, centered with overwhelming physical command before the vast height of a great, empty entrance hall. He was dressed in soft brown trousers and a loose shirt, with the sleeves rolled up. His large, intense eyes were astonished and somber, raking her with intentions that seemed anxious, welcoming—or victorious. As he judged the look on her face, he arched a brow and asked, "Jehovah's Witnesses? Avon calling? Taking donations for the Daughters of Nazi Stormtroopers?"

His careless dismissal broke the dam. Lily flung herself at him, grasping the front of his open-collared shirt, jerking at it, slamming into his chest so forcefully that he staggered back several steps as he grabbed her by the shoulders.

"You bought that damned teapot back," she yelled. "You couldn't keep from interfering in one of the few free choices I had left, could you?"

"You had no right to sell it," he answered, his voice brutal. "That silly teapot represents something important to both of us, something I won't allow you to forget."

"You won't *allow* me?" She kicked him in one knee, and his leg buckled. They went down in a heap on the cold stone floor.

He cursed and forced her hands into balls inside the hard grip of his own, then wrestled her furiously contorting body as she drew up her knees and jabbed the heels

of her thick leather shoes into his thighs. His sharply inhaled breaths conveyed pain and shock, and with a sudden growl of fury, he rolled away and wound one hand
into her tangled hair. He got to his knees and held her at
arm's length, while she tore at his hand and tried to writhe
upright. He pinned her head to the floor. She couldn't see
him. His ragged breaths came between muttered obscenities and warnings that finally trailed off into "Crazy . . . absolutely certifiable . . . I've never . . . God!"

She made a keening sound and dug what was left of
her work-torn fingernails into his wrist. "If I have to be a
bitch to make you leave me alone, I can do it!"

"Thank God for one thing," he said with another deep
breath. "You're fighting like the woman I remember."

She wrung her head and struggled against the fistful of
hair, the side of her face mashed painfully into the rough
stone floor. "You want everything to be the way you remember it! But that means pretending Richard never
existed!"

"I wish to God he never had. My sister would be alive,
and there'd be no guilt and duty to keep you and me away
from each other." He let go of her. She bolted upright and
crouched, heaving, her hands clenched on her knees. They
felt raw against the hard floor, even through her jeans, and
her head ached at the crown. Through a haze of rage and
frustration she saw Artemas kneeling in front of her with
undaunted anger on his face.

Lily shook her head fiercely. "Julia is dead because she
bullied and threatened people unmercifully." She curled a
hand to her chest. Misery hunching her over, she cried,
"You think you can coax me into forgetting that. You'll always protect your family, even if it hurts me!"

He caught her by the shoulders and made a bitter
sound deep in his throat. "If I felt that way, I would have
turned my back on you from the moment I knew Richard
was incriminated. Every time I try to help you, I risk losing my family's respect. But that doesn't stop me from trying. Dammit, Lily, you have to believe that."

She pushed herself to her feet. "When I was nineteen,

I wanted to believe you loved me more than anyone or anything else in your life. I learned a hard lesson then. I've never forgotten it."

She whirled around and started out the door, her legs shaking. Behind her was the sound of swift movement, then his footsteps on the stone. "We need to have one helluva long talk about my motives and your attitude," he said softly. A hand latched onto the back of her shirt.

Lily yelled and twisted, but by then he'd already enveloped her with his other arm. He pinned her arms to her waist and lifted her off the floor. Her back and hips were crushed against his torso. "Come and see the house," he said, his voice tight with exertion. "You always wanted to see it."

He half carried, half dragged her through the dim, cavernous hall. It opened on one side to a court with a small fountain in the center, on the other to a grand marble staircase, and flowed through a wide arch into a huge main-floor gallery—stark, empty except for a baby-grand piano near rows of towering glass Palladian-style doors that opened onto the loggia. The walls were stripped of paper, the enormous wooden floor unstained. But the bare, stately house was magnificent, and the gallery simmered with late-afternoon light that poured through the doors.

Lily's dazed attention focused on the piano. The blue-and-white teapot sat there. She struggled until they were both panting. He wound a hand into her hair and held her still. She felt his heart hammering against her back. "I've dreamed of taking you on a more genteel tour, but this is the best we can do." He pushed her against the piano. "Pick it up," he ordered, shoving her toward the teapot.

"I'm beginning to feel I should wear it around my neck on a chain. Like a porcelain albatross."

He flattened her against the keyboard. A discordant crunch of sound echoed through the room. "Pick up the damned teapot with one of your claws," he repeated. "Or by God we'll stand here until the F-sharp goes flat."

He had her pinned just above the elbows. Lily maneuvered one hand up and finally managed to grasp the delicate little vessel by the handle. Bending his head beside hers, he said grimly, "We're going to sit on the loggia with our albatross and enjoy the sunset."

His arm still around her, they stumbled out a pair of the open doors to the windswept loggia into the long, soft rays of the sun, which hung just above the distant mountains. "Sit," he ordered, when they reached the loggia's marble steps. When she stood rigidly, her feet braced apart, he shoved one of her legs out from under her with his foot. They both sat down hard on the wide steps, her sliding down between his legs to the step just beneath his. She cradled the teapot in her lap protectively.

His arm mashed her breasts as she tried to get up, then released her. His hand sank into her hair again. She twisted between his thighs and stared up at him.

They traded a violent, searching, bewildered look. His face was flushed; the tiny mole beneath his right eye stood out on the tight skin. His black hair hung over his forehead in disarray, and a muscle popped in his cheek. He lowered his hand from her hair. She didn't move.

"Truce," he said sharply. "Please."

She searched his eyes and tried to assess the heated, vital roar of blood through her body. Afraid of that feeling, she turned and faced forward. The air was cool and bracing on her flushed skin. Below the loggia's stone steps sat the trio of old fountains. The ground around them had been chewed by workers' feet, and all that remained of the pine forest was a patch along one side of the corridor, a dark and secluded spot draped in wisteria.

"How do you like it?" he asked, his tone grim. "It needs your attention."

"I don't belong here—not as someone you hire to rebuild the gardens, and not as a guest." Her hands curled tightly around the old teapot. She exhaled wearily, got to her feet, and hugging it against her stomach, went down the stairs, toward the fountains. He followed.

The warm, prickling sensation in her muscles whispered that she was alive and vital, not the helpless shadow she'd felt like for so long. It was seductive and frightening to realize he was the source of that energy. She walked to the balustrade at the end of the fountains' terrace.

"Does restoring it mean so much to you anymore?" she asked tersely. "How can it be worth the price you've paid to save it?"

"It means even more to me now than before. Maybe it's become a symbol of my family's survival." He paused. "And yours. Because even after all that's happened, you're here."

"This place is not a sanctuary for either of us anymore."

"I'll never accept that, Lily." He gripped her shoulder and forced her attention back to him. He swept a hand toward the section of garden that hadn't been cleared yet, where the scrub pines had been enveloped by wisteria. The fat vines were full of leaves, and they cascaded down in shady umbrellas over the matted grass. Someone had cut a narrow space under them. It was shadowy and private.

"There was a wooden arbor there when I was a boy. I used to hide inside the wisteria when vacation ended and I had to return to New York. Of course, my grandmother or her servants knew exactly where to find me, but I never stopped hoping that I'd become invisible." He added gruffly, "You see, if I'd been invisible, I could have stayed here forever and done exactly as I pleased."

"You're still not invisible. You have responsibilities to everyone who depends on you, everyone who trusts you to do what's best for your family and your businesses."

He scowled. "There has to be room for what's best for *me*. And for you. That could start right now—today—if we agree to stop tearing each other apart over the past."

"All I want from you is respect for what I had with Richard, for the son I loved dearly, and for what I believe about Richard's integrity. Until I have that, there's nothing else."

"You have that respect from me. I don't have to agree with your beliefs to honor them."

He touched her face, very slowly, his fingertips almost

but not quite motionless on her cheek. "Don't," she begged.

As if helpless to stop, he gave the faintest shake of his head. "I'm not asking you to forget him. I'm asking you to remember me."

"That's the same thing."

"Lily." His voice was the barest of whispers. "No matter what else you feel, I don't think you can say you stopped loving me, even after you were married."

Grief and guilt exploded. She jerked back. The teapot slipped from her hands. With the awful, stunning sound of something delicate and irreplaceable meeting harsh stone, it fell against the balustrade and broke into pieces.

The horror in her sharp gasp was echoed in Artemas's low sound of distress. They stared at the ruins in shared misery. Lily dropped to her knees. Picking up a shard of porcelain, she closed her hand around it and bowed her head. "I didn't mean to. I swear."

He knelt close beside her and carefully pried open her hand. A tiny smear of blood marked where she'd pressed a sharp point into her palm. He took the piece into his hand and studied it with an anguished gaze. She cried out softly as he gripped it. When he opened his fingers, his palm bore a similar dab of red. Dropping the shard, he clasped her hand, melding their blood together.

Lily murmured his name with violent despair. He pulled her to him and ground his mouth on hers. Hard and wild, they fed on the provocation, his heat exploding into hers. She felt everything, every warning and alarm, screaming that she'd gone too far and couldn't go back. Didn't want to go back.

We can't. It won't change anything, she tried to say, but the words came out in a ragged moan.

He picked her up and carried her to the dark tunnel of wisteria. Under it, hidden from all view, they turned to each other with ferocious hands. He pierced her mouth with his tongue, and she was enveloped in the deep, searing heat of a blindness she'd known only with him. She clung to it, to him, twisting her mouth on his, recklessly acknowledging that he could give her something no one else could.

Suddenly she was an animal that had to have him, and he was taking her wildness with stunning precision, his hands in rough sync with hers, his eyes burning with blind need as she pulled him to the ground. He dragged her jeans and cotton underwear down and jerked them off over one of her clumsy boots, while she sank her hands into his thick hair. They were both making guttural, furious, sexual sounds.

Lily dived forward and lightly sank her teeth into the swath of chest exposed by his open shirt, gripping the hard flesh over one of his nipples, then just as quickly putting her teeth to his stomach. He shuddered and jerked her to him, but she shoved him away, then latched her hands into his trousers. She tugged frantically as they caught on his soft leather shoes. The rip of the trouser hems brought a victorious sound from her throat.

But he grabbed her hands as she reached for the thick, greedy flesh jutting between his thighs. He pushed her onto her back, then raked his teeth and lips over her stomach and down to her sex, plunging his tongue between her spread legs. She writhed and arched her back. The scent of musky sex and wisteria joined in her brain. When she moaned helplessly, he slid upward, slower now, no endearments necessary, the feeling of being both lost and discovered simultaneously holding her as tightly as his hands.

In the next second he shoved her shirt and bra up and took her breasts with rough, scalding tenderness. She scooped her hands between their bodies and brutally massaged the fettered muscle and coarse hair of his chest and belly. He covered her breasts with hard, sucking kisses, wild in his possession, a possession that erased everything but the masculine incense of his sweat and the heavy weight of him, the complete and primal love she felt.

We can't. It won't change anything, she tried to say, but the words came out in a ragged moan.

He slid his arms under her bare back and down to her

buttocks, lifted them to his belly and thighs, tested her with a quick, expert hand high up between her legs, and when she cried out with pleasure, her head thrown back and eyes shut, he buried his head beside hers and arched into her with a swift, hard stroke.

She was already writhing under him and raising her hips convulsively. He came down on her with a gentleness she hadn't expected, and tears burned her eyes. Lily wrapped her arms around him and shuddered with waves of sorrow and release. He met her in one last frantic, bowing arch of his body, his lips twisting against her cheek, his hands pulling her upward into the deep penetration, then holding her there, as they struggled together. It was done. Completed. Lost.

There was no peaceful relaxing after the fierce physical need faded. Frozen, they clung to each other harshly, her legs locked around him, his knees half under her, keeping her hips pillowed on his thighs. His arms still circled her so that only her shoulders touched the ground. His heart hammered against her breasts. She drew ragged breaths with the soft, damp texture of his hair against her mouth. Minutes of stark, fragile silence passed. Neither of them wanted to break the spell.

Guilt without shame. Love without pleasure. They merged as intimately as her body had joined with his. Slowly he drew his head up. The conflicting emotions had been waiting beneath it all, as inescapable as the warm fluid between her thighs, the tender but uncompromising look of triumph on his face. Victory. There was nothing brutal or careless about his expression, but the conquest, no matter how well-meaning, was there.

Lily turned her head to one side and shut her eyes. Shut him out. A different brand of tension infused the stillness in his body.

"Don't," he said.

"We've only made the problems worse."

Pulling away, he lay on his side next to her, but when she started to move, he held her against his body. Lily twisted to lie with her back to him, quivering. Finally she realized he was guiding her shirt together over her breasts. "Let's go inside," he said gruffly. His voice seemed hollow, frantic. "Let's try to make sense of this."

"I have to go home," she said desperately, sitting up. Artemas moved with her, closing a hand around her arm. "You are home."

Tears that had not been possible before now slid down her cheeks. She hunched over her bare legs and pulled her clothes to her. His semen, warm and smooth and pungent, covered her inner thighs.

"You are home," he repeated.

Lily twisted toward him. His open shirt made him as vulnerable and exposed as she. The urge to communicate her torment and gratitude made her reach out, brushing the backs of her fingers down his chest; then she quickly withdrew her hand and looked away.

His face mirrored her anguish, but she knew they couldn't go any further. He lifted a hand to stroke her hair, but she froze, and he dropped his hand to his side. He looked at her grimly but said nothing. Her nerves jerked. Shivering, she dressed hurriedly, trying not to look at him as he dressed also. They rose at the same time and bumped into each other. "We're not exactly graceful romantics," she said in a lame attempt to sound casual.

He snatched her into his arms. His face was etched in deep lines of anger and sadness. "It's only a matter of time. I'm not willing to sacrifice my happiness anymore. Or yours."

"Maybe we had our only chance years ago, and we lost it."

"You mean I threw it away. You've never forgiven me for that."

She knotted her hands in his shirt. "You made your choice then. And you didn't choose *me*."

"There was so much about that I couldn't control. I know you don't understand why, but I'll never be trapped like that again."

"You're trapped now. Between your family and me. Between what you believe about Richard and what I believe about Julia. And if you have to choose again, I'll lose this time too."

"No. Stay with me. Fight for *us*. Give us that chance, and there won't be anything we can't overcome."

"I don't have that faith anymore. I don't have that strength. I don't know if I could survive losing anyone else I—" Lily hesitated, choking.

"*Love*," he finished for her. "Anyone you love. Can you say that, at least, that you love me?"

Lily flinched. *I can't do that to Richard.* "I loved you when I was eighteen. I love what I remember about you. But in so many ways, you're a stranger now."

"A stranger?" He let go of her. He looked toward the shadowy cavern they had shared beneath the wisteria. His face was set in a hard mask. "You can lie to me, but don't lie to yourself."

Lily touched his arm. She was desperate to tell him how much she wanted to forgive, and trust—and love—him, but she couldn't. Her mind was filled with specters of a future that would tear his family away from him, and self-respect from her. His siblings would never comprehend her bitterness toward Julia, because they hadn't seen how their sister's vindictive harassment had tormented Richard and the others.

"For a few minutes we were invisible," she told Artemas, the words whispered and hoarse.

She walked past the fountains, past the broken teapot, down the stone stairs dropping to the slope below the mansion, and followed a muddy path to the lake and the woods beyond. When she reached them and was certain he couldn't see her anymore, she sat down in the darkening forest and, crying, put her head in her hands.

Twenty-three

Cassandra was hungry, thinking of the bowl of consommé she'd had for lunch and wishing she'd eaten more. Paradise was a place where women with no cellulite ate mounds of buttered rolls without gaining weight. Their plastic surgeons and diet doctors were in a special hell, along with Jenny Craig and Richard Simmons and Jane Fonda, perpetually reaching for bags of cookies held by fat, grinning demons.

She thought of Elizabeth, who had been slender and gotten plump but didn't mind, and, with deep loneliness, of Julia, whose perfect weight had been maintained by frenetic energy. Julia.

Brooding, she smoothed suntan lotion over her bare breasts, hitched up the sides of a shimmering red bikini bottom, then moved Princess Di off her stomach. "Does Mother's little baby want to get out of the sun?" The Yorkie, a reddish ball of hair with eyes, panted and stretched out in the shade under the lounge chair. Cassandra fussed over her, cooing, then settled back and shut her eyes wearily. Animals were trustworthy. She trusted them and her family, and no one else. The lake water lapped softly at the pavilion's stone deck, and birds made small sounds in the trees. The July heat scorched the air.

Artemas was right about one thing—this secluded old estate made a person feel lost in a separate world. There were no self-serving men staring at her with greedy eyes, wondering what they'd have to do to curry her money and clout. There were no preening, ambitious artists sucking up to her to win her attention for their china designs, and no meetings to run for Colebrook International.

She draped one hand onto the warm male body stretched on the lounge chair next to hers, tugged at the chest hair, then at the beard, and when that brought only a sleepy groan, planted her fingers over the soft bulge covered in tight black swim trunks. "Armande." She wanted to stop thinking about Julia, and about the tension in the family these days, with Lily Porter living nearby.

Armande laughed in his careful, elegant way but sat up immediately. "Your wish is my command." He yawned.

He knelt beside her chair and began drawing his hands over her long torso from breasts to thighs. She smiled and arched her hips. Armande pulled her suit's bottom off with his teeth.

When he reached her feet, he slung the tiny bit of red material aside. Spreading her legs apart, he kissed his way back up, until finally his coyly moving head was twisting from one thigh to the other. He plunged his face into the center of the black hair between them. Cassandra laced her hands behind her head. *Bingo*.

She had discovered Armande two years ago, when she'd come to Atlanta to select a house. Someone had invited her to a party, and there he was, dark eyes flashing at her, black hair slicked back above the diamond stud in one ear, tight jeans, too much chest hair showing above the buttoned yoke neck of his silk shirt. He was a record producer—silly New Age jazz performers with names such as Moon Lover and Raine Forrest—but she forgave him that. He was local. Convenient. She needed a bed warmer in this new city Artemas had coaxed the family to adopt.

Ah, but Armande had become so much more than convenient. He was accommodating, polite, and always ready.

Eventually she'd invested in his business, to reward him. She didn't trust Armande, but she depended on him.

She pulled him up to her and kissed him. He made a sighing sound she took for pleasure, then kissed her back just as intimately. She pushed him onto the other lounge and stripped off his swimsuit. His erection was as reliable and accommodating as the rest of him, poking out grandly from his bearish brown fur. Cassandra drew her fingertips over it. Now she had him at her mercy. "Armande?"

"Hmmm, my angel, what is it?"

"Are you enjoying my brother's estate?"

"Yes, it's a lovely old place."

"I'd like you to come here with me often."

"Whenever that's possible, my darling."

"If my brother knew you have a wife, he'd never let you set foot here again."

"You should have told him long ago."

"He's a little old-fashioned on the subject. The rest of my family is too." She curled her hand around him and stroked expertly. "I think it's time you left your wife. I loathe sneaking around my family this way."

Armande gaped at her. "Leave my wife for you? Such an idea! Why would I do that? She would hate me." He shrugged with European nonchalance. "I have a very nice wife."

She sat back on her chaise and stared at him. Humiliation soaked into her like the hot sun. Why did her relationships always end up in conversations such as this one? "Armande, I don't care if you love me, but I expect consideration."

"You're in a strange mood, my darling. Sometimes I see through your sophistication and think you're naive. I'm very considerate to you. I do everything you ask. In return, you enjoy my, hmmm . . . attentive company."

"You seem to think that's enough."

"This is funny, coming from a woman who wants men to be only ornaments."

"But look at what you get in return."

He laughed. "You're over thirty, you're skinny, you're

not beautiful, and you have the personality of one of those hot-tempered crazy racehorses you own in Kentucky. I enjoy your spirit, my angel, but I'd never trade my nice, normal wife for you."

She punched him in the gut. It was a good, solid punch, and he lurched upright, coughing. Cassandra got up and wrapped a long print sarong around herself, knotting it over her breasts, then jabbing her feet into black sandals.

Armande shook his head and laughed harder. "Don't be upset. Come here and have sex with me. That's all you need. The rest would only make you nervous."

Princess Di's yips and the patter of her manicured toenails scrambling on the blue slate distracted Cass. Whirling, she saw the tiny dog leap off the terrace's edge and scurry into the forest. "Di! Di, come back!" Her innocent little dog would probably get mauled by a squirrel. "I'll deal with you later," she flung at Armande.

Cassandra strode after Princess Di. The Yorkie shrieked with excitement, raced down an incline, and disappeared into a grove of laurel that stretched along the rim. Cassandra ducked into a narrow deer trail between the huge bushes, cursing and shoving at the branches. "I'll skin you for earmuffs, you stubborn little—*oh, my God.*"

A black bear was loping toward her up the narrow hollow.

Princess Di circled it and yipped frantically. The bear, small and plump, crashed to a stop at the sight of Cassandra. Growling and turning, it poked at Princess Di with a paw as big as the Yorkie, then bolted away, disappearing over a knoll. Princess Di raced after it.

"Di!" Cassandra screamed. She turned and ran back to the pavilion, where one of the estate's Land Rovers sat in the paved lane that wound around one end of the lake, toward the mansion. As she leaped into the vehicle and slammed the door, she shouted to Armande to find his own way back to the estate house.

To hell with him. She'd grown up being humiliated by

her mother and ignored by her father, and she'd never let anyone have that power over her again.

The loud rustle of leaves and tree branches and the sound of dogs barking in the distance made Lily look up quickly from mulching a bed of hostas she'd planted along the greenhouse wall. Whipping her hat off, she peered across the dirt road into the forest. At the same time she heard the approaching rumble of a car coming too fast down the road into the farm's wide, flat hollow. Huckleberry shrubs, honeysuckle, and small trees had turned the forest floor into an impenetrable wall of greenery for the summer; her gaze strained toward the swiftly rising sounds of dogs giving mad chase through it, then up the road. The animal and the car were on a collision course.

Lily dropped her shovel and ran toward the road. One of the estate's brown Land Rovers burst into view, slinging gravel and trailing a cloud of pink dust. At the same time a panting black bear broke through the forest's undergrowth and galloped madly toward her clearing.

Staring in amazement at the first bear she'd seen since childhood, Lily stumbled into the roadside ditch and halted. Tall daisies bobbed their yellow heads against her arms as she flung out her hands, shooing the small, terrified bear away. It shied off toward the woods at the farm's perimeter.

She would have laughed when the tiny, yipping ball of red hair with eyes shot out of the forest in pursuit, but the Land Rover was racing toward it. Lupa followed blindly, fat and big and determined to keep up.

Lily felt her lungs caving in with horror. The Land Rover's driver slammed on the brakes. The heavy vehicle slid sideways, slowing, but still plowing forward helplessly. Its front bumper caught Lupa behind one shoulder. Lily was already running forward, fixated on the dog's yelp of terror and pain as the impact tumbled her into the ditch.

Not like Sassy. Please, God, no. Lily shoved the jungle of daisies aside and dropped to her knees. Nettles stabbed at her skin beneath cutoff overalls. Their sting was lost in her desperate concentration.

Lupa whined and huddled with one front leg hanging limp in the brambles. Lily crooned and ran frantic hands over her side. She was dimly aware of the errant driver hurrying up to her, feet crunching on the road's gravel. Lily turned with furious intent. "You stupid—"

Cassandra Colebrook stared down at her, mouth open in distress. One long, tanned leg peeked from a saronglike wrap of gauzy, brightly colored material. She looked as if she belonged on an island with a piña colada in one hand.

Lily shuddered. "You fucking *idiot*."

Cassandra sank to her knees beside her and put a trembling hand on Lupa's head. "I swear I didn't—my dog, Princess Di, I had to—I'm *sorry*."

"She's all I have," Lily said brokenly, turning back to Lupa. "She's my son's pet. She was, she is—God, can't you people leave me alone? Isn't anything safe from you?"

"I adore animals. I wouldn't—"

"Get out of here. Get out of my sight."

"Come *on*. We'll take her to a doctor."

Lily shoved her grasping hands away. "I don't want your help."

"Don't argue. We can put her in the Land Rover right now. If she's bleeding internally, she doesn't have much time."

Acknowledging that was a swift and merciless defeat. Lily gathered Lupa into her arms. Cassandra cradled the dog's head and front legs. Lupa cried and struggled. Together they carried her to the Land Rover and laid her in the backseat. Lily climbed in beside her. "Where's the local veterinarian?" Cass demanded.

"Just turn this thing around and drive. I'll show you when we reach the main road."

The bedraggled little Princess Di trotted up. Cassandra tossed her into the front seat. "You're a bad girl. Bad girl." Her voice, filled with plaintive rebuke, wavered uncharacteristically.

Lily stroked Lupa's head and listened in disgusted wonder. Cassandra Colebrook cooing maternally to a lapdog was the last thing she'd expected.

"I didn't mean to hit your dog," Cassandra said loudly, as she guided the Land Rover back up the lane, sliding around the curves. Her sarong fell, but she drove on heedlessly, naked from the waist up. "There was a bear—"

"Don't talk to me!" Lily snapped open the shoulder straps of her overalls, tugged her T-shirt over her head, and threw it over the seat. "Here. Even a Colebrook can't run around town with her tits hanging out."

Dr. John Lee Sikes was settled in a respectable, fortyish bachelorhood in MacKenzie, with a lucrative veterinary practice, two junior partners, a piece of rolling land with handsome pastures and barns, a large stone house, and a dozen purebred quarter horses on which he doted. On some dark nights he still remembered Vietnam, but that had been more than twenty years ago, and the memories had mellowed with time. On one beefy forearm he bore a tattoo from an ass-kicking marine company, of which he was proud. In his wild days during veterinary school and for a few years afterward, he'd partied with bikers, and once, for a few heady months, he'd lived in a commune with women who wore gold studs in their noses.

He'd seen a lot and enjoyed the majority of it.

But here, in his examining room, huddling over him as he expertly probed the dog's fractured shoulder, was a sight to rival everything. He knew Lily Porter, having given her ugly dog its shots and worming back in the spring. Never one to pass up a chance, he'd tried to excite her with a dose of the Sikes crotch-driven charm, thinking she'd be a nice change from women who stitched little beer emblems on their panties and collected posters of Garth Brooks.

She had given him a firm but classy *"No, thank you."* He liked her style.

Now, she stood here, her face screwed into anguished lines, her curly red hair tangled sensually around her shoulders and arms, wearing cutoff overalls with only a white bra underneath. The big doll had a pair of fine, pink-skinned, freckled knockers, by God.

But she wasn't the main attraction. The bitchy, braless one with the thin T-shirt and the skewed, sheer whatever-it-was hanging jauntily from one hip was the winner. She looked like Morticia Adams on a cheap cruise. The way she kept sweeping her dark straight hair swept back from a widow's peak, so that its blunt ends whipped the tops of her shoulders, made him think of a glossy mare tossing its head angrily. Her nipples made beautiful little points under the white shirt.

He could take a woman like that home to Mother, but dear old Mother had long ago died of alcohol poisoning in the drunk tank of a two-bit Texas town. Still, it was a pleasant thought.

"Are you waiting for mold to grow on your ass?" she asked suddenly.

"Shut up and let him do his work," Lily told her.

John Lee arched a brow. As he continued to probe the dog's shoulder, he scowled at the stranger. "How about I forge your name on a veterinary degree and let *you* take over?" Feisty, this one. Since Lily didn't care whether he talked like a saint or a marine, he added, "You need your attitude poked."

Her eyes widened. "You balding, potbellied, tattooed prick."

"You noticed. I'm flattered." John Lee turned his professional persona toward Lily and said, "I'll take some X rays and make sure there are no internal injuries. This shoulder isn't too bad, I think. The best thing for you to do is go home and give me a call in the morning."

Before Lily could answer, the other one popped her delicious mouth open and snapped, "I'm calling my veterinarian in New York. If this dog's not cared for properly, I'll close this little two-hole crapper of yours down and have your license revoked."

John Lee gaped at her. "You go ahead and call your private ass-wipe, lady, and see if I care."

"I'm Cassandra Colebrook. Don't you dare talk to me this way."

"A Colebrook, hmmm? Well, keep quiet before I bite your tasty little rich-girl hiney off and hang it on my door for a trophy."

She formed a snarl like a cornered rat. Lily stepped between them. "Cassandra, I said *shut up*." She bent over the dog and cradled its head in her hands. At the other end of the table the tip of its tail twitched with affection. "I'll be back," Lily whispered brokenly. "I love you, old dog."

Straightening and brushing at her eyes, she met John Lee's gaze firmly. "Nobody'll bother you. You do what you can."

"Thank you."

"Or else," the other one warned.

John Lee was already lifting Lupa into his arms. He shot her a wicked look. "Beat it, Cassandra Who-Gives-a-Shit Colebrook. I'll deal with you later."

Lily had to drag her out the door.

Artemas checked the old leather-bound watch on his wrist. When the family was together, they gathered for dinner promptly at six. Cassandra knew that. Family times were sacred. He'd ingrained that rule over the years. He left the others in white wicker chairs under the loggia's pleasantly churning fans, sipping wine, and walked through a side door into an intimate little dining room. Its creamy, figured walls and old rosewood furniture were as he remembered them from his childhood, when he had taken meals there alone with his grandmother. His quiet pride was tortured by knowing that he wanted Lily to see this room and all the others, to sit with him here, gazing out the tall, narrow windows at the land they both loved.

He went to an intercom on the wall near a service door and called LaMieux's office downstairs. No, LaMieux said, Cassandra hadn't phoned. Artemas frowned darkly and went back to the windows, looking toward the loggia, where the others were watching Elizabeth's boys play with one of the estate's black Labradors. He'd brought the dogs down from a farm he owned in Connecticut. He would also bring in cats, rabbits, birds—especially birds in the palm court, which hadn't been finished yet—a friendly menagerie of creatures to fill the place.

James was restless, glancing back at the loggia's enormous glass doors, probably saying to the rest that Cassandra was late. They had pondered Armande's sudden departure for Atlanta. They only tolerated the man and were pleased, like Artemas, that he and Cass had obviously had a fight.

Mr. Upton, the butler, who'd come down from the Connecticut house, too, appeared at an inner doorway. "Miss Cassandra has arrived," he said somberly, but his face was flushed. In a low, worried voice he added, "Sir, she's with your neighbor. Mrs. Porter asks that you come to the front door and, well, 'take care of your sister.'"

Artemas strode past him. "Take care of her?"

Mr. Upton whispered, "She appears to be intoxicated, sir."

Lily held on to Cassandra's arm to keep her from swaying and stared upward at the Tiffany skylight in the entrance hall. It glowed like a kaleidoscope. Her heart contracted with painful awe. Mama and Daddy had described that exquisite domed cap of multicolored glass so many times. The sound of hurried footsteps made her jerk her attention down.

Artemas entered the darkly elegant arena with a force of presence that sank into her to the core—a hard, rugged man made no less primitively masculine by soft gray loafers, soft gray trousers, and a gray shirt, fashionable, with no collar and tiny pearl buttons at the chest. If anything, the casual finesse of his clothing emphasized the contrast.

Cassandra teetered from foot to foot. "Shit, it's Artemas," she said sadly, and covered her face with one hand. Her Yorkie lay by her sandaled feet, bedraggled but devoted. Artemas halted in front of them, staring from his sister to Lily, who pushed Cass forward firmly. "She's been at my house for the past hour. She drank an entire bottle of homemade peach wine Aunt Maude gave me."

"Why?" His interest seemed torn between the sight of his sister in an old T-shirt, bikini bottom, and skewed sarong and Lily's unexpected visit to the house.

She looked stoic but drawn, clownish in an oversized work shirt buttoned over something—overalls?—with baggy cutoff legs. Her legs were scratched and dirty above sagging white socks and blunt work shoes.

He wanted to find it all unappealing. Instead, her uncared-for appearance made him sorry, and angry on her behalf, ready to attack anyone who disparaged her. It had been inevitable that she and his siblings would encounter each other, but like this? What the hell had happened between her and Cass?

Lily explained about Lupa, watching his expression segue from dismay to an authoritative, intense concern that burned her skin, then finally to bewilderment. She didn't explain how Cass had come to be drunk on peach wine. There was so much more to the story, hurtful and private, and she wouldn't say it in the middle of this grand foyer with Cassandra wobbling beside her and the butler watching.

"I need to lie down," Cassandra announced. "Or I'm going to—what is it they say on television? I'm going to *hurl*."

Her blunt, drunken humor didn't bring even a hint of a smile from Artemas. He gestured for the neatly suited little butler, who had been hovering in the background. "Help my sister to a couch in the the gallery, please."

As the butler took Cassandra's arm formally and guided her away, she looked back over her shoulder at Lily. "You think you can worm your way into our lives like this. Don't forget what I told you." She took a deep gulp of air, then added grimly, "But I didn't mean to mash Loopy."

Lily knotted both hands in her shirttail and gave Cassandra a look of weary disgust, but said nothing.

When she and Artemas were alone in the hall, he led her to a small, sumptuous sitting room and closed the door. She exhaled and studied him with shadowed eyes. "Cassandra mouthed off at the veterinarian, and he fought back. I didn't think your sister was the sensitive type, but then, I don't know her very well. I guess he upset her. By the time we got back to my place, she was almost in tears. She muttered about being treated badly by men, and hitting Lupa, and"—Lily shrugged, uncertain why she felt sorry enough for Cassandra to care—"and I ended up giving her the bottle of wine. I didn't expect her to drink the whole thing in less than ten minutes' time."

Artemas thought of Armande and knew there must be a connection. "And then?" he asked, stepping close enough to Lily to see the feathering of unhappiness around her eyes, urging himself to keep the conversation centered on his sister.

"She said I'm causing disagreements in your family. She said that's the revenge I want—to cause you to fight among yourselves."

He shut his eyes for a moment, and when he opened them, they were the stained soft gray of forgotten pewter. Lily took one of his hands between hers. She could only whisper—her throat was too tight for more. "Even with the bitterness I feel and the stand I'll always take, I never want to see your family torn apart. That's not the answer, to me. Hurting *you* won't ever make me happy. This has to stop."

He covered her hand. They were poised at a dangerous edge. "They'll understand, in time. They'll *know* what's between you and me, if you'll help me prove it to them."

Before she could answer, the door burst open. James stepped inside, bracing himself with his cane. Alise had her hands on his arm as if she'd tried to stop him. Behind him, Michael and Elizabeth looked regretful also. James's expression was furious as he studied their intimate scene. Lily withdrew her hands and faced him. He said grimly, "I've never seen my sister in a drunken stupor before. What did you do to her?"

Artemas stepped forward, his face set in harsh lines. "Lily was kinder to her than she deserved. And I'm going to be more patient with you than you deserve, despite the fact that you've broken into the middle of a private conversation."

"Are you getting what you want, Lily?" James continued, limping toward her, ignoring the rage and surprise rising in Artemas's eyes. "When will it stop? When you've played this martyr act so well that my brother forgets why our youngest sister is dead, and why I have to walk with this cane? You're not a martyr—you're a goddamned parasite. *Here,* try walking with this for the rest of your life, if you want to have people pity you." He threw the cane at the floor in front of her feet. The violence of his actions unbalanced him. He stumbled and fell against a chair. Alise, Elizabeth, and Michael leaped forward and caught him as he slid to the floor, his bad leg angled hideously beneath him.

Elizabeth's five-year-old wandered into the frozen tableau. When he saw his uncle on the floor, he ran to Elizabeth and clutched the skirt of her pink sundress, then stared at everyone fearfully and began to cry.

Lily's heart had stopped at the sight of him. Painful chasms broke open inside her. She couldn't bear to see a child hurt, even in a small way. She started past Artemas. He reached for her. Lily moved out of his range.

She walked swiftly through the hall, found her way into the huge gallery at the back of the house, then ran to the doors of the loggia and outside. Artemas caught her at the steps below. "I don't want—don't, please," she said. She looked up at him desperately. "You would never forgive yourself if you lost their respect. Go back to James. Make things right."

"You will always be welcome in this house," he said, holding her arms, his eyes filled with fierce promise. "Come back inside."

"Oh, Artemas," she said, groaning his name. She pulled away violently, brought his hand to her lips, and kissed it. "I meant what I said. Don't make James hate me more than he does. Go back. It's the only way. If you care about me, then go hug your brother."

His hands dropped to his side. She turned and went down the hill. Artemas went to the balustrade of the fountain terrace and watched her as long as he could.

Twenty-four

The beer-gutted, balding bastard had asked for trouble, and Cassandra would make him regret it. She turned off the road outside town beside a handsome wooden sign bearing MACKENZIE VETERINARY HOSPITAL in raised white letters, stopped the car, and studied the setting like a general surveying a battlefield.

She'd been too busy to notice the details two days before, with Lily glaring at her and Lily's dog whimpering pitifully in the back seat. A long paved lane curved between beautiful pastures outlined in white wooden fences. Glossy, thickly muscled quarter-horse mares and foals grazed in the knee-high grass. Lush, forested hills rose behind the pastures. The lane ended at a cluster of pecan trees and a handsome white clinic. Beyond that was a large, rustic house of stone and wood, with a wide veranda, a long, modern stable, and neat outbuildings. A shiny four-stall horse trailer was parked near a gleaming black truck outfitted as a mobile veterinary unit. An old red Corvette was stored inside a small stone shed near the house.

The place was handsome. It had class, serenity, charm. It certainly didn't reflect its owner.

She clenched the steering wheel of the black Jaguar

she'd brought up from Atlanta. By God, if Artemas expected the family to visit the old estate regularly, she wouldn't drive around in one of the homely Land Rovers anymore. And if Dr. John Lee Sikes thought he could intimidate her, she'd leave Jaguar tracks on his beefy, over-indulged body.

If she hadn't let him upset her on top of her humiliation over Armande's insulting behavior and her guilt about Lily's dog, she'd never have taken the bottle of wine from Lily, never have babbled to Lily about the family's private discussions of her motives, never have gotten so drunk that Lily had to drive her back to the estate house, where that awful confrontation between Artemas and James had occurred. The family was still tiptoeing around each other, James acting grim but humble, Artemas keeping to himself. Artemas and James had talked, alone, for an hour after Lily's departure. The result had been only a pathetic truce, not an understanding.

Artemas was disgusted with her for what she'd said to Lily. She was disgusted with herself. Something about her anger toward Lily wasn't clicking anymore. Dull respect modified it. That didn't mean Cass forgave her, but—oh, hell, who knew what to think anymore? Lily appeared to be minding her own business. It was Artemas who couldn't stop pushing for reconciliation.

Reconciliation with anyone was the last thing on Cass's mind. She drove up the lane, squinting at Dr. Sikes's handsome home and untangling the windblown red scarf from her hair. The hot summer wind billowed under her thin blouse and long skirt. Her toenails, peeking from open white sandals, were painted the same violent red as her fingernails. Let him stare at her and make lewd comments today. She would chew him up and spit him out in small, hairy, tattooed pieces.

Horse halters and leads were draped over the veranda's railing. A brown boxer with a face like a flat scowl lounged on the stone walkway that bisected a small lawn, proudly licking his enormous assets.

He needs to have his balls cut off, Cassandra thought,

jerking the car to a halt in the yard and scowling at the doctor's home. *And his dog does too.*

It was Sunday, so she didn't look for him at the clinic building. She climbed stone steps to the veranda, got no response when she rang a bell beside a handsome door with leaded-glass insets, then marched out to the barn. The boxer followed, sniffing at her bare ankles and licking the hem of her skirt.

She walked into a long, low hallway between large stalls and spotted her nemesis. He was leaning over a stall door, watching something on the floor inside. She scanned him with a breathless little catch in her throat, cataloging his, what—appeal? Threat? Old western boots, run-down at the heels. Tight jeans on lean legs. A sweaty white undershirt of the tank-top variety, revealing brawny arms and too much chest hair. The jaunty belly that had been graced by a plaid sports shirt the other day made a hard curve over the jeans waistband. His face was blunt but intelligent, and the thinning, closely cropped brown hair was sun-streaked. The scalp under it had tanned the same toast color as his leathery face.

"Keep quiet and come here, Cassandra," he said.

Cassandra flinched in astonishment. He'd never looked her way. "Are you psychic, Dr. Demento?"

"I saw you drive up. And now I can smell you." He continued studying the mystery inside the stall. "I remember your perfume." He gestured lazily with one hand. "Come 'ere."

Hypnotized, she walked to the stall and peered inside. A fat calico cat was curled in a mound of wood shavings. Several slick newborn kittens were nursing as she cleaned them. "What's her name?" Cass whispered. "Or do you bother to name your pussies?"

His eyes flickered at the obscene taunt. A sly smile crept over his mouth, but he still didn't bother to look at her. "Doesn't matter what her name is. My pussies come when I call them. Just like you did."

Cassandra inched away from him and snatched at the small white purse that hung from a thin strap on her shoulder. Opening it, she pulled out a wad of money. "I'm here to pay the bill for Lily Porter's dog. Tell me how much it is."

"You Colebrooks have a peculiar interest in Lily's life. Your brother Artemas was here yesterday, offering to pay."

Cassandra grimaced. "Our relations with Lily Porter are none of your business."

"Some say you want to drive her away. Some say she wants to tear up your family. Seems odd to me that either you or your brother would care whether her dog's bill gets paid."

"I was the one who hurt the damned dog. I take care of my responsibilities."

"Forget it. Lily and I worked out a barter."

"Yes, I just bet you did."

He turned slowly, nailing her with an amused, admiring gaze. "She's going to put in some new shrubs and flowers around my place. God, you're suspicious and territorial. I like that, if it doesn't go too far. You've got nothing to worry about."

"You think I care what you do?" He took one step and was suddenly so close that the scent of sweat and horse hair was an invisible steam. He was no taller than she, but he seemed overwhelming. His expression was bawdy and profane, as coarse as a diesel engine. Her heart pounded with excitement. He leaned toward her, his eyes half-shut. "I asked Lily all about you. The funny thing is, she didn't have a bad word to say about you or your family. She respects you a helluva lot more than you think. But from what she told me about your parents and your upbringing, sounds like you were a defensive little fat girl trying to survive any way you could. I think you still are."

She shivered. *"Fuck you,"* she said between gritted teeth.

His voice became gentle and persuasive. "Well, little fat girl, I see through your bullshit. I grew up with a drunk for a mother, and a father who beat the hell out of me every chance he got. I understand you better than you understand yourself."

Her fingers trembling, she threw a handful of bills. They fluttered against his chest and fell to the sawdust-covered floor. "If you won't take that for your shitty little services, then donate it to the local humane society. And by God, you'd better do it too. I'll check. If I find out you used the money to take some slut on a spending spree at Frederick's of Hollywood, I'll put your balls in traction."

"I love it when you talk dirty. You're incredible."

"Men usually ask for more money before they suck up to me."

He pulled a lighter from a back pocket, bent gracefully, and scooped the bills in one bearish hand. Then he set them on fire. Cassandra gasped as the flames curled through them, eating closer to his clenched hand. His deep, mocking gaze held her riveted. When the flames were licking his skin, he casually dropped the burning money on the floor and crushed it with the toe of a boot. She threw more money at him. "Wrap that around your tiny little cock and set it on fire."

He jerked her purse off her shoulder and tossed it aside. "You don't have to pay for it. It's all yours, Queen Bee. It was yours from the first minute I saw you."

She darted past him, but he caught one of her hands. Snarling at him under her breath, she elbowed him in the stomach. It was like hitting hard rubber. They went down on their knees, wrestling wildly. She pounced on her purse. He snagged her from behind and pulled her against him, clamping her arms to her sides.

His breath was hot on her cheek, his belly and thighs pressed tightly to her hips. Blindly cursing, she noted the hard mound of his erection and the amazing desire coursing through her body like mercury.

"Apologize," he hissed into her ear.

"Make me."

He circled her with one arm, holding her still. One hand crept under her voluminous skirt, inserted itself between her lower thighs, and began a slow progression upward. "Apologize," he whispered.

"Make me," she repeated.

His fingers slid higher. "Garters. How wonderful." He delved under her sheer silk panties and began stroking her. She bucked against him. "Wet," he purred. "Wet and hot. *Apologize.*"

"Make me." Her voice was now a low rasp. She wasn't helpless, she was taking what she wanted from this man, she told herself. Just as she always used men.

The heat and sudden, plunging intimacy of his fingers poured into her senses and made her shudder. Helpless. Helpless and dazzled by his raw attention, she shut off rational thought. Her legs were spread in uncaring recklessness, her knees digging into the sawdust.

He pulled her skirt to her waist and continued to stroke her, murmuring crusty, explicit endearments. Sensation built inside her quickly, luxuriously, riding the movements of his fingers and urged onward by the throaty, rapid pulse of his breath. She had him, had him right where she wanted him.

The explosion inside her shattered around his careful, thrusting hand. She moaned, shocked and angry and delirious when he pulled his hand away. They were both on their knees. He bit the back of her neck gently. Dimly she heard the quick, rough sound of her panties tearing, then his zipper sliding down, and then reason fled in the immediate, smooth ramming of his body into hers. He slammed into her with short bursts of power, and his hoarse sigh of delight drove searing victory into her mind. She had him. He had her. The taking was confused now. Exquisite volleys of pleasure assaulted her again. Rocking against him, she forgot to hold back, to force her way. Her whole body hunched in wild, graceless welcome.

He poured into her to the hilt, his hand caressing her hair, the other twisting deliciously into the waistband of her skirt, pulling her hips upward so that they hung impaled on him.

Coming down was slow and delightfully obscene, with him grinding languidly into her, his hands releasing her only to grasp her buttocks and spread them, making her gasp with pleasure as he sank even farther into her. The harsh duet of their breathing filled the hallway. She sagged forward, her head resting in the sawdust. When he withdrew, she sighed with the loss.

He kissed the top of her head, then slapped her lightly on the bare rump. The slap became a luscious squeeze, then he smoothed his fingers up and down in the tender, soaking crevices between her hips. Cassandra twisted to her side and lay there in a stupor, wondering how she'd ever look at another man without thinking greedily of him.

Suddenly he pushed something soft and bulky into her hand. *The money.* "Take it back. Keep it for next time," he said wryly.

She shoved herself upright and jerked her skirt down, smiling at him, beckoning him with one forefinger. He handed her purse to her. But when he leaned forward to kiss her, she dodged his head and caught one of his ears between her teeth. He shouted in pain and lurched backward.

They stared at each other, his ear crimson and indented with deep furrows. The slow, amazed smile that lifted his mouth sent shock waves of pleasure through her. "You are the woman for me," he said.

He wasn't like Armande. He wasn't like any other man she'd known. For once in her life she couldn't think of anything cynical to say or do, any plan to keep a man under control. She'd never let him know how frightened she was. When he took her hands and kissed them with absurd gallantry, and she blushed, Cassandra knew she was in trouble.

Hot air puffed through the low, open shed from humming attic fans set in the rafters, carrying the scent of summer and suntan-lotioned vacationers, and the sweet, smoky aroma of a barbecue stand. Lily leaned back in a lawn chair, trying to catch the breeze on her face and studying the crowded aisle from behind dark sunglasses. Old shade trees hung over the building, making a cool canopy, inviting people to wander away from the bright sidewalks and sunny shop doors on the town square.

She looked forward to these Sundays at the flea market, where fifteen dollars rented a cubicle and a chance to rest. Most Sundays she sold almost everything she brought—vegetables, bedding plants, and willow saplings, and went home with a couple of hundred dollars in her pocket, to be divided, fifty-fifty, with Mr. Estes.

The money was important to her—so far, her split of the profits was the only income she had—but she craved the human contact more. She soaked up the shoppers' serenity, admired their children, and made carefree small talk with other vendors—the bohemian young artists selling custom jewelry and wooden flutes, the potter with his earth-stained hands and creaking, foot-pedaled potter's wheel, the old couple weaving split-oak baskets, and all the rest.

For one day a week she was forced to live outside herself, to smile at someone's red-haired little boy when she wanted to cry, and pretend that the sight of couples holding hands or with their arms draped comfortably around each other's waists didn't make her ache with loneliness.

She pulled a wide-brimmed hat lower over her eyes and rose to help someone who was asking about the willow saplings, which stood like a dozen short, delicate sentinels at the edge of a table, their rootballs bound in burlap bags. Lupa stretched and licked her bare ankle above her tennis shoes. The sleepy golden dog lay flat on her side under a wooden table sagging with fat, glossy vegetables arranged in small baskets. The market's dirt floor had been covered in a deep layer of pine shavings. Each time Lily scratched her head with the toe of a shoe, Lupa's bushy tail swept tiny curls of sweet pine back and forth.

She sold a sapling and handed the man a sheet of handsomely typeset planting instructions and botanical information. Last week she'd unpacked the computer and printer she'd saved.

Slipping his twenty-dollar bill into the pocket of her loose khaki shorts, she pulled a small pad and pen from the same pocket. As she jotted a note about the sale, she glimpsed a tall, lanky man from the corner of her eye.

Topsiders with no socks, tan trousers, a white golf shirt with the tail out—her distracted assessment rose to his lean, handsome face, sandy hair, and large eyes. A jolt of recognition. She swiveled toward him, her hand motionless over the pad.

Michael Colebrook stood close by the table, studying her with his head slightly tilted, his expression pensive. "Hello, Lily."

She put her pad and pen away, stalling for time to analyze him and her reaction. He and Elizabeth Colebrook had always seemed like thoughtful, gentle souls compared to James, Cass, and Julia. She remembered that he'd stood up gallantly as she'd entered Marcus DeLan's office last year. And that neither he nor Elizabeth had ever said anything accusing or cruel to her.

Michael did not look hostile now. In fact, he seemed respectful as he glanced from her to the tables, then at the snoring Lupa underneath them, and the willows. "I hope you're doing well here."

"Do you?" she blurted, but there was no sarcasm in it. He had sounded sincere. She wanted to believe at least one of Artemas's siblings didn't hate her.

"Yes."

They traded an awkward silence. She removed her sunglasses and hung them from the neck of her loose white tank top. "I assume you're visiting at the estate."

He nodded. "All of the family's there for a few days." Michael paused, watching her closely. "You must be worried that you'll be invaded by suspicious, hostile Colebrooks again."

"It's always a possibility."

"This isn't an invasion." He fumbled with a pocket of his trousers and pulled out a sleek leather wallet. When he opened it, she saw one of her new business cards tucked inside. The card was pale blue with a willow etched on it in black, beside BLUE WILLOW NURSERY AND GREENHOUSE, in script. Mr. Estes was listed as the owner, with her name, Lily MacKenzie Porter, and *Award-Winning Landscape Designer,* beneath. "I picked this up when I was having a cup of coffee at a diner," he said, frowning mildly. "I met a garrulous old fellow who was thumbtacking one of the cards to the community bulletin board by the door."

"Mr. Estes," she said, her tone tense but droll. "He's in charge of publicity."

"He didn't know I was one of his hated Colebrooks. I'm sure he would have tried to stick a thumbtack in my forehead if he'd realized."

"I'm afraid so."

"He volunteered that your place isn't open to the public yet."

"No, not yet. We're just trying to drum up some landscaping accounts." She hesitated. "It's the first time we've used the Blue Willow name publicly. If you're here to confront me about that—"

"No." He fumbled with his wallet, scowling, his hands as lanky as the rest of him. A laminated photo fell out and landed under the table, near Lupa's nose. The dog licked it with a curious tongue. Michael ducked down along with Lily, who reached the photo before he did. Lily winced when she saw the pleasant, bespectacled young woman smiling benignly at her. His dead wife? Tamberlaine had told her once about the loss and how devastated Michael had been.

Lily stood quickly, as he did. The distress on his face touched her. "I'm sorry," she said, placing the photo in his outstretched hand.

"No harm done." He wiped it with the tail of his shirt, almost as if polishing it, his head down, while Lily watched in silent sympathy. "I'm sorry about your wife," she amended. "I understand."

He put the photo and his wallet away, then looked at her with troubled, searching eyes. "I'm sure you do. You've been through hell in the past year and a half. My family is aware of that."

"But you'd all be happier if I'd move to Timbuktu or someplace equally outside the Colebrook social circle."

"Maybe. But you're not about to leave, are you?"

"No."

"Then I, for one, am telling you that I don't consider you an enemy, and I wish you and my brother could live near each other in peace." He studied her shrewdly, but without accusation. "Lily, our faith in our sister isn't a slap in the face to you and all you've lost. Please don't take it that way."

"Are you speaking for James and Cassandra too?" He looked defeated. Lily wavered. The kindness and respect he had offered her meant more than she'd admit to him. She said gently, her throat burning, "I wish you were. And I wish Artemas weren't caught in the middle."

He dipped his head in subtle acknowledgment. "Your friendship with my brother—" he began carefully.

"Is something I miss," she finished.

"I'm certain my brother wants to help you. That's not something I oppose. This family can certainly survive any gossip your friendship might cause." He arched a brow. "Believe me, our reputation has survived much worse."

"You're a romantic. I appreciate that."

"Yes, I am a romantic. I've lost someone I loved, someone I can barely live without, and if I thought my brother had lost—"

"Stop now. You're going off down the wrong road, and it's a dead end. Don't let your imagination run away with you." Lily couldn't breathe. She wanted this conversation over, before she said too much, or the wrong thing. "Excuse me. I have a customer waiting over there." She called to the pleasant, round-faced little man who had been shifting anxiously from foot to foot, and now appeared to be trying to hide behind a display of macramé at another booth. "How are you doing, Mr. Canton? I remembered to save all the cucumbers for you this week."

"I, I, oh my," Mr. Canton said, turning red. Michael lifted his gaze in Mr. Canton's direction and stared at him. Mr. Canton waved his hands mysteriously, turned, and fled into the crowd. Lily rubbed her neck and watched in openmouthed dismay. She felt Michael's gaze on her. When she met his eyes, he asked slowly, "He comes here every week?"

"I think he runs a restaurant over in Victoria. He buys at least half of my vegetables." Astonished by Mr. Canton's strange behavior, she added, "Either he's had a fit of shyness or he's got a secret past as a gun-runner, and he thinks you're an FBI agent."

Michael searched her face. When he seemed convinced she meant what she said, he told her, "He doesn't run a restaurant. He runs the kitchen at the estate."

She felt the blood draining from her face. Speechless, alarmed, and struck with guilt for no reason except the feeling of being exposed—it was as if the karma Little Sis believed in had come home to roost with scalding irony—she shook her head numbly. "You're mistaken." A weak denial was better than none at all. "He told me—"

"I'm not saying you knew. I can see that you didn't." Frowning thoughtfully, Michael touched a basket of tomatoes. "I'll tell Chef Harvey"—he looked at her dryly— "that's the title he likes—I'll tell him that I have no problem with his choice of produce suppliers. He always buys the best. I'm sure Artemas would approve. If he knew."

Lily sat down limply in her chair. Michael smiled at her reassuringly and walked away.

Artemas draped one arm across the convertible's torn vinyl seat and steered with the tips of his fingers. He couldn't rationalize why he'd bought a '57 Chevy convertible with rusty tail fins and no muffler, except that when he'd seen it sitting in the yard of a service station with a FOR SALE sign stuck to the windshield, he thought, It's almost as old as I am, and it looks the way I feel.

He took the narrow road to the estate's gate. As he rounded a curve, he saw Lily ahead, walking along the grassy roadside.

Her hair streamed down her back in a ponytail. She looked like a redheaded scarecrow in long, baggy, denim shorts and a floppy T-shirt. She was magnificent, nonetheless.

And she was leading an enormous pig.

He geared the growling convertible down to low and approached at a careful pace. Lily, her eyes covered in black sunglasses and a tractor cap pulled low over her brow, glanced over her shoulder at him and stopped. The pig heeled obediently. It wore a black leather harness and leash. It had a Harley-Davidson tattoo on one shoulder, and a double set of obscenely flopping teats.

When Artemas halted the car, the animal ignored Lily's hard tugs and shuffled over to the passenger door, then thrust its snout over the doorframe, snuffling and grunting.

Artemas pulled a paper bag filled with apple turnovers out of the animal's range. Yes, he'd take any excuse to talk to Lily. This obscenely grunting conversation piece wouldn't be in front of him if fate intended otherwise. He cut the engine. "Nice pig."

Lily was silent. Behind the glasses, her eyes were unreadable. Finally she said, "It's a hog. Pigs are smaller." Thank God, she was able to pretend, as he did, that they could speak to each other casually. "Is it yours?" he asked.

She exhaled, as if concluding that they couldn't escape each other and might as well attempt nonchalance. "As of today. Name's Harlette. She's a pet. The old boy who owned her is moving to Michigan to run a florist's shop with his cousin. I was the only person he could find who'd promise not to sell her or eat her. I traded him a couple of pounds of ginseng roots."

"Ginseng? It grows wild around here?"

"The old folks call it man root," she said dryly. "It's worth about a hundred dollars a pound in the health food stores in Atlanta. And yes, if you know what to look for, it's here."

"I'm taking a large risk to say this, but why is it called man root?"

"It's shaped like a gnarly little man with his legs spread." She removed her glasses and did a slow scan of his car. "Nice pig."

"It's a vintage '57 Chevy. I'm going to restore it. I bought it for five hundred dollars."

"I thought you Colebrooks had an inborn aptitude for making smart business deals."

"I'm an expert at recognizing potential."

There were subtle implications in that. It seemed impossible not to communicate on a deeper level with her, no matter how inane the subject. The look she gave him was pensive but gentle. "I like your old junk heap. You need some toys in your life. What you have to do next is get this thing fixed up with a sound system, play some vintage Elvis real loud, and cruise for babes."

"It's working already." He nodded toward Harlette, who was rooting a torn place in the seat back. "The babes can't resist."

Lily pushed the hog's head aside. "Sorry."

"How's Lupa?"

"Doing fine. She's limping a little, but almost as good as new." She paused, her eyes somber. "How are things with your family?"

"Polite."

She winced visibly. "That doesn't sound good."

"I don't want to discuss it. Since I can't change anything except my taste in cars, I'll—" He halted, knowing he was only upsetting them both. Rubbing his forehead with one hand, he nodded toward the passenger seat. "Be brave. Accept a ride back to your driveway with me."

"I have a hog here, not a speedwalker."

"I'll drive slow. It's only about a hundred yards."

"Artemas, if anyone saw us—"

"They'd probably be too stunned by the sight of a hog with a Harley-Davidson tattoo to gossip about you and me. Come on. I want to talk to you about my sister and Dr. Sikes."

She hesitated, then nodded. His eyes gleamed. "You'll have to climb over. The passenger-door latch is broken." He leaned toward her and held out a hand. Grasping it slowly, she climbed over the door and settled next to him. His fingers pressed briefly into her palm before he let go.

Her heart pounding, she laid one arm on the rusty doorframe with the hog's leash wound around her hand.

Artemas cranked the engine and let the car inch forward. Harlette walked dutifully beside it, tail twitching. "John Lee is a respectable hellion," Lily offered.

"Do you know that Cass has spent a lot of time with him in the past few weeks?"

"I've seen her with him when I've been working on the yard at his clinic."

"What does she say to you?"

"Not much. We keep our distance. She asked me why I told him so much about her." Lily related the conversation she'd had with John Lee about Cassandra's childhood. Pulling her cap off and running a hand through the errant red curls feathering her forehead, she added, "He wanted to know all about her. I guess I wanted to see sparks fly."

"Mission accomplished?"

Without missing a beat, Lily drawled, "Well, the last time I saw them together, he was showing her how to examine a pregnant mare, and she had her arm up an equine vagina. If that's not romance, I don't know what is."

Artemas wanted to laugh. He wanted to put his arm along the grimy seat back and rest his hand companionably on Lily's shoulder, as if they were people who were free to enjoy each other, and the hot summer day, and an old convertible. Instead, he could only say with somber disbelief, "You'll have to get affidavits from a dozen witnesses before I can accept the image of my sister playing horse gynecologist."

"For better or worse, I'm responsible for her meeting Dr. Sikes."

"If that means Cassandra has finally met someone she can't abuse and can't discard, you've done something that none of us has ever been able to do."

Artemas turned the old convertible onto the farm's road and stopped. The woods were shadowy, weighted by the summer heat, throbbing with the slow music of insects and birds. He cut the engine again and twisted toward her. "Why don't I drive you the rest of the way to the farm?" His voice was gruff and deceptively casual. His large gray eyes never shifted from her face. "For once let's just be to-gether without regretting everything."

"Mr. Estes is at my place. He's building tables for the greenhouse. He'd see us." The dejection in her tone soft-ened the words. "I'm sorry."

Artemas leaned back. His face became shuttered. "How is he, these days?"

"There's a kindler, gentler Mr. Estes somewhere under all the grizzle. I catch glimpses of him more than I used to. I cook dinner for him a lot of days, and Little Sis comes over to ogle him. She brings him bran muffins. He claims she's got a fixation on whether or not he has healthy bowels."

Artemas laughed.

Lily shook her head and smiled thinly. "For now, we're building our stock, buying plants from wholesalers, and talking about a mail-order brochure and ads for next spring's gardening magazines." She studied Artemas again, searching his eyes. "When I was working at Dr. Sikes's last week, a retired couple stopped by on the way out of the clinic with their cat. They were curious about my work, and me—looking for someone to landscape the yards around their vacation home up here. They took one of my cards."

He brightened a little. "You're saying you've got your first design job then?"

"I don't know." Measuring every word, she added, "I may have insulted them. I grilled them for personal infor-mation until they probably thought I was an undercover loan officer running a credit check." She paused, holding his intense scrutiny and returning it. "I was afraid they were another one of your secret offerings."

"No, but I've considered doing that."

"Don't."

"But I know you're living hand-to-mouth, and it makes me crazy."

"I have a huge garden. Mr. Estes gave me an old freezer he had in his basement. I'm freezing and canning every-thing in sight. I'll never go hungry, and I have enough money for necessities. I'm happy this way. It's basic, and it takes all my energy to keep things going, so I don't have much left over to think about Stephen. And Richard."

Richard's name sounded like an afterthought, and that upset her. She repeated it in a stronger voice. There was the slightest flinch around Artemas's eyes. Casting his attention into the woods—thin air, hidden territory—his expression was troubled.

As she looked at him, the woods' heavy, sweet melancholy settled in her chest. It couldn't be wrong to want him, to want to remind this old car of couples who had been seduced by its deep, wide front seat on summer days such as this one.

It wasn't wrong to think of that, and him. It was only wrong to hope for it, or indulge blind selfishness. He was thinking the same thoughts, she suspected.

Lily wanted to stroke his dark, windblown hair, or feel his hand in hers, or kiss him very slowly and lightly on the mouth. None of that was possible, but she knew it showed in her eyes. She was locked on him, sad and wishful.

But reality was a rusty hulk of a car with torn, faded seats, a hog tugging impatiently on the thick leather leash, and an estate security guard who would drive by on patrol sometime soon. Reality was the wall of problems in their lives.

The rumble of a vehicle approaching on the public road snapped the tension. Lily glanced back and stiffened with dread as Mr. Estes's battered truck pulled in behind them. Mr. Estes sat still for a long second, staring at them. Then his face compressed in anger, and he shoved his door open.

Artemas got out of the convertible before she could and faced his furious advance. "Good afternoon."

"Good afternoon, *hell*," Mr. Estes replied. His accusing gaze latched onto Lily. "I go to town to get some more lumber, and I come back, and what do I find? You sitting here with *him* like you're on a picnic."

She held Mr. Estes's outraged gaze firmly as she

climbed over the convertible's passenger door and stood.
"Mr. Estes, are you telling me I can't even *speak* to a Colebrook? That's not fair, and it does nobody any good."
Harlette snuffled her hand noisily. Dark, giddy humor rose
in Lily's throat. It wasn't a pleasant sensation. Everything
seemed ridiculous, frustrating, and bitterly out of kilter.

He pointed at her. "I'm telling you that I don't want no
dealings with any of 'em, and you work for me, and you
better remember it. And he"—Mr. Estes jerked his head toward Artemas—"he may act like he wants to be friendly,
but he's a snake in the grass. A snake in the grass waiting
for you to look the other way, so he can strike! Just like he
did to Joe! You trust me, Lily!"

Her shoulders sagged. "I can't fight you and everyone
else. If the day comes when you don't trust *me*, you can
tell me to leave."

Mr. Estes sputtered. His anger had a current of distress
in it that bewildered her. "You don't understand. You just
don't understand what this man is like!"

"I understand very well," she answered. "He'd be a lot
happier if he never had to deal with either you or me
again." She met Artemas's eyes. The flicker of communication was private and sympathetic. He shrugged
elaborately.

"She's absolutely right," he told Mr. Estes. "Excuse
me. I have better ways to waste my time."

He slid back into the old car, backed out past Mr.
Estes's truck, and left. Lily felt as if every muscle in her
body were being drawn after him. When she and Mr. Estes
were alone, frowning at each other, he flung out his hands.
An odd brand of anxiety radiated from him. "He takes
what he wants, and he don't care who he hurts. He'll ruin
you, and if you help him do it, it'll be your fault, not mine.
You hear me? *It's not my fault.*"

The bizarre conversation made her head swim. "You go
on to the farm. Harlette and I'll take a while to get there."

Mr. Estes stammered, coughed, and finally blurted,

"You been better to me than I deserve. I wish I could do more for you. But I *can't*, you hear? I just can't—except I can try to keep you away from Artemas Colebrook. I'm right. You'll see." He climbed into his truck and drove off down the lane in a cloud of dust.

Twenty-five

Labor Day weekend was caught between the sleepy heat of late summer and the faint scent of autumn in the air. People filled the mansion's loggia and the terraced garden of the fountains. From her quiet sitting place among the trees beyond the lake Lily strained to catch glimpses of Artemas. While his guests moved incessantly from the canopied bar and buffet to the small tables set up around the fountains to the dance area in front of the band, he kept to a spot near the terrace's stone balustrade.

He didn't have to mingle. People came to him.

The band played bluegrass music, which drifted to her in soft snatches when the wind was right, like a mountain ghost who couldn't decide whether to visit her or not. The trio of fountains gushed into the bright afternoon sun.

She felt forlorn in her rumpled khaki shorts and brogans and T-shirt, her hair stuffed into a knot of tangled, fuzzy curls at the back of her neck, her face, arms, and legs sticky with sweat and bug spray. It hurt to be an outcast, an unwelcome witness to others' pleasure at the house she had loved and defended during all of her childhood.

She was startled when Elizabeth's two small boys and a stout, efficient-looking young woman in a white skirt and blouse walked down the hill, following the lake path. The woman, who must have been their nanny, carried the three-year-old and led the older boy by the hand. A colorful beach blanket and a cloth tote bag hung from her shoulder.

Lily parted the huckleberry shrub next to her and watched as the nanny spread the blanket on a shady spot behind a clump of laurel. A small white beach curled around the lake's edge. The nanny pulled off the older boy's shirt and tennis shoes. Dressed in bright print swim trunks, he ran to the water and waded in. The nanny helped the younger child undress as well, then carried him to the water, kicked off her sandals, and sat with him between her feet in the shallows. The boys squealed and splashed.

Lily propped her chin on one hand and stared at the scene through slitted eyes, paralyzed with misery. She'd never yearned for children before Stephen, had never been one of those women who loved to be around children in general or thought she needed to have a child to feel complete. But watching Elizabeth's boys brought the barely submerged grief back to the surface, and she would have given anything to cuddle them and pretend she had Stephen back.

Long, leaden minutes passed. Her heart sank when the nanny took the boys back to the blanket and began patting them dry with a towel. The younger boy curled up beside her, and yawned. She stripped off the five-year-old's trunks and began dabbing the towel at his groin.

The woman curled one hand between the boy's legs and massaged him, smiling as she did. Lily's head snapped up. Shock and disbelief froze her. The boy frowned and tried to twist away. The nanny slapped him on the back, pulled him to her, and gave him a long kiss on the mouth, cupping his small, bare bottom in both hands and holding his wriggling body against her side. Finally she let go of him, brought a dry pair of shorts from her bag, and helped him dress.

Lily brushed a hand over her eyes. *I'm in a strange mood. Did I misinterpret what that woman just did?*

Lupa nuzzled her cheek with a wet, inquiring nose, as if sensing her distress. That contact snapped the unreal feeling. Certainty washed over her, then rage. *I'm not crazy. I'm right.*

Lily got to her feet. The nanny couldn't see her through the deep undergrowth. Gathering the younger boy and her belongings in her stout arms, the woman took the older boy's hand. The three walked back up the path to the house.

Lily cursed in desperation. Would Elizabeth believe her? Would anyone, except Artemas, and perhaps Michael? Would James accuse her of meddling and lying, trying to cause trouble where none existed? She had promised to stay away from them all.

But finally, one overriding thought hammered at her. *If someone had touched Stephen that way, nothing could hold me back.* She was already walking forward, hurrying toward the lake path.

Artemas walked into the gallery. He couldn't linger outside by the terrace balustrade any longer, using any excuse to gaze toward the lake and the woods that separated the estate from her land. He wanted this exercise in hospitality to end, so he could stop pretending to enjoy it. Ironically one of his dearest dreams had been to see the house this way, alive with music and laughter, admired by all. Lily's absence, as always, reduced the feeling to a shell.

He started through the enormous room, hoping to slip into a hallway at the other side where a discreetly locked door led to the stairs up to his private wing of the house. He would go out on the balcony of his bedroom, where he could look across the lake in peace.

Guests approached him as he made his way through the throng. Keeping up small talk had never been easy for him; Cassandra was a natural at party banter and usually performed that service with inexhaustible energy at the family's business-related events. But Cassandra had fled to some hiding place with Dr. Sikes, and had not been seen for over an hour. Artemas almost smiled at that. He approved of the rough-cut veterinarian, who seemed gleefully able to deflate anyone's pretensions, especially Cass's.

Just as he reached the other side of the room and sighed with relief, Michael strode in through one of the enormous, open glass doors and headed straight toward him. One look at his brother's strained expression halted Artemas. "Lily's here," Michael said to him, in a low, urgent tone. "There's some kind of trouble."

When Artemas got outside, she was standing below the terrace's stone steps, involved in an obviously heated conversation with James. One of the estate's security guards had her by one arm. A large group of guests were staring avidly from the terrace. As Artemas descended the steps, she looked past James to him, and he saw both stark determination and anxiety in her eyes. Artemas stepped between them and gave a quick, almost imperceptible jerk of his head. The guard immediately let go of her arm and stepped back.

"I need to speak to Elizabeth," she said between clenched teeth.

"The hell you do," James replied. "You're not going to invade this house in the middle of a party and create some ridiculous scene."

"James," Artemas said. There was lethal warning in the softly spoken name. James turned toward him, clenching the handle of his cane with white-knuckled anger. "Don't take sides against us. For God's sake, I thought we'd agreed."

"I agreed to keep my temper. You agreed to keep yours. You seem to have broken that agreement already."

Lily made a hissing sound of disgust. "Get Elizabeth, please."

Artemas frowned at her. "What is this about?"

"That's between Elizabeth and me. She can tell you later, if she wants to."

"If you need to see her, then you will. With me."

"*No.*"

Anger and frustration graveled his voice. "You're putting me in the position of wondering if James is right to keep you away. If you've got a complaint about our sister, this isn't the time or place for it."

She stared at him as if he'd deserted her. Her eyes were shimmering blue ice, melting with a look of betrayal, then hardening just as quickly. "Don't worry about your damned party," she said in a soft, scathing tone. "I'm not here to embarrass you. But I'm not leaving until I talk with Elizabeth. *Alone.*"

James leaned toward her. "You're an embarrassment to this family whether you're standing in front of us or a thousand miles away. But we're not going to allow you to make it any more public than you already have."

"Don't bet on that. If you want to see me wrestle with a guard, I'm ready. You can tell your morbidly fascinated boot-lickers that it's one of the local customs."

Artemas held up a hand. He felt trapped, furious, despondent over her unreasonable behavior. "You can tell me what you want, or by God, I'll drag you back down the hill myself."

She looked stunned but answered, "I'll come back. And I'll *keep* coming back until I get what I want."

"That sums up your whole goddamned plan neatly," James said.

Artemas turned toward his brother with deadly calm. "Shut up. I'm ashamed of you."

James looked as if he'd been slapped. Never in their lives had Artemas spoken to him that way. His face white, he said softly, "You see what she's reduced us to?"

Artemas saw all too well that everything he loved was crumbling around him. It was in Lily's wounded, contemptuous eyes, James's fading respect, and the gut-wrenching repulsion at feeling the eager, gossipy intent of the crowd watching from the terrace a few feet above them. He snagged Lily's arm. "We're going to walk back down the hill," he said.

"Don't try it." The threat in her voice matched his.

His fingers tightened. He felt the muscles of her arm contract. One more second and the first social event at Blue Willow in more than three decades would earn a unique and ugly place in the estate's history.

Elizabeth, Alise, and Michael hurried down the steps to them. "Stop this. Please, stop this," Elizabeth begged. "What's wrong?"

"I have to talk to you," Lily said quickly. "In private."

"To me?" Elizabeth looked astonished and fearful, as if Lily might be carrying a hidden weapon. Lily leaned past Artemas, grasping his shoulder hard, and ignoring James's grimace. "Please. *Please.*"

"But . . . I haven't done anything to you." Elizabeth clasped her hands in front of a pale blue shorts outfit.

"It's not about you. It's about your children."

Elizabeth gasped. "But they're fine. Their nanny just took them upstairs."

"They are *not* fine."

Artemas eased his grip on her arm. He stared at her in bewilderment, with the sense of having misjudged her in ways she'd never forgive. Elizabeth burst into action, pushing at him. "Let her go!" She reached past him to take one of Lily's hands. Artemas stepped aside. Lily glanced at him bitterly, then followed Elizabeth up the stairs.

The family waited tensely outside the closed door of a butler's pantry. Artemas felt as if his nerves were being ground to raw ends. Cassandra strode in, with Dr. Sikes at her heels. "What the hell is going on?" Cassandra flung a hand toward the door. "Why is Lily in there with Lizbeth?"

Any answers were prevented by an audible shriek from behind the pantry's heavy white door. It flew open, and Elizabeth ran out, her hands clenched and eyes wild. She pushed through the group. Michael and Artemas caught her. "Lizbeth," Artemas said, horrified. She seemed uncontrollable, crazed. She stared up at him. "Ellen molested him! *Jonathan.* Lily saw her do it. She touched my son! I'll kill her. I'll *kill* her."

Chaos took over. Cries of alarm, guttural oaths. Everyone closed in on Elizabeth, who struggled fiercely. "I'm going to the nursery. I'm going to strangle that bitch. No one can do that to my son. Oh, *God.*"

"You're not going up there alone," Artemas said. Lily stood in the pantry's doorway. His distraught, searching eyes met hers. She looked exhausted. He loved her more at that moment than he could have put into words, even if there had been any way he could tell her. "You need to come with us. Please." She nodded.

Surrounded by the sheer emotional force of angry Colebrooks, the children's nanny confessed. Lily had no pity for her, but when she thought of the legal machinery the family would bring to bear, she shuddered. She knew their unyielding revenge too well.

Elizabeth was too upset to question her son—the others convinced her she'd only frighten him. Artemas gently carried the bewildered little boy into a playroom filled with toys, joking with him, tickling his bare feet, making him laugh and relax. Lily had seen such poignant strength and such intuition for a child's feelings only once before: in Richard.

After talking to Jonathan alone, Artemas returned to them, his voice calm, but his face lined with fury. Jonathan had described the sort of touching Lily had witnessed. The nanny had coaxed him to play her game several times before.

Elizabeth was a wreck. Michael sat her down in a chair and tried to talk with her. She buried her face in her hands and shook her head. James stood behind her, his hands resting protectively on her shoulders. Cass stroked her hair.

Tears clouded Lily's vision as she watched them close ranks around their sister. Artemas came to her and took her arm. Yielding to the gentle pressure of his fingertips, she left the room with him. When they were alone in a hallway, he faced her. Lily choked on the memory of the accusing words he'd spoken to her at the terrace steps. He studied her expression intently, and she knew he was reading the caution there. "You could have told me why you wanted to see Elizabeth," he said without rebuke.

"You could have trusted me."

"It was lousy communication, not lack of trust."

"No, you thought James was right about my motives."

"I had been thinking about you, all day. Wishing you were here. You showed up, as if you knew—as if you needed to be with me as much as I—" He halted. "Then everything went to hell." He spoke with harsh, weary emphasis. "Just as it always seems to, because one or both of us can't break through the wall of pride."

"At least something good came out of the effort. Elizabeth believed my story, and her children are safe now."

"No one doubted your story. Not even James. Thank you for protecting Elizabeth's children. I'm sorry I made it so difficult for you."

She felt his hand stroking her hair, and couldn't make herself tell him to stop. When he pulled her into a deep, comfortable hug, she rested there gratefully, her head on his shoulder, her arms slipping around his back. It was reassuring—no fireworks, no threat, no questions. The seconds passed in slow, protective regard.

Her arms tightened around him in silent acceptance. During this brief truce she would cherish being pressed against his body, loving the warmth and intimacy between them.

"Excuse me," Michael said softly.

Lily jerked her head up. Artemas did not immediately loosen his hold on her, so she stood there awkwardly, close to him, looking at Michael, who gazed back with discreet scrutiny. "What is it?" Artemas asked.

"Will you talk to Elizabeth? The rest of us aren't having much effect. Maybe you can calm her down."

"Of course. I'll be right there."

Michael nodded and walked back into the nursery.

"You go on back now," she told Artemas. "Whatever gratitude they feel toward me will evaporate if you don't. They need you. Especially Elizabeth."

"And you'll never admit you need me." He looked

down at her with weary resignation. "That's where the honesty between us stops."

She let her silence give an answer. His eyes darkened. They turned from each other, the spell broken.

Late the next afternoon, Lily hurried out of her house anxiously, at the sound of Lupa's barking. Elizabeth stood at the base of the porch steps. Her blond hair was disheveled and her face sweaty with the afternoon heat. She wore a wilted shirtwaist dress and white jogging shoes, as if prepared to take flight from a garden party. The lush flower beds framed her on both sides of the front path, and the shade trees dappled her with shadows, like the voluptuous centerpiece of a living Monet.

"I told everyone I was going for a walk," she explained. She hugged herself and looked distraught. "They're watching me like mother hens. They think I'm having a nervous breakdown. Maybe I am. Maybe it's irresponsible to show up here without warning."

"No," Lily said slowly. "You love your children, and it'll take some time to deal with what happened to Jonathan. I don't mind you coming here—depending on *why* you're here."

"I never thanked you. What you did took so much courage. If you really hated us, you'd have ignored what you saw."

Lily shivered. "I don't hate you. And even if I did, I wouldn't take it out on your children." Her voice faltered. Very few things were clear to her, but that was. Lifting her chin, she added, "I'd like to believe any of you would have done the same for my son."

"Oh, yes, *yes*." Elizabeth, her shoulders hunched and eyes glazed with inner turmoil, seemed to be on the verge of withdrawing into some personal hell.

At a loss and feeling sorry for her, Lily gestured toward the door. "Come inside. I promise not to tempt you with peach wine, like Cassandra."

Elizabeth swayed. "There's so much I can't say to my family. I shouldn't be here, trying to tell you."

"I'd think you could say anything to your brothers and sisters. Y'all are so close."

"That's why I can't tell them . . ." Her voice trailed off. Clearing her throat, she moved tentatively up the steps, then halted, searching Lily's eyes. "If you don't want to be bothered with me, I'll understand."

"No. Come on inside." Elizabeth looked at her with relief. Lily sensed she was desperate to talk. "Anything you say to me is just between us. If that's what's worrying you, relax."

Elizabeth began to cry. Lily guided her inside, and she collapsed in one corner of the couch. "I thought I was safe. But now I know I've never been safe. I've been lying to myself. All these years. Lying. I am such a coward."

Lily sat down on the hearth across from her. "What do you mean?" Her question brought a moan of anguish from Elizabeth. "I drove my husband away because of it. I see that now. I shut him out, over and over, until he was so confused and hurt that he left." She sobbed. "I couldn't let him get too close. I hid. I loved him, and I didn't want to drive him away, but I couldn't help myself."

Her ambiguous confession made Lily fear that she really had disconnected from reality. Moving beside her, Lily clasped her shoulder. "But if you still love your ex-husband—"

"I do. But the way I treated him was something I couldn't control—and still can't." She swiveled on the couch and grasped Lily's hands. "You have to swear to me you won't repeat this. Whether you think I'm right or wrong, I think I'd die if my family ever found out. We went through so much when we were growing up."

"You have my word."

Elizabeth closed her eyes. Then, in a small voice drenched with misery she whispered, "Yesterday brought back a lot of horror. I can't ignore it anymore."

"What horror, Elizabeth?"

Her eyes flew open; they looked bleak and terrible. "My father. He used me. He *molested* me, when I was a child." Elizabeth flinched. Lily quickly took her by the shoulders. "It's all right. Keep talking."

"I said it. For the first time in my life, I've told someone." She sounded stunned.

Goosebumps scattered down Lily's spine. "When did it start?"

"I was about seven."

"Elizabeth, I'm sorry. I'm so sorry."

"Poor Artemas—I'd sneak into his bed at night, to sleep with him, for protection. He didn't know; he was embarrassed to have his little sister crawling into his bed. He made me stop. It would kill him if he knew what Father had done to me."

Elizabeth crumpled. Lily put both arms around her and held her as if she were still a heartbroken child. In many ways, she was.

But she thought of Artemas, too, and her throat constricted with fierce tenderness. He'd devoted himself to saving his brothers and sisters from their parents' careless cruelty. She didn't want him to know what had happened to Elizabeth.

Elizabeth leaned against her gratefully. Lily took a shaky breath. "How long did it go on?"

"For years. Until my father d-died." Her body shook. "I thought I was free then. I thought I'd forget what he'd done and be just like other girls. By the time I entered college, I'd suppressed the memories so much that I was convinced they didn't matter. But the first time I slept with a man, I realized I'd never be normal. Sex was the most terrifying, disgusting thing. I pretended to enjoy it, but it made me sick. I decided I'd never escape those feelings. I took a handful of pills and tried to kill myself."

Lily rocked her. "And you suffered alone rather than tell your brothers and sisters, even then?"

"Yes."

"You're one of the bravest people I've ever met."

Elizabeth leaned back and stared at Lily. Her eyes flickered with surprise. "How can you say that?"

"You've lived with a terrible secret all these years. And you've survived. You're a good person, a gentle person. Your whole career is centered on helping others through Colebrook projects. You take care of your children devotedly. And you tried to spare your family a lot of pain, at your own expense. That takes a rare form of courage."

"But . . . I should have *done* something to stop my father. I let him use me. I was so stupid—the only way I fought back was by eating. I wanted to gain weight so he'd leave me alone. I wanted to be fat, like Cass. He thought Cass was repulsive." Loathing and fury tortured her voice. "I was his *special* daughter, he said."

Lily was frozen in thought. "What about Julia?"

Elizabeth winced. Pulling her hands away from Lily, she covered her face. "You think I'm brave? Julia asked me once, when we were older, if Father ever visited me at night. I *knew* what she meant. I knew he must be doing it to her too. But I said no." Elizabeth moaned. "I let her think it was just her, because I was too ashamed to admit he did things to me."

Lily died inside. What emotional scars had Julia borne? Suddenly Julia's broken relationship with Frank took on new clarity. What had Julia expected from men? Like Elizabeth, had she walked a tight line between fear and a desperate desire to trust them? Lily didn't doubt that she'd loved Frank and had thought he loved her in return.

When his interest had cooled, it must have been an unbearable violation. Reacting with vicious, blind vengeance must have seemed reasonable—desperately self-protective—to Julia.

Elizabeth was watching her, Lily realized. She dragged her attention away from the tortured speculation and asked as calmly as she could, "Where is your ex-husband now?"

"He's in Oregon. He produces documentaries. He has his own film company." Elizabeth shuddered. "He'll be coming back through Atlanta in a few weeks to see the boys. He's never ignored them—he loves them so much. God, what can I tell him?"

"Do you think he still cares about you?"

"I don't know. He's always kind to me. But I never give him anything to hope for."

"Then give him a chance. Don't wait. Take your children and go see him. Tell him what happened to Jonathan. And what happened to you. If he's worth loving, he'll respect you. He'll understand so much about the way you've behaved. It's a place to start. You've already proved you can do it by telling me."

Elizabeth sagged back on the couch. There were glimmers of amazement in her eyes as she considered what Lily had just said.

Elizabeth stayed for the next two hours, talking, reworking everything in her mind, trying to believe she'd come to a turning point in her life. When she rose to leave, she hugged Lily. "I'll walk back. I feel stronger in a way I never expected. Thank you. Thank you so much. I don't know why you did this for me. But somehow, it's not surprising."

"I only said what you needed to hear. The rest is up to you. I know you can do it."

They went out to the porch. Lily sat down on a step and watched Elizabeth stride through the yard. Elizabeth stopped, turned to face Lily once more, and called, "I want things to be right between you and my family. I'm going to work on it."

Lily inclined her head slightly, acknowledging the sentiment without revealing the pain it caused. A door had opened slightly, enough to let her glimpse possibilities but not reach them.

Twenty-six

Mr. Estes had dredged up a talent as sly as a fox's. Sitting beside Lily in a little Queen Anne chair that looked incongruously elegant for his bulky, grizzled self, he hunched over an office desk strewn with wholesale price lists, their project proposals, and Lily's landscape designs. Lily kept her back straight and remained calmly aloof. The fact that the man sitting across from them was intent on keeping a clawlike hold on every penny of his investment in the restoration of one of Victoria's largest inns only infused her with a sense of challenge. Parts of her life could be solid with confidence and enthusiasm again, and if she nurtured that, it helped overcome the bleakness when she thought about the rest.

"Me and my partner may have to go outside and arm-wrestle over this, Mr. Malloy," Mr. Estes told the man, sighing. "She can argue the horns off a brass billy goat."

Malloy looked at his watch. "We've been haggling for thirty minutes. I have other concerns besides landscaping to take care of. Your budget's too high. That's all there is to it."

Lily shook her head solemnly. "If we cut our overhead on installation, we can't justify bringing in a full crew." A *full crew* was only the difference between Mr. Parks and two sons or Mr. Parks and one son, but it sounded important. "I just can't do it," she added, crossing her arms over her chest and sighing.

Mr. Estes jabbed a blunt forefinger toward their prospective client. "Lily, you are bein' too hard on this feller. He's got two whole acres he wants torn up and redone from the word go. We've got to cut him some slack."

"Nope. If we can't budget a full crew, we'll never get the job done before winter. We've got to recontour the back section before we do any planting. We'll run into cold weather before we can set all the shrubs and bulbs out."

Mr. Estes rolled his eyes. "I say we can still make the schedule and give Mr. Malloy the budget he wants. I'm willing to go along and drop the bid by four thousand dollars."

She shook her head again. "We'll end up with a bunch of frostbitten plants that won't look decent next spring." She sighed heavily and gazed at Mr. Malloy with regret. "No can do. We have our reputation to think of."

The man threw up his hands. "Could you come down two thousand?"

"Well, I don't know—"

"Aw, Lily, don't be hardheaded," Mr. Estes interjected.

She pretended to study the proposal for a minute, tapping her fingers on her forehead, tugging at her hair, chewing her lip. Finally she exhaled in defeat. "Okay. I can manage that."

Mr. Estes pounded the desk. "Thank the Lord!" Malloy shot Lily wary glances as he grabbed the contract they'd provided. "Let's get this deal signed and sealed before *someone* starts arguing again."

Lily tried to look abashed.

When she and Mr. Estes were safely inside her truck, he slapped his knees and began chuckling. "He never knew what hit him!"

Lily clamped her hands to the steering wheel. She felt weak with relief. Colorful autumn leaves floated down from the roadside trees, and she watched them skitter across the truck's hood. For today, at least, she wasn't like them. She wasn't aimless, frantically searching for a safe place to land. She smiled with satisfaction. "He wanted good, fast work at rock-bottom prices. He got a fair deal, and so did we."

Mr. Estes looked positively elated. "We've finally got ourselves a big foot in a big door. You were right, Miss Tiger Lily. This is goin' to be a success. And it's fun too. I didn't expect anything to be this interestin' again." He rubbed a hand over the sheepskin vest that covered his flannel shirt. "Whew. I got indigestion from all the excitement. I got—" His ruddy face began to pale. Sinking back on the seat, he said in a tight voice, "I got chest pains." He winced and shut his eyes.

Lily cranked the truck quickly. Trying to sound nonchalant, she told him, "We'll just run by the hospital."

"Yeah. Let's do that." His lack of bluster and protest scared her.

Little Sis bounded into the examining room, took one look at Mr. Estes lying on a gurney with EKG electrodes nestled among his fuzzy gray chest hair, and gave a little shriek of dismay. Lily rose from a stool beside the gurney and waved both hands at her in warning. Mr. Estes, ashen-faced and worried, lifted his head and stared at Little Sis. "You think I'm dying," he said out of the corner of his mouth to Lily. "You called the vulture."

"*Shush,*" Little Sis said. She slipped past Lily and bent over him. "You'll short-out your wires if you start fussing." Her distraught tone softened the tart words. She put a trembling hand out and stroked the graying hair back from his forehead. "You old fart," she added tenderly. "You're not having a heart attack. I won't let you. You haven't even asked me out on a date yet."

"His blood pressure's high, but not too bad," Lily interjected. "They gave him a nitroglycerin tablet. That eased most of his chest pains."

Mr. Estes rested his head on the pillow and stared up at Little Sis with fading bombast. "I feel like I've used up all my chances," he said in a gravelly little voice. Little Sis mewled sadly and tugged at his hair in reproach. "Old fart."

Mr. Estes looked wistful at the endearment. Clearing his throat, he said in a stronger tone, "Lily, come 'ere."

Lily stepped closer and laid a hand on his bare, freckled shoulder. "Yes, sir?"

"Get me a piece of paper and a pen. I want you to write out a change in my will."

Little Sis scowled tearfully. "That's negative self-talk. Think positive. Close your eyes. Concentrate—"

"For God's sake, woman, if I die, you can tie a crystal around my neck and say bad energy done me in. But not right now. *Lily.* Get that piece of paper."

Because he was growing agitated again, Lily fumbled in a pocket of her nylon jacket and grabbed the notepad and pen she always carried. "Go ahead."

"Just write out something that says I leave the old MacKenzie place to you, and everything on it. I can't die knowing that I kept it from you just because of revenge for what Colebrook done to Joe."

She lowered the pad. "No, sir. I can't be a party to this."

His eyes flickered with shock. *"Why?"*

"Little Sis is right. It'd be bad luck."

"What do you care? It's *good* luck for *you*."

"I don't want my luck that way."

"Why?"

Little Sis moaned with disgust. "We like you. Can't you get that through your thick head?"

Mr. Estes looked teary and unnerved. "Helluva time to find it out."

"I ought to skin you alive for being such a fool," Little Sis said, crying. She grabbed him by both ears. Lily tried to pry her hands off.

A dusky-skinned middle-aged woman in a white lab coat came into the cubicle. "Good gracious, don't threaten my patient," she said when she saw Little Sis hovering like a ferocious honey bee. She spoke cheerfully, with a lilting

Indian accent. Lily gently guided Little Sis out of the way
as the doctor began studying the EKG printout.

"How is he?" Little Sis asked plaintively.

Scrutinizing the graph, the doctor grunted mildly.
"What did you have for lunch, Mr. Estes?"

He glanced at Lily accusingly. "Turnip greens, peas.
Corn bread. Lily and me stopped at a diner. I wanted fried
chicken but she talked me out of it. Said it'd clog my ar-
teries." His lower lip trembled. "I'm already clogged. Now,
you see. There ain't no hope. Might as well have had the
chicken."

Lily frowned at him. "He ate about a gallon of hot onion relish, too, even though I told him not to do it."

The doctor sniffed in amusement and laid the EKG
printout down. "Mr. Estes, please promise me that you'll
take your blood-pressure medication regularly from now
on. You know you have angina. You must have aggravated
it today."

"It's not too late to be good? I'm not a goner?"

She pulled a packet from her coat pocket and held it
so he could see. "No. For now, I'm sure this miracle drug
will save you."

He craned his head. "What is it?"

"Antacid tablets. You aren't having a heart attack.
You're having heartburn."

There was stunned silence. Little Sis leaped forward
and pinched one of his nipples, which made him jump as
if the electrodes had backfired. Her expression was furious.
"You scared me over *onion relish*?"

"I, I—"

"And now you'll go back to your cranky ways and be
as much of a son of a bitch as ever." She whirled on one
heel and stomped out. He sat up, speechless, his mouth
working. Lily took his shirt from a peg on the wall and
held it out, silent with diplomacy. Mr. Estes's alarm turned
to a look of bitter regret. "I *will* fix things, somehow," he
muttered. He stared at Lily as if she were the source of his
misery, too, and snatched his shirt away.

•   •   •

Stephen must be bouncing a ball on the floor. He was going to play Little League in the spring. The sound reassured Lily. But when she looked into his bedroom, he wasn't there. Instead, she heard his voice whispering, *Mommy, why are you still so sad?*

Lily woke up, sweating and disoriented. Rain whipped the house. Thunder rumbled behind the mountains. A tree branch was thudding against the room's outside wall.

She sat up, sank her hands into her hair, pressed her fingers into her temples, and tried to force the dream away. The familiar anguish washed over her. Had he been conscious and terrified until the last moment, under all the jagged concrete? Suffocating and broken against his father's bloody chest, had he tried to call out to her?

She stumbled out of bed and ran into the main room, her cotton nightgown molded, cold and damp, to her body. Lupa bounded up from a rug on the fireplace hearth and whined. Lily switched on a lamp by the couch and stood, shivering, fighting for control. Would these nightmares never stop?

Some instinct propelled her to a stack of boxes in one corner of the nearly empty room. She searched through them frantically until she found a small, lumpy cloth bag with a drawstring top. Lily sank onto the couch and cupped it in her hands. She knew its contents by heart, and hadn't been able to look at them after Richard and Stephen's deaths.

She untied the tight little bow and reached carefully inside. Withdrawing an oval of white plaster, she ran her fingertips over the imprint of Stephen's tiny foot, made the day they brought him home from the hospital. Cupping that keepsake in one hand, she pulled others from the bag. His first baby tooth, inside a delicate, enameled pillbox that had belonged to Richard's mother. A lock of his hair, from the first time she'd cut it. It made a small bright red curl, tied with a bit of white ribbon.

Her trembling fingers found Richard's fraternity pin next. He'd given it to her the night they'd made love the first time, in his room at Georgia Tech. She laid the treasures in her lap. The bag also contained a brooch Daddy had given Mama. It was a tarnished spray of flowers, and Mama had worn it even after some of the minuscule chips of garnet had fallen from the petals.

The bag should have been empty. It wasn't.

Frowning, Lily delved into the bottom. A rectangular object no bigger than a matchbook met her bewildered touch. It was wrapped in a sheet of white notepaper and bound with a rubber band. She examined it for several seconds, testing the hard surface beneath the paper. Whatever it was, she hadn't placed it in the bag.

The mystery made her heart pound. Her reluctance bordered on fear, without reason. Rebuked by her morbid and irrational reaction, she unwrapped it quickly.

A miniature cassette tape lay in her palm. She stared at it, perplexed. Then recognition snapped into place. The breath rushed out of her lungs, and her vision clouded.

It had fit the answering machine in their office. Richard had said the machine was broken. He'd thrown the tape away, he said.

But he hadn't thrown it away. He'd put it with her most cherished mementos. To hide it? To protect it?

Lily ran back to the boxes and shoved desperately through their contents until she found the answering machine. She sat on the hard wooden floor and jammed the plug into a wall outlet. The tape pressed neatly into the machine's console. When she turned the volume up and touched the playback button, there was an efficient *whir*, followed by a beep signaling that someone—Richard—had begun recording a conversation.

Lily knelt over it with her hands knotted against her stomach. Frank's honeyed drawl, clipped and angry, burst forth. *You stupid bastard, why did you tell Julia about the bridge?*

Mr. Tamberlaine looked strange—out of kilter without his pinstripes. He was dressed in soft black jogging sweats and bedroom slippers. But after all, she'd awakened him in the middle of the night and told him a garbled, shocking story.

He surveyed her from head to toe, the jumbled hair, the hollow eyes, the shirt stuffed haphazardly into her jeans, one tennis shoe unlaced. "You've been driving for over an hour. You look absolutely on the verge of collapse. Please let me fix you some toast and tea."

She shook her head and said, her voice little more than a rasp, "You have to hear this tape first. I need your advice."

"Very well." He guided her into his living room of white-and-gold antique French mixed with African sculpture, and she sank down on a plush couch. He busied himself attaching the answering machine to an extension cord, while she watched dully.

Finally, when he was seated beside her with a notepad and small gold pen in his hands, she pressed the playback key. "There are several different conversations," she told him. "Frank and Richard, Richard and Julia, Richard and Oliver Grant, and a conference call between all four of them. About thirty minutes, total." Lily propped her elbows on her knees and dropped her head into her hands. Tamberlaine made notes, at first. But he slowed, then stopped. The pad fell off his knee and he ignored it, leaning forward, listening. When she glanced at him, she could tell he was too stunned to do more than that.

Her back felt as if it would break with tension. She knotted her hands in her hair. Richard's voice, his anger and distress, and finally his terrible compromise, tore into her.

When the tape ended, she turned the machine off and leaned back on the couch, shutting her eyes. Tamberlaine sighed as if all the energy were being released from his body. "What a god-awful paradox this is," he said.

She stared at the room's creamy, filigreed ceiling, fixated on the pattern, trying to find some pattern to her thoughts. "Richard warned Julia that he couldn't guarantee the bridge's safety. He told her there was a possibility the concrete hadn't been allowed to cure properly. He told her they'd have to take core samples to determine whether it was strong enough. And that if it wasn't, the bridge would need extensive repairs. But Oliver and Frank convinced her that Richard was being too cautious. And she was so anxious to open the building on schedule that she believed them."

Tamberlaine got up and paced. "Ah, Julia, Julia." Disappointment and sorrow graveled his voice. "Why did she let pride overwhelm her own judgment? The risk must have been obvious, even to her."

"Richard should have stopped her."

"The others gave him very little choice," Tamberlaine reminded her. He added grimly, "Nor did Julia give him much, with her threats. She forced him to choose—was he being overly cautious? Was that caution worth risking a lawsuit for delaying the construction schedule and going over budget?"

Lily dug her fingers into her hair. Her scalp was tight, squeezing like a rubber band. "He allowed Stephen up on that bridge with him. Obviously he had no idea that the structural flaws he suspected could have such immediate, catastrophic consequences. Obviously he was worried only about the bridge over many years. If only he hadn't let Stephen stay up there."

Tamberlaine rewound the tape partially, searched until he found Julia's phone call to Richard, and played it again.

Listen to me, Porter. If Frank says that bridge is safe, it's safe.

Julia, he can't be certain of that. Frank's desperate. He's scared to death you're trying to ruin us in retaliation for his lousy behavior on the personal side. He's letting that distort his common sense. And Oliver is nervous too.

Good. If Frank's that frightened of me, he's not lying about the bridge being structurally sound. He wouldn't dare.

Dammit, you've punished Frank for months. Isn't that enough? Are you willing to take foolish chances just to twist the screws a little more?

I'm not going to let him make me look incompetent in front of my family!

For God's sake, Julia, this is business, not your personal crusade. All you have to do is inform your family that there are going to be delays, while we check the bridge out and do whatever's necessary.

The bridge is safe. My family is never going to know about this. Do you understand? I'd feel dirty for the rest of my life.

Dirty?

Stupid, inadequate, feeble, foolish—all because I let Frank Stockman screw up my life.

Julia, that doesn't make any sense. Your family won't look at it that way. That's crazy.

My family's respect is more important to me than your damned opinion of my sanity. The building will open on schedule. If it doesn't, and if you let even one word about your concerns get back to my family, I'll run you and Frank into the ground. You'll be lucky if anyone asks you to design a doghouse.

Tamberlaine stopped the tape.

Lily hunched over, her hands steepled against her mouth. *I'd feel dirty for the rest of my life* echoed in her thoughts. Those were the words of an abused child. She started to tell Mr. Tamberlaine, then realized she'd have to reveal who had given her the information about Julia's abuse, and why. *Oh, Julia, I understand now.* Julia hadn't known how to ask for help. She was accustomed to suffering alone. Feeling ashamed, alone. She couldn't trust anyone but herself.

"She felt she had no choice," Lily said finally. "In essence, she was convinced she was solely responsible for the building."

"You're being very generous. More than the facts warrant." His movements leaden, Tamberlaine sat down across from her. "Artemas and the family will have to accept the fact that Julia was capable of this inexplicable vanity and pettiness, and that she had so little integrity that she let her personal vendetta against Stockman overwhelm common sense."

But that's not true, Lily wanted to tell him. The roller-coaster emotions tortured her. They'd judge Julia unfairly, unless Elizabeth helped them understand what she and her sister had gone through as children. Only Elizabeth had the right to reveal that history, but Lily doubted she would. Elizabeth had just begun coming to terms with it herself, and Lily vividly remembered Elizabeth's determination to keep her brothers and sisters from ever knowing.

There was no satisfaction in attacking Julia any longer. Richard had left the tape for her in case anything happened, though he must have known it wouldn't pardon him. For the first time she felt a sad brand of serenity. It was still possible to love all that had been good and decent about Richard. She couldn't forgive him for Stephen's death or the others, but she could go on with her life.

Tamberlaine was watching her intently. "Your husband let Julia's threats overwhelm his convictions. You have the strength to deal with that sorrow." He paused. "Just as Artemas has the strength to accept Julia's failings."

Artemas. His pain was so entwined with hers, there were no boundaries. Help herself. Help him. Protect herself. Protect him. But revealing the tape would accomplish neither.

Lily straightened and gave Tamberlaine a direct, uncompromising look. His eyes widened. He began shaking his head. "You can't keep this information from Artemas."

"Knowing the truth doesn't change what Richard did. The fact that he had good intentions doesn't make him less guilty. If this tape had shown that he was innocent, I'd want the whole world to hear it. But that's not the case."

"But Artemas and the others need to know that Julia bears part of the responsibility. They have to be told, Lily. It might cast a different light on your problems with them. It might help you."

"It might. We can't be certain how they'd react. But I know one thing—if they hear this tape, it will hurt *them.* I don't think it does any good for them to know she was afraid to come to them for help. In a way she wanted them to accept the responsibility too, if anything went wrong. That's exactly what will happen. Artemas will blame himself."

Tamberlaine considered that in troubled silence. "Are you asking me to say nothing to him about this tape?"

"Yes."

He sighed. "You have my word."

"I'm sorry to do this to you."

"It's what you're doing to yourself and Artemas that I question."

"I'm doing it because I love him."

"I know." Tamberlaine looked pensive. "This time, however, it will haunt you."

Lily couldn't argue with that. But so many ghosts whispered to her. She had room for one more.

Artemas strode down a hall through the labyrinth of bright, airy kitchens and pantries and laundry rooms in the house's basement level, carrying a dark tie he had not yet slipped under his shirt collar. Cool, clear morning sunlight filtered through large windows. A helicopter was waiting on the bare back lawns to take him to Atlanta for the day.

He bounded into a room filled with tables and shelves. Masses of cut flowers stood in buckets of water. The shelves were filled with vases, baskets, and floral supplies. "Good morning, Maria."

The small dark-haired woman smiled from her place at a desk. "Good morning, Mr. Colebrook. You look so happy."

"Really? That's a shock to you—and me, as well."

Her four-year-old daughter, Anita, darted out from behind a table and ran to him. Lifting the girl into his arms, he said, "Maria, I'm having the whole family in for the weekend. I want the house full of flowers."

"*Si*, no problem." Maria's eyes glowed with plans. "I'll call my supplier as soon as his office opens."

Artemas grinned at the little girl, who had befriended him. She attended a nursery school for children of the estate's staff. He often wandered down to the classrooms before leaving for the office each morning, to speak to them. As he had gotten older, his own childless state had become one more regret. He tried not to think of the redheaded children he and Lily might have had together.

"Chef Harvey is cooking funny things for breakfast," Anita said solemnly. "They look like rocks."

Maria shushed her. "He's boiling pots full of oysters, for some kind of seafood salad," she explained to Artemas. She clucked her tongue at her daughter. "You are too curious for your own good."

Artemas set the child down and ruffled her dark hair. "Go tell Chef Harvey to make you some oyster pancakes."

Giggling, the girl ran out of the office. When they were alone, Artemas said to Maria in a low voice, "Call Mrs. Porter. Ask her if she'll sell you some of those incredible flowers she has growing all over her place."

"But, Mr. Colebrook, I've tried to coax her before, and—"

"Tell her it's for Elizabeth—Elizabeth and Leo. I doubt she can resist, in this case. Tell her I said that she had a hand in creating this celebration, and if she won't participate with us any other way, she can at least contribute some flowers."

"Ah. She will understand this message, yes?"

"She will."

He thanked her and walked back into the hall, his head bowed in thought. Elizabeth and Leo were trying to work out their problems. They were living together again. Elizabeth would only say that Lily had given her the courage to try. He was so proud and pleased. If only Lily could participate in his celebration. If only . . .

He stepped into the main kitchen. The room was empty except for Anita, who was perched on a stool at one of the gas stoves.

Steam hissed from an enormous steel pot on a front burner. Anita stood on tiptoe, a bulky oven mitt looking ridiculously large at the end of her arm. Curiosity had gotten the best of her. Artemas watched in alarm as the child clasped a handle on the boiler's side and tried to peek over the edge. The boiler slid to the edge of the stove.

"No!" Artemas vaulted toward her. She jumped in

surprise, stumbled on the stool, and fell, pulling the huge pot after her.

He caught her in his arms and sank to one knee, shielding her. Scalding water poured over his right shoulder and arm.

Artemas lay atop the jumbled covers of his bed, trying to read a stack of company paperwork one-handed, groggy from the pain pills he'd taken. his gauze-wrapped arm still throbbed.

Mr. LaMieux, small and lean, as elegant as a greyhound in his gray trousers, vest, ever-perfect white shirt, and neatly knotted tie, came into the main room and halted by the bed's far side. "You have a visitor. I'll show her in."

He stepped back out before Artemas could ask who it was. Such evasive behavior was not LaMieux's habit. Frowning, Artemas slid up on the bunched pillows behind his back and laid his papers aside. The doors clicked again; the visitor had entered.

With his good hand he gingerly pulled the sheet across his black jogging sweats and bare chest. Every movement sent small agonies up his arm and shoulder. Leaning his head back on the pillow, he listened to the rubbery clump of heavy shoes on the entrance hall's wood floor. It couldn't be a surprise visit from someone in the family, because he'd told them all not to come.

Perhaps he was more like James than he cared to admit. He was uncomfortable being helpless.

Lily entered the room. She halted, her blue eyes shuttered in a face as pale as cream. She wore a sweater and long T-shirt with faded cutoffs. Her hair hung around her face and over her shoulders in luxurious red waves. In her hands was a bulky cardboard box dotted with holes.

"How are you?" she asked, her voice low and husky.

He felt as if a Mona Lisa in denim and brogans had just appeared, asking him to comment on her transformation into living, breathing flesh. Wordless with conflicting emotions, he was aware only that he'd been ignoring a fierce need to see her again. "Parboiled," he said finally.

She winced. "Mr. Tamberlaine called me. He said it wasn't serious, but it sounded bad to me." There was unmistakable concern in her eyes, and Artemas couldn't stop looking at her. "How serious is it?" she asked.

"Just superficial, but I could enter the blisters in the *Guinness Book of World Records*. I'll be back in commission by next week."

"The child you pushed aside . . . wasn't burned at all?"

"No. Thank God."

She nodded, her gaze liquid and admiring.

This was dangerous. The pain medication should have deadened all sensation, but it was no match for the arousal curling through his blood. He gestured toward the box with his good hand. "A baby bear?"

Her face relaxed a little. "No, two baby wildcats." She came forward tentatively and set the box on one corner of the bed. "They'd taken up residence under Aunt Maude's house. I was planning to adopt them, but I decided you could use the entertainment."

Artemas's gaze remained riveted on her as she opened the box and reached inside. Two kittens bounded past her hands and landed on the bed. Looking around with the inane mixture of curiosity and arrogance of which only cats are capable, they spotted the subtle twitch of the exposed fingers of his bandaged arm, and jumped on them.

He inhaled sharply and pushed at two fiery balls of determination, who saw his movements as intriguing and began scrambling over him, catching wrinkles in the coverlet between their paws.

"Oh, my God," Lily said. She hurried to his side of the bed as he tried to move his injured arm out of their range. One sprang at the expanse of white gauze and hung there, gnawing at the bandages. Lily bent over him, her hair brushing his face, her hands working swiftly to unlatch one kitten from his injured arm and corral the other, who ran madly up his chest.

When she had them both safely cupped in her hands, she looked down at him in abject apology. "I'm so sorry."

Artemas collapsed on the pillows, breathing heavily. "I

could laugh at this if I weren't thinking of ways to cut my
arm off at the shoulder."

She sat down limply near his feet and set the kittens on
the floor. "Tamberlaine said you needed distractions. I'm
sure he didn't mean painful ones." Her face colored, and
her eyes narrowed in distress. She started to rise. "Don't
go," he said quickly. His tongue was thick, his hunger unleashed. Instead of killing the sensation, the pain only
made it seem welcome.

He grimaced and rearranged his arm on the pillow. The
way her gaze went over him, hinting at unspoken distress,
made him look away from her and straighten the scattered
papers on the bed. She exhaled softly, a gentle, weary
sound. His attention was drawn back to her like a magnet.
He saw her tired face and the chapped hands she clasped
on her knees.

"You've been working as hard as ever, I s'pose," he said.
"Let me see." He reached across his body with his good
hand, beckoning her. She was soft around the edges to his
hazy mind—no frown of censure, no stiffening, just a
warm, beautiful gift who ought to grant him her hand
for a moment. "Goddammit, don't be prissy," he said
with a glibness he was certain she would find funny and
compelling.

Instead, she bent over him and grasped his chin
fiercely. Holding him still, she said, "I haven't been in this
room five minutes, but you're already exhibiting very bad
form."

He was pleased to study her up close—the wide, luscious curl of her mouth, the blue eyes glimmering over
flushed cheeks, her breath pulsing against his face. "I think
the lady is suspicious of her own motives, not mine," he
said.

"Your pupils look like two black dimes. Is anybody
home?"

"I'm not sure. I take half the medication that's pre-
scribed for me, and all it does is make me stupid." He
pulled her hand away from his chin, held it over his eyes,
scrubbing his thumb over the hard palm and trying to fo-

cus. Her fingers stood out stiffly, trembling. The small quakes traveled through him. Warning and self-control made him let go of her abruptly.

She seemed mollified by his condition, or at least resigned. She sat down in a chair nearby. He languidly turned his head to one side, watching her. Lily knew how tenuous his restraint was; she was the one person who could make him prove that. In a way it was comfortable to be exposed.

The kittens scampered wildly around the room, and Lily tracked them with a pensive gaze, using the excuse to study the place. It had a handsome wood ceiling with a network of beautifully carved beams. Large glass doors opened onto a stone balcony, and tall inner doorways with naked hinges, still waiting for the magnificent doors that would be hung there, led into various areas, one of which appeared to be a kitchen.

His bedstead was made of some dark, rich wood, but the style was simple, with plain, blunt posts and no headboard. On the nightstand beside it was a brass lamp, a sturdy black office-style phone console, and a plastic fastfood cup filled with gold pens and chewed yellow pencils. A stereo receiver and compact-disc player were stacked on the hardwood floor nearby, and a pair of five-foot-tall speakers sat unceremoniously atop wooden packing crates. Free weights were stacked on a rack in one corner. Cardboard cases crammed with paperback novels were scattered around the floor, and issues of *The Wall Street Journal* vied with the latest, liberal *Utne Reader*—a strange contrast.

"Not exactly hedonistic yet, is it?" Artemas said with a strained attempt at humor.

"It's an interesting, messy place," she said. "What kind of music does a tycoon listen to?"

"When I'm lifting weights, Jimi Hendrix, or the Grateful Dead. When I'm feeling intellectual, a little opera. And everything in between."

"Dear Lord, not Barry Manilow or Madonna. No, no, I can't stand the thought."

He chuckled and winced.

She leveled a look at him that could split hair, but there was also an earthy humor, an easy arch to her red brows, and that voice! He could imagine it saying, with perfect, drawling sassiness, *I've got no use for you, rich boy.* He could also imagine her swigging whiskey and flipping aces in a poker game, or stirring grits in a smoky kitchen with an old chenille bathrobe wrapped around herself, or slapping him on the bare ass with lusty good humor but then, in the next instant, turning him inside out with a kiss.

Waving his good hand, feeling expansive, he announced, "The problem with you and me, Lily, is that we're too much alike. Territorial. Have to mark boundaries all the time, chase off invaders, protect our clans."

"I've tried putting my scent around the farm. But, personally, I find it difficult to pee on the side of trees."

"Takes coordination."

"And balance."

"But it keeps the males from poking around your life and leaving their mark on your plans."

"I hope."

Artemas frowned. "Someday, MacKenzie, you'll see that you can't close yourself off from other people and live like a hermit."

The light mood crumpled. Her expression tart, she said, "Oh, I expect I'll tease my hair up eventually and hang out at a motel lounge, looking for unsuspecting men to beat up and drag home for a little entertainment."

"Does Mr. Estes know about this?"

"About my plans to be a floozy? No."

"You know what I mean. Does he know you're here?"

"No. Little Sis coaxed him into going with her to take Big Sis to a doctor's appointment in Atlanta. Big Sis is having trouble with arthritis in her knees again. She's seeing a rheumatologist."

"Would you have come to see me regardless?"

Lily stared down at him darkly. "Yes."

"Good."

She couldn't resist straightening the sheet across his chest, carefully keeping her fingers from touching his skin, but wanting to touch him. "Tamberlaine said you're too stubborn to rest." She glanced at the pile of paperwork lying beside him. "I came to see for myself. He also said you don't want the family coming here to look after you. Why?"

"Makes me uncomfortable, being helpless."

"Ah, I see where James gets his attitude."

"Hmmm." He was too lethargic to take offense at that, apparently. "They've got work and personal lives of their own. Besides, Cass is off somewhere with John Lee. Vegas, I think. Very mysterious, these past few weeks. I don't want to disrupt everyone's lives."

"What unlucky soul is in charge of bullying you then? Who changes your bandages and makes sure you don't trip over your own feet on the way to the bathroom?"

"I asked for Mary Poppins, but she wasn't free." He scowled. "I could have hired a nurse, but I don't like strangers fiddling with me."

"Well, somebody needs to. Have you eaten anything lately?"

"Not hungry."

"How will your thick, stubborn hide heal right, if you don't eat?"

"I can call down to the kitchen anytime I like."

She nodded toward his private kitchen. "Is that just for show? Is there food in it? Does the stove work?"

"I can *cook,* and I do cook. It's fully stocked."

"Then I'll make you some lunch." The unmistakable flicker of surprise and relief in his eyes sealed her decision. Studying the tube of antibiotic ointment and the rolls of gauze and tape on the bedside table, she asked, "How often do your bandages need changing?"

"Once a day."

"I'll do that after you eat, then." She hesitated. "If you want me to."

He raised his good arm, laid his hand over hers, and

asked gruffly, "Is this going to be another emotional hit-and-run?"

Lily went very still. "No, this is going to be two old friends making the best of a bad situation, with no illusions. I ought to pretend I don't worry about you, but the idea of you lying up here alone—in pain, too stubborn to rest, and fumbling around trying to help yourself—is more than I can stand." She turned her hand upward and slid her fingers through his. Her voice softened. "I want to be with you for a little while in peace and quiet and privacy, with nobody condemning us. I want to take care of you the way you've always tried to take care of me. That's all we can hope for."

Artemas searched her eyes. What he saw in them—a mystifying blend of serenity and sorrow—was new. "I love having you here," he whispered. "Stay as long as you can."

"She's there, goddamn her. She's with Artemas." James replaced the phone on a small lamp table and leaned back in his chair, his fingers biting into his thighs. Through the burgundy silk of his pajama bottoms he felt the long indention of a scar on his bad leg.

Alise stepped out of the bath, her hair wrapped in a towel, a thick white robe knotted around her waist. He looked at her standing uncertainly across their large, dimly lit bedroom. A brooding antique armoire loomed on the wall nearby, making her seem more delicate, more ethereal, too vulnerable. "What are you saying?" she asked, frowning.

James slammed a fist against his leg. "Lily's sequestered in Artemas's private wing at the estate. She's been there with him for the past two days. Playing nurse. Cooking for him. Changing his bandages. A new maid went into the bedroom suite by mistake yesterday morning and found Lily asleep on the bed with him."

"How do you know all this?"

He was too angry to care that he'd been indiscreet about his methods. Pushing himself up—thank God, he no longer needed a cane—he limped to a large dresser and jerked one of its drawers open. "I asked one of the servants to let me know if Lily ever visits the estate."

Alise gasped. "You mean you *bribed* someone, don't you? You bribed a servant to spy on your own brother?"

"If that's what you want to call protecting the family's reputation, then yes." He retrieved a slender, leather-bound book and shoved the drawer shut.

She ran to him as he returned to the phone. James turned, scowling with impatience, as she grasped his arm. The look on her face stabbed him. Disgust and fury glittered in her eyes. "Have you lost all of your self-respect? You can't justify this."

"Do you think I enjoy doing it?" A muscle throbbed in his neck, and he wrenched a hand over it, squeezing hard. "I hate going behind Artemas's back. But what about the way he's disregarding the family's concerns? Goddammit, I'm not going to let him throw away the good name we spent years rebuilding. I'm not going to have it overshadowed by gossip and innuendo about his relationship with the widow of one of the men who was responsible for Julia's death."

Alise cried out and shoved at his bare chest. "What you're doing is more damaging to the family than any compassion and loyalty Artemas has shown Lily!"

"If Richard Porter had murdered Julia with his own hands, would you want to see Artemas involved with Lily?"

"Oh, *James.*" She moaned with frustration. "You can't honestly believe that's a reasonable comparison. There are too many shades of gray. What happened was a mixture of mistakes, poor judgment—"

"Don't. It's bad enough to hear that kind of shit from Elizabeth and Michael. Cassandra is starting to retreat too. They don't want to admit that Artemas could let a personal obsession drag him down."

"He's needed someone important in his life for years. He's been so lonely since Glenda died. Let him have a chance to find some happiness. He's not a fool, and I don't believe Lily is bad for him."

"That's a risk I'm not willing to take."

Flipping the book open, he reached for the phone again. "I'm calling William DeWitt. He may be the only one who can make Artemas recognize the brutal reality of this situation."

Alise stepped back, her hands falling to her sides. "I don't know you anymore. I don't know what you're capable of." She left the room. James slung the address book down and followed, but couldn't reach her before she entered a guest room down the hall and shut the door. As he halted before it, he heard the smooth click of the latch bolt, a shocking, obscene sound of distrust and separation.

Sweating, sick to his stomach, he leaned against the door. He would make all of this up to her, somehow. She'd see that he was right.

Lily woke to the feathery touch of a tiny paw patting the tip of her nose. Artemas sat on the bed beside her, smiling. He held up a long strand of her hair, rubbing it between his fingertips. Clearly the kitten had been provoked.

The warmth in his eyes was affectionate and provocative. The faint light of a lamp across the large room cast shadows on him, making his dark hair meld with their background, reflecting old silver in his eyes. The room had a hushed, middle-of-the-night stillness about it. She was hypnotized.

"Is your arm hurting again?" she whispered finally, rising to one elbow. A soft, down-filled comforter slid down her chest. It made a sensuous weight, pressing her over-sized flannel shirt against her breasts. Her legs felt contentedly relaxed inside a cocoon of old gray sweatpants.

"I'm fine. I want to take you downstairs, and now's the best time. No one will see you with me. You won't feel uncomfortable."

She sat up and studied him, silent and thoughtful, her pulse kicking into a rapid patter of excitement. A narrow white sling made a sharp contrast to the dark hair of his chest. It cradled his burned arm at the wrist. He'd draped a dark blue robe around his shoulders and somehow managed to don a pair of soft old jeans and white socks. He read her thoughts and said, "If any of the live-in servants are awake at this time of night and wandering where they shouldn't be, they'll assume we're sleeping together, regardless of how we're dressed."

She glanced at the oversized bed, with its black coverlet and white sheets pulled back on his side. She lay on top of them, an arm's length from his mound of large white pillows. "The Puritans would be proud of us."

Artemas glanced grimly at his arm. "I have a built-in bundling board. Blistered, drugged on pain pills—it's a helluva way to get you into bed." Before the discussion moved into even more hopeless territory, he took her hand and tugged gently. "But it's a start. Come on. Let's go downstairs. I have something to show you."

She stood beside him in front of a pair of overwhelming, heavily carved doors in the darkness. "I'm lost," she whispered. "Where are we?"

Artemas took an ornate key from the pocket of his robe and fitted it into the doors' gleaming brass mechanism. "It's a surprise. Cover your eyes. Don't peek."

She did as he said, feeling a little foolish. The slight chill of the polished wooden floor crept up through her heavy socks. She heard the smooth, ponderous sound of the doors opening. He took her by the elbow and guided her forward. The sweet, earthy smell of flowers and plants was easily identified. The air cooled. Water, gurgling languidly somewhere, was unmistakable.

There was a sense of having stepped into a vast space. Shallow steps met her feet, some type of stone. As he nudged her downward, she felt the glasslike surface of tiles. She judged their square perimeter with her toes.

"One more second," he said, his voice as low and private as a caress but also threaded with anticipation. She heard the doors closing, and the barely audible click of a switch. He took one of her hands in his. "Look at your palm court, Lily."

Her chest ached with poignant recognition. A sigh of

pleasure and surprise burst from her. He had transformed the vast, ruined, glass-enclosed room into the luscious heaven she had always tried to imagine.

After decades of loneliness, the little stone girl poured water from her fountain pedestal. A pampered forest of palms formed a background for ferns and a glorious variety of flowering plants. Tiled pathways wandered through their midst. Beautiful white-ceramic urns replaced the broken vessels she remembered.

"It's wonderful," she whispered. "Even better than I dreamed."

She heard the melodic chatter of sleepy, disgruntled parakeets roosting in the trees. Artemas lifted her hand. One bright yellow bird swept down and landed there. Lily studied it wistfully. Perched atop their intertwined fingers, it was as delicate and proud as a memory.

Twenty-seven

The ruthless old bargain hung in the air like the scent of the pine logs burning in the music room's fireplace. The room was softly lit and comfortable, the stately baroque pieces soothed by overstuffed couches and chairs, a baby grand gleaming like sculptured onyx by tall, filigreed windows.

Artemas leaned back in an armchair, a tumbler of scotch ignored on the table beside it. His arm, cushioned on a pillow in his lap, itched and hurt like a hundred sunburns. He'd taken no pain pills since the senator's arrival. It was unwise to be less than alert around the man.

The senator nursed an ornate pipe and stared, slit-eyed, into the flames. Stretching one leg over the other on the ottoman in front of his own chair, he looked deceptively benign. Finally he took the pipe in mottled, elegant old hands and studied it as if seeking enlightenment. "Since I've retired, I have entirely too much time to think," he told Artemas. "And one of the things I've discerned, in my infinite wisdom, is that your continuing kindness and respect since my daughter's death are more than I deserve."

Artemas measured his words carefully. "We've paid our debts to each other."

"No resentment, my boy? You have no inkling of disgust for the dreadful old bastard who manipulated your life?"

"I chose to accept your offer. I could have walked away."

"As I recall, it was a threat, not an offer. I was desperate. I can't be pious in my old age and say I'd have been forgiving if you'd turned me down. I assure you, I would have done everything in my power to ruin you. Don't tell me you doubted that." The senator smiled thinly. "It would insult my ego."

"Whether I felt trapped or not, I kept my word. And you kept yours."

"And now I sound as if I'm a frail old sinner asking for redemption." The senator made a derisive sound at the thought. "In fact, I'm here to meddle in your life again." When Artemas straightened in the chair and studied him with deadly intensity, the senator shook his head. "You are far too powerful to fear me now. Relax, my boy. I've come here to listen and advise, not to threaten. I'm concerned about you and this woman—this Lily Porter."

His teeth clenched, Artemas said softly, "I don't owe you an explanation of my personal life."

Cupping the pipe on the lap of his trousers, the senator settled deeper into his chair. "I understand you've known this woman since both of you were children. I can only assume her friendship is well worth the risk of alienating your family."

"She hasn't caused the problems. She's done her best to avoid hurting me or my family. Which is more than I can say for how we've treated her."

The senator contemplated that in silence. "I've never doubted your loyalty to my daughter. I don't now. But I'd like an answer to one question. Were you involved with Mrs. Porter—Miss MacKenzie, at that time—were you in love with her when you married Glenda?"

"Yes."

"But you gave her up to honor our agreement?"

"Yes. Lily and I didn't see each other again until after Glenda died. By then, Lily was married and had a son." Artemas held the senator's gaze. "Lily is not the kind of person who ignores her vows. And I never asked her to."

"And now that those vows are not an issue?"

"I'll draw her into this family. I'll convince her that the past can be overcome. I'm going to prove that to her if it takes the rest of my life."

"And what if your hopes are never realized? Are you prepared to choose her over all that you've worked for, and all those who love you?"

"Yes."

"My God." The senator sighed. "I came here to remind you of all you've sacrificed to secure your family's stability and success. I feared your feelings for Mrs. Porter would make those noble efforts meaningless. It seems I was mistaken."

"Completely," Artemas replied. He said nothing else. His love for her was something he didn't want to discuss further. He had so few private treasures. Lily was his greatest sacrifice. Having her with him again would *give* meaning to it all.

Mr. Estes sidled over to Lily as she was hanging bundles of dried flowers on pegs along the greenhouse wall. She wanted flowers to put in her house all winter, even dried ones. "You are *never* still," he complained.

She grunted. "Always got work to do. Unlike some folks I know, I don't see the use in mully-grubbing around in a bad mood."

He scowled and leaned against a table, lost in thought. The cloudy light of the autumn afternoon cast him in a pewter tint, like an old photograph. But his eyes gleamed vividly, shifting to her and then away. His moods had been more mercurial than usual since that frightening day at the hospital. She couldn't penetrate them. "That empty pad of concrete outside is starting to get on my nerves," she said lightly. "We ought to use most of the profit from Malloy's project to build a shop. Mr. Parks says we could put up the shell for under five thousand dollars."

"It's too late in the year to fiddle with construction." Mr. Estes's voice sounded strained, distracted. He rubbed his jaw and stared at the tables and shelves filled with plants. He wandered outside. Lily watched him walk among long rows of shrubs and willow saplings. Their outside inventory covered almost an acre, forming a neat patchwork. When she looked at it, she thought of the old quilts she'd put on her bed yesterday. Mama's and Grandma's handiwork had the same loving order to their patterns.

He ambled around, thumping his hands against his trousers like the fat red rooster who was standing on a pile of mulch, preening for his hens in a beam of sunshine that had burst through the clouds. When Mr. Estes finally came back into the greenhouse, he wandered up and down the aisles between the tables, muttering. "Winter's coming. I feel it in every bone of my body."

"Joe's up for parole in January. You've got a lot to look forward to."

He halted, staring at her with unfathomable distress, the way he did any time Joe's name came up. "You don't," he blurted.

She jerked a piece of twine tight around a clump of lavender. "I can't say he's one of my favorite people."

"He's the only flesh and blood I have. You *got* to understand that. Don't you hate me for taking his side."

"I never said I did." She gave him a puzzled look. "How'd we get off the subject of building the shop?"

"I said it's too late in the year to fool with it. You . . . you don't need to be putting your profit from the Malloy job back into this place. You need to save some money."

"Nope. I've got a place to live, food to eat, and a new electric space heater to keep my toes from freezing in the house this winter. I'd rather put the money into a shop."

"We'll talk about it later."

"Okay. We'll talk about it in January, after I sign a new lease. I want two years on the next one."

His voice rose. "You just can't stop jabbering about the future, can you? I don't want to talk about it!"

"All right, let's talk about Little Sis."

His shoulders sagged. "I don't know what to do about her. I don't know what to say, or how to say it."

Lily dropped to her heels beside a basket and pretended to concentrate on bundling her flowers. "Do you sincerely want to try? Is that what's making you so unhappy—that you want to change things, but you're too shy?"

He waved his hands loosely. "It won't last. I'm caught in the middle. You just don't understand. She'll end up hatin' me."

Lily would never understand his dark, vague mutterings. She was tired of trying to decipher them. Rising like a threat, she pointed at him firmly. "Go home and take a bath and put on a nice shirt and a pair of slacks and your dress shoes. Then go to the florist's shop and get a half-dozen red roses wrapped in paper and tied with a nice ribbon. Then you go over to the sisters' house and give the roses to Little Sis and ask if she'd like to have dinner with you at a nice restaurant over in Victoria. She'll say yes."

He snorted. "You just want to see me make a fool of myself."

"Somebody has to look out for you."

"I ain't your granddaddy."

She put her hands on her hips. "I ain't holding my breath for you to adopt me either."

"Meddler."

"Not long ago, when you thought you were dying, you looked like a man who wanted a second chance."

He wavered, exhaled, then said wearily, "I do."

"Then don't wait around. Don't worry about what's going to happen next. Make hay while the sun shines. Don't look a gift horse in the mouth."

She waited. He stalled. Finally he wrenched his hands together and swallowed hard. "What'll I talk about at dinner?"

When her astonishment passed, Lily nodded with ap-

proval. "You don't have to talk. She'll talk enough for both
of you. You just listen like your life depended on it and
answer when she asks you a question."

"She's got more words than a dictionary."

"After you get used to her, you'll feel like talking too."

"If it goes all right, I won't know what to do next."

"Send her flowers in the morning, and then call her
and ask her if she wants to go bowling."

"Will she?"

"Yes."

"Oh, my God. This kind of sticky-sweet stuff is for
kids. I've seen it on *Love Connection*."

"Well, if you're going to think of yourself as an old
man, then let me go get a rocking chair for you and cover
you with a blanket before your arthritis starts acting up."

He stomped to the greenhouse door, looking rusty and
rakish, like an aged Willie Nelson with short hair. He
scowled at her as he flung the door open. "I can't be any
worse off than I already am."

She held her breath. "A half-dozen roses. Don't forget."

"I'm not *senile*." Distress radiated from him like smoke
from an old engine. "I won't forget." He went out and
slammed the door behind him. Lily sat down on the hard
concrete floor and laughed wearily. Mr. Estes and Little Sis.
Cass and John Lee. Elizabeth and her ex-husband. Her
laughter faded into lonely regret. She seemed destined to
be a catalyst for other people's romances.

One of the estate's black limousines pulled into her darkening yard. Peering out the window at it worriedly, she
tossed a handful of kindling into the fire she'd just built
and rose quickly from the hearth. Lupa trotted ahead of
her to the porch, giving a latent *woof* of territorial alert.

Lily stood on the porch, wary and watchful, as the
driver opened a back door and helped an elegant white-
haired man from the car. His beautiful old suit and overcoat were as stately as his face. He walked with careful
grace to the base of her steps and looked up at her with
somber regard. "Mrs. Porter? Forgive my unannounced in-

trusion. I am William DeWitt. I'd like to speak with you. May I come in?"

Artemas's father-in-law was the last person she'd ever expected to invite into this house. Her first thought was that Senator DeWitt had come to see the Colebrook dilemma for himself. The senator returned her silent, cautious scrutiny. "I'm not here to pass judgment, Mrs. Porter. You'll hear no speech of righteous indignation from me. And I assure you, Artemas has no idea I've come." Arching a white brow, he said over his shoulder to the stocky little driver standing at attention by the car, "Isn't that right, George? We're simply on our way to the airport, aren't we?"

"Yes, *sir*. We never took a detour."

Gazing at Lily again, the senator gave a slight bow. "Whether you choose to reveal this meeting to Artemas is up to you."

Confused but polite, she nodded and opened the porch door for him.

When he was seated on the couch, waving aside her offer to take his coat, she sat down on the hearth. He swept a curious look around the spartan, dimly lit room then returned his attention to her. Lily remembered going to the library at Agnes Scott during the months after Artemas had married his daughter and searching out a photograph of her in the society pages of a New York newspaper. Glenda DeWitt had been a small, waifishly pretty woman, as elegant as a piece of the finest Colebrook china. Glenda DeWitt Colebrook. The woman to whom Artemas had devoted himself. The woman Artemas had loved enough to marry.

She hated the prickle of self-conscious discomfort she felt. She was suddenly too tall, rangy, and indelicate in jeans and a work shirt, with her hair tangled down her back. Not fine porcelain, like Glenda DeWitt, but thick, sturdy stoneware, unbreakable but ordinary. "Why did you come to see me?" she asked the senator, her head up.

He took an ornate pipe from the pocket of his coat, stroked it, frowned, then put it away again, and leaned forward. His narrowed eyes simmered with the pensive reserve of a man who had thought long and hard about what he wanted to say. "I took so much away from Artemas. And from you," he answered slowly, his gaze burning into hers. "I came here to give the future back to you both."

Wearing only white pajama bottoms, Artemas stood in the open doors that led from his bedroom onto the low stone balcony, his head tilted. He studied the panorama of autumn mountains over the balustrade, blue-tinted, rust-and-gold in the early light. He was puzzled without knowing why.

His restless sleep had been filled with Lily's presence even more than usual, both melancholy and promising, half-seen yearnings rising like a morning arousal. The dawn air was cool on the feverish skin of his arm.

The two kittens scampered past him. Their sporadic shenanigans through the night had woken him at least once, and he recalled them sitting on a table near the doors, silhouetted in the moonlight, fixated on some mystery beyond the beveled-glass panes.

He walked out onto the balcony, flexing his burned arm, deciding gratefully that he was comfortable enough to dress and go to the office. He needed the routine, the work. Having Lily with him for even their brief time made his solitude more painful. After the senator had departed yesterday, Artemas had debated calling her, but he'd known she wouldn't return.

Stroking a hand through his disheveled hair, he pulled a heavy iron chair to the edge of the balcony. He craved the cigarettes he'd crumbled over a trash can yesterday. He'd open a new pack later, smoke one, throw the rest away.

He started to sit down, then halted, astonished, disbelieving, as he studied the ground below the balcony. A section of the mansion's looming stone walls jutted out, giving him a private area. In his childhood it had sheltered a small, secluded flower garden. He'd had the space scraped clear of brambles and pines, like the rest of the lost gardens around the house.

During the night it had been reclaimed.

A thick bank of azalea shrubs, their summer greenery not yet subdued by an autumn frost, nestled against the wall. Other shrubs, which he couldn't identify, bordered the private space. The earth in front of them had been mulched with pine straw, creating curving, empty spaces dotted with wooden stakes. The stakes bore small paper notes. Artemas hurried down the stone steps and dropped to one knee, to read them. They promised a spring show of irises, daffodils, tulips, and lilies.

Her signature. He wanted to go to her, ask her if there was some special meaning, something new. But he wouldn't. She had her reasons, and she'd explain when the time felt right to her. He imagined her slipping back and forth through the dark woods between the estate and her place, carrying her gifts, working beneath his balcony, his bedroom, in the moonlight. Telling him in this simple, profound way that she was with him.

Lily woke to the sound of Mr. Estes bellowing her name. She jerked upright, disoriented, and looked around her bedroom wildly. She lay on top of the quilts, with the corner of one pulled halfway across her body. Bits of pine straw clung to her jeans and shirt. Her socks were stained with dirt. Her hair lay in matted disarray over her shoulder, an elastic band jumbled in the strands. She'd fallen asleep in the middle of unbraiding it.

Then she remembered—Senator DeWitt's visit, and the reason Artemas had married his daughter. Knowing made her feel both better and worse. Nothing else had changed, but that one, very deep sorrow was gone.

"Lily! Where are you? Get out here, girl!"

She stumbled into the main room. Mr. Estes stood there looking at her with gleaming, mischievous eyes. "It's ten A.M., girl! What's wrong with you, takin' a nap on a beautiful morning like this?"

Scrubbing a hand over her face, Lily absorbed his astonishing cheerfulness. "You're not Mr. Estes. Aliens must've switched him for someone who smiles."

"Ask me," he ordered, giving a proud little jerk to the open sides of his work jacket. "Ask me how it went."

"Your date with Little Sis? Tell me."

"Went good," he said, suddenly shy and gruff. He pulled his hat off, and twisting it in his hands, stared at the floor.

"Did you order flowers to send to her today, like I said?"

He shifted from side to side. A sheepish tilt curled his mouth. "Didn't have to. Gave her some before she left this morning."

"Left where?"

His face colored, and he began running a hand over the back of his neck. He shot her an exasperated glance. "It went *real* good."

As the implication sank in, Lily bit her lower lip to keep from smiling. "Well, I swear. I *swear*." She bounded over and hugged him. After a startled second he returned the hug. She stepped back and scrutinized him. "I'm glad for you and her."

"I know you are. I know it never woulda happened except for you."

"Oh, I doubt that. Little Sis would never have given up."

"But I . . . I needed a kick in the pants. You got me out into the world again." He halted, his mouth working silently, his Adam's apple bobbing up and down. "You been more like family to me than my own son." Suddenly distressed, he moved away, clutching his old felt hat in front of him. He walked slowly through the room, his distracted, scowling gaze going from her to the family photos on the fireplace mantel. He turned toward the fireplace. "I'd rather burn in hell," he muttered.

"What?" Lily moved closer and leaned on the back of the couch.

He turned, went to the door, then blurted, "I gotta go.

I got, uhm, things to do. I'll see you over at Malloy's place this afternoon, but, well—"

"Tell Little Sis I said hello."

He sighed. "Okay, okay, I'm going back to my house. When I left, she was cleanin' out the freezer. If I don't hurry back, she'll have throwed out all my TV dinners. I better go, uhm, get her mind off changin' my diet."

Lily went to him and kissed him on the cheek. "Watch out now, because if you end up marrying Little Sis, you and me will practically be related. If I treat you like a grandpa, you won't be able to fuss about it."

Mr. Estes looked at her somberly. "Maybe a new family is the best thing I can have waiting for Joe when he comes home."

She hid her dismay. She didn't want to be Joe's family. "If there's any way to help you get Joe straightened out, we'll do it."

"I'll deal with Joe," he said darkly, and left.

Twenty-eight

The table brimmed with a Thanksgiving feast, crystal, silver, and the finest Colebrook china. Oak logs crackled in two ornate fireplaces at either end of the room. Artemas sat at the head of the massive table in the estate's magnificently restored dining hall, surveying the surroundings and his brood with strained pride. It was wonderful to see Elizabeth with Leo, and Cass with John Lee. James and Alise sat stiffly, always subdued, but together. Glancing at Michael, he thought his youngest brother looked heartier than usual. Even Tamberlaine, who often joined them for holidays, looked peaceful enough.

But there would always be one person missing, the one he needed most, the one they would never accept. "Here's to our first Thanksgiving at Blue Willow," he said, lifting a glass of champagne and trying to inject more serenity into the words than he felt. He noticed that Cassandra merely sipped hers and put it down. Her face pale, her black hair pushed back from flushed cheeks, she looked nervous. Next to her, John Lee downed his champagne in one swallow, then reached for hers and drank it as well.

"I have—*we* have an announcement," she said suddenly, glancing at John Lee. Everyone was silent, a little taken aback. Cass rose to her feet. John Lee stood beside

her. She rapped her knuckles on the table, then blurted,
"We're married. And pregnant." And sat back down. John
Lee was left to buffer the wave of frozen surprise. Troubled, he stared down at Cass and said dryly, "That wasn't
real diplomatic, darlin'."

She faced forward, staring at the roasted turkey in the
center of the table as if she knew how it felt. "They were
going to be stunned, no matter how I said it."

Artemas rose and asked as calmly as he could, "When
did this happen?"

One of her dark brows flew up. She looked rattled.
"The pregnant part? About two months ago. The married
part? A month later. In Las Vegas."

Elizabeth dropped her napkin on the table and pressed
both hands to her chest in wounded dismay. "Why didn't
you tell us, Cass? Why didn't you want us at your
wedding?"

"That's my question also," James interjected, his face
bleak and angry. "Has this family degenerated into complete, self-serving secrecy?"

Alise leaped up. Her hands jerked out, knocking her
champagne glass over. "Don't you *dare*," she said to James
in a tight little voice. "Don't you dare accuse your sister of
your own faults."

"Sit *down*," he ordered, flashing her a look of both fury
and distress.

Michael stood then. "We haven't even heard Cass's explanation. James, this is not the time for stupid comments."

Artemas knew he was losing control over the loyalties
he'd spent his entire life building. Frustrated and alarmed,
he gestured curtly for silence. "I won't have this kind of
hateful bickering." He looked at Cass. "Why didn't you
want us to know before now?"

She flattened her hands on the table. They were pale
and stiff against the white linen cloth. "Because I was
afraid you'd all misunderstand. You'd all just accuse me of
being reckless, I thought."

"There seems to be ample evidence of that," James said.

"You've known the man only slightly longer than you've been pregnant by him."

The remark had the effect of a hard slap. Everyone stared at James as if he'd called Cass a whore. Artemas turned toward his brother, struggling with rage over the thoughtless condemnation. Before he could speak, John Lee interjected in a murderous tone, "You can trash me all you want, but if you talk to your sister that way again, I'll break your neck."

James's eyes narrowed. "What, precisely, do you hope to gain by marrying into this family?"

John Lee held his own with a hard look that met James's reproachful one. "Not a goddamned thing, if you mean money. All I want is Cass, and I'd want her even if she was a piss-broke nobody. And I'm going to be the best old man our kid could ever have."

Cass made a garbled sound of affection and grasped his hand. "How could I not love this sweet idiot?" she asked. "And I intend to stay with him. You can all think this is just another one of my flings if you want to. But it's not. I'm going to move into his house next week."

Artemas exhaled wearily. "We would have understood. And we would have liked to have been there at your wedding."

"How could I expect everyone to approve? Especially since every argument we have seems to center on Lily, and Lily's the one who's responsible for my meeting John Lee."

"She does have a way of infiltrating the family and causing endless grief," James said, his eyes narrowed. "It seems she's struck again."

Alise shoved her chair back and left the room. James flinched, rose awkwardly, and went after her. Artemas looked at the shambles of the family dinner—the empty places, Michael hovering at his place, coughing and reaching in his coat pocket for his inhaler, Cass gazing sadly up at the furious John Lee, Elizabeth bending her head to Leo's shoulder, while he stroked her hair sympathetically. Tamberlaine was scowling at the scene as well, but with a brand of thoughtful anguish that hinted at deeper worries.

Artemas towered over the end of the table, his jaw clenched, his hands in fists on the tabletop. "You are *welcome* in this family," he told John Lee slowly. "If you can stand the mess it's become."

Alise called downstairs a few hours later and asked Mr. LaMieux to have a car sent out front immediately. Artemas, sequestered in his study with the silent, brooding Tamberlaine, heard Alise's request from a startled LaMieux and ran downstairs as Alise strode into the entrance hall with her suitcase. She looked as if she'd been crying since dinner. James limped after her. He had discarded his coat and tie; his dress shirt hung open, missing several buttons. Artemas grimaced at the scene. God, what kind of battle had they been through?

Alise whirled at the sight of them and said to Artemas, her voice broken, "I've had all I can take. He won't stop until he destroys himself, and me, and everything all of you love. I'm leaving him. I'm going to our apartment in London. I won't be back."

"You can't," James said hoarsely, reaching for her arm. She snatched it away.

Artemas stepped between them. "Alise, will you sit down with me—just me—and talk about this?"

"It's useless." She looked up at him with frantic sorrow. "I've tried. I've tried so hard to believe he'd change. But he hasn't. I can't bear to watch him sink any deeper into self-pity." She staggered. Tamberlaine and Artemas caught her. Pushing away from them, she said bitterly to James, "You think I'm upset because Cass is pregnant and I'm envious. Yes, I'm jealous. I want a baby, too, and you won't agree to it. And I'm hurt because all you could do tonight was ruin her announcement. You don't want anyone to be happy. You blame everything on Lily, as if she controlled our lives. She *doesn't. You* do. But not anymore. Not my life."

James, a muscle popping in his jaw, lunged past Artemas and caught her by the shoulders. "If you want a baby, then by God, don't leave. We'll have one, if that's what it takes."

"A consolation prize?" she asked, her voice rising. "You think that's the reason we should conceive a child—so I'll be distracted and mollified enough to ignore the fact that you don't care about our future, that you can't stop tearing yourself apart over what happened almost two years ago? What kind of father would you be? I don't want our child raised with your attitude of blind self-interest!"

James pulled her off-balance. They swayed together. "Trying to keep this family's reputation intact is not blind self-interest," he said through gritted teeth.

Alise groaned in defeat. Her gaze darted past him, to Artemas. "James called Senator DeWitt. It was James who wanted him to talk you out of associating with Lily."

Artemas gave an indignant cry. The idea that his feelings for Lily had been discussed that way behind his back brought rage to the surface. James let go of Alise abruptly. A fierce shield dropped over his expression.

Alise read it accurately and shivered. "I broke your confidence. That's all you see. You don't understand that I did it because I love you."

"Perhaps you'll be happier in London." His voice was low and icily dismissive. He turned to Artemas. "I'm not ashamed of anything I've done."

Artemas wound a hand in his shirt and looked into his eyes with brutal warning. "Your wife is leaving you. Are you just going to let her go?"

"I'm not like you. I don't know how to compromise. And I can't conjure up forgiveness at the expense of everything I believe in."

Alise destroyed their tense confrontation by turning and walking to the doors. Mr. Upton, the butler, reluctantly opened one of them and took her bag.

James's agonized gaze tracked every step. Artemas released him and stood aside, praying that he'd go after her. When he didn't, Artemas told him, "Nothing I can say or do could condemn you more than what you've just done to yourself."

James turned and walked from the hall, his shoulders squared.

Tamberlaine found Artemas on the loggia, standing alone in the darkness. The cold November sky shimmered with a canopy of stars.

"Lily may never forgive me for what I'm about to tell you," Tamberlaine said wearily. "But this madness will certainly escalate if I don't take the risk. James cannot go on this way. I see, now, that he'll never stop fighting for his misguided vision."

"What do you mean?"

Tamberlaine took a breath of the chilly air. Then he told Artemas, as precisely as he could remember, about the taped conversations Lily had never wanted to reveal.

Her hands were trembling on the truck's steering wheel as the guard waved her through the enormous gates at Blue Willow. The sunlight felt harsh against her eyes. Lily followed the paved lane through the forest. The woods closed in, almost bare of leaves, gray silhouettes against a bright blue sky. She rounded a curve and entered the park's large clearing, with its circling drive girdling the enormous willow in the center.

Artemas stood by the massive old willow where they had met so tempestuously as youngsters, its leafless tendrils making a delicate lacework behind him. The sight of him affected her like a seductive drug.

Lily got out, slamming the truck's door. Was this the best they could ever hope for—furtive, mysterious meetings?

She flung out a hand angrily. "I was in the middle of mulching a bed of tulip bulbs at the Malloy Inn. Aunt Maude showed up looking like General Patton on his way to the front. I thought the Parks boys were goin' to salute her. She told me I had to come here *right now* and see you. Like the sky would fall if I didn't. You want to explain how you convinced Aunt Maude to play messenger for you?"

He halted in front of her. One dark brow arched, he said, "I've been planning to donate money to the library. I suppose it softened her mayoral heart."

"How convenient."

"Please," he added. "Just come with me, and listen." Lily looked at him in bewildered anguish, her heart kicking into a higher gear at the urgency in his expression.

His silence hypnotized her as they walked to the tree. Her gaze fell on the new bronze plaque set in a rough stone pedestal at the tree's base. THE BLUE WILLOW. PRESENTED BY THE MACKENZIES TO THE COLEBROOKS, 1900. MAY IT ALWAYS GUARD AND INSPIRE THOSE WHO LOVE IT.

He faced her and took her by the shoulders. He exhaled raggedly. "You can't protect me or my family anymore. God, I love you for what you tried to do. But it's time to face all the truth, Lily."

"What—"

"I know about Julia. I know what you tried to do, for my sake."

Lily gave a sharp cry of defeat. "*No.* Why? I thought he understood—"

"Julia wasn't innocent. You were right. Did you think I wouldn't accept that? That I'd hate you for forcing me to face the truth?"

She slumped a little. "Yes. That was part of my reason. I know how much it must hurt you."

"Yes, it hurts. I wanted to believe my sister knew nothing about the problems with the bridge. But I won't let you defend her, just to protect my feelings."

"What good does it do for you to know? It doesn't give me any satisfaction. I prayed that Richard was innocent. He wasn't. Hurting you and your family won't change that."

"You were willing to live with what you'd learned about Julia, letting my brothers and sisters go on rejecting you because they think you accused Julia unfairly— letting me continue to believe you were wrong to defend Richard?"

"I've come to terms with what Richard did. He made a terrible mistake. He lost sight of right and wrong. I understand why, and even if I can't forgive him for it, I can live with what I know. But I can't ask you to forgive him."

His struggle for composure was painfully obvious. Finally, his voice low and full of sorrow, he said, "Just as I won't ask you to forgive Julia. But should that make it impossible for us to love each other?"

His words swept through her like a cleansing fire. Lifting her head, she searched his eyes desperately. The look on his face destroyed her. She had to break the barriers, burn the past, so no other tragedies could come between them. "I have loved you all my life," she told him, her voice breaking. "And no matter what happens, I'll love you for the rest of my life."

He kissed her. She cried out in welcome and relief. His hands swept over her hair and caressed the sides of her face, and the drugging affection of his mouth hypnotized her.

Their struggle had the fast, wrenching consequence of pain and pleasure. He lifted her against his chest, and she stroked the back of his head fervently. She cried out, a soft, urgent sound. "I know why you left me before." The words were tumbling out recklessly. "I know why you married Glenda DeWitt."

"How? Who—" His eyes burned into hers. Understanding sank into the gray depths. "The senator. He told you?"

"Yes. He came to see me before he left for New York. He did that for you. He said he was giving us back our future." Her sorrow and frustration crested in a shaken moan. "And all I could do to show you how much it meant to me . . . all I could do was plant a few miserable flowers and shrubs outside your bedroom, such a pathetic way of telling you that—"

He kissed her again. She clung to him, winding her arms around his neck, sinking into him with welcome and forgiveness, absorbing the gentle violence of desperation and pouring it back into him.

"We're going to be together," he said, his voice low and desperate. "Not in secret, not in hiding, and not with regrets. Together, the way we should have been years ago."

She smiled at him, calm but torn down, trembling

inside, starting from a new place, summed up from the instinctive gifts of their childhood, and everything this old willow represented.

A universe of sensation existed between them—skin against heated skin, the weight of the soft old quilts and blankets on her bed; the smoothness of the white cotton pillowcase against her face as her head moved from side to side, receiving the slow, intimate caress of his lips and the stroke of his fingertips. His gentleness wrapped her in languid excitement, every discovery revealing stunning kindness and desire.

Lily drew her hands over the expanse of his chest and down the thickly muscled wall of his abdomen, curling her fingers lower, glorying in his quivers of pleasure and low sighs. She raised herself to him again and took him into her with a plaintive cry, and he gave back deep, infinite servitude, until only heat and trust existed between them.

He was speaking to her, maintaining her hypnotic trance with a voice so low and private and filled with ecstasy, it might only have been his thoughts she heard.

They held each other fiercely at the last, exquisite moment, shivering, merged so completely that sight and sound faded into a soft blur of elation. When he drew his head up from her damp shoulder and met her eyes, she saw the satisfaction of old promises brought to fulfillment and the quiet knowledge that they would willingly share a future neither he nor she could predict.

The mansion had a life of its own, and even in the deep stillness of the night she woke with a vague, disturbing sense that restless forces were at work. Lily raised herself to one elbow in the jumbled landscape of Artemas's large bed and looked at his empty place. The moon shone high through the tall windows and the row of glass doors to the stone balcony, making a silver sheen on the bedsheets and black coverlet.

The two kittens she'd given him, which were now

lanky adolescents, made soft weights on the bed coverings just beyond her feet. Lupa was snoring on black cushions on the floor by the bedroom fireplace.

Everything was asleep and content, except her and Artemas. She listened to the benign ghosts of water running somewhere in the mansion's labyrinth of pipes, the faint sigh of a floor creaking, or a thick, beautifully carved door shutting with whispering precision. As her mind cleared, she realized she'd woken to the click of Artemas shutting a door behind him.

She climbed from bed, drew one of his long silk robes around herself, and padded to the balcony doors. Pulling back one edge of the sheer white curtains that covered them, she saw him standing at the balcony's stone balustrade, his back to her, his bare feet braced apart, his arms immobile by his sides. He wore only his thin black robe in the freezing night air.

His solitude tore at her. She knew he must be brooding over his brothers and sisters—how to soften the information about Julia. He led his life like the great, proud Colebrook clock at the crossroads, keeping his family's time, and now hers. He'd told her about Cass's startling announcement, and that Alise had left James.

Lily stepped onto the balcony. At the click of the door he turned, a dark, broad-shouldered form against an overcast night sky. She went to him and wound his robe's lapels in her fists. "Santa Claus won't show up for weeks," she said with feigned amusement. "It's too early to wait up for him."

"I want to direct him to the right chimney." His voice was gruff. He put his arms around her waist and pulled her to him with a vehemence that was both loving and rough. Stroking a hand down her hair, he whispered, "You need your rest. God knows, we've gotten very little sleep the past two nights."

"Sleeping's for people who've got nothing better to do." She kissed the grim line of his mouth, then realized that there was no scent or taste of cigarettes, and there hadn't been yesterday, either. "There are so many small things I don't know about you yet," she said. "Have you quit smoking?"

He was silent for a moment, nuzzling her upturned face. "I was trying, without great success. Suddenly it's become easy to stop. I've developed a strong desire to live to be a hundred."

"Good," she whispered.

"Don't worry about my phantom-of-the-night wandering. This is when I do my thinking."

"Looks to me more like worrying than thinking. If you're going to run your engine overtime, I'll stay out here with you and make sure you don't blow a gasket. And keep you from freezing your piston."

He brushed a kiss on her forehead, then dropped a deeper one on her mouth. "You're shivering." He moved his hands inside the robe.

"Keep your hands where they are and I'll be warm enough." Lily pulled his robe open a little and laid her face against his bare shoulder. "I keep asking myself if there's really a good reason to tell your brothers and sisters about the tape."

"If I don't, they'll never know the truth about Julia. They'll always believe you were searching for an excuse to blame someone other than Richard."

"In time we could come to some kind of mutual truce on that subject. Elizabeth and Michael want to make peace with me, and even Cass—"

"You'd let them go on thinking the worst about Richard? You don't owe that kind of sacrifice to my family." He paused, then added sadly, "And certainly not to Julia. As much as I loved my sister, I won't make excuses for her. If I had known what kind of impossible pressures she was putting on Richard and the others, I would have stopped her."

Lily thought about Julia's childhood, and the terrible secret Elizabeth had confessed about their father. Certainly the abuse had colored Julia's reactions to men, but to what extent? Elizabeth's desperation to keep it from Artemas and the others was a decision Lily still didn't have the right to violate.

She slid her hand down his chest, placing it over the slow, steady throb of his heart. This was a man who'd fought to defend and nurture his siblings since he himself was little more than a child. A man who had salvaged their lives from a legacy few people could have overcome. He took such pride in that accomplishment. He didn't deserve to torment himself over horrors he'd never suspected.

Lily finally realized, through a light-headed haze of distress, that Artemas was speaking her name, his tone filled with concern. "You're shivering harder," he said. "Let's go inside."

Her low moan of confusion and grief brought his arms around her. He bent his head to hers. "What is it? Is it Stephen?"

"Richard stood on that bridge with our son in his arms. If only—"

"He made a mistake, Lily. He died for it."

"But my child died too. And so many others."

At his urging, she lifted her head. He wound a hand through her hair and held her very still. She could feel his gaze piercing her. "We can't bring Stephen back. God, I wish we could. I'd love to have your son with us."

Tears slipped down her cheeks. "And I know you'd treat him as if he were your own. I *know* that without asking, and I love you for it."

"I know Stephen can't be replaced." His voice was low and careful, gruff with emotion. "But there can be a very happy place for other children in your life. Our children. Do you want that for us as much as I do?"

"Yes."

Holding each other close, they went back inside. He guided her to a chair near the fireplace, tempered the darkness with the light of a small Tiffany lamp on his dresser, then stood in front of her, stroking his fingertips over her upturned face. "Wait here," he whispered. "I'm going to bring you something from the safe in my study."

He left through a hall that snaked through the cluster

of rooms that made up his private wing. When he returned and she saw what he was carrying, she looked at him with wonder. He knelt and set the old Colebrook teapot on her lap, "I've been waiting for the right moment to give it back to you." He watched her expression intently, as if worried that she'd find his gesture maudlin. "There are great advantages to having expert china artisans at my beck and call."

She feathered her fingers over the delicate blue-and-white pattern. "I can hardly feel the broken places."

"I had faith that it could be restored."

Moving with exquisite care, Lily set it on a small table beside her chair, then slid to her knees and put her arms around him. "It has been," she said.

Por Dios, Maria thought desperately, closing the door to her workshop deep in the maze of service areas beneath the mansion's main floor.

She was sorry for what she had seen in the palm court this morning, as she was removing a basket of flowers from the breakfast table set near the fountain. The chef had cleared the dishes himself—how mysterious. No one had been allowed there but him. But so much time had passed—Maria had thought she should take the table flowers away before they wilted.

The sound of laughter had startled her, coming from somewhere inside the vast, sun-dappled room filled with tall shrubs and plants, as if happy spirits had somehow made a home there. She had jumped with alarm when Mr. Colebrook and Mrs. Porter had suddenly emerged on one of the narrow pathways, not aware that she was watching, their arms around each other. He was pulling leaves from Mrs. Porter's red hair, and she closed the fastening of his trousers, smiling at him, letting her hands do more down there than just fix his clothes.

Maria had wanted to hurry away without them noticing, but they had turned her way too quickly, catching her. "I'm sorry," Maria had gasped. "I did not mean to interrupt—"

"No, it's all right," Mr. Colebrook had assured her, though he was frowning. Mrs. Porter looked as startled as Maria, but then Mr. Colebrook recovered his authority and took her hands. "It's all right," he repeated to Mrs. Porter, and after a moment she had given him a little nod of agreement.

Maria had rushed out of the palm court.

Now, locking the door to the shop, she rummaged among vases of fresh lilies—lilies of all kinds, exotic ones, ordinary ones, filling her coolers and spilling onto tables everywhere, because Mr. Colebrook had told her he wanted his private rooms filled with them. She pushed aside a jumble of florist accessories on one of her work tables and finally found the phone.

She did not want to be part of this awful spying on Mr. Colebrook, who had been so kind to her and her little girl. But the other one, the devil, James, he had learned of her cousins who were living with her and her husband at their house in Victoria. He knew her cousins were illegals. He had said they would receive green cards if she helped him. He had not said what would happen if she did not, but Maria was certain she knew.

She crossed herself and promised to speak of this in confession. But then she called him, the devil, and told him what she'd seen.

Twenty-nine

James slung the contents of his glass into the fireplace. The brandy burst into a blue flame. "You can dislike my methods, but not my results," he said grimly. "Yes, I had someone at the estate report to me. Yes, it was an ugly thing to do to Artemas. But now you see why it was necessary."

Elizabeth and Michael turned in their chairs, tense and frowning as they watched him. Cass leaned back on a sofa, studying him through slitted eyes, her hands molded to the slight bulge of her abdomen. "I see why Alise left you," she said. "You're despicable."

James stiffened. Tamberlaine rose quickly from a chair near the window, took the glass from James, and carried it to the bar in one corner. "I suggest that you neither consume more nor throw more into the fire," he told James. "And as for your reasoning, there is no excuse for spying on your brother."

James leaned against the mantel, as somber and elegant as this room in his vast, empty, brooding home, deceptive in his stillness, like a wounded panther, Tamberlaine thought. Wounded to the point of blind desperation. "The question is," James said, "am I the only one who won't passively tolerate this situation?"

"I think you are," Michael said. He stepped to the center of the room. Cass watched with mingled pride and surprise. A different brand of confidence had emerged from Michael's mellow, contemplative self during the past months. It was as if he'd come to terms with his wife's death. He had always been their peacemaker, but with an almost saintly distraction that brooked no conflict. Now, he seemed ready and willing to do battle with anyone who opposed him. He surveyed everyone with grim regard. "If Artemas loves Lily, and he asks us to accept that, I'll do so with open arms."

James said with soft vehemence, "And you'll accept the fact that she'll always throw her accusations about Julia in our face?"

"She has a right to her beliefs," Elizabeth interjected, studying James sadly. "She could hate us for defending Julia, but she doesn't. She never has."

James shot a hard look from Michael and Elizabeth to Cass, who stirred, stroking her stomach and eyeing him unhappily. He had apologized for his ugly outburst toward John Lee, but she'd been uncertain of him since. "You have to admit that she's been kinder to us than we've been to her," Cass said. "It was a damned strange way to retaliate. Lily's willingness to put up with us has never really made sense unless you consider the possibility that she loves Artemas."

James replied, "Have any of you considered the possibility that there was a helluva lot more than friendship going on between them *before* her husband died?"

Cass grimaced. Elizabeth shook her head adamantly, and Michael whipped toward his older brother with an expression of sheer disgust. "I can't believe you've reached the point where you'd accuse Artemas and Lily of that."

James flinched but held Michael's furious gaze. "I've always found the story about their quaint childhood friendship more than a little hard to swallow."

Tamberlaine straightened ominously. *"Enough."* Everyone turned toward him. His eyes glittered. *"Enough.* I *cannot* let this kind of filthy suspicion take hold."

Cass sat forward, personifying the hushed astonishment with her wide, alert eyes. "You know much more about Artemas and Lily's past than you've ever admitted, don't you?"

"Yes." Tamberlaine paused, sorting through all the years, finding the right words, the right starting point. Finally he knew exactly what it was. He sat down in a chair near the hearth, weary and troubled. He began, "She was nearly nineteen and Artemas just twenty-six, when she came to New York to see him. . . ."

The sofa was covered in blinking Christmas lights. Hopewell took the last string from the jumble in a cardboard box, plugged them into an extension cord, and grunted with satisfaction as they flashed. He hadn't expected any of the old lights to work after years of disuse, but they did. Like him, they still had the know-how. He couldn't wait to decorate for Christmas.

By God, he'd cover the whole house with lights. He'd put up a tree, and set out Ducie's little crinoline angels on the mantel, and hang mistletoe from every doorway. Not that he and Little Sis needed excuses to get romantic. The woman nearly wore him out sometimes.

Chuckling, he moved around the old house, taking pride in how clean and orderly it was now, fluffing the pillows in the bedroom and fiddling with the silly sticks of incense she kept in a little pottery jar on the nightstand.

Thinking about Joe getting out of prison in two months sent a dark chill through Hopewell. He knew what he had to do. He'd help Joe any way he could, but not at Lily's expense. As long as she stayed away from that Colebrook bunch, Hopewell couldn't ask her to leave the old farm.

He heard a car crunching along the gravel on his driveway and hurried to the front door, expecting Little Sis. Instead, he found a rusty old van with duct tape plastered over a hole in the passenger-side windshield. The driver, sporting a long, ragged beard and dirty-looking hair, flicked a cigarette butt out the side window. The passenger door opened and someone got out, but the van was angled so Hopewell couldn't see who it was. "Thanks for the ride, man," a startlingly familiar voice said.

The van's driver crunched the gears and backed up the driveway.

Joe stood there, a smirk on his face, a canvas tote hanging from one hand, tight trousers and a shiny windbreaker emphasizing a bull-necked, lean-hipped body that had been built in a prison weight room. "Hello, old man," he said. "Shit, you don't look too happy to see me."

"How—how come you're out?"

"They let me go early. Had to make more room for no-accounts and niggers. Don't worry—I ain't lying. I got papers from my parole officer."

An invisible fist closed around Hopewell's throat. Terrible images flashed through his mind—Lily and Little Sis learning the kind of deal he'd made with Artemas Colebrook's lawyer, hating him for it, of his life reverting to its miserable, lonely state. No. *No.* He'd talk to the lawyer—tell him he'd changed his mind. He'd help Joe some other way. Joe wouldn't know the difference.

Hopewell walked numbly into the yard and hugged him. "Welcome home, boy."

Joe draped a beefy arm around his shoulders and smiled. "Goddamn, you're a smart old thing, ain't you? Twistin' the knife. Cuttin' a piece right out of Colebrook's guts." Hopewell staggered back and stared at him. Joe laughed and nodded. "That lawyer come to see me. Told me all about it. Said he'd get me out early, if he could."

Hopewell nearly strangled. "It doesn't seem trashy to you to take handouts from the man who set the police on you and got you put in jail?"

Joe's eyes narrowed to slits. "Don't you get righteous on me. Colebrook owes me for what he done."

"You don't care that he's doin' it to put Lily MacKenzie off her own homeplace?"

"*Her* homeplace? Old man, that bitch hasn't owned the place for years. *You* own it. And I'm your flesh and blood, and you better do what's right by *me*. You get her ass off that land, and you tell Colebrook to pay up."

"Her lease isn't up till February. I never said I'd kick her out before then."

"Well, you just break that lease. I'm not sittin' around here for two months."

"Joe, this is your home. You got a place to live. I can get you a job. Hell, I'll pay you to work for me and Lily—"

"You think I'm gonna break my back for chickenshit, when Colebrook said he'd give me anything I want? You set this deal up for me. Why are you bitchin' about it now?"

"I can't do it! I was wrong. This isn't no way to get you straightened out. You're worse than you were before you went away."

Joe shoved him, then snapped a hand around his shirt collar and looked down at him with calm menace. "I'm gonna be rich, old man," he said softly. "If you fuck it up for me, you'll be sorry."

Hopewell jerked Joe's hand from his shirt. "You can't do nothing worse to me than you've already done. I'm tellin' you, it's *over*. You either live with what I say, or get out of my sight."

"You don't want to mess with me. I'll give you a few days to get that through your head." Joe strode into the house. Hopewell charged after him. Joe went to the desk in the living room, pulled a bottom drawer open, and smiled thinly. "Still got your little cash stash, don't you?" He snatched a wad of twenties from the drawer and shoved them in his pants pocket. Hopewell grabbed the fireplace poker and drew it back. Joe pulled a pistol from the drawer. The hammer clicked back with a soft, deadly sound as Joe pointed it at him. Joe grinned. "Still keep your gun in the same place too."

"Put all of that back. Put it back, damn you."

"I'll pull the trigger, Daddy." Joe's voice had a taunting lilt. "I got nothing to lose but Colebrook's money. And I ain't gonna lose that."

"I'd rather be dead than see you this way." The sound of a car made Hopewell jerk his arm down and glance out the window. Little Sis's red Cougar was coming down the drive. Joe followed his gaze. He hid the gun inside his jacket and kicked the drawer shut with one foot. "You got a visitor. Now you don't want other people to know what we're up to, do you? We're gonna make this deal with Colebrook and keep quiet about it. Because if we don't, if we don't, old man——" Joe smiled and let his voice trail off. He went to a key rack by the door, flipped a set of truck keys into his hand, and said lightly, "I'll be over at a motel in town, *Daddy*."

Hopewell's mute desperation was the only answer Joe needed. Laughing, he walked out of the house.

"That was *Joe*," Little Sis said, standing over him and pointing back toward the front door, as if he didn't know. "I passed *Joe* on the way in. What's he doing out of prison? I called out to him, but he just laughed at me. Why are you sitting here on your bed, in the dark?"

"Be quiet, woman." His voice shook. He pulled her down beside him and held her hand. She must have seen the despair in his face. "What happened?" she cried, stroking his cheek frantically. She would never be quiet. He should have known. He'd grown to love her chattering and her questions. Oh, God, he couldn't tell her what was wrong. "He got out early. He come home. My boy came home, Sissy."

"Lord, you look like it's the worst thing that ever happened."

"He's bad, Sissy. He's bad to the core, and I've lost him."

She murmured something sad and pulled his head to her shoulder. "Don't talk like that."

He couldn't tell her why. He could only wait and think, and then, when he was forced to, make the hardest decision of his life.

Snow began falling, a rare sight this early in the season, even in the mountains, where winters were mild and the occasional white blankets of January and February sent everyone into hibernation for a day or two. Lily stood in the wintry new gardens of the Malloy Inn holding a plastic cup filled with champagne, snowflakes settling on her face like soft, wet kisses and giving a white patina to the bare shrubs and dormant flower beds. Aunt Maude and the sisters were clustered around her, with Mr. Malloy, Mr. Estes, Mr. Parks, and his sons, who had gulped their celebratory champagne with typical silent appreciation.

Mr. Malloy surveyed the finished work and nodded. "I can't wait to see it in the spring."

"You're gonna love it," Mr. Estes assured him. Though there was a subdued, almost bitter look on his face, he waved a champagne bottle with one hand and clapped the other on Lily's back. "This lady knows her business. You'll have the prettiest damned garden in Victoria."

Lily smiled dully and caught Aunt Maude's worried glance. Lily had told Aunt Maude and the sisters about her and Artemas. Little Sis was certain Mr. Estes had mellowed enough to accept their relationship, even if he never forgave Artemas for helping put Joe in prison. Knowing that Joe was back in town made Lily nervous. She wasn't sure of anything.

The champagne created an acid taste in her throat. Artemas was waiting for her at the estate. By the time she arrived there this afternoon, his brothers and sisters would be at the house too. They had no idea why he'd asked them to come. Before this day ended, they would know. Her stomach churned, and she poured the last of the champagne onto the ground.

"I want to talk to you about a maintenance contract," Malloy said to her and Mr. Estes. "I'll call you next week to discuss the details. With the reputation your work is getting, I don't want you to be too busy by spring to accommodate me."

"Yeah, spring," Mr. Estes echoed, his brows drawing together. He shuffled his feet, frowned, then shoved the champagne into Mr. Parks's startled hands. Suddenly brusque, he said, "Well, let's get this show on the road, before we all get covered in snow."

Malloy pulled a check from one pocket of his overcoat

and handed it to Lily. "There's your last payment. Merry Christmas. Thank you for a job well done. Here's to the future." Lily raised her empty cup. After Malloy shook their hands and hurried back into the inn, she tucked the check into Mr. Estes's hand. "You can give me my part in a few days, after you pay Mr. Parks and his boys. I've got to run. I'll see you later."

Mr. Estes peered at her. "I thought you was goin' to Maude's with us. I mean, we got some celebratin' to do. We ought to have *something* to celebrate," he added in a grim tone. He took Little Sis's hand awkwardly. His gaze skittered when she gave him a wistful look. "You can't leave me alone all afternoon decorating a Christmas tree with this gaggle of pushy women."

Big Sis spit tobacco juice. "Lily's got better things to do than referee your social life."

"Like what?" Mr. Estes demanded, alert and almost fierce.

"Sssh. She's not welded to us old folks," Little Sis interjected, tugging at his hand.

Lily managed a smile. "I'll see y'all later."

His scowl deepened. "Something's going on here. I want to know what it is. Why aren't you coming to Maude's?"

Aunt Maude stuck her jaw out. "Hush, you nosy old groundhog. Lily, you take off. This isn't the time or the place to get into an argument."

"Why, it damned sure is the time and place," Mr. Estes retorted.

Lily felt the hopeless confrontation rising in her chest like a jackhammer. She leveled a troubled gaze at him. "You might as well know right now. I'm going to Blue Willow. Artemas is expecting me."

Mr. Estes gaped at her. "You been seeing *him* behind my back?"

Before Lily could answer, Big Sis snorted. "How else could she see him? You've been holding your feud with him over her head all this time, making her think you'd turn your back on her if she so much as said a kind word to the man. Artemas Colebrook's not your enemy, you bull-headed coot. Joe's problems are Joe's own fault, and I thought you'd figured that out. He's treated you like dirt since he got home."

Little Sis pushed in front of Mr. Estes and gazed up at him. "Hopewell, Lily's been good to you. She's made her peace with Artemas Colebrook. She loves him, and he loves her—ever since they were kids, they were meant to be together. It's finally come full circle. It was just a matter of time."

"He don't love her," Mr. Estes retorted, his face livid. He stared at Lily. "Were you waitin' until this job was finished to tell me the truth?"

"There wasn't anything to tell, until recently." Lily held out her hands, beseeching him. "Please try to understand. He and I have tried so hard to do what was best for everyone else. Now, we have to do what's best for us too."

"You listen to me. He's just scheming to ruin you all over again."

Lily continued to hold his outraged gaze without blinking. "You're wrong. If you can put your stubborn ideas about him aside long enough to get to know him, you'll see that. I've never asked you for anything but a fair chance. Will you give me that?"

"I'm trying to keep you from making a terrible mistake."

"I want to keep working at my family's home. I want to keep working with you. You have to tell me whether that's going to be possible."

Mr. Estes sputtered. "Just like that? You drop this news on me and think it don't change anything?" Little Sis gave a soft cry of alarm and disappointment. "Hopewell, you *wouldn't* trash what you and Lily have accomplished. You can't. I know you're not capable of that."

"I don't know what Colebrook's up to, but I intend to find out. Y'all believe me, there's more here than meets the eye. You'll thank me for trying to keep Lily away from him."

Lily felt the pulse jumping in her throat. "I've made my choice. Do you want me to move out of my house?"

"What do you care about your house? You'll go live in that mansion of his and let him own you. Mark my words, he'll make you sorry."

"Why in the world would you say that?" Aunt Maude asked, throwing up her hands. "If I've learned one thing about Artemas Colebrook over the years, it's that he'd give his soul to keep from hurting Lily. This talk about him scheming *against* her doesn't make any sense."

Little Sis leaned toward him, scrutinizing him desperately. "What makes you say such terrible things? Is it because Joe's come back so much more hateful than he was before? Oh, Hopewell, don't poison your mind because of your son."

Mr. Estes swallowed hard and stared at Little Sis as if he were seeing the last beautiful sunset of his life. He shook his head. "Sissy, Artemas Colebrook is the coldest, most conniving bastard—"

"Stop," Lily commanded, her throat tight. "I'm asking you again, Mr. Estes—I've got until February on the lease you gave me, but if you can't accept my relationship with Artemas, then tell me now, and I'll make plans to leave."

Breathless tension hung in the cold, snowy air. Mr. Estes straightened. "We had an understanding about the Colebrooks, and you broke it." His tone was anguished and bitter. "You done it to yourself. It's not my fault."

"Hopewell, *no,*" Little Sis begged. "I'll never forgive you if you do this god-awful stupid thing." She hurried to Maude's station wagon at the street, got in, and slammed the door.

His mouth trembled. He jerked Malloy's check from his coat pocket and thrust it at Lily. "Take it. It oughta cover the money you spent fixing up the house. Consider it a settlement."

"You keep it. Pay Mr. Parks and his sons," Lily answered, her voice low and controlled. "Throw the rest down a hole, if that'll make you feel better. I don't want any money from you. I want respect and understanding."

She walked away. He called after her, his voice hoarse, "It's not me you'll hate! It's Colebrook!"

Thirty

Artemas was waiting by the doors to a private entrance below his rooms, and he flung them open before she stepped from the truck. She wore a simple gray dress and low pumps, with no coat. Snowflakes dusted the bright red mass of her upswept hair. He went down the stone steps to her, took one look at the fatigue and sorrow in her eyes, quickly put his arm around her, and led her upstairs. When they were inside an anteroom to the main suite, he brushed his fingertips over her hair and kissed her gently. "Rest a few minutes. I'll get you a drink."

"No, I'd just like to sit down a minute." Her hand wrapped in his, they walked into the library, and she sat on a couch before the fireplace, rubbing her arms through the dress's long, slender sleeves. He settled beside her and took her cold hands. "I wish I could make you feel more comfortable—that this could be easier."

Lily leaned her forehead against his. "I'm fresh out of inspiration." The defeat in her voice made him tilt her head back and study her shrewdly. "You've had trouble with Mr. Estes today."

She nodded. She told him what had happened. He sat back on the couch, steepled a hand to his forehead, and listened, his eyes darkening. When she finished, he said,

"Don't ask me not to fight this. I'll talk to him. I'll offer him money. Whatever he wants for himself, or Joe—"

"My fight, my home, my decision," she said, shaking her head. She stroked a hand over his hair to soften the words. "Stay out of it."

"Not this time. You're not going to lose everything again because of me."

Lily grasped his shoulders. Staring at him hard, she said, "It's just a damned piece of land. Just dirt and trees and sentimental stories"—her voice broke—"and I'm done with it. *Done* with it. It will never be more important to me than you are."

Artemas stood quickly and pulled her up with him. "There's one thing I *can* do, and it's what I want more than anything I've ever wanted in my life." His eyes were harsh but loving. "After my grandfather died, my grandmother lived alone in this house with her dreams, believing that someday someone would love this place and fill it with the kind of happiness she'd lost."

Lily rested her hands over the center of his chest and looked up at him tenderly. "She found that someone. You."

"No. You and me." He reached inside his jacket and took something from the pocket.

The ring had the unusual hue of old rose gold. Filigreed tendrils of gold as delicate as willow branches held a cluster of small diamonds and sapphires. "This was my grandmother's engagement ring." When Lily made a low sound of distress, he touched a fingertip to her lips, a silencing caress.

"Don't say it's too soon—not when it's been the path we've followed from the first day you looked up at me with those blue eyes." Watching her reaction intensely, every nuance measured, loved, and, finally, assured, he took her left hand and slipped the ring into place. "Welcome home," he said.

James and the others waited in a room that radiated comfort and old-world charm, evocative of class as well as money, dark woods soaring to high ceilings, soft old Aubusson rugs covering the polished floor, and deep chairs as plush as a king's robes. The snow filtered silver light through tall, arched windows.

Their conversation halted as a heavy door swung open with a slow, melodic purr of fine wood on well-oiled hinges. Artemas entered the room with Lily beside him. James watched the way they moved, close without touching, in sync, intimacy and strength wrapping them in an invisible bond. Grief stabbed him. He and Alise had been that way once.

Lily went to Elizabeth, squeezed her outstretched hand, then to Michael, and Tamberlaine.

Tamberlaine held out his hands to her. "I only pray you can forgive one well-intentioned breach of confidence."

Artemas watched, close by. Lily took Tamberlaine's dark hands and gave him a pensive but affectionate look. His anxious expression relaxed a little. "I've waited years to make up to you for the part I played in hurting your relationship with Artemas," he said. "Have I done it?"

Her throat tight, Lily nodded. "Thank you."

"I see the concern in your eyes. Please trust me on this as well."

"I'm trying very hard to hope for the best."

He added softly, "I also see the remarkable strength and love you share with Artemas."

Cass rose from the couch, faced Lily with a curious, almost pleasant expression in her eyes, and said, "I suppose Artemas explained what's happened between Dr. Sikes and me."

"Yes."

"You told John Lee everything you knew about me, after that first, disastrous encounter we had. You gave him a lot of ammunition."

"Looks like he hit the target."

Cass's eyes flickered with approval. Her pleasure over John Lee and their baby was impossible to contain. For the first time in her life there were no sharp edges.

Lily turned toward James. He returned her scrutiny

without a hint of warmth. She stepped closer to him. A muscle worked in her throat. "I want you to know something," she told him. "Before anything else is said today." She paused, wincing a little, then continued, "My husband was a good person, with good motives, but he could have prevented what happened at the Colebrook Building, and he didn't. I'll never ask you to forgive him."

"Lily, don't," Artemas said, coming to her. He took her arm and gave her a troubled look. "Not this way."

James felt as if a fist had slammed into his stomach. "Why the confession?" he asked. Regardless of all Tamberlaine had told them about her and Artemas, he'd gone too far to retreat now. "Second thoughts?" he said, his voice tight. "Or has it merely become convenient to demonstrate a change of heart?"

Her sharp inhalation cut through the silence. Artemas pushed between them. "You've walked a very thin line with me for a long time," he said to James, his voice low and brutally controlled. "I've pampered you because of your leg. That's not pity," he added, as James tensed. "I made allowances for your bitterness, and I tried to understand it."

"Don't patronize me," James answered through clenched teeth. "I despise it."

"Then stop acting as if your injury excuses every goddamned cruel word you say to the rest of us."

James went still as a statue, unyielding, his stony gaze shifting to Lily's resigned one. He felt the truth in his brother's assessment—it burned. A lifetime of rigid, defensive pride refused to let him say so. His silence was the only sign of truce. A veneer of disgust as hard as diamonds gleamed in Artemas's eyes. Artemas turned from him abruptly.

James's gaze remained locked on him as Artemas touched a hand to Lily's back, guiding her to a chair. As she sat down, she and he shared a brief, private glance as loving as it was tormented. Any doubts James had about the nature of their relationship evaporated. What

Tamberlaine had said was true. They had loved each other since childhood.

"Begin, please," Artemas said to Tamberlaine.

Tamberlaine went to a writing desk between the room's windows and unlocked its shallow drawer. There were looks of bewilderment among the family as he removed a small, sleek answering machine and plugged its cord into a wall outlet.

Lily clutched the arms of her chair. Her nerves were brittle. Artemas positioned himself beside her. He rested a hand on her shoulder.

Tamberlaine faced James and the others. Then, his magisterial voice flowing with a measured cadence, he told them how she'd come to him with the tape, and whose conversations it had revealed.

"What kind of conversations?" Elizabeth asked. Her stunned expression mirrored Michael's and Cassandra's. James's eyes had become even more chilling and alert.

Michael stared at the answering machine. "Julia's voice is on that tape? Why?"

Tamberlaine hesitated. Sorrow radiated from him. He seemed to have trouble answering.

Artemas said for him, "There were discussions about possible hazards involving the bridge."

Lily had to force herself to look at the others, as they realized the implication. Horror. Denial. Pain. It was as if Julia were dying before their eyes, again. James made a stiff movement forward, then halted. "Are you saying . . . you're saying Julia knew it might not be safe?"

Artemas's hand tightened on Lily's shoulder. "Yes. She knew. She insisted on going ahead with the building's dedication."

Elizabeth cried out. Cass wavered, then sat down limply on the couch. Michael stared at Artemas in speechless supplication. James whipped toward Lily. "You think we'll believe this? You drop some contrived revelation about Julia in our laps and expect us to accept it without question?"

"There's so much more to the truth than simple blame

or exoneration. I'm not asking you to pass judgment on your sister."

"Lily didn't want any of you—or me—to know about this tape," Artemas said.

Tamberlaine cleared his throat. "That's true. I urged Lily to give the tape to Artemas, and she refused. I was the one who revealed its existence to him."

Cass bent forward, her hands splayed toward Lily. "Why did you feel that way about it?"

Lily found herself looking at Elizabeth instead. "When you hear it, I hope you'll understand. Julia was a complicated woman, and she was too emotionally involved to be objective. She didn't see the danger. She despised Frank, but she wanted to believe him. He convinced her to ignore Richard's warnings."

The confusion drained from Elizabeth's ashen face. The secret torment she and Julia had suffered as children hovered in the gaze she and Lily traded. She knew why Lily was protecting Julia.

James made a low sound of dismissal. "You seem to have developed the most mysterious intuition about our sister."

"Be quiet!" Elizabeth ordered, her voice strained. She sat on the edge of her chair, trembling, her eyes filling with tears. "Play the tape. I have to hear what Julia said."

Michael strode to James and gripped his arm. "Save your questions until we've listened to it."

For the first time James seemed shaken. He pulled away from Michael and crossed the room to Tamberlaine. Leaning on the table, he braced his hands on either side of the answering machine. "Go ahead."

Lily looked up at Artemas. He met her gaze. His large gray eyes were shadowed.

The tape whirred. Lily shut her eyes. The answers to nearly two years of terrible doubts and recriminations began to unfold. Frank's angry, determined voice burst forth. *You stupid bastard, why did you tell Julia about the bridge?*

Lily glanced at each face around her. The drama played out in their eyes, and she saw the devastation. A half hour later, when silence replaced the eerie voices, Tamberlaine turned the answering machine off and sat down, massaging the deep grooves of tension in his forehead.

Since no one else seemed capable of speaking, Cass bent her head to her hands and asked, her voice hollow, "What now?"

Artemas looked at them all sadly. Lily saw a lifetime of authority and grace, the leadership that had been pressed on him as a child, now coming to its harshest test. "We talk. We cry. We forgive."

Michael leaned back in a chair and exhaled. "I'm glad we know."

"What do we know?" James countered. He looked at Lily. "We know that your husband and the others convinced her that the bridge was safe."

Artemas's eyes narrowed. "We know that she ignored Richard's warnings and badgered him to accept Stockman and Grant's assessment of the risk."

James cursed. "You can condemn her for accepting recommendations on technical matters no layperson could judge?"

"I don't condemn her. She made a mistake—a mistake that turned out to be disastrous. I believe she was driven by reckless pride. Nothing mattered to her but seeing the building open on schedule. I wish to God I could understand how she justified it. I wish I knew why she didn't simply come to us and explain that the opening needed to be delayed. No one would have accused her of mishandling the project." Weariness settled on him, slumping his shoulders. "That's the question we'll never be able to answer—why she felt she couldn't ask for our help and advice."

James smashed a fist onto the answering machine. The plastic shell gave way with an ominous cracking sound. Artemas reached him as he pounded the device again. Slinging off Artemas's hands, his face contorted with rage and grief, James limped to a window and stood with his back turned, gripping the handsome wooden casing, his head bowed.

Elizabeth moaned. "It's hard—you become so accustomed to thinking no one can possibly understand your feelings—your feelings about *anything*. You become so afraid to admit any doubt. Your self-image is so fragile and confused. *You think, I have to keep everyone from knowing how terrible I am.* There's no room to ask for help."

Her rambling speech brought anxious looks from the others. James turned quickly, staring at her. Michael knelt by her chair and put his arm around her. "Easy now, Lizbeth," he said carefully. "What are you trying to say?"

"I'm not losing my mind," she answered with dull conviction. "I'm trying to tell you—God, I'm trying"—her gaze shifted to Lily—"I think I know why Julia couldn't trust anyone in a crisis. Lily, *you* know what I mean. That must be why you don't hate her. You understood." Lily froze, recoiling from the tragic decision in Elizabeth's eyes. *No, don't, they're hurting so much already.* But she couldn't say that to Elizabeth, couldn't ask her to hide the final piece of the puzzle.

"Lizbeth, what are you talking about?" Cass demanded brokenly.

Elizabeth got to her feet. Lily felt smothered by dread. There was no room to breathe.

There was only the crumpling of Elizabeth's defenses and her low, raw voice. Certain words had a sick power that overwhelmed the rest. *Father. At night. Julia and I. Mother let it happen.* Even though Lily already knew Elizabeth's story, each word stabbed her. How much worse was it for Artemas, who was hearing it for the first time? She went to him, watching his face, taking his hand gently.

When Elizabeth finished, the weight of shock settled like a blanket. Artemas's stark gaze met Lily's. He was lost, needing some evidence of sanity in the world, some guide. "Go over and hold her," Lily told him. "You don't have to say anything right now. Just go put your arms around your sister."

Elizabeth covered her face and cried as he reached her. "Do you believe me?" she asked.

"God, of course we do, Lizbeth."

"Oh, Liz," Cass whispered, and came to her. Michael looked devastated. He moved woodenly to his twin, and then he bent his head to hers and cried with her. "Why didn't I suspect?" he asked. "I should have felt something was wrong. I've always known when you were unhappy."

"I shut it out of my mind," she whispered.

James stood in leaden distraction, as if lost in his own shock and agony. Artemas studied him sadly over the others' heads. Stepping back from Elizabeth, he looked at Lily. "After Elizabeth confided in you, she asked you not to tell me?"

Lily closed her eyes for a moment and nodded. "I'm sorry."

"It's all right. I understand."

"I would have died of shame," Elizabeth cried. "But Lily convinced me to tell Leo, at least. Leo has been wonderful. Now he knows why I was so damned paranoid about our relationship. He's helped me feel whole again. He talked me into going back into therapy. That's why I had the courage to tell the rest of you."

Artemas said slowly. "I agree with Michael. How could we not have suspected? And about Julia—" He halted, his control fading. Elizabeth quickly touched his arm. "I'm sure Julia didn't want you to know either. How could any of you have recognized what was happening when it was years before I realized that Father was abusing Julia as well as me?" She strangled on a sob, caught her breath, and added bitterly, "Mother told me if I ever said anything, I'd be sent away. She must have threatened Julia like that too."

Tamberlaine, who had been quiet for a long time, had tears on his face. "You grew up in an era when no one even imagined that such heinous things could happen. It's not surprising that it never came to light."

"What could any of you have done about it?" Elizabeth asked, leaning against Michael and holding Cass's hand. "I had these terrible ideas—that no one would believe me, or that something violent would happen." She looked at Artemas with distraught affection. "I pictured you killing

Father and being sent to prison. That's the kind of fear that kept me quiet—Julia, too, I'm certain. It was almost worse to think about being discovered."

James made a tortured sound—less human than animal. His face was ravaged, his eyes bleak. He reached out blindly and braced himself against a chairback. His stark gaze met Artemas's. "I knew what was happening to Julia."

"Oh, my God," Elizabeth moaned.

"And I didn't do anything about it."

The others seemed speechless. Lily found herself stroking the back of Artemas's hand, seeking that small, reassuring contact. He asked James finally, "You knew what Father was doing to her, and you never said anything?"

James looked beaten. "I'll tell you how you react when you walk into a room and find your little sister on a bed, half-dressed and sobbing, and your father's doing something to her that instinctively makes you sick. You pretend it didn't happen."

"How old were you when you saw this?"

"About fourteen."

"Then Julia was only *six*."

James leaned on the chair as if he'd collapse without it. "When you're older, you realize that you watched your sister being raped, and that you were too frightened of your father to tell anyone." He gagged, then scrubbed a hand over his mouth. "You know you're still too afraid to try to help her. And you hate yourself. You hate yourself so much that it colors everything about your life from that day on." His ravaged gaze moved to Lily. "You defend your sister in every way you can, to make up to her for the betrayal you can never change."

Elizabeth ran to him and threw her arms around his shoulders. "Don't blame yourself, Jimmy. I couldn't help Julia *or* myself. I pretended we could forget. That's what children do when something is too horrible to live with. I've learned that much."

James lifted his head and looked regretfully at Artemas. "I wanted to be like you. We all did. You wouldn't have let Julia or Elizabeth suffer alone."

Artemas lifted a hand, then let it fall. "I thought we were invincible—that no one could hurt us because we could depend on each other. How incredibly naive." He turned toward Michael and Cass. "Is there more? What about the two of you?"

"I have no secrets," Michael said wearily. "I despised being sheltered because of my asthma, and I've always rejected the theory that asthma can be a form of psycho-somatic defense. But now I wonder if it was."

"Cass?" Artemas's voice grated with painful expectation.

She shook her head. "I had an armor of fat. Father ignored me. Do you know how hearing the truth about Elizabeth and Julia makes me feel? God, this is insane. I was jealous because he paid so much attention to them. I thought they were lucky. I never knew I was the lucky one."

Lily could not take her eyes off James. He met her gaze and held it. He said slowly, "Perhaps I've dealt with it by turning my self-hatred toward anyone who threatened my brothers and sisters. Especially anyone who threatened Julia."

Was this an apology, a plea for understanding, or a warning that his animosity toward her was too deeply in-vested to overcome? But this wasn't the time to inject that question. Her problems with James were insignificant for now. She was looking at a family that had just been ripped open for emotional surgery.

"James," Elizabeth spoke gently, "you did the best you could." She started toward him, hands out, arms open. James backed away. "I'm not asking for sympathy." He choked. "Liz, I'm sorry for what you went through."

"Then why can't I feel sympathy for you?"

"No. I don't want that." His gaze shifted to each of the others, finally coming to rest on Artemas and Lily. "From anyone." He walked out of the room.

The snow had stopped, and at the top of its dome, the sky was clearing. The sunset made a faint magenta haze behind the low clouds that drooped, like a smoky mist, among the mountains.

Lily sat on an overturned bucket outside Harlette's pen. The hog grunted happily and stuck her wide pink snout through the wire for more cinnamon cookies. Lily hugged one of Mama's old quilts around her shoulders. She had changed from her dress into jeans, a sweater, and her boots. More normal. She needed every small, familiar reassurance, after today's revelations.

Lupa snuggled on a corner of the blanket and leaned against her legs. One cookie for Harlette, one for Lupa. Then a crumbled cookie for the chickens to peck at. Back and forth. They were attentive companions, as long as the cookies kept coming.

Artemas walked up the knoll to her. His face was gaunt with exhaustion, and her heart went out to him. His lips crooked in a slight smile when he saw the cookies in her hands. She held one out. He shook his head. "Harlette and Lupa would never forgive me."

His smile faded. He looked down at her pensively. "Why didn't you tell me you were coming here? I thought you'd gone up to my suite. Then LaMieux brought me the message that you'd decided to leave."

"I needed to feed my critters." She stood, divided the rest of the cookies between Harlette and Lupa, then put her arms around his waist and kissed him. "I knew you needed to stay with the family."

"I need to be with you too." She enclosed him in her blanket and put her head on his shoulder. He pulled her close against him, his body warm and solid along hers.

"What a nice cocoon," she whispered. He made a soft, weary sound of agreement, and angled his head so that his cheek brushed lightly along hers. She was soothed by the warmth and scent of his skin, the coarseness of his faint beard shadow, the weight of his hands on the hollow of her back. "Has James said anything else?"

"No. He's keeping to himself. As always."

"And the others?"

"They're still in shock, I think." His voice was gritty

with fatigue. "We keep going over the details of everything James and Elizabeth said, and everything we heard on the tape."

She lifted one side of the patchwork quilt. "It takes time to stitch the pieces together. But at least all the pieces are in place."

"I like that analogy. I hope you're right."

After a moment of troubled silence, she said, "This is going to sound morbid—or like one of Little Sis's whimsies—but I've been thinking about Halfman. Do you remember his legend?"

"Oh, yes." His arms tightened around her. "The peddler who gave the first blue willows to Elspeth."

"And then foretold her death. Halfman disappeared into the mountains after she died, but Grandma always warned that he'd become an evil spirit, watching us, waiting for any excuse to come back and cause more grief."

"Your grandmother told me that story too. I think it was designed to keep children in line."

"It did. I had nightmares about Halfman when I was growing up."

Artemas lifted his head. She followed his gaze. He was looking at the old place, the snow-covered barn looming over them, the willows draped in lacy white, the handsome old farmhouse. A muscle worked in his cheek. "You must wonder if Halfman has come back, then. To make you leave this place again."

"Maybe he has worse things in mind. I feel . . . oh, I'm just ragged out. It's been a rough day. Your family may not realize it yet, but they built some strong bridges today. I only hope that James—"

"He will. He will come to his senses. He took several large steps in the right direction." Artemas lifted her slightly, so that she was on tiptoe, their bodies fitting together in all the soft curves and hard angles. She wound her arms around his neck. They were both desperate to push the unknown and its sorrows into the shadows, for a little while. "Halfman was just a story from our childhood," Artemas whispered, his breath feathering her lips. "He can't hurt us."

Lily stretched upward, returning the caress of his body. On a silent cue they turned and walked down the knoll.

Her bed was their haven, a warm, safe place where their coupling brought comfort and release. They took each other again and again, lost in savage, elegant, re-affirming possession filled with all the nuances of lust and affection, and in the quiet interludes they talked about anything and everything, safe inside the open-hearted trust.

Afterward she lay quiet, drowsy in his arms, but when she slept, she felt the dark specter near them again.

Joe stood in the woods, frustrated and cold, watching the house.

He slipped away, smiling contemptuously. He'd hunted these woods for years, grown dope in the hollows—getting to Lily's place without being seen was easy. If Artemas Colebrook hadn't put the law on him, he'd still be here, making money.

Oh, yeah, tomorrow he'd be back, when no one was around, and he'd leave a little message. Lily might suspect it was from him, but she'd never prove that. His old man would know who'd done it, though. His old man would understand that he meant business. That was the important thing, because Joe wasn't going to let him back out on the deal he'd made with Artemas Colebrook. Colebrook had to pay. One way or another, the bastard had to pay.

James sat at a desk in the downstairs library, surrounded by shadows, the small pool of light from a desk lamp shrouding him in a sense of secrecy he loathed. But that was almost past. He would conquer this insanity with the same fierce dedication that had created it. It wasn't too late. It couldn't be. His hands rested on the phone in front of him, strong and certain.

He called Beitner. The lawyer was paid too well to resent being contacted at home by his most powerful client.

"I want you to meet with Hopewell Estes and his son, as soon as possible. Tell them you're ready to close the deal and give them everything you offered. It's urgent."

After a moment of surprised silence Beitner asked, "And you want the same condition as before—that Mrs. Porter be asked to leave the Esteses' property when her lease ends?"

"No. She stays. For good. With the open understanding that she can buy the place back if she wants to."

"Let me make certain I understand. You no longer wish to prevent Mrs. Porter from associating with your brother. You want the exact opposite."

"Yes. Take care of it immediately."

"All right."

James hung up. His hands trembled. He lifted the phone again and called London. The housekeeper answered at his and Alise's apartment. It was maddening. She said she'd have to see if Mrs. Colebrook was free to come to the phone. That meant Alise was still screening his calls.

"Hello." Alise's soft, steely voice cut through him. Every time he talked to her, she sounded as if she despised him a little more. But then, he hadn't given her reason to expect anything but arrogance, arguments, and demands.

He'd rehearsed an eloquent, logical speech, but it deserted him. James bowed his forehead against the heel of one hand, hunched over the desk, and told her everything that had happened that day. The words rushed and tumbled. It felt like a free fall in a nightmare, where either hell or a safe new morning waited at the bottom. He was afraid to pause, afraid she'd wake him up before he finished, and he'd never escape from purgatory.

He told her about Julia, about his cowardice, the demon that would always cling to him, hobbling every step he took. He told her about the ugly plan he'd harbored toward Lily, and that he'd already put the steps in motion to stop it.

When he finished, he felt dazed. Her muffled crying was all he heard, like the distressed whispering of angels, deciding his fate. Dignity had been burned out of him; he was a beggar. *"Alise."* Her name was a plea. "I love you. I know I've never said it enough. You have no reason to believe I can change, but—" He had hoped for too much, too soon. "I'll come to London. I'll leave tonight. Just think about all I've told you. We'll take it slow, and maybe in time I can prove to you that—"

"*No,*" she cried.

He was plunging to the end, taking his last breath. "Alise, *don't*—"

"I'm coming home. It's that easy, if you trust me."

He leaned back in the chair, shutting his eyes against the tears, then letting them go. The deepest peace came at the end of a nightmare, when all was safe. "It's that easy then," he said.

Thirty-one

There was a place for her at the table, adjacent to Artemas's place at its head. Lily stood behind her chair, looking tentatively at the others, who stood behind theirs, waiting for Artemas to sit down. But he continued to stand, his gaze shifting from each person to the next. Cass and John Lee, Elizabeth and Leo, Michael, James, and Tamberlaine. No one had any appetite for breakfast, but it was a ritual everyone needed.

"Some of you may feel that we opened a Pandora's box yesterday," Artemas said. "But we can move forward now. There's no need to pretend it will be easy to find our balance again. There's no need for any kind of pretense. I think that's a blessing."

He pulled his chair back. "Wait!" Cass said. "There's something we need to do." She left her place and walked around to Lily. Lily looked at her with a twinge of the old wariness. Cass saw it and shook her head. "Welcome," she said. She held out her hands.

Formality dissolved into tears and emotion. Lily hugged Cass, and then Elizabeth came to her, and Michael. Tamberlaine waited for the others to return to their places, then walked over. She hugged him, too, and whispered "Thank you," in his ear, and he mumbled something like this time he had not needed to initiate anything, it was spontaneous.

James had not moved. But now he walked over to her and halted, staring at her with a terrible sorrow on his face. He started to say something, but Mr. Upton appeared in the dining-room doorway. "Excuse me," the butler said excitedly. He smiled at James. "She's arrived, sir."

Lily grabbed one of James's hands. "Go see Alise."

He seemed startled by her touch. "Thank you." He left the room without a backward glance. She and Artemas traded a troubled look.

He held Alise close, so close that even the damp heat of sex had been less intimate. Her bare legs were tangled with his, one lying over his scarred thigh, and for the first time he loved the sleek feel of her skin on it, without any sense that he hated having her touch the damaged part of himself.

They were in the plush bed of a guest room on the mansion's second floor. It was the quickest privacy they had been able to find, and Mr. Upton had been left with a stack of Alise's luggage in the entrance hall, trying to figure out where they'd gone.

She rose to one elbow and took his face between her hands. "I have to tell you something." She hesitated. Her fingers were very still on his cheeks, but he felt the tremors in them. She cleared her throat and said in a low, careful tone. "I was so disappointed, so afraid we had no future, when I left you."

"I know. I understand," he said, his chest tight with regret.

"You *can't* entirely understand why I felt so desperate to change your attitude," she continued, studying him sadly. "Because you don't know my other reason." She hesitated. "We were fighting so often—sometimes we didn't touch each other for weeks. I was so angry and hurt. Toward the end I threw my pills away. There seemed to be no point in taking them." Taking a deep breath, she finished, "We're going to have a baby."

The immediate conflict of joy and anguish was a claw inside him. Alise saw his mysterious dilemma and sighed. "I'm sorry."

"*No.*" He pulled her head down to his shoulder again, caressing her hair and the tense slope of her back. "You have nothing to be sorry about. *A baby,*" he said with slow wonder.

"Do you really feel happy about it?" She sounded astonished.

He shut his eyes. "I want to be a good father . . . the best father in the world. I'm afraid I won't be."

"Yes, *yes,* you will be, if you're happy about our having a child."

James rolled her to her back and looked into her worried eyes. "I am *very* happy."

They made love again, slower this time, and when they were quiet and still once more, he lay with his head on her abdomen, imagining he could hear the beat of an embryonic heart.

He couldn't bring their child into the world with any shadows over it.

Lily loved the solitude of the farm. The house and greenhouse and barn roofs were still covered in snow. The land was as smooth as a white porcelain plate. The willows' bare branches were sheathed in crystals that caught the last glimmer of light.

She parked the truck in the yard, put her arm around Lupa, and pulled the old dog to her for a hug. Lupa licked her cheek. Nuzzling her head against Lupa's, Lily told her, "You're the simplest old friend I've got right now. I'm going to change clothes and feed the critters, and then you and I are going to sit in front of the fireplace for a while."

Lupa followed her out of the truck's cab but immediately veered off to one side, sniffing the unbroken snow. Lily watched her hustle around in anxious circles, checking out some unknown scent. "It was probably just a deer," Lily told her.

Lupa continued her frantic scouting as Lily went into the house and turned on a lamp. She changed hurriedly in the cold air, trading a dress for a heavy sweater and overalls, sliding thick socks and ankle-high brogans over her feet. She flicked on the floodlights at the corners of the house as she went back outside. Lupa was still racing around. As Lily walked up the knoll toward the barn, the dog rushed past her, head down.

Lupa galloped to the barn door, snuffled furiously at its base, then drew back, growling. Lily halted a few feet away and frowned. This was something other than excitement over the invasion of a deer or two. Maybe a fox, a hungry opossum, or—or what? She didn't like the prickle of fear on the back of her neck. Arguing with herself that her nerves were frayed and it was a silly, suburbanite thing to do, Lily went back to the house and got the shotgun she always left standing in a corner near the front door.

With it balanced in the crook of one arm, she hurried back to the barn. Lupa whined and scratched at the barn's double doors. Lily flipped the wooden latch and pulled one of the heavy doors open as quickly as she could. Rather than bolting inside as Lily had expected, Lupa advanced a few inches with stiff-legged uncertainty, then halted.

Staring into the dim interior, Lily saw only the earth-floored central hall as it had always been, lined with yard tools, stacks of plastic pots, and other mundane items. Chicken wire rose above the sides of a large stall at the far end. It was too dark to tell whether any of her chickens were at roost on the two pine poles that stretched across the enclosure at head height.

Lily stepped inside and pulled a chain connected to the bare bulb overhead. The barn's interior filled with reassuring light, but it showed that the roosts were empty. She took the shotgun in both hands, pumped a shell into the chamber, and moved forward slowly. The stall that served as the chicken roost had a small door on its back wall, leading to a large, fenced pen. The chickens should have been on the roosts by now.

Harlette's stall, across the hallway, had a larger door to her pen. Lily glanced into it and saw that it was empty, the deep bed of hay hardly marred by droppings. Through the opening to the pen she saw nothing but snowy ground and a glimpse of the fence.

The silence was eerie. The stillness made her hands clammy.

And the smell. She grimaced. Then she recognized it, and her stomach lurched. The smell of butchering time. Acrid. Natural but unnatural. Blood.

She vaulted forward and stared down through the chicken wire. They were all dead, all lying in mangled clumps of dark red feathers, their necks twisted at impossible angles. Lily whirled and ran back outside, wanting to gag but swallowing it. She circled the barn and stopped outside Harlette's large pen, bile rising in her mouth again.

She forced herself to open the gate and walk inside. Harlette lay on her side, a black apron of dried blood fanning out from under her head. Shaking, Lily dropped to her heels and looked at the awful gash in the hog's throat.

With sick regret, she thought of James. *No, please not him.* She tried to shove the idea out of her mind. But who else would want to do this to her? Her breath caught. *Joe?* Why? Did he hate Artemas that much and therefore her? She had to find out. Tonight.

She jumped to her feet, her hands clenched on the shotgun. Blind rage and grief overwhelmed her. She walked swiftly down the hill, patting a hand on the bulging thigh pocket of her overalls where she'd stored extra shotgun shells. If the person who'd done this had stepped from the shadows at the moment, she would have shot him without a second thought.

Lupa crept along beside her, frightened by her furious energy. Lily caught her by the ruff and held tight. "Halfman isn't going to get us, *goddamn him,*" Lily shouted. She dragged Lupa into the truck's cab.

A few minutes later they were on the public road, roaring toward the estate's entrance, where tall, handsome lamps cast bright light on the snow and the majestic wrought-iron gates. Lily slid the truck to a stop and got out, leading Lupa by the ruff again. The elderly guard came outside, squinted in the truck's headlamps, then smiled at her.

Hiding her distress, she politely asked him to call the house and leave word that she'd gone to visit Aunt Maude. The small lie would keep Artemas from worrying while she took care of this mission in her own way, for her own pride's sake. She asked the guard to keep Lupa until she returned.

Then she drove on, the shotgun hidden behind the truck's seat.

Hopewell opened his door and stared at Lily with poignant welcome. It took a second to notice that her face was ashen and angry, a cold white mask centered in her mane of tangled red hair. "What is it?" he asked.

She looked him straight in the eyes. "I went home a little while ago and found all my chickens with their necks wrung, and Harlette with her throat cut."

He recoiled, grasping at the air with one hand, then sinking it into his hair. *Joe.* She studied his reaction and made a low sound of rage. "It was Joe, wasn't it?" she asked. "You think so too. Why?"

It was a death. Hopewell felt it to the marrow of his bones. Joe was dead to him. He loved the son he'd raised, but the monster that existed now was not that son. His shoulders drooped. "Joe. *Joe,*" he mumbled. "I tried to fix everything for him. I gave up all my pride. I was willin' to hurt innocent people to help him. God forgive me."

"What do you mean?" she asked desperately.

"He's tryin' to scare you off, so he can get what he wants. But it's over. I won't back down again. It has to be over, this time."

"*What does he want?*" She clutched his shoulders. Her eyes glittered. "Did he come home expecting to live at the farm again? Is that why you have to make me leave?"

Hopewell shuddered. "I don't want you to leave." He

dropped his hands limply. "Colebrook does. And Joe knows that."

"*What?* What kind of crazy idea is this?"

"Joe wants money. All the money Colebrook has been promisin' him since right after you moved back to the place."

"What are you talking about?" Her dazed expression gave way to a frown. Hopewell tried to speak, but the words had barbed hooks that caught in his throat.

Lily watched his torment with distracted shock, while what he'd just said about Artemas promising Joe money made a dizzy spiral in her mind. She remembered the time in September after the incident with Elizabeth's children, when Artemas had urged her to let him use his money to help Joe—to encourage Mr. Estes to let her stay at the farm, or even buy it back. She remembered all the other attempts he'd made to help her without her knowing. She remembered that even before he'd given her Grandmother Colebrook's ring, he'd said that he wouldn't let her lose her old home again because of him.

She felt as if a vise were squeezing her chest. Had he gone behind her back after she'd trusted him to honor her wishes? Was Joe's viciousness the result of some misguided deal? *Oh, no, please,* she prayed. *So many dreams have died because of the best intentions.*

Mr. Estes was still hesitating, his florid, rusty cheeks flinching with the effort to talk without breaking down completely. Lily's knees felt weak. She latched a hand onto the doorframe. "Whatever Artemas did, it wasn't meant to hurt me," she told Mr. Estes.

Her defensive words freed his voice. His eyes were tearful, but he thrust his jaw forward belligerently. "Oh, he's got you convinced, but it ain't true. He sent a lawyer to see me last spring. This lawyer said all I have to do is kick you off your place when the lease is up, and Joe'll never have another worry as long as he lives. That Joe would be cared for, so he'd never be tempted to go back to his old ways." He jabbed a finger at himself. "I can't go through with it.

Joe's tryin' to scare me into agreein', and he's using you to do it."

Lily felt cold to the pit of her stomach. A terrible fear flashed through her. Maybe Artemas *had* wanted, at one time, to drive her away.

No. Even had their past few days together not been absolute proof of faith, the man she had loved since childhood wasn't capable of what Mr. Estes claimed.

Lily leaned against the doorframe, feeling sick to her stomach. "This lawyer told you who'd sent him?"

"Hell, no. He was too smart for that. But I knew. It had to be one of the Colebrooks. It has to be Artemas."

Not Artemas. Please, not Artemas. A stark suspicion slammed into her thoughts. *James?*

After what she'd learned about James yesterday—had it only been yesterday, when it seemed centuries ago?—she knew his pain, his confusion, the shame that had made him fight so hard for Julia's reputation.

She had to believe she'd witnessed his turning point. His openness, his vulnerability, the reassurance Artemas and the others had given him—he was poised to close a door on the past. He hadn't shown overt remorse for his bitterness toward her, but she had sensed strongly that he no longer considered her an enemy.

What did he intend now? To end his hateful scheme or let it play itself out? God, if she told Artemas about this, it would tear the family apart for good. Artemas would never forgive him.

Mr. Estes was speaking to her, she realized. "I know you love Colebrook," he was saying frantically. "I can see how much the bastard's conniving hurts you. I wanted to keep you from believin' in him, Lily. I tried—"

"It's not Artemas," she said, straightening and meeting his gaze firmly. "I'll never believe that."

He held out his hands. "Aw, Lily, *please* don't let that man ruin your common sense. I stop what's happened with Joe, but I can't fight your battles with Artemas Colebrook for you—"

"I think I know who is responsible." His brows shot

up. She shook her head. "That's between me and that person."

Mr. Estes gaped at her. She could see the wheels turning behind his shocked, shrewd eyes. They narrowed. "It's that crippled brother of his you suspect, isn't it? There ain't no way of knowin' for sure, Lily. You think either one of 'em would admit it to you?"

She gave him an unrelenting stare. "If you really care about doing what's right, you'll never tell another soul what you just told me. You'll let me handle it my own way."

He looked as if she'd asked him to cut off his own hands. Then his tattered dignity began to find itself, and he lifted his head. "That's one thing I *can* do. I swear it."

"Good. I'll take this one fight at a time. I want you to tell me which motel Joe's staying at."

His eyes widened, then became determined slits in a harsh frown. "I know you, Lily MacKenzie. I've knowed what kind of grit you was made of since that time you tried to chase Joe out of the woods at the Colebrook place and got shot for it. I ain't gonna let you do something crazy on his account again. You ain't gonna end up maimed or dead or in jail, no, ma'am."

"If you won't tell me where he is, I'll go to every motel in town and ask until I find him. I want him to admit what he did. I don't care what it takes."

"You get yourself over to your Aunt Maude's, and you tell her and the sisters—you tell Little Sis—about everything. You do that for *me*, 'cause I love that little gray fox and I want her to know it, even if she never forgives me for what I done." His throat worked. "And then you *wait*," he ordered desperately. "I'm gonna call the sheriff. All I've got to tell him is that Joe stole money and a gun from me." Tears crested in Mr. Estes's eyes and slid down his lined cheeks. "He's done broke his parole, see? I'll have him put back in prison."

She put her arms around him and gave him a hard hug. Stepping back, she said hoarsely, "You do what you have to, but I have to face Joe myself."

He grabbed her hands. "If you really believe you got a future with Artemas Colebrook, you'll fight for that future, not for some proud foolishness. Haven't you learned nothin' from me, Lily?"

He struck a chord as deep as her love for Artemas. After all these years, after all the heartaches and mistakes, with hope and triumph at last within reach, had it come down to this—risking everything for a petty, violent confrontation with someone like Joe? He wasn't worthy of it. He was nothing compared to the menace of unanswered questions about James and her fear that she couldn't resolve them without destroying Artemas's love for him.

Mr. Estes was studying her intently. Sadness and satisfaction softened his face. "Believin' in somebody else is the bravest thing a person can ever do. Now, if you believe in Artemas, then you let me handle this thing with Joe."

She looked at him with tears in her eyes, and nodded.

Artemas stood by a window in the gallery, a gold-framed photograph in his hands. But his attention was lost in the darkness outside the window. The serenity of the distant mountains sleeping in white splendor under a half moon contrasted with the turmoil he felt.

When the guard at the front gate had called with Lily's message, Artemas had been tempted to follow her to her aunt's house—which would ruin the private time she obviously needed—so he forced himself to wait.

James entered the room and walked over to him with halting steps, the limp a grim reminder of the scars they all carried. James looked at him as if he feared exactly that kind of response. Artemas quickly adopted a neutral expression. "Where is Alise?"

James's expression softened a little. "Asleep."

Learning that Alise was pregnant had been a delight to everyone, especially when they could see how much it meant to James. Artemas put an arm around his shoulders. "Elizabeth and Michael have gone with Cass. She wanted to show them the room she and John Lee are remodeling as a nursery." He paused. "Leo took the children back to

Atlanta. They're puzzled and frightened by the closed-door discussions we've been having."

James grimaced, his eyes feathered with lines of unhappiness. "One big happy family. All talking about the unrelenting truth."

Artemas frowned but said nothing. The truth was all they had, and James would have to accept it. Slowly James's gaze shifted to the photograph. He winced. "How old were we?"

"I think I was about fourteen. That makes it twenty-four years ago."

James held out both hands. He looked tortured. Artemas gave him the photograph and followed his gaze to Julia's piquant little face. "I let her down once," James said. "I couldn't let myself do it again. I couldn't let anyone threaten her."

"I understand. Thank God, we all finally understand."

James asked carefully, "Does Lily?"

Artemas met his gaze without yielding. He couldn't stop thinking about the suspicion and humiliation James had heaped on her during the past two years. "She's certainly trying, for my sake."

"She's put up with a lot from us—from me—for your sake."

"That's how it is when two people always want what's best for each other. If you still doubt us, I want to hear it. I want to know what we have to face, before she comes back here tonight. By God, I may understand why you thought she was your enemy, but I won't permit you to punish her any longer."

James squared his shoulders. "Then let's settle this. I'll go see her—right now. I'll make certain she understands that . . . I'm different." He swallowed roughly. "That I was wrong."

Artemas looked at him carefully. "I've never been more proud of you." He meant it. James bowed his head. His silence was fraught with emotion. Artemas gently clamped a hand on his shoulder. "Wait a little while before you go. She's at her aunt's house. I think she needs that privacy.

She needs her own family. Do you realize that Hopewell Estes intends to banish her from the old MacKenzie place because of her involvement with me? Do you understand that she's accepted that—because she loves me?"

When James lifted his eyes to Artemas's again, they were shadowed. "There must be a way to persuade Estes that his vendetta against you is misguided." James smiled grimly. "I'm an expert on misguided personal attacks."

"Lily says when Joe showed up two months early, Estes hardly seemed happy about it. Considering what I've heard about his son, I find it hard to believe he thinks Joe's honor is worth defending."

James stared straight ahead, as if prepared for execution. "People might say the same about me. That I'm lucky to have a family who cares."

"Look at me." When James did, Artemas said gruffly, "I've never doubted that you're worthy of this family's trust and love. I've never wished you weren't my brother."

James laid the photo on a table and braced himself with both hands. He cursed. Artemas gripped his arm. "What is it? What's still eating at you?"

"Last spring I offered Mr. Estes a deal." James spoke through gritted teeth. "We agreed that when his son was released from prison, he'd receive money, help. In return Estes agreed not to renew Lily's lease."

Artemas stared at him in speechless disbelief. "It's true," James told him, every word edged with disgrace. "But please believe me when I say I'm doing everything I can to change it."

Artemas swung James to face him. "You're the reason Estes told Lily she has to give up her farm. You're the goddamned reason she's going to lose the greenhouse and nursery business. You betrayed someone I love dearly. You betrayed my trust. And you betrayed this family's integrity." He jerked a fist back, then hit James—hard, in the mouth—without thinking, without restraint.

James was driven back a step by the force. He winced but continued to face Artemas. "I only ask you to let me rectify the situation."

"And how are you going to do that?" Artemas's voice was low and furious.

"My lawyer is probably talking to Estes right now. I'll keep my end of the offer provided that he allows Lily to continue as before—"

"And what about Lily? How do you think she's going to feel about this? *Damn you.*"

"I'll speak with her immediately, at her aunt's house." James hesitated, searching Artemas's relentless gaze for some hint of understanding. There was a slight slumping of his shoulders, a deadening of his eyes. "Afterward would you prefer that Alise and I return to Atlanta for the night?"

"Alise is welcome here. But you"—Artemas bent his head to one hand, agonized and bitter—"I don't know if you'll ever be welcome here again."

James made a low sound of defeat, then nodded and left the room.

After Lily left, Hopewell pulled on his coat, then went into his bedroom and hunted through a drawer of keepsakes in the dresser. He put a picture of Joe as a little boy in his pocket, along with a little gold cross that had belonged to Joe's mother. He went to the bedside table and picked up the quartz crystal Little Sis had left there. She'd meditated her love into it, she'd said. He put it in his pocket too.

Then he opened another drawer and rummaged through handkerchiefs and socks until he found a small revolver. That went into his pocket last.

He met a car on the way out. James Colebrook's lawyer, coming to see him at night. That could only mean more trouble. Hopewell ignored his frantic waving and drove on.

Little Sis sat, motionless and despondent, on the divan, and Lily's heart went out to her. She looked like an endearingly eccentric granny doll, dressed in red stirrup pants and a long red sweater with hand-painted holly and silver bells across the chest. Only her eyes moved, shifting from

Lily to Big Sis and Aunt Maude as if they were bumpers in a pinball game, while they talked and gestured frantically.

Lily stopped pacing in front of the sisters' Christmas tree and went to her, dropping to her heels and taking Lit tle Sis's hands. "He wanted you to know that he loves you," Lily told her gently. "He hasn't been deceiving any-one about *that*."

But Big Sis fished a wad of tobacco from one cheek, dropped it in the spittoon by her chair, and looked at Lit-tle Sis evenly. "You old sexpot, you've been traipsing after a man who intended to keep Lily out of everything she's worked for."

Aunt Maude scooted to the edge of an ottoman and glared at Big Sis. "Oh, shut up." She angrily plowed her hands into the skirt of the wool jumper that sagged be-tween her knees. "Hopewell's probably got the sheriff at Joe's door by now. He's turning his own son in. That's about as big an apology to Lily and Little Sis as a man could offer."

Looking at Lily, who rose wearily and sighed, Aunt Maude continued, "The bigger problem here is how's Lily going to handle what she found out about James Colebrook's nasty little scheme. Now, us three"—Maude waved at herself and the sisters—"we're not going to stand by and let him sabotage you, Lily. But if you don't want this story to go outside this parlor, it won't."

Lily nodded. "Y'all have to be patient and let me take care of it."

Big Sis snorted. "If you were trying to save a sick tree, you wouldn't think twice about cutting off a rotten limb. If James is rotten, you hand Artemas a saw."

"Nice wedding present," Aunt Maude retorted. "Telling Artemas something that will make him hate his own brother. Driving the brother out of the family." Giving a curt little nod for emphasis, she added, "Nice relations with your new in-laws then."

"I'm hoping that James feels differently about me now," Lily said. She leaned against the fireplace mantel and rubbed her forehead. "I'll confront him, but Artemas is never going to know about it. Not even if James intends to fight me the rest of our lives."

"Lily!" Big Sis and Aunt Maude said her name in unison, and with matching rebuke. Aunt Maude threw up a hand. "That'd be like ignoring a rattlesnake under your house."

Lily laughed dully. "I'll never trust him. I'll just stay away from the basement."

"Yeah, and James'll slither out when you're not looking and sink his fangs into you."

Little Sis finally moved. She bent over and propped her chin on her hands. Tears slid down her cheeks. "You won't have to live with the rattlesnake, because you've forgotten one thing. You think Joe won't talk? Oh, yes, Hopewell can get him sent back to prison, but Joe'll hire some greedy lawyer to sell his story. Hell, by New Year's he'll be on *Geraldo* telling how one Colebrook plotted against another one's ladyfriend."

Lily hadn't had time to sort through everything and arrive at that hopeless conclusion. It hit home like a sledgehammer.

Hopewell stood outside the motel room's door, his breath puffing swift white clouds in the frosty air. Neon lights from the motel sign blinked down on him. The motel was cheap and dingy, the kind where upstanding locals did things they wanted to keep secret. They thought it was the last place their wives or husbands would suspect them of being.

He could hear the TV going inside. He knocked on the scratched-up metal door. The TV noise snapped off. "Who the hell is it?" Joe bellowed.

"It's your daddy."

Eventually Joe opened the door. His face was ruddy. His eyes glistened. He wore an old black sweatshirt and jeans with the zipper half-undone. He smelled like liquor and sex. "You got a woman in there?" Hopewell asked.

"Nah." Joe smiled thinly and gestured obscenely with one fist, pumping it up and down. "Makin' do, old man.

Drinkin' cheap bourbon and jerkin' off. Waitin' to get rich."

Hopewell shoved him back and stepped inside, then slammed the door. The revolver made a heavy weight in his coat pocket. He put his hand in the pocket and clasped it tightly. "You tell me the truth, boy. Ain't no use tryin' to lie. You went over to Lily's place today, didn't you?"

"Goddammit, why do you always talk like she owns it? It's ours. Yours and mine."

"It's *mine*. Your name ain't on no deed. Never have been. And you got no right to go there." He stepped toward Joe. "You killed all her stock, didn't you? It was you."

Joe's gaze shifted. He shrugged. "I warned you. You ain't gonna tell nobody."

"You're coming with me, boy. I'm taking you over to the sheriff."

Joe stared at him. The sly, lax expression vanished. "It's too late to back out on that Colebrook thing, old man. You want me to make killin' a few chickens and a hog look like a Sunday school lesson? Hell, I will."

"We aren't dealin' with Artemas Colebrook. I was wrong—it was the other one—his brother, James. Artemas ain't goin' to hide behind a lawyer and money. He'll come right into the open—and then he'll chew you up and spit you out, boy."

Joe's stunned expression became a mask of fury. "You talked. You told—you told somebody. You told *her,* didn't you? Lily. And she'll go to him with it, and he'll screw me over. But he'll get you, too, old fool. Nobody cares about you."

"You're wrong. Even if you weren't, I'm through with you. Now, be a man. Get your stuff together and come with me. You been drinkin', you stole from me, you did that god-awful thing at Lily's. You never even tried to live up to your parole. You never meant to."

Joe shoved him. Spit flew from his lips. "I was goin' to have protection! I was goin' to have money! You set it up for me, and then you took it away!"

"You never earned nothing by honest work in your life. You can't claim what nobody owes you."

Joe raised a fist. Hopewell stepped back and drew the gun from his pocket. Pointing it at his son's chest, he said, "Get your stuff together. I'll shoot you if I have to."

Joe gaped at him. His fist dropped. He looked beaten. He went to the rumpled bed and sank down on the foot of it, his hands lying limp on his thighs. "Please don't send me back to prison, Daddy."

Hopewell thought his heart would shrivel and disappear from the misery. He knew it was foolish to let Joe get to him, but his hand wavered a little. Tightening his grip on the revolver, he said between clenched teeth, "Don't call me Daddy and sound pitiful."

"You don't know what it was like in there." Joe's mouth trembled. "If you got to know why I'm so desperate . . . why—oh, I never wanted you to know, Daddy."

"What? Tell me."

"Don't send me back. I . . . I got raped in there, Daddy. They ganged up on me. It happened a lot."

The sick, slow horror pressed on Hopewell's lungs. He lowered the gun and stood in numb silence. "Son. Oh, Son."

"I got nothing now, Daddy. Nothing but bad memories. Please, don't you turn against me."

Hopewell slipped the gun back into his coat. "You got to leave this town, boy. Just leave. And don't come back. That's the best I can do for you."

Joe sighed and got to his feet. Moving leadenly, he gathered clothes that were scattered around the room and put them in his canvas tote bag. He zipped his jeans and pulled his jacket on. Then he opened the drawer of the cabinet beside the bed and retrieved the pistol he'd taken from Hopewell. "Not that gun," Hopewell said. "You give that back to me. It'll only cause trouble for you, boy."

Joe carried it over, but stopped just out of reach. The hard amusement snapped back into his eyes. He tucked the pistol into the waistband of his jeans. "You're a bigger fool than I thought you were, old man." He vaulted forward. His fist slammed into Hopewell's jaw. Hopewell slumped to the floor. Blackness spread like spilled ink over his vision. He tried to wipe it away with one hand. Dimly he realized Joe had knelt beside him. Joe's breath and whisper were hot in his ear. "Colebrook won't let me just disappear, and you know it. My life's ruined for good this time, and you helped him do it. You know what else? I might as well go out in a blaze of glory. Make a name for myself. You be proud of your famous son now, you hear? I'm gonna go kill an important man."

Hopewell moaned bitterly and tried to push himself upright. Joe hit him in the temple. The blackness deepened, and took over.

Thirty-two

Lily's shoulders ached with the tension. She stared at the portable phone in Little Sis's hands. Little Sis stood in the parlor doorway, clutching the phone as if it might explode if she used it. Aunt Maude stood up impatiently. Big Sis hunched forward, watching.

"You want me to call?" Maude said.

Little Sis shook her head. Looking defeated, she punched the number in and slowly brought the phone to her ear. "Bertie? It's Sissy. Bertie, has the sheriff gotten a call from Hopewell Estes tonight?" Little Sis was silent, listening. Shock and fear pulled fine lines together between her brows. "Thank you, Bertie," she whispered, and dropped the phone on the floor. "Hopewell never called the sheriff."

Lily took a deep breath. The inevitable sank into her bones. There was no way around it. "I'm going to find Joe," she said, and walked out.

By the time she reached the street, Aunt Maude and Little Sis caught up with her. Big Sis tottered on the porch, rapping her cane on the snowy railing, while she glared at the slick porch steps. "I'm not about to be left behind!" she called.

Lily jerked the truck's door open. Little Sis grabbed her

arm. "Let's wait. Maybe Hopewell just hasn't made up his mind yet. Oh, that fool, that dear old fool—"

"Don't you dare leave," Aunt Maude commanded, pushing all her considerable girth between Lily and the cab. "We'll go call the sheriff back and get him to take care of it."

"You call him," Lily told her. "But I can't stay here and do nothing."

Aunt Maude leveled a hard gaze at her. "You're avoiding the thing you don't want to do. You've got to go to Artemas and tell him about his brother. It'll come out sooner or later, Lily. Don't let him find out from somebody else."

Lily made a sound of fury and despair. "I can't give up. I'm not going to throw away everything he loves on the chance that Joe Estes can't be kept from talking."

Little Sis tugged at her fiercely. "You can't reason with Joe! You've got nothing to bribe him with either."

"Yes, I have." Lily stuck out her left hand, fingers splayed. The diamonds and sapphires in Grandmother Colebrook's magnificent ring glittered in the light of a street lamp. Lily choked at the ethereal promise, the gift that represented so much sacrifice and devotion. But it was an empty symbol unless it saved them.

Her teeth clenched, she said softly, "If this is enough to make him keep his mouth shut and leave town, then I'll give it to him without a backward glance."

Maude asked darkly, "And if it's not enough?"

Lily met her eyes. "One way or another, I'm going to stop Joe."

The flash of headlights turning down the street made them all freeze. Little Sis shielded her eyes and cried. "It's Hopewell's old truck! It's him! Thank God!"

She broke away and ran to the truck as it slid to a stop in the slush along the curb. But as she put her hands on the door handle the door swung open, almost knocking her down.

Joe leaped out and snatched her by one arm. Little Sis gasped in pain as he wrenched it behind her back. Lily shoved past Aunt Maude, reaching into the cab of her truck and slamming the seat forward. She had her hands on the shotgun when Joe yelled, "I'll kill her! Get out of that truck, or I'll blow her damned brains out!"

Lily halted, her fingers tingling on the shotgun's stock. Beside her, Aunt Maude was cursing and shaking the truck's open door with both hands, her rage and fear trapped into futile gestures.

Joe had the muzzle of a pistol jammed into the hollow below Little Sis's ear. He glanced at Big Sis on the porch and yelled, "You keep still, too, old lady!" His deadly gaze flicked back to Lily and Aunt Maude. "I need a little help with something I gotta do. Looks like I'll get more than I expected. I ain't leaving any of you bitches here to call and warn everybody."

He jerked his head toward his truck. "Come on. All of you. I mean it. I'll pull this trigger. Come on."

Little Sis struggled and twisted toward the house. "Run!" she yelled to Big Sis. "Call the sheriff!"

Joe shook her and gave a harsh shout of laughter. "Why don't you tell her to throw down her cane and sprint like a rabbit?" His mouth curled sarcastically. "Old lady," he yelled to Big Sis, "you hobble this way as fast as you can, 'cause if you don't, I'll kill everybody and come after you next."

"Dead's dead," Big Sis retorted, but her voice shook. "If you're going to shoot anyway, what difference does it make where you do it?"

"I don't want to kill none of you. Y'all can get out of this alive, but you better do what I say. We've got a little trip to take."

Lily moved slowly around Aunt Maude, her hands knotted by her sides. "I'll go with you. You don't need the others."

"Hell, yes, I do. You always was crazy. You'd just as soon drive us both into a tree, if it was just you and me." He dragged Little Sis toward his father's truck. "Get in." He shoved her into the cab and kept the pistol pointed at her.

"Come on, Lily. Goddammit. You other two get in the back."

Big Sis held the railing of the porch steps and descended with choppy, fast steps. Aunt Maude walked forward helplessly. Lily stood in the middle of the street, trying to form a plan, seeing nothing but the lethal set of Joe's flat, thin lips. "Where's your father?" she asked.

Joe's eyes flickered without regret. "Don't talk to me about my old man, you thievin' cunt. You made him think you was more important to him than me. He got what he deserved. Everybody's gonna get what they deserve tonight."

Hopewell plowed his old Chevy into the curb in front of Maude's house. He staggered through the empty rooms, disoriented, his head full of pain, the scent of dried blood rising from his lips, his vision blurring. He kept trying to remember what Joe had said at the last. Where had Joe gone?

When he saw the phone on the floor, he sank to one knee, dizzy, fighting to remain conscious. Images refused to form a complete picture. The door of Lily's truck, standing open. The door of Maude's house too. The empty rooms. The phone.

He grabbed it and tried to focus on the console. Call the sheriff. But the blackness stained his sight again.

"Hello?" someone called from the front hall. A man's voice, deep and solemn, unfamiliar. "Is anyone there?"

"Here! Here," Hopewell gasped. "Help me." He sagged, turned limply toward the parlor door, and squinted. A tall, dark-haired man appeared in the door—angel or devil, a stranger in clothes like the men's magazines said rich people wore when they relaxed. The man came to him, limping a little, a long cloth coat flinging back from the bad leg, bending over him, grasping his chin. Hopewell recoiled. *James Colebrook.*

"What's going on here? I came to see Lily." Colebrook stared at his face. "You're Hopewell Estes, aren't you? Who did this to you?"

Hopewell swayed and threw up a hand to ward him off. "Hurt her. You'll hurt her. Hurt me. Afraid—"

Colebrook hurriedly pulled him to his feet and held him steady with a brutal grip. "*Talk to me.* Where are Lily and the others?"

He was the enemy. Hopewell couldn't trust him. But what if—what if Joe had been here? *I'm going to kill me an important man.* Hopewell moaned. "Joe's took 'em, somehow! And I know where he's gone! He's gone to kill your brother!"

"Stop the truck." Joe's voice cut through Lily's frayed concentration. She stepped on the brake. Beside her, Little Sis shivered. Joe sat on the far side of the seat, with the gun jabbed into Little Sis's side.

They were on the road to the estate. Nothing but snow-drenched forest stretched ahead and behind, a ghostly tunnel. Joe cranked the window down and yelled over his shoulder, "*Get out.*"

Lily glanced back into the bed, where Aunt Maude struggled to help Big Sis slide toward the lowered tailgate. She met Joe's cruel stare behind Little Sis's head. "They ain't gonna cause any trouble out here in the middle of nowhere," he said lightly. "You can thank me for lettin' 'em go."

"They'll freeze. I'm giving them my jacket," Lily told him. Her hard tone sullied Joe's control. Watching him tensely, she shrugged her quilted jacket off, opened her door, and held it out. Aunt Maude, breathing heavily, helped Big Sis along the truck's side. "We'll be all right," she said, taking the jacket. "Dear God, do whatever he says, Lily."

"Until you get the upper edge," Big Sis interjected, craning her head to look in the dark cab. "Then kill him. Kill him and spit on his dead face." Her voice broke. "Sissy, Sissy, I love you," she called.

"We'll have a fine story to tell around the fire, when this is done," Little Sis answered, staring straight ahead, afraid even to turn her head toward them.

Joe grunted. "Let's go. Shut the damned door."

Lily gave Aunt Maude and Big Sis a shamed look. Aunt Maude patted her arm. "Go on. You can't do any different."

Lily closed the door and drove on slowly, stalling for time. "Why are we going this way?"

"I got business down here."

"You had business at my place earlier today, didn't you?"

He laughed softly, the sound creeping over her skin. "You know, they came right up to me. They was as tame as pets."

She gripped the steering wheel until her hands ached. "I expect you knew how to get in and out through the woods without any of the estate's guards catching you on my road."

"Hell, yes. I hunted those woods for years." He laughed again. "Shot me a nosy little shit of a girl once too. Grew dope in the hollows. Had it good." His laugh became a low hiss. "Until Artemas Colebrook found out. Goddamn him. I been cheated out of my rights. Cheated by him. Cheated by my old man too, 'cause he turned on me for your sake. And for *yours*," Joe added, leaning toward Little Sis and whispering the words near her face.

"Where is Hopewell?" Little Sis asked, her voice small and strained.

"He was gonna take me to the sheriff. Held a gun on me. Didn't have the guts to use it."

"What did you do to him?"

"I beat the shit out of him."

Little Sis moaned. Lily saw the distant glow of the lamps at the estate's gatehouse, a faint light around a bend in the road. Joe saw it, too, and leaned back. "Now, you listen to me good, Lily. When we get to the gate, you better damned sure make certain we get past the guard without him suspectin' nothing."

It was the bleakest moment, a flash of resistance so overwhelming that Lily stomped on the brake. "No."

She heard the ugly, muffled click of the pistol's hammer. "I'll do it," Joe said softly. "Don't push me."

"Tell me why we're going to Blue Willow."

"If you don't shut up and go on, I'll kill both of you and still find a way to get in. At least this way, you give your man a chance to see me coming. Maybe he can even make things right—talk his way out of trouble. The other way, I just slip up in the woods and wait for him to step outside, and I put a bullet in him."

Lily pressed the gas pedal again. The truck crept along. She was screaming inside, working on the cold numbness of battle, alert and ready, and she forced herself to think rather than feel.

Little Sis blurted, "Your quarrel's not with Artemas! It's with his brother, James! It was James who got your hopes up!"

Lily bit her tongue. Could she protect Artemas by turning Joe's revenge toward James? James had brought this terrible situation down on them. James should be the one to pay, not Artemas. And finally, she knew she had no choice. She would save Artemas any way she could.

"Yes, it was James," she agreed. "Artemas's brother is the one you want to confront. He's the son of a bitch who schemed without any consideration for you *or* me. He held out all sorts of fantastic promises to you, when he *knew* the whole thing would fall apart as soon as the truth came out. He didn't care if you got caught in the middle. It doesn't matter to him that your dreams and hopes are ruined because of your father's change of heart. There's no point in you hating Artemas. It's James you want. But James isn't even here. He's . . . in New York. He left for New York tonight."

Little Sis gasped at the lie but added dully, "That's right. You should go to New York and find that bastard."

"Ladies, ladies," Joe said, giving the word a filthy lilt. "Colebrooks are thick with each other. Hurt one, you hurt 'em all. And I'm gonna make 'em all hurt."

They were at the gate. Lily looked at the neat little stone house and tall iron willows with despair. Joe said softly, "You get us in, or there'll be blood everywhere."

"I'll have to give the guard the names of my guests. It's

a rule. He'll be suspicious if I argue." That was another lie. She had the same privileges as Artemas or his family members. The guard would never question her. But he would, as a matter of routine, call the house and alert Mr. Upton to open the front doors. And Mr. Upton would relay her arrival to Artemas.

"You think of something safe to tell him," Joe warned.

She rolled down her window as the guard walked out. Lupa bounded out with him and leaped up, planting her paws on the truck's door, her tail wagging wildly. The guard raised his brows at Lily's unfamiliar vehicle but said politely, "Hello, Mrs. Porter." Seeing Little Sis, he brightened and said, "Why, and hello to you, Sissy. I've been reading that book on psychokinesis you sold me, but I still can't bend any spoons by looking at them."

"Mind over matter is a capricious thing," Little Sis replied grimly. "It takes faith."

He laughed. "At least I can open these gates for you." He fumbled with the remote control on his belt.

Lily stifled a flash of panic. If she blurted out information he hadn't requested, Joe would immediately suspect her motives. Lupa whined and scratched the truck's door, accustomed to being invited wherever Lily went. Lily's breath rattled in her throat. "Lupa! Stop clawing the finish off Mr. Halfman's truck."

Halfman. The name of the specter from her family's past, mysterious, a harbinger of doom. It came to her as if the evil had always been waiting at the edge of her mind to destroy her dreams, as it had destroyed Elspeth MacKenzie's future with the immigrant English china artisan she had loved so dearly, the man whose name and legacy had finally come full circle in Artemas. Halfman had returned.

"Mr. Halfman, I'm sorry about this damned dog," Lily continued. She put an arm out and shoved Lupa down. Lupa's tail drooped. Lily glared at the guard. "I thought I told you to keep her inside the gatehouse. If she gets run over, I'll have your job. I've warned you before. You never listen."

He blinked in astonishment, because she'd never spoken to him with anything less than courtesy or asked him
to keep Lupa before. "Ma'am?"

"Now she's put scratches in Mr. Halfman's door. Just
open the damned gates and get her out of the way."

He grabbed Lupa's ruff and backed off. The gates slid
open with slow grace. "I'm sorry, Mrs. Porter!" He glanced
at Joe. "I apologize, Mr. Halfman."

Lily scowled at him. "You'll be even sorrier after I tell
Mr. Colebrook how incompetent you are."

"Mrs. Porter, you're mistaken. I'm sorry!"

"Sorry doesn't cut it." She gunned the engine and
drove up the paved lane into the woods. Her pulse hammered in her throat. *Please, God, let him be so upset he tells
Mr. Upton every detail. And let Mr. Upton tell Artemas.*

The estate's forest closed in around them.

Artemas kept the sleek black phone to his ear and paced
in front of the doors to the loggia. "Could you try again,
operator?"

"Sir, the line is out of order or the phone has been left
off the receiver. I can't get through."

He told himself it meant nothing, but not being able to
call Maude's house stirred a sense of foreboding he
couldn't shake. James must be there by now, talking with
Lily. Artemas couldn't ignore the protective instincts of a
lifetime. Tonight, burdened with so much evidence that
those instincts had failed him with Elizabeth, Julia, and
James, he was more determined than ever.

He wouldn't risk failing Lily too. He'd go to Maude's,
check on the situation, but discreetly attempt to appear
casual about it. Lily wouldn't be fooled, but she'd understand.

Frowning, he thanked the operator and cut the connection, then strode out of the gallery. He went to the
entrance hall, intent on telling Mr. Upton to have a car
brought around to the front.

"Artemas?" He turned at the soft sound of Alise's voice.
She came down the grand staircase, floating, it seemed, in

a pale silk robe that reflected just a hint of color from the Tiffany skylight at the dome of the entrance hall. It was a lovely sight, as if she were moving through a rainbow, and her gentleness only made him angrier at James.

She halted at the landing, looking puzzled. "I woke from my nap and called downstairs to find James. Mr. LaMieux said he's gone into town."

"I'm sorry, I thought you knew. He's gone to see Lily, at her aunt's house."

The barely concealed tension in his voice alerted her. Alise raised a hand to her throat. Her eyes darkened with distress. "Is everything all right?"

"I assume he told you what he'd been planning to do to Lily."

She shut her eyes, then looked at Artemas with a sheen of tears in them. "Yes. When he called me in London yesterday." She stepped forward quickly, holding her hands out in supplication. "I know how horrible it must have sounded to you. But he's changed so much. If you could have lived with him, with his confusion and pain, the way I have for nearly two years, and then heard the difference in his voice yesterday, and then today, today, after I arrived, when we"—she hesitated, her reluctance to disclose James's private moments apparent in her eyes—"oh, Artemas, he's very different from before."

Artemas couldn't bring himself to tell her that his fury and disappointment seemed endless right now. "He's gone to apologize to Lily. His scheming may have ruined her business relationship with Mr. Estes permanently—and worse, her chances of recovering her family property someday. A great deal will depend on how Lily feels about that."

"I understand, but please, give him a chance."

"I've told him he's not welcome here at the estate for now. He'll be leaving for Atlanta tonight."

"Oh, Artemas, *no!*"

"You're a much-loved part of this family, and you've done nothing wrong. You may stay if you wish."

"I'd never do that, without James." She clutched the ornate wooden balustrade with both hands and gave him a beseeching look. "All these years—ever since I was a little girl who tagged along after James—I've always seen how strong the bond was between you. I won't believe it's broken."

Artemas looked at her wearily. "Right now, I honestly don't know if it will ever be the same."

Crying, she turned and went back upstairs. Artemas watched in grim, miserable silence. The swift opening of a small door off the entrance hall drew his attention.

"Oh, marvelous, sir. I was afraid LaMieux would never locate you." Mr. Upton strode out of the anteroom that served as his office. Looking agitated, the butler said, "Sir, I've just had a very strange call from Louis, at the front gate."

Artemas regarded him with dull interest. "What?"

"Mrs. Porter came through a few minutes ago. She said some very bizarre things to Louis. Sir, Mrs. Porter has always been the most courteous person, even last spring. That's why Louis is so puzzled."

Artemas's first thought was that her conversation with James had gone terribly wrong, and she was upset. But she would never take it out on a member of the estate's staff. "What did she say?"

"She accused Louis of not caring for her dog properly. She called him incompetent."

"What had he done?"

"Nothing, sir. And she made it sound as if he'd treated the dog carelessly before. But he's never kept the dog for her before."

Bewildered, Artemas scowled and went to the massive front doors, sliding the bolt and wrenching one of the ornate handles. He'd wait for her on the front steps. "I'll take care of this. Call Louis back and tell him not to worry. I'm sure she didn't mean to insult him."

Artemas pulled one door back. Cold, snow-scented air curled around him. The outside lamps cast ethereal light on the apron of stone landing and the shallow, wide steps that led down to the cobblestoned courtyard. Beyond the white expanse of the front lawn the entrance drive curved into the forest. He searched the dark wall of trees and listened for sounds of her approach.

Mr. Upton followed him anxiously. "There's something else, sir."

Artemas pivoted and stared at him. "Yes?"

"She wasn't driving her own vehicle. Louis said it was an old pickup truck belonging to one of her passengers."

"Passengers? Who? Did he know them?"

"One of them, sir. Her aunt's sister. The lady everyone calls, uhm, Little Sis."

"And the other one? The owner of the truck?"

"A, uhm, Mr. *Hoffman*, I believe Louis said. She was very upset because Louis allowed the dog to jump up on the door of the gentleman's vehicle. Though Mr. Hoffman seemed unconcerned. Frankly, sir, Louis was a little concerned about Mr. Hoffman's appearance. I hope you don't think this is forward of me to mention it, sir, but, well, Louis isn't one to comment on a guest's appearance unless it worries him."

"How did Louis describe him?"

Mr. Upton shifted uncomfortably. "Louis said, and I quote, 'If I were in a Seven-Eleven late at night, and that guy walked in, I'd get my ass out of there before I got robbed.'"

Artemas went very still. But reason argued with vigilance. This Hoffman was probably some local man Lily had known since grade school, someone like Timor Parks's hulking but benign sons. The Parks boys' appearance might send customers hurrying out of a convenience store too.

"*Hoffman?*" Artemas repeated, musing over it. "I've never heard that name." He shook his head in dismissal and went down the steps. The first, faint rumble of an engine came to him, from beyond the distant wall of trees. "No need for you to stand out here in the cold too," he called to Mr. Upton. "I'll usher them into the house."

Mr. Upton gave a slight bow and turned back to the open door. But then he halted, tapped his forehead and said, "Ah! Excuse me, sir. It wasn't a Mr. Hoffman. She said his name was *Halfman*. Mr. Halfman."

Lily shivered with hope when she saw the house. There was no one on the steps. The looming walls and windows on either side of the entrance were in deep shadow extending out to the barren areas where the gardens had been in the old days, then merging with the darkness of the woods.

Only the steps and the wide stone landing were bathed in light, creating an eerie sense that a bright stage had been set. Her worst fear had been that she'd find Artemas waiting for her there, unsuspecting. Had her warning gotten through? Had he interpreted it accurately? Or was this a false reprieve? Perhaps Elizabeth, Michael, and Cass had returned. It was possible that he and the family were involved in another round of intense conversations about their childhood, and he couldn't break away.

She feared that dapper little Mr. Upton would swing one of the doors open at any second and come out to greet her. She slowed the truck to a crawl. Little Sis sat rigidly, mashed tight to Lily's side, and Lily felt her tremors. Joe was staring at the house, his eyes half-shut, his face contorted with preparation and disgust. "You're gonna get me into the house," he told Lily. "The three of us are gonna walk up to the door, and I'll be back of ol' Sissy here, and you better say all the right things again, Lily."

Lily stopped at the base of the steps and cut the engine. The silence ticked in her nerves like a time bomb. She braced her hands on the steering wheel and was very still. The dilemma was tearing her apart. She could not escort this evil into the center of Artemas's family. She thought of Elizabeth, Michael, Cass, even James. And of Little Sis. But always, first and last, of Artemas.

A flicker of movement, reflected in the rearview mirror, riveted her. Artemas slipped forward, from the shadows, behind the truck, on Joe's side. He bent low beside the bed, his hands splayed on the frigid metal, moving steadily and silently toward the passenger door.

"Lily, let's go," Joe said, with a low, grinding threat in his voice. She did not move. "You're going to kill him," she said.

"If you do what you're supposed to, it'll only be him. Helluva choice, ain't it? Maybe you can fight me, Lily. Maybe you can keep me from gettin' him. But little Granny here won't make it. And you won't make it, either. And anybody else that crosses my path will pay. Think about it, Lily—is one man worth everybody else's lives?"

Yes. Screaming it inside her own mind, Lily knew the answer was savage and loving and impossible. *He's lived for everyone else. I won't let him die for us too.*

But she had Little Sis to think of.

Little Sis raised her chin. Lily realized she was staring into the rearview mirror also. "You know, Lily," she said in a chirpy, sad little voice, "I'm sure I'm going to be reincarnated." She looked at Joe. "I'll be back," she intoned. Then she jammed both hands between him and her, where the pistol was, and wrenched it upward. The fleeting shock on Joe's face signaled his surprise. He jerked the pistol away and fired. The blast was deafening. The windshield exploded.

Lily lunged across Little Sis, clamping both hands onto Joe's and the gun. He jerked the trigger again. Sparks flew from the dash gauges. Bits of metal and plastic showered over them. She bored her thumbs into the soft hollow of his wrist. The gun's muzzle was suddenly pointing at her face. "Bitch!"

His door was flung open, and Artemas had both hands on him, jerking him backward. Another explosion. The window of her door shattered.

Joe twisted, swinging the gun and his free fist toward Artemas. Lily shoved her door open and pulled Little Sis out that side. "Get! Go! I'm fine!" Little Sis cried, falling on the cobblestones. Lily ran around the truck.

Joe fired again.

Artemas's head slammed backward. The force pushed him away from Joe. He collapsed.

She screamed—a wrenching, guttural cry of fury and

despair. Joe had already righted himself and stood with his feet braced apart, the pistol gleaming at the end of his outstretched arm. Lily leaped at him and hit him full body. They fell in a heap. The pistol jerked. A bullet screamed off the cobblestones.

She heard the roar of another car, sliding to a stop inches away. She got her fingers between Joe's legs and wrenched with every ounce of strength. He cuffed the side of her head. His bile flew on her face. She knew she'd given him the rage and impetus to kill her. And after her, Artemas.

Punching, kicking, Lily got away and scrambled to her feet. She threw herself toward Artemas.

He lay on his back. She knelt and cradled his head in her arms, using her body to shield him from Joe. "Don't be gone," she begged, sobbing. "Don't let Halfman win this time." He moved groggily, one leg shifting a little, his eyelashes flickering. Blood seeped through his hair and down the side of his neck. There was hope. It wasn't over.

There was the sound of footsteps scraping on the cobblestones.

"Stop!" Joe yelled. "Or I'll finish it right now!"

Whoever had arrived halted at the warning. Lily looked over her shoulder. *James.* He stood there, hands clenched by his sides, staring at her and Artemas with the torture of the damned on his face. Behind him, holding each other, were Aunt Maude and the sisters. Mr. Estes clung weakly to the front fender of his truck, his face bruised and his mouth stained with dried blood, absolute devastation in his eyes as he looked at his son. Joe was crouched on the cobblestones, one hand trembling over his injured groin, but he kept the gun pointed at Lily and Artemas.

One of the mansion's heavy front doors swung open a few inches. Mr. Upton thrust out his head and shouted, "The security people will arrive at any moment! And I've called the sheriff!"

"James!" Alise darted past Mr. Upton. She looked like

a terrified angel in her pale robe. Mr. Upton snagged her by one arm, but she jerked away from him.

"Go back inside," James yelled.

"No!"

"I love you. Please go back inside."

Mr. Upton latched onto her. She struggled with him, and he planted himself firmly between her and the threat below.

Joe began shrieking, "Don't do it! Don't you fuckin' do it!"

Alise called James's name, a begging, tormented sound. A shadow fell over Lily and Artemas. She turned her head, seeing James from the corner of her eyes. He had his back to them. He stood between them and Joe.

Joe staggered to his feet, keeping the gun pointed at Lily and Artemas. Hunched over in pain, his face contorted, he stared at James and gasped, "I've got one. One left. One shot." He glanced toward Artemas, who moved again, trying to sit up. Lily pulled him close to her and sheltered his head against her chest. Joe yelled, "Get away from him, bitch!"

"Lily," Artemas murmured. He tried to push her aside, but he was too weak. He focused on her, aware now, holding her gaze with his life. His lips moved, giving a faint, groggy whisper filled with determination. "Love you . . . all these years . . . not to lose you."

"I said move!" Joe yelled. "Both of you! Get away from him!"

Lily bowed her head against Artemas's and held him tighter. His blood was wet against her cheek, the ugly furrow in his scalp inches from her mouth.

"It's me you want," James said. His voice had a low, melodic certainty, like the chime of the Colebrook clocktower. Lily shivered. He had measured time dearly and accepted his midnight. "Pull the trigger," he continued. "Have the guts to do one thing right in your miserable life."

"So he wasn't here, huh, Lily?" Joe taunted. "So I'd

have to go to New York to find him, huh? Well, looks like the cripple surprised us."

Mr. Estes moaned. 'Joe. Don't you hear them sirens comin'? I love you, boy. Put the gun down."

"I hear 'em, old man," Joe answered. There was rage and defeat in his voice. "You want to be the hero, huh, cripple? It ain't gonna change nothing."

James said softly. "You can't get around me. You can only kill me."

Artemas latched his hand onto Lily's shoulder and lifted his head, groaning with the effort. "No, James."

"I love you, big brother," James said. "And . . . Lily. *Lily,* I'm sorry for everything. I tried to stop it, but I was too late."

She caught a sob in her throat. "I know that now."

Joe gave a rancid laugh. "You want glory, cripple? Then here it is."

He swung the pistol toward James's chest. The fierce shrieks of Aunt Maude and the sisters filled the air, like the sirens pealing through the night. Artemas's hands dug into Lily's sweater. She cried out and pulled his head into the crook of her shoulder, sheltering him from the horror that hung on the next second.

The shot snapped like a willow breaking at the core.

Beyond James, staring up into his eyes, Joe had a look of shock. Then his face convulsed. He folded, slowly, to his knees, slid backward, and sprawled with slow grace, blood bubbling from his lips, to the cobblestones. Behind him. Mr. Estes wavered, moaned like an animal in pain, and let a small pistol drop from his hand.

Thirty-three

Strangers were fiddling with him, which he disliked. A nurse dabbed antiseptic on the line of stitches in his scalp. The emergency-room doctor hummed lightly as he studied an X-ray, saying something about Artemas being fortunate.

Fortunate, yes. Because Lily was sitting on a stool close to his side, her elbows propped on the gurney, her hands wrapped around one of his, and even though his blood was on her sweater and the bib of her overalls, and her hair was tangled wildly around her gaunt face, she was looking at him in a desperately pleased way that made the pain and the strangers unimportant.

Artemas was satisfied simply to continue lying there in private, loving communication with her, letting his thoughts settle into orderly patterns. His sisters and brothers were waiting in the hall outside, with Tamberlaine. James was there. Safe. Everyone was safe. Artemas sighed with relief.

Joe Estes was in surgery, though the paramedics who'd brought him from the estate had told the family that he'd never survive. Artemas found himself thinking, with bitter gratitude, that he hadn't wanted Joe to die on the steps at Blue Willow. The grand old house had escaped that ultimate infamy.

The troubling scene came back to Artemas in hazy pieces. His helpless rage. The fear for Lily, and James. Her fierce protection, her arms wrapped around him and her head bent over his, shielding him so that the sickening crack of the gunshot was muffled, the consequences hidden from his sight.

Then the soft thud of someone falling, and Lily's cry of shock and excitement when she turned to look. Artemas had been able to see then, too—to see that James was unhurt, that Joe Estes had been stopped by his own father.

Events after that were blurred, because adrenaline had stopped flooding his pain and he hadn't been able to overcome the dizziness or disorientation anymore.

"Stop thinking so hard," Lily whispered now. He was surprised to find that the nurse and doctor had left during his troubled reverie. "Stop thinking about it," she repeated. She was teasing him a little, though her voice was hoarse. "You'll pop a seam. Need extra stitches." A muscle worked in her throat, and the amusement in her eyes faded into their stark blue depths. "I came so close to losing you. I'm afraid it's just a dream that you're alive."

He squeezed his fingers around hers. "Halfman isn't coming back, Lily."

She shivered, slid closer to him, and rested her head against the side of his chest. He stroked her hair gently and shut his eyes.

Eventually he realized that someone was walking toward them, and he recognized, with sorrow and pride, the uneven rhythm of the step. Lily heard it, too, and sat up. They looked at James, who stood a little distance from them. He seemed awkward, agonized. "Am I intruding?" he asked gruffly.

"Not a bit," Lily said. She beckoned him with a slight nod, and only then did he step closer, stopping beside the gurney. James looked from her to Artemas. "I'm responsible for what Joe Estes did tonight."

"No," Artemas replied, brushing a hand over his forehead and wincing at the pain. "You can't blame yourself for Halfman's intentions."

James frowned and glanced at Lily. "Is he still groggy?"

She almost smiled. "A little. But he's right. I'll explain about Halfman to you, sometime." She stood and faced James squarely, her head up. "Listen to me. You stepped into the middle of a lot of history that had nothing to do with you. Joe has been in and out of trouble as long as I can remember. He's always blamed everyone but himself. I expect you know that when I was a little girl I caught him hunting on the estate, and he fired at me, like an irresponsible fool. He shot me in the arm."

James nodded. "I've heard that story from Tamberlaine."

Lily continued, "Well, Joe blamed it on me. And he never forgot it. Then he blamed Artemas for having him arrested when he was growing marijuana on the estate." She exhaled. "And when he got out of prison, the last thing he could accept was that I was living at the farm again. He wanted Mr. Estes to kick me out. When Mr. Estes wouldn't do that, Joe reacted the way he always had"—her voice broke and she slumped a little—"only he made a god-awful mistake when he thought he could accomplish anything by . . . by what he did to my animals.

"Joe thought his father would defend anything he did. But Mr. Estes was going to the sheriff. Even if we couldn't have proved that Joe killed my livestock, he'd already violated parole by stealing from Mr. Estes. He knew he was going back to prison. It made him crazy."

She was finished. She leveled a hard, meaningful gaze at James. "There's the only truth that's important, James. Pure and simple. If you embroider it with more details, it won't be any better."

James slid his hand roughly through his hair. He had tears in his eyes. "You don't owe me this kind of loyalty."

"When I think of you now, I think of what you did for Artemas and me tonight. I don't think about the rest. And neither does Artemas."

His gaze shifted quickly to Artemas. James sat down beside the gurney, his eyes urgent and shadowed. Artemas lifted a hand slowly, cupped it around the back of James's neck, and James bent his head to his brother's shoulder. Lily watched silently, her throat tight.

"You are the best," Artemas whispered to him. "The very best. We needed you, and you were there. That's all that matters."

James made a tragic sound—relief and defeat, joy and anguish. "I wasn't there when Julia needed me. That's why I swore I wouldn't let anyone down again."

"Then you've kept your promise." James lifted his head. Artemas repeated softly, "You've kept your promise."

Cass, Alise, Michael, and Elizabeth pushed through the double doors to the treatment area and advanced on them. "We can't wait outside any longer," Michael explained. "We had to see how Artemas is doing."

"I've never felt better," he answered. From the pride on his face as he surveyed his brood, Lily knew he meant it.

Lily went upstairs, where Joe Estes was in surgery. Aunt Maude met her as she stepped out of the elevator. "Lily. I was coming to find you. How is Artemas?"

"He's fine."

"He and James—"

"It's all right."

Aunt Maude sighed. Her sturdy face was as solemn as an owl's. "The surgeon just came out and told us. Joe's dead."

Hopewell fumbled inside his jacket and found the small, rumpled snapshot. He held the photograph in the palm of one hand. "My poor little boy," he whispered. Joe's face had a smear of blood on it, and he scratched at it with his thumbnail.

He rubbed his thumb over the photo again, rougher and without much effect on the dried blood. When Little Sis saw what he was doing and how badly his hands shook, she gently took the picture from him. She dabbed a fingertip to her tongue and wiped the blood away. Then she laid the picture back in his hand. "There. Not a speck of stain on him anymore," she said softly.

Her kindness tore him open. Hopewell cupped the picture in his hands and cried silently. "He took and he took from me and Ducie, and she died from the grief, and then he took every good feeling I had left, and then . . . he almost took you from me. He did take you, 'cause things'll never be the same between you and me."

Little Sis made little shivering sounds of distress and held on to his arm with both hands. "Don't you give up like this, Hopewell Estes!" She jerked his arm harder with each word.

Hopewell fumbled with the photograph, put it away carefully in his side pocket, and sat staring at the floor.

When Aunt Maude and Lily arrived in the doorway of the hospital's waiting room, Little Sis looked up gratefully from her place beside Hopewell on the couch. Then she saw James Colebrook with them and froze.

But he didn't appear too tough or devious now. No, she sensed a sad, dark blue aura around him. Or maybe it was something she saw in his eyes—those big gray eyes like his brother's, now cloudy as yesterday's sky.

Big Sis pushed herself up from a chair in one corner. She'd lost her cane in the confusion, so she clung to the chair's back and stomped one foot for attention. "I need a chew," she said. "Maudy, you help me down the hallway. Help me find that orderly with the can of Red Man in his shirt pocket. I'm going to bum a chew off him."

Little Sis gaped as Maude helped Big Sis totter from the room. For once in their nosy, meddling lives they weren't going to inject their two cents' worth. After they left, she smoothed the backs of her fingers down Hopewell's bruised cheek and whispered, "You want to talk to Lily alone?"

"No, you can stay. Please stay." He straightened and stared at James. "You too."

James shut the door and waited nearby, his hands sunk into the pockets of the overcoat he'd never removed. Lily came to the couch and dropped to one knee in front of Hopewell. She looked up at him sympathetically and covered his hands with hers. "I wish Joe had given you a different choice," she said.

"He didn't. He never did. I'm so sorry for what he done, Lily."

James said, "You wanted to let him shoot me." It was a flat statement, not accusing, almost as if he couldn't fathom why Hopewell had not let that happen.

Hopewell scrubbed a hand across his swollen eyes. "You don't know me very well if that's what you think."

"I wouldn't blame you for it," James replied, astonishment filtering into his eyes. "I take full responsibility for the mistakes I made that led to your son's death."

"Confession ain't good for the soul if it doesn't do nothing but hurt people." Hopewell looked at Little Sis. "More than anything, I wanted to keep you from knowin' how weak I was, how I planned—at first—to turn Lily out for Joe's sake. Then I tried to fix things, and I didn't want nobody to know the truth." He swiveled toward James again. "But you want to spread it to the whole world."

James stared dully at him. "There's something else you have to know. Yesterday I called Beitner and told him to settle the deal. To pay Joe off in return for you letting Lily stay on her land. If I had done that sooner, Joe might be alive right now."

Stunned silence sank into Hopewell's grief. "So that's why Beitner was coming up my driveway."

"You saw him tonight?" James asked.

"I ignored him. Drove on past. I was headed out to get Joe. To take him to the sheriff." Hopewell gave Lily a regretful look. "I couldn't let somebody else do what I had to do, as Joe's father."

She grasped his hand. "I understand."

The door burst open. Artemas stood there, leaning heavily on the doorframe, the thick white patch of a bandage standing out in stark contrast against his dark hair. The others—Cass, Michael, Elizabeth, Alise, even Tamberlaine, who'd been outside the hospital lobby speaking with the the sheriff—were behind him.

"This should be a family meeting," Artemas said, staring hard at James.

Tamberlaine looked over the others at Lily. "You know, he's impossible to stop."

Lily leaped to her feet and went to him, putting an arm around his waist. He braced himself against her and walked into the room. The rest crowded in as well. Alise took James's outstretched hand. James never took his eyes from Artemas.

The silence was oppressive. Lily looked urgently at Mr. Estes. "If James had never influenced Joe's life in any way, if Joe had come home from prison with just ordinary expectations, how would things have turned out differently?"

Hopewell wished he could say that Joe would have been a model son, a model citizen, but that kind of blind loyalty had burned out. "He would have got into trouble again," Hopewell said, slumping in defeat. He shut his eyes and leaned back on the couch. "He would've hated seein' that I'd let you move onto the farm, and hated Artemas the way he always had, and there would've been trouble of some kind. I can't say things would've turned out any different than they did."

Little Sis chimed in, "Let that story stand, all of you. Some people are born broken and can't be fixed." She took Hopewell's hand gently. "That's the way Joe was."

James leaned against a wall. His chest rose and fell roughly. Lily walked over to him, tentative at first, then halting in front of him with quiet acceptance.

Artemas stepped up beside her. He gestured toward everyone else in the room, including Hopewell and Little Sis, then at Lily, and finally at him. "This is your family. You risked your life to protect it. Ultimately that's all that matters."

James moved into the circle of his brother's arm.

Hopewell found himself being pulled off the couch by Little Sis, and then, to his amazement, he was being surrounded, taken in, and comforted by Colebrooks.

Lily shut her eyes and exhaled gratefully. Very old sorrows and fears were fading away.

• • •

Artemas woke with a grimace, his head aching, all the events of the day and night before creeping out of unpleasant dreams. But then he realized where he was, and with whom, and that there were no shadows.

Lily was beside him. In his bed. *Their* bed, at Blue Willow. Carefully lying close to him with her face nuzzled against his jaw, she rose to one elbow and kissed him as his eyes opened. She tucked the covers around him a little better and stroked his hair, studied his bandage, fussed with it a little, then kissed him again.

Golden morning light seeped in through the curtains of the balcony doors. She was as warm and soft as the light.

She whispered to him, maintaining his hypnotic trance with intimate suggestions in a voice so low and private and filled with love, it might only have been in his thoughts. Artemas looked at her in wonder. She pulled the covers aside and took him so gently that he forgot the pain and the bad dreams.

This, she was telling him, was how their ancestors had started it all.

Midmorning sun softened the room's old paisley hues. Hopewell had opened the heavy drapes. He couldn't bear the somber light from the wall sconces over Joe's coffin. Melting snow trickled from the eaves outside, and the drops of moisture gleamed like falling diamonds behind the window's lace sheers.

He looked at himself in a gilt-framed mirror. His black suit was snug around the gut; he looked robust and strong, while he felt ancient and shrunken. And alone.

He went to a sofa and sat down. The scent of flowers throbbed in his head. There were plenty of flowers in the room. He had forgotten how many friends he had. But they were the kind who would come here to sign the register and stay for a few polite minutes only because they pitied him. They would leave casseroles and cakes on his front porch, because that was the respectful thing to do.

They would stick sympathy cards inside the warped screened door and hurry away.

No one would stay.

"Hopewell?"

Little Sis eased into the room, her hands clasped on a little black purse. Her neat, trim brown coat and dress were almost conservative, except for the bright red embroidery down the dress's front and the red Christmas bow tied girlishly around her gray hair.

She was the dearest sight he'd ever seen, but he didn't know how to tell her so. He didn't know what he'd ever say next to her, to make up for the horrible time Joe had put her through.

She settled next to him, not quite touching, and faced forward. "I couldn't sleep a bit last night," she said. "Not after you left the hospital without so much as a word to me about where you were going. I finally found out you came straight here."

"I couldn't talk to you. Still can't. There ain't no words that can say how I feel." They were all stuck in his throat, stinging his eyes.

"I see," she said, her voice strained. "Couldn't you have gone home, or called me or something, so I wouldn't be worried?"

"I couldn't bear to go back to my own house. I see Joe and Ducie in every room. I'm thinkin' I'll move into a trailer. Maybe I'll move over to Victoria—"

"No, you're not moving away! You come to Maude's house. We've got an extra room. And nobody'll say anything if you only pretend it's where you sleep."

Swaying, he looked at her. "I'm not gonna live in sin with you!"

"Then marry me. *Marry* me."

He looked across the room at Joe's closed coffin. This ought to be all wrong, to be talking about such things in the room with his son's body. But then, Little Sis had never done things right. She'd just always done what was best for him, and he finally saw that.

He got to his feet, shamed and grieving and happy, and

he took her hand and pulled her along beside him, out of the room, out of the little building, into the melting snow and bright sunshine. "I love you," he said then.

She cried harder and threw her arms around his neck. "I love you too."

They were kissing each other and crying together, and eventually he looked over and saw the funeral director frowning at them from the doorway. So he scooped a handful of snow into a ball and threw it, and it splattered on the doorway, thank the Lord, but it drove the nosy bastard back inside.

He and Little Sis made their way to a bench on the lawn and sat with their arms around each other and their heads bent close. He could grieve for Joe and not say any more, because she would do all the talking. "My phoenix rising from the ashes," she called him.

And that was exactly how he felt.

Artemas and Lily stood in the yard of the house, looking toward the barn. He had sent workmen to remove the carcasses, but it wasn't as easy to erase the ugly memory. Artemas kept his arm around her. Her sorrow seeped into him. "I wish I could tear it down and give the lumber away," she said. "I don't want to set foot in there again."

He was grateful for the sound of a car, a distraction. Lily turned, puzzled, and watched Little Sis's bright red Cougar come up the dirt lane and turn onto the farm's drive. "What?" she said, frowning. "What's this?"

"A surprise," he said gruffly.

Little Sis parked under the willows. Mr. Estes opened the passenger door and got out, and she took his hand as they walked to Lily and Artemas.

"Thank you for comin' to Joe's funeral," he said to them both, halting in front of them. He looked at Artemas. "Thank you for havin' your whole family there."

"It was their decision. I didn't have to insist."

Mr. Estes reached into a pocket of his coat and pulled a folded document from it. "Lily." She glanced at the paperwork and made a small sound of amazement. He held it out with a trembling hand. "The deed's all worked out, in your name. It's a weddin' present. I asked Artemas to make sure you'd be here, so I could give it to you."

She took the deed as if it were fragile. "Thank you."

"You and me, we can still make a go of things here. If you need a crusty old man for a partner."

"Oh, yes, *yes*." She put her arms around him. He snuffled in embarrassment but hugged her back. "I know you ain't goin' to live in the house here no more—"

"I'll be at Blue Willow." She looked at Artemas. "But the two aren't separate anymore."

He smiled tenderly. "The Colebrooks and MacKenzies have been neighbors for over one hundred and fifty years. If the legend is true, there wouldn't be a Colebrook family in America if Elspeth MacKenzie hadn't taken care of Old Artemas when he was injured. Our families have managed to come back where they started—together. No, we're not separate anymore. We're never going to be separate again."

Little Sis cleared her throat. "What would you say if Hopewell and I got married and wanted to keep an eye on this place for you?"

"Live here?" Lily asked. "Would you like that?"

Mr. Estes studied her sadly. "Would you want an Estes livin' in your family's house?"

"I'd like family here. I'd want you and Little Sis here."

"Then . . . then that's settled." When she moved to hug him again, he waved her away. "Got to go. Got to go."

"He's shy," Little Sis explained, as if it were needed.

They left as quickly as they'd arrived. Lily tucked the deed in the breast pocket of Artemas's coat. "There's my wedding present to you," she said softly.

Epilogue

She sat cross-legged on the brown winter grass outside the granite mausoleum, under a bright, cool winter sky, her hands jammed tightly in the crook of her jeaned legs, the light breeze curling inside her open jacket and chilling her through the heavy sweater she wore. The events of the past two years seemed as distant as a bad dream but as fresh as yesterday; in the odd contrast of grief and acceptance she was beginning to find serenity.

The soft hum of a car engine rising over the knoll of the cemetery's narrow paved lane made her look up dully. A car crested the knoll and stopped. Artemas got out.

She rose and brushed a hand over her damp eyes as he walked up the hill to her. "I went by the farm," he said as he reached her. "Mr. Estes said you'd left work early. He told me you'd driven down to Atlanta, and why."

"He's become as fussy about me as an old hen."

"He adores you." Artemas held out his hands. She took them and looked up at him in silent misery. "Why did you come here alone, without telling me?"

"I wanted to talk to myself, and to Stephen. And to Richard too. I feel as if I'm still inside a long tunnel, but there's light at the end now." She paused. "I've only begun to see that light in the past few months. You put it there."

"I'm with you now, in the darkness, and I'll be with you when you reach the other side."

She stepped into his embrace. "I wish there was something I could say or do for Stephen that would make sense of everything," she whispered, her throat tight. "A way to let go of the pain but keep the memories, without feeling that I'm forgetting him. I never came back here before because I was afraid it would kill me to . . . to imagine him being alone. I found this inside the mausoleum, sitting on the floor." She slid a hand into her jacket pocket and removed a tiny brown teddy bear. Meeting Artemas's shuttered gaze, she asked, "Did you bring this here?"

He nodded. "During all those years that you and I were growing up, separately, there were small gestures that kept the connection. They may seem simple, even maudlin, now, but—"

"No. They meant everything to me. They still do."

"I can't bring Stephen back for you, but I can tell you that his memory will always be welcome to me."

She took his arm. Together they walked to the mausoleum. She opened the wrought-iron door, and they went inside. Lily sat the tiny bear back in its place on the floor, then touched her fingertips to her son's name, carved on the stone plate next to Richard's. "You are always with me," she whispered.

She touched Richard's name too. Artemas said nothing, but kissed her hair gently.

They went back outside, and she closed the gate. He pulled her to him and held her with comfort and sorrow and mute appreciation. After a while Lily looked up at him and smiled. It was time to go back to Blue Willow and start the new year.

Dawn light, rose-hued and clear, filled their bedroom. Artemas frowned at the empty space beside him and eased out of bed. He threw a robe around himself and went through their suite, looking for her. The air was cool and silent, the rooms empty.

He returned to the main one, stared at the bed as if she

might have reappeared during his search, and called her name. A soft, cool breeze scented with earth and sun touched his face.

One of the doors to the balcony stood slightly ajar. He walked outside. The sky was pink and blue, meeting the mountains at a misty line along their ridges. Eternity clung to moments like this, a brief halt in time, offering no answers.

He went to the balustrade and strained his eyes toward the forest and lake, wondering if she were gone on some mission she might never share with him.

"Good morning." Her voice was a sweet and compelling bell. He glanced down quickly, to the wintry garden beneath the balcony, where she'd cleared a space and planted flowers last fall, in secret. She was kneeling there, barefoot and wrapped in a blanket.

In the middle of the garden she had added a blue willow. A strong little tree, and delicately beautiful.

Artemas caught his breath. She called, "Spring'll be here soon. I'm going to plant the most incredible gardens around this house."

Leaning against the balustrade's sun-warmed stone, he smiled at her. "You picked the perfect place to begin, my love."

"It'll be happy here," she answered, nodding toward the willow. "This is going to be the prettiest willow you've ever seen. We'll enjoy watching this tree grow."

"I'll enjoy every day of it. Every year. Every decade. This is exactly where it belongs."

She lifted her head and studied him solemnly. Then she got to her feet and ran up the balcony steps, and he held out his arms—graceful, gallant, causing her eyes to fill with devotion. "You're not just talking about some little old tree," she drawled, before she kissed him.

The promise of a blue willow was theirs.

About the Author

A former newspaper editor and multiple award-winner for her novels and contemporary romances, **DEBORAH SMITH** lives in the mountains of Georgia, where she is working on her next novel.